SINS
OF THE
FATHER

JEN BLOOD

Adian Press
Maine

Cover Design by Travis Pennington
www.probookcovers.com
Author Photograph by George Glum

Visit the Erin Solomon website:
www.erinsolomon.com

For Mike
"There's no other love like the love for a brother.
There's no other love like the love from a brother."
- Terri Guillemets

ACKNOWLEDGMENTS

There are quite literally too many people to thank here, for the success of All the Blue-Eyed Angels, assistance with research, spreading the word about Erin Solomon, and providing encouragement as I continue on the indie path. But I'll try. My deepest gratitude to Jan Grieco for inviting me to the Northern Maine Community College and introducing me to such wonderfully supportive, enthusiastic new friends; to my mom for the endless list of things she's done to help me achieve this writing dream; to my dad for his consistent cheerleading and occasional harassment of every bookstore owner and mystery lover in a hundred-mile radius; to the rest of my family for excusing me from family functions and understanding when I've vanished in the middle of birthday parties, weddings, and graduations to jot down a random plot point; to my fellow fangirls—Alanna, Liz, Sherry, Cheryl, Jillian, Biba, Philippa, Jenn, Jess, Liz, Amy, Katie, Heather, and so many others—for their unflagging enthusiasm, support, and humor; to Bonnie Brooks for featuring *Angels* in her store, and for her phenomenal support throughout this wild ride; to Heidi Vanorse, Chuck, and the whole gang at the Loyal Biscuit for opening their store to me and helping me find the perfect face for Einstein; and to the wonderful writers I've met as I've embarked on this indie publishing journey—DV Berkom, Pamela Beason, Joanne Lessner, Susan Russo Anderson, Darcy Scott, Elizabeth Wilder, and Desmond Hall—for their willingness to share their knowledge, contacts, and empathy. To my phenomenal old friends here in midcoast Maine—David Mills, Nikki Demmons, Lynn Barboza, Rick LaFrance, and an endless slew of others… Having you in my corner truly means more than I can say.

A very special thank you to Jan Grivois for her invaluable information on all things northern Maine. Anything that rings true about that area in this novel is entirely thanks to her. If it doesn't ring true, of course, it's all on me.

PART I.
LITTLEHOPE

Chapter One

I first met Hank Gendreau at the Maine State Prison in Warren, twenty-five years into a life sentence. It was hotter than hell in midcoast Maine, and I was damp from the humidity and cranky from spending an hour and a half in summer traffic, crawling along a bottle-necked stretch of Route 1 that ran the full thirty miles from Bath to Waldoboro.

When I finally hit Warren, I parked Einstein—my faithful canine compadre—with a sympathetic neighbor I knew from back in the day, thus saving him from baking in the hot car while I went about my business. Then, I drove another half-mile up Route 97 and turned right at a section of brick wall taken from the original state prison in Thomaston, before it was replaced by the fifty-thousand square foot "Supermax" I was about to enter.

According to the official prison visitor's rules of conduct, shorts and a tank top are too much for the average lifer to handle, so I opted for khakis and a button-up blouse. The ensemble was cooler than jeans, but still too warm for the dog days of summer. Once inside the building, it took forty-five minutes to get through the metal detector, a lengthy list of questions, and a thorough frisking more intimate than any date I'd been on in recent memory, before I was allowed into the belly of the beast. The sun was blazing outside, but that light didn't make its way into the stark visiting chamber where Gendreau waited for me.

A few other inmates were already scattered throughout the room, visiting with friends and family. Gendreau sat behind a wood-veneer table with his hands folded and his eyes on the clock. Unlike movies or TV, there was no protective glass between us. He wore a blue denim shirt with faded jeans. No shackles. His hair was graying at the temples, and his brown eyes were clear and soulful. At first glance, they didn't look at all like the eyes of a man who'd tortured and killed his seventeen-year-old daughter in a hallucinogenic frenzy.

I sat down in a plastic chair on the opposite side of the table. He smiled, his teeth even and surprisingly white. In another life, he would have been an attractively innocuous sixty-year-old man living out an attractively innocuous life. Someone you might remember for his good manners, but not much else.

I introduced myself and managed a good two minutes of small talk—a personal record—before I got down to business. The guards had confiscated my bag before I was allowed inside, but they let me carry a letter in with me once they'd assured themselves I wouldn't pull some kind of Ninja death-through-origami stunt.

"I know your final appeal was just denied. I'm not sure what you expect me to do about that," I said. I tapped the letter with my index finger. "What did you honestly think you'd get by writing me?"

He didn't seem ruffled by my tone. "You came. That's something."

I opened the envelope and took out the blurry photo I'd received with it two days earlier. Someone had scrawled the words *Jeff, Will & Hank, Summer 1968* in sloping penmanship on the back. In the photo, three boys mugged for the camera. Two were dark-haired, the other a redhead, probably between fourteen and sixteen years old. The picture was too out of focus to tell much beyond that, however.

"I've had that for a long time," he said. "But it didn't click for me 'til last week, when I was reading a story about the Payson fire in the *Globe*. They had a picture of you and your father in there, when you were younger."

I'd seen the article; it was one among many these days. Three months earlier, I'd bungled my way through an investigation that had ultimately proven the alleged cult suicide by fire of the Payson Church of Tomorrow— the religious community where I spent the first nine years of my life— hadn't been suicide at all. In the process, I'd learned that my father had been harboring a secret that, for reasons I still didn't understand, had inspired him to fake his own death ten years later. For the past three months, I'd been searching for some hint as to what that secret might have been... And where, exactly, my father was now. Gendreau's letter was the first lead I'd gotten with any real potential in months.

"And you recognized him after all those years?" I asked.

"I wouldn't have if you hadn't been in the picture with him. But you looked just like him when he was younger." I didn't care for the way he was looking at me: Like I was some ghost of Christmas past, come calling in the dead heat of summer.

"I don't know how you think this picture would convince me of anything—I can barely tell these kids are kids, much less that one of them might have been my father forty-five years ago. Besides which, my father's name was Adam, not Jeff."

I waited to see if he took the bait. I knew full well my father wasn't born Adam Solomon… I just needed to know if Gendreau did.

"Maybe he was when he had you—after he joined that church," he said evenly. "But when we were kids together, it was Jeff. He had a birthmark behind his knee shaped like South America, and a scar on his left forearm. You remember?"

I nodded, but said nothing. I reminded myself to keep breathing.

"He got that scar when we were out fishing one day—we were about fifteen," Gendreau continued. "There was this pond with some of the best trout in the County, but we had to climb over a fence to get to it. Somebody saw us. While we were trying to get away, Jeff got his arm snagged on the barbed wire. I'm telling you the God's honest truth: the boy in that picture is your father."

I'm not above taking the word of a crazed psychopath, but I try not to make a habit of it. Facts don't lie, though: My father did have a scar on his left forearm, and he'd told me almost exactly the same story about how he'd gotten it. And while as a kid I'd always thought the birthmark behind his knee looked more like a dancing hippo than South America, I could see where someone might get confused.

"In your letter, you said you could give me answers." I hesitated. There were a couple of prisoners at a neighboring table seemingly lost in their own conversations, but I'd learned the hard way that there was a very determined, as-yet-unidentified faction out there who'd go to great lengths to keep me from finding the truth about my father. I leaned in closer and lowered my voice, comforting myself with the knowledge that it's only paranoia if there's no one out to get you.

"How did you know him? Where did you two grow up?"

He pushed the letter and photo back toward me and wet his lips. Like that, his eyes changed. Either thirty years in prison had made that pleasantly innocuous sixty-year-old a hell of a lot harder than he would have been otherwise, or I was getting a rare glimpse into the true Hank Gendreau. He never took his eyes from mine.

"I'll make a trade," he said.

"What kind of trade?"

"I don't have any money left to hire anyone. My last appeal's been denied. But I read about what you did with the Payson fire—how hard you worked to find the truth." He looked like he expected me to argue the point. I kept quiet. "If you'll look into my daughter's murder, I'll tell you about your father. Whatever you want to know."

"What was his last name?"

"Not until you bring me something. Will you look into that day?"

I'm not an idiot—I knew he could be lying. Maybe he and my father had known each other when they were kids, and that was the end of the story. Maybe he'd never known my father at all.

"What if all I uncover about your daughter's murder is that you did it?"

"I didn't," he said. His eyes hardened, but he didn't flinch and he didn't look particularly offended by my words. He looked around for the guards, then waited a second or two, until he'd assured himself they weren't listening. "There's something else," he said. "Something I didn't mention in the letter."

I waited for him to continue.

"Did you hear about the bodies they found up at the border last week?"

"In Canada?" I asked. "Sure, who hasn't?"

A week before, a couple of hunters had gotten off track in the deep woods along the border between Maine and Quebec. In the process, they stumbled on a shallow grave… And then another one. And another. By the time they made it back to civilization, they reported that they'd found half a dozen of these unmarked graves. It turned out that all six belonged to high school and college girls who'd gone missing sometime in the '80s. There weren't a lot of details beyond that yet, but the story had been getting plenty of air time ever since.

"You're telling me that whoever killed those girls is the same one who killed your daughter," I said. I didn't actually come out and say he was full of shit, but it was certainly implied.

"They were all Ashley's age. All tortured. Strangled." He stopped. The hardness vanished from his eyes. "They all died the same way," he said softly. "Five of the bodies have been identified as girls who'd gone missing from central and northern Maine at around the same time Ashley was killed."

"According to the stories I've heard about this case, you'd taken three tabs of acid the day your daughter was killed," I said, unmoved. "They found you with the body, covered in her blood. And correct me if I'm wrong, but there's the little matter of a confession that keeps cropping up in all these appeals you've been filing."

"I didn't know what I was saying—I was out of my mind by then. The drugs were still in my system. And even if they hadn't been, finding

Ashley that way…" His eyes filled with tears. If his grief was an act, Hank Gendreau deserved an Oscar. "I was out of my mind," he repeated.

"So, what changed?" I asked. "How are you so sure of what happened now, twenty-five years later? How do you know you didn't stumble across your daughter on a path in the woods that day in the middle of some epically bad trip and just lost control? And then when you came to, the reality of what you'd done was so horrifying you just blocked it out."

"I didn't kill my daughter," he said. "You don't have to believe me—take a look at the evidence. The DNA and blood samples as much as prove it."

I'd heard rumblings about this, but I wanted to hear the details from him before I formed any opinions. "If you have DNA evidence proving you're innocent, why are you still in prison?"

"The judge says it's tainted; he ruled it inadmissible. But I had tests done. There were blood and skin cells under my daughter's fingernails. They weren't mine."

"They can't tell whose they were?"

"There wasn't enough to come up with a match—most of the evidence got tossed after the first trial. But it didn't come from me; that much has been proven. Someone else did this. I couldn't do something like that…"

I took a few seconds to think about that. The room was hot and overcrowded. There were sweat stains at the neck of Gendreau's denim shirt and under his arms. A little boy with dark hair played with a plastic truck in one corner of the room, a rail-thin, dark-haired woman not far from him. She chewed gum and held hands with a built blond guy with some seriously disturbing tats extending from his upper arm all the way up his neck. He caught me staring and met my eye. Smiled. I looked away.

"I'm not a detective," I said, my attention back on Gendreau. "I'm a reporter. Which means whatever I find, chances are good that I'll shout it from the rooftops. You're prepared for that?"

"That's part of the reason I contacted you. You think if I had any doubt about whether or not I'd done this, I'd call a reporter to investigate? Would I order DNA tests if there was any question in my mind that I might've just blacked out? I'm telling you." He leaned in so close that I saw one of the guards take a step toward us. "Find the man who killed those girls and buried them in Canada, and you'll find Ashley's killer. He did this."

"Look, Mr. Gendreau—" I began.

He held up a hand to stop me. "Whoever murdered my little girl is still out there. I have two other kids I watched grow up from behind prison bars. They won't speak to me. My wife filed divorce papers an hour after I was convicted. I lost everything the day my daughter died."

I glanced at the photo again, not sure how to respond. It took maybe fifteen seconds before I'd made up my mind. "If I do this, I'm doing it my way."

"That's what I expected," he assured me. "And for every piece of information you bring me, I'll answer anything you want about your father."

"I won't do anything until you give me at least one scrap about my dad," I insisted. "Last name. Where he was from. Something."

"Black Falls," he said. "That's where I met him. You want to know more, you'll need to work for it."

I got the same sweet-as-sugar rush I always get when I have a lead, and stood. Black Falls. "Fair enough. I'll be back in a few days."

He nodded. Something about his story still bugged me—aside from the fact that if Hank Gendreau really was innocent, the wheels of justice had skidded horrifically off course. Or maybe it was just something about *him* that bugged me. At the very least, I didn't trust him. The guard who'd been about to intervene on my behalf a minute or two earlier flashed me a smile as I left the room. When I looked back over my shoulder, Gendreau was sitting where I'd left him, his gaze fixed once more on the seconds ticking by.

◊◊◊◊◊

After I'd retrieved Einstein, my next stop was to the *Downeast Daily Tribune*, where I cut my teeth as a reporter way back when I was still wearing combat boots and too much eyeliner. That meant returning to Littlehope, of course—the hometown I'd been avoiding since the aforementioned horrifically bungled Payson investigation in the spring. The second we crossed the town line, Einstein was on his feet, whining at the window. He darted past me as soon as I opened the car door in the *Trib* parking lot, made a quick rest stop at a nearby shrub, and headed straight for the front door without me.

I wasn't feeling quite so eager. I wiped my sweating palms on my khakis, checked my reflection in the glass door, and did what I could to wrangle my red hair into some kind of discernible style. That never actually panned out, so I eventually gave up and pulled it back into a ponytail, straightened my top, took a breath, and went inside.

The *Trib* is a no-frills operation; most days, you're just grateful the plumbing works, so A/C is out of the question. The concrete walls were sweating and the linoleum was slick with humidity as I headed down the hall to the newsroom. Not a soul was in sight.

I was still a few feet from my destination when the newsroom door opened and Daniel Diggins, editor-in-chief, stepped outside. He had his head down, focused on some paperwork in his hands. Einstein gave a hysterical yelp of joy and was off like a bolt of furry lightning as soon as he caught sight of him. Diggs looked up from his papers, then just stood there for a split second, like he wasn't sure I was actually there. Once he'd assured himself I was no mirage, a smooth, slow grin touched his lips.

He knelt to give Einstein a proper greeting while I bridged the distance between us. He had on shorts and an Arcade Fire t-shirt, his wavy blond hair as untamed as ever. His blue eyes sparkled when they met mine. Diggs is eight years older than me, and forty never looked so good as it did on that man. He straightened. Stein wandered off to make sure all was copasetic with the rest of the paper.

"I wondered when you'd show your face around here again." He said it with a smile, no trace of the awkwardness I was afraid I might find.

"I've been busy. You know how it goes."

He looked amused, like my absence was exactly what he'd expected, my return right on schedule. I felt a flash of irritation that vanished when he took a step closer and tucked a tendril of hair behind my ear.

"You look good, Sol," he said.

If I hadn't been about to melt from the heat before, the look in his eyes was enough to finish the job. "You too," I said.

My voice didn't sound like mine and the flush in my cheeks didn't have a thing to do with the weather. In the good old days, we would have hugged hello and he would've given me hell for staying out of touch so long. Now, thanks to a two-minute conversation while I was pressed against his desk in this very building three months ago, I was blushing like a virgin bride.

I cleared my throat, took a step back, and made a concerted effort to get a grip. "I was in town on a story—figured I'd pop in."

"And steal our Wifi?" he guessed correctly.

"I'll buy you lunch for it; that's not stealing."

"Deal." He nodded toward the newsroom. "Snag a desk, or you can set yourself up in my office. I'll be back in ten."

He didn't tell me where he was going, and I didn't ask. After three months without so much as an e-mail to let him know how I was, I figured I didn't merit much in the way of explanations.

Einstein and I went into the *Trib's* newsroom, but the heat and the faint smell of sweat and stale Cheetos drove me straight to Diggs' door. His desk was uncharacteristically neat, complete with a labeled inbox, a new computer monitor, and a jelly jar of wildflowers looking somewhat worse for the wear. Diggs isn't really a wildflowers kind of guy; the sight didn't sit well with me.

I set myself up with my laptop on his leather sofa so I could make the most of the tiny bit of relief provided by an old box fan in the window. I'd already logged into the network and was looking for everything I could find on Hank Gendreau by the time Diggs returned.

He tossed a plastic-wrapped sub sandwich on my lap and handed me an extra-tall iced coffee.

"I thought I was buying lunch."

He waved me off, his attention already on my computer. "Next time. So, what's the big story?"

I set the laptop aside for the time being. The sub was from Wallace's—the town general store—which meant it tasted like the best thing this side of heaven but probably took five years off my life. Einstein parked himself at my feet with his chin resting on my foot, gazing up at me with profound faith that I'd do right by him. I tossed him a pickle.

"What do you know about Hank Gendreau?" I asked.

Diggs perked up. "The guy who claims he was framed for raping and murdering his own daughter? That's who you were visiting?"

"I got wind of some anomalies in his case, heard there might be a story there," I said. "I figured I'd talk to him first and see what I could find out. And there was no rape," I added. "His daughter was tortured and strangled... No sexual assault."

"Ah. Well, I guess if all he did was torture and strangle her, it's no big deal." He bit into his veggie burger and took his sweet time chewing before he continued. "They just turned down his last appeal, didn't they?"

"Yeah. But there's been a lot of interest in his case over the years. There's some DNA evidence the jury never heard about, apparently."

Diggs got that look he always gets when he sees more than I intend on showing. "What's your interest? I thought you were focusing on your dad's story for a while."

"I still need to pay the bills." It was the truth. Basically. "People eat this shit up, you know that. So, what's your take—is there a story or isn't there? Do you think he did it?"

"They got a confession from him, right? He was in the woods tripping balls the day it happened, then they found him later covered in his daughter's blood. Definitely a slam dunk case at the time."

"He says they found someone else's DNA under her fingernails."

Over the course of his career, Diggs has somehow managed to retain the details of just about every news story on all seven continents for the past century—something I tend to view as either incredibly helpful or just plain annoying, depending on circumstances. He didn't even blink at what I considered fairly weighty evidence in Gendreau's favor.

"There've been a couple of cases in the news about that lately," he said. "The thinking now is that the nail clippers CSU used back then might have been contaminated from other victims."

I read farther down before I shook my head. "They were using disposable clippers by then, for just that reason. Whatever scrapings they found had to come from under Ashley Gendreau's nails."

Diggs scratched his stubbled chin, thinking that over.

"Have you met him?" I asked.

"Gendreau? Once. I was doing a story on one of the job programs he spearheaded over at the prison. He's done a lot of good work in there."

"Everyone I talked to so far over there loves him," I said. "Maybe times have changed, but the last I checked, guys accused of torturing and murdering their own kids aren't real popular 'round the cell block. The consensus on the inside is he got railroaded."

"Maybe he's just a good actor," Diggs said. He sat back in his chair and finished his burger. "He could be a sociopath. Split personality. Anything's possible."

"He's seen shrinks for the past thirty years. You don't think one of them might have picked up on that?" I pulled up the story Gendreau had turned me onto during our visit.

"And then there's this," I continued. I read aloud from the screen. " 'Five of the six bodies discovered buried in the woods along the Maine/Quebec border have now been identified as young women from the central and northern Maine area reported missing in the early '80s.' "

"And you think whoever killed these girls is the same guy who killed Ashley Gendreau?"

"It's a theory. They were all the same age. All kidnapped, strangled, and buried."

"Except Ashley wasn't buried."

"Maybe her father interrupted the killer. Whoever did it had to run before he could haul the body away to his burial ground."

He arched an eyebrow. "You're reaching, Sol—this guy's desperate.

Since when did you become such an easy mark?"

I bristled. "I'm not an easy mark. There are plenty of unanswered questions here—I'm not alone in thinking maybe Gendreau got caught in a shit-storm with a bunch of cops out to string up the first suspect they found after they saw everything that had been done to this girl. You honestly think anyone could have been impartial after seeing that?"

He thought that over for a few seconds, then settled in behind his desk and fired up his own computer. "So, this mysterious killer who was murdering girls in the '80s... Do they have any leads on who he is? Any clue where he might be now? Or why he just stopped killing for no apparent reason?"

"How do we know he stopped?" I asked. "He could have more burial sites than just the one they found. Or maybe he got caught. Maybe he died."

We both fell silent, scanning the innumerable websites that detailed the brutal slaying of Ashley Gendreau in 1987. At the time, the public had been ready to skip Gendreau's trial entirely and get straight to the lynching. He'd gotten hate mail, death threats, been segregated from the general population... And yet despite all that, somehow over the years he'd been able to change a lot of minds while he'd been inside. I wasn't ready to dial up the governor for a pardon just yet, but looking into the matter didn't seem like quite the colossal waste of time I'd thought it would be when I first got Gendreau's letter.

I spent the afternoon and evening in Diggs' office researching the Gendreau murder and the discovery of the bodies in Quebec. Hank Gendreau had given his lawyer permission to talk to me, so I set up a meeting for the following day. I checked the map to figure out where his daughter was killed and sketched out a time to visit the site later in the week.

I was in the middle of jotting down notes on the other victims when Diggs got up from his desk and turned off the fan.

"All right, Sol, I'm closing up shop."

I glanced at the clock on my computer screen. "It's not even seven o'clock—what happened to burning the midnight oil?"

"Not tonight. Your mutt's wilting, and I'm teetering on the brink of heat stroke over here. First we swim, then we eat. This'll wait until tomorrow."

Einstein *was* looking pretty sad, and I was feeling a little damp myself. I peeled myself off the furniture and packed up my stuff. So far I hadn't broached the subject of where I was planning to crash for the night—another thing that had changed since my last visit. I glanced at the flowers on his desk again. Usually, it was a given that Diggs would be putting me up during my stay. I wasn't so sure about that anymore.

"I was thinking about giving Edie a call," I said. "And maybe spending the night there tonight." I'd been going for cool and casual; I fell considerably short.

Diggs flashed a brilliant smile my way. "Oh?"

"It's not really fair of me to just show up out of the blue like this, and expect you to… You know."

He folded his arms over his chest and leaned back against the doorsill, clearly enjoying himself. "No, I guess it isn't."

"You're not gonna make this easy, are you?"

"Not if I can help it." He straightened, grabbed my backpack, and tossed it over one shoulder. "Come on, Sol—I'll race you to the car. We can fight about it there."

Einstein was already out the door, hot on Diggs' heels, while I was still trying to figure out my next move. It was pretty much a foregone conclusion, though: I'd been following Diggs since I was knee high to a toadstool. I wasn't about to stop now. I grabbed the rest of my stuff and locked the door behind me, feeling undeniably nostalgic for those hot summer nights of my youth.

Chapter Two

Halfway to our old swimming hole, Diggs took a left and headed in the wrong direction entirely. We'd taken his Jeep; the top was down, the air was warm, and Einstein's ears were blowing in the breeze. I had the uneasy feeling that what had started as the perfect evening was about to take a turn.

"You're going the wrong way."

"I thought we'd grab a bite first. We can swim later."

"I'm not hungry."

"I am," he said, with nary a glance my way. "Humor me."

"Are we dining alone?"

His fingers tightened on the wheel. "More or less."

I groaned. "Dammit, Diggs. I'm not in the mood for this tonight."

"Have you even talked to her since she got out of the hospital?"

The 'she' to whom he was referring was my mother: Dr. Katherine Everett, pediatric surgeon extraordinaire. Or she had been, until she was nearly killed during that same catastrophic story that had almost done the rest of us in three months ago.

"I've talked to her on the phone."

"When?"

I had to think on that. I'd been taking care of Kat's house in Portland while she ran the Littlehope Medical Clinic during her 'convalescence,' but most of our interactions over the past few months had been through her partner, Maya.

"I don't know—somewhere along the lines I must have."

"Nice."

"Hey, she didn't call me, either."

He pulled into the parking lot at Bennett's Lobster Shanty with a long-suffering sigh. "Come on. I promised Maya I'd drag you over here. We don't have to stay long."

I would have put up more of a fight—or resisted entirely—but since I'd just found out about the potential link between my father and Hank Gendreau, I was actually anxious to see if I could learn anything more from Kat. She was notoriously close-mouthed about my father, but there was always the chance she'd slip up. It was right up there with hell freezing over and pigs taking flight, but it was a chance all the same.

"All right—sure," I agreed. "What the hell. But if a war breaks out between the two of us, don't blame me if you get caught in the crossfire."

He grinned. "Don't worry. I packed my Kevlar."

◊◊◊◊◊

The best thing about Bennett's Lobster Shanty is the lighting, which does patrons the kindness of keeping things so dim you can't see whatever might be crawling away with your bread basket or skittering across your feet. As the only restaurant in twenty miles, however, it's never hurt for business.

By seven-thirty on a Wednesday night, most of the folks who'd come for dinner were long gone. The TV mounted in the corner was tuned to the Red Sox, half a dozen fishermen at the bar drowning their sorrows while Buchholz pitched what was looking to be another losing game. Kat and Maya were late—partly because Kat was always late and partly because, I was sure, she was dreading this dinner even more than I was. Diggs and I sat in a corner booth with a votive candle in a red glass bowl flickering between us.

"So, I'm assuming you still haven't found the connection between your father and Jane Bellows," he said, thereby officially introducing the conversation I'd been dreading all day.

"Nothing," I said. "So far every road I've gone down has been a dead end, just like while we were out there. Nobody recognizes his picture. No one's ever heard of the Paysons beyond what they've seen on the news. I can't find any connection between Dad and any investigations Senator Bellows might have done..." My frustration bled through before I could contain it. "She'd never even been to Maine before. Other than a thing for organic tomatoes and an investigation she did into cults in the late '70s, I can't find a single reason why their paths would have crossed."

Diggs nodded. "Well... You'll figure it out one of these days."

"Or I'll die trying."

"I think that's what we're all afraid of."

Jane Bellows had been a senator in Washington state back in the '70s and '80s. I had inadvertently connected her home address with my father last spring, when it turned out reports of his death had been greatly exaggerated. She'd been murdered just days after I'd called her home and spoken—very briefly—with my supposedly-dead father. Diggs and I had gone out west together once I got news of Bellows' murder, rendezvousing with Special Agent Jack Juarez for a very unofficial inquiry. From there, it took only two days before I followed my last solid lead about Dad straight into a brick wall. Then there'd been a whole stupid mess between Diggs and Juarez and me and a blessedly angst-less romantic triangle I was still trying to figure out—one that, thus far, all three of us had managed to avoid actually addressing in any way, shape, or form.

Until now, apparently.

"So... Have you heard anything from Juarez?" Diggs finally asked, when the woolly mammoth in the room proved impossible to ignore any longer.

My eyes slid from his to the bread basket between us, now almost empty. "A couple of times."

I could tell he knew that was a lie; I hedged before he could call me on it. "Maybe more, I don't know. He calls." *And I answer* was all I meant by that. Diggs didn't take it that way.

"I would have called," he said. "But the last time we talked, you said you needed some space. I figured you'd pick up the phone when you had a reason to."

His instincts had been good on that count—I *had* needed space. And time. Even Special Agent Jack Juarez, steamy Fed that he was, hadn't been able to convince me I was ready for anything beyond a few racy phone calls. Of course, Diggs had no way of knowing that.

"I know," I said. "I'm sorry—I was just getting my head together."

"And Juarez was a big help in that department, I suppose."

"Watch it, Diggs. If I didn't know better, I'd say you were jealous."

He looked me dead in the eye. "And if I was?"

I almost choked on my breadstick. Before I could come up with a witty retort—or recover the power of speech—Kat and Maya arrived, continuing my mother's longstanding record of epically bad timing.

Maya was easy to spot in a crowd: tall and slender, with curly grey hair and a smile that radiated good health and good humor. My mother was a few inches shorter, with dark hair, a few more curves, and an unnerving tendency to say whatever popped into her head. She slid into the seat beside

Diggs while Maya sat next to me.

"Sorry we're late," Maya said. "There was an unexpected delay." She hugged me warmly—something she did a lot of. I'm not the huggy type, but in the few short months that I'd known Maya I'd learned to make allowances. Kat already had her menu open, but she looked up at her partner's words.

"Work," she said briefly, as though the single word explained everything. She looked from me to Diggs and back again, her eyes narrowed. "Did we interrupt something?"

"No," we said at the same time.

"Right," she said dryly.

I couldn't see a trace of a scar from the emergency surgery she'd had months before, now hidden beneath her close-cropped hair, and her green eyes looked as sharp as ever. The only sign I could see of her recent brush with the Reaper was the way she clearly favored her right hand.

"Thanks for inviting us out," Maya said. I glared at Diggs, who ignored me entirely.

"Sure thing," he said. "This'll be fun."

Kat snorted, but otherwise kept her nose buried in her menu. I looked for the closest exit, and prayed for a diversion.

Diggs and Maya chatted like over-caffeinated schoolgirls through most of dinner. Kat and I, on the other hand, were silent through most of the meal. She was distracted, and more withdrawn than I'd ever seen her. She looked tired. Older.

"I'm working on a new story," I announced finally, at a little after eight o'clock. We were almost through dinner and Kat had been eyeing the exit for a while. If I didn't bring it up now, I knew I never would. "The Ashley Gendreau murder." I directed the statement at Maya, who clearly didn't have a clue what the hell I was talking about.

"She was still living out West when that happened," Kat said. For the first time all evening, she looked interested in the conversation. "Did you meet Hank?"

"You know him?" I asked.

"Of course. Everyone around here knows Hank." She returned her attention to Maya. "His daughter was murdered back in…" She looked at me.

" '87," Diggs and I supplied at the same time.

"Right," she agreed. "Hank was out doing mushrooms on the back forty when it happened. He confessed—well," she amended, "they said he confessed, though I always thought that was bullshit."

"So you think he's innocent?" I asked.

"What idiot doesn't?"

I looked at Diggs pointedly.

"I didn't say I don't think he's innocent," he said. "I just think you should tread lightly."

"How do you know this guy, exactly?" I asked Kat. She was obviously playing for the other team now, but back in the day my mother had a reputation for loving and leaving men of all ages and economic persuasions. I was hoping we weren't about to add another long-lost "uncle" to the list.

"Smartass," she said. "I did a little work at the prison a few years ago. We hit it off." Her eyes drifted from mine, a sure sign that she was lying. Interesting.

"Did you ever talk to him about his childhood?" I asked. "Or... You know, your time with the Payson Church?"

"I was checking his prostate, not doing a psych eval. And why the hell would I ever mention the Paysons if I didn't have to?"

"So, you never mentioned Dad to him?"

Now it was Diggs' turn to look baffled. "What does your father have to do with the Gendreau murder?"

"Don't you know by now, Diggs?" Kat asked. "All roads lead back to Daddy with this one. Always have."

Maya shot her a glare.

"Sorry," my mother said. She even seemed sincere. Kat wasn't the kind of woman who apologized easily... Or at all. She looked around the room restlessly. "I didn't mean anything by it."

"Hank told me he and Dad grew up together," I said. "Did Dad ever mention a place called Black Falls to you?"

"He didn't."

"He must have said something, though," I insisted. "He never told you anything about his family? You never wanted to meet his parents?"

"He said the Paysons were his family, and I didn't push. They were more than I could handle in the in-law department, anyway. He always said the present was what was important, not what came before."

It was the most I could remember her saying about my father in years. I tried to think of a follow-up question that wouldn't spook her, but Maya beat me to it.

"What about that story you told me—about the man who came to visit when you two were first married? You said you thought he might be family."

Now it was Kat's turn to glare. Maya didn't even flinch. "I don't know what his name was, though," she said.

"Are you sure?" I asked. "What did he look like? Are we talking parent or sibling?"

Her lips tightened into a thin line. The waitress came by to take our dessert order. I waited impatiently for her to leave, knowing this new, chatty Kat wouldn't last long. As soon as the waitress was gone, I pounced.

"What else can you tell me about this guy who visited Dad?" I looked at Maya. "Do you remember what she said when she told you the story?"

Maya started to say something, but my mom stopped her with a glance.

"I wish you'd let this go," Kat said to me. She sounded dead tired, in a way I'd never heard before. "Your father loved you. You had nine good years together—that's more than a lot of kids get. He's gone. Trust me when I say he's never coming back. You really want to ruin the good memories by digging up everything that came before, and obsessing over all the shit that came after?" She shifted in her seat again. I noticed a tremor in her right hand. "Just leave it alone."

Maya put her hand over Kat's, but my mother withdrew quickly. Diggs looked at me. I sat there for a second or two, silent, trying to figure out how to address the unexpectedly human stranger my mother had become.

"I can't," I said finally. It came out little more than a whisper. I cleared my throat, trying to get my voice back. "I have to know what happened. Where he is. Who he was. I can't stop until I have some answers."

She didn't look happy, but she didn't look all that surprised, either. The waitress came over with two plates of blueberry pie for Maya and Diggs, with two extra forks. Kat and I both declined their offer to share.

"This man who visited Dad," I tried again. "Is there anything at all you can tell me about him?"

She shook her head. Her jaw was set, a look I knew well. "No," she said. She stood and looked at Maya. "I think I'll just walk back to the house—I could use the fresh air." I expected Maya to argue, but she just nodded. Then, Kat looked at me again. "I know you won't stop, but I'll be damned if I'll help you get yourself killed. You've seen where this road leads. I won't be part of it again, and I sure as hell won't be responsible for opening that door for you."

If she'd screamed at me, threatened me... Hell, if she'd just made a joke, I would have known how to handle her. But there was no anger in her tone, and there was definitely nothing funny about what she'd said. I watched in stunned silence as she left the restaurant, noticing for the first time that she walked with a slight limp now. Maya waited until she'd gone before she said a word.

"She's trying," she said quietly. "Communication isn't a gift of hers, but she cares about you. She wants you in her life."

Rather than argue, I let that one go. "There's a tremor in her right hand," I said. "You never mentioned anything. How much longer will she be like that?"

"It might get a little bit better, but she'll always have it," Maya said flatly. "She didn't want you to know, but frankly I think you've got enough secrets between you. She'll never operate again. The clinic is good for her right now because she can stay here and do some good, make a difference, without constantly being reminded of what she's lost."

Steady hands, a good memory, and a strong stomach, I suddenly remembered my mother saying to me. I was maybe twelve at the time, assisting her in the dead of night after a boating accident in Littlehope. *That's all it takes to be an ace surgeon. As long as you know how to cut, you'll know who you are. Your place in the world.*

She'd been so steady, so sure of herself. I had no clue what to do with this new version of my mother—this damaged woman who would never hold a scalpel again.

"How long are you in town?" Maya asked, saving me the trouble of having to come up with an appropriate response.

"I'm not sure. Probably just another day or two."

"Where are you staying?"

I hesitated. Diggs and I still hadn't technically tackled the question. I started to panic at the thought of being forced to bunk with my mother, new leaf or not.

"She's staying with me," Diggs said, before Maya could offer their place.

I could have kissed him. His eyes caught mine and he gave me that little secret smile he's been giving me for years.

"Yeah—I'm staying with Diggs."

"Well, come by the house before you leave, would you? She's changed… you'll see that if you just spend some time with her. I know you have a long, complicated history, but she really is an amazing woman. She deserves a second chance."

"I will," I said. "I mean, I'll at least try. I'll do what I can."

She gave me another hug, dropped a kiss on the top of Diggs' head, and then left us to our blueberry pie.

◊◊◊◊◊

I left my car parked at the *Trib* and Einstein and I hitched a ride back to Diggs' place in his Jeep. Darkness usually meant a welcome dip in temperature, but so far that hadn't panned out. More of the same was in the forecast: high humidity, thunderstorms, and record temps. I wasn't looking forward to any of it. That night, though, there was at least a moderate breeze, and the sky was filled with stars. Diggs' Jeep smelled like leather and coffee and whatever the aftershave was that he'd been wearing for as long as I'd known him. I'm not a huge believer in the afterlife, but if heaven smelled half so nice I'd definitely consider giving up my heathen ways.

He'd barely turned down the rutted drive to his house before he started in with the questions.

"You really think Hank Gendreau knows anything about your father?"

"He says they grew up together."

"And you believe him."

"He has a picture of them…" I amended that. "Well—okay, he has a shitty shot of three boys who could be anyone. But he knew things about my father that no one else would."

"Such as?"

"A birthmark on his leg. Scar on his arm, and how he got it—the same story my dad used to tell me. How would he know that?"

"So, I guess that explains the sudden interest in the Gendreau case."

"You don't have to sound so disappointed," I said. "Gendreau said he'll give me information about my father if I'll investigate this link between his daughter's murder and the bodies in Canada. I have to at least give it a shot."

"I know," he agreed. He actually smiled a little. "I wouldn't expect anything less."

He pulled up in front of the house, then grabbed my pack and hopped out without another word. I let Einstein out for a quick run around the yard before I went inside, still stuck on the conversation at Bennett's. Maya might claim that my mother wanted me in her life, but I still couldn't get my head around that one. For as long as I'd known her, it seemed that what Kat wanted most in the world was for me to just drop off the face of it entirely. Near-death experiences are supposed to change people, sure, but I doubted St. Peter himself could turn her around that dramatically.

Diggs was rummaging through the freezer by the time Einstein had done his nightly business and we'd meandered inside. He'd gotten furniture since I'd visited last—a grab bag of used, salvaged, and homemade pieces that would never make the pages of Better Homes. Somehow, he made them work.

"I didn't have time to make the bed," he said, looking over his shoulder at me. "But I got some fresh sheets out for you. And I'll dig out an extra blanket in case you need it."

"In this heat? Unlikely." I came over and stood beside him at the freezer, letting the cool air wash over me.

"Wishful thinking, maybe," he said. He glanced at me when I didn't say anything. "You okay?"

"Yeah. I'm good. It's just… I've never seen her like that," I said. "Kat, I mean."

"Like what?"

"I don't know—like an actual human being. She's usually all sharp edges and smartass remarks. Now she's all… " He looked at me, waiting for me to finish. I waved my hand around inarticulately. "Weird," I finally finished. "And not in the normal way she used to be weird."

"That was a better way to be weird?" He raised an eyebrow, clearly amused.

I shrugged. "Maybe not. I don't know… This whole lesbian thing is a pain in the ass. The worst the guys she used to bring home would do when I was a kid was make a pass at me or occasionally pee in the sink. No one ever tried to make me forge a friggin' meaningful bond with the woman."

He laughed. It sounded good—like a favorite song I hadn't heard in too long.

"Come on. It's cooler outside." He grabbed a couple of popsicles from a box in the corner of the freezer and handed me my favorite—grape—without having to ask. Then, he led the way outside to a porch swing on the back deck that hadn't been there when I'd visited last.

He was right, it was a little cooler outside. Einstein circled at our feet before he found a spot and settled with his chin on his paws, his eyes sinking shut fast.

"So, what about you?" I asked once we were both seated on the swing, looking out over a surprisingly well-manicured lawn. I'd never really pinned Diggs as a porch-swing-and-yard-work kind of guy. "How's life in Littlehope?" I'd been back ten hours, and it was the first time it had occurred to me to ask the question. Nice.

He shrugged. "It's good. Or the same, I guess." There was a weight on his shoulders I hadn't noticed before. "Nothing new to report, really."

"The paper's going okay?"

"It's a dying industry in a long-dead town. What do you think?"

"Wow. You guys are a laugh a minute around here."

He cracked a smile and looked at me sideways. "Sorry. Just feeling a little... bored, I think," he said, to my great surprise. "I don't think I was meant for the editor's desk."

"I could've told you that." I took a couple of bites of my popsicle, careful to affect my most casual, do-whatever-you-want tone when I spoke again. "You could help with this Gendreau thing, if you want."

"What about what Kat said?"

"What about it? She knows I'm not giving up—I'll get my answers one way or the other. If I can't get them through her, I might as well see what I can find out from Hank Gendreau."

I could see his wheels turning. He set the swing rocking gently as he stared out into the night. "I do have a few Canadian contacts I could call about those other bodies," he said after a few seconds. I did my damnedest not to appear too pleased with myself.

Diggs looked at me, just a hint of a spark returned to his baby blues. "Don't kid yourself—you're just as big a pain in the ass as your mother, you know." He paused. "I'm still glad you're back, though," he said quietly.

"Yeah?" We were close enough to touch, but not quite there yet. "Me too," I said.

His hand fell to my knee and stayed there as he leaned in. My eyes drifted shut and the night slowed to a sweet, bone-deep ache.

Until his lips brushed my cheek.

"We should probably get some sleep."

My eyes popped back open as Diggs stood and extended his hand. I couldn't read his expression—I was pretty sure there was regret in there somewhere, but there was also something veiled that I hadn't expected. I took his proffered hand, thrown off kilter. It wasn't like I'd been expecting him to fall all over me as soon as I hit town—especially since that had never been our M.O. before. I wasn't sure what I *had* been expecting, though. Or what I wanted, even.

I let him pull me up, inadvertently brushing a little too close when I was on my feet again. Something that might have been desire or might have been indigestion flickered in his eyes.

"I'll see you tomorrow, then?" I asked. I sounded as befuddled as I felt.

"Bright and early," he agreed. "You'll find that extra blanket in the chest at the foot of your bed, just in case."

I thanked him, particularly since what had started out as a steamy night had gotten unexpectedly chilly. I might need that blanket after all

Chapter Three

I decided to run into town the next morning, because sleeping alone hadn't been enough punishment the night before. I got a stitch in my side halfway there, and another ten feet down the road Einstein spotted a rogue golden retriever and took off running, pulling both of us into an overgrown ditch directly in front of the Mobil station, thus ensuring that my ass-over-teacup tumble be witnessed by half of Littlehope. I staggered into the *Trib* at a little past nine with a bloody knee, a couple of bee stings, and a hell of a lot less enthusiasm than I'd left the house with.

Diggs was at his desk with a pencil behind his ear and phone in hand. The wilted flowers had been replaced with fresh ones, and a snazzy straw fedora rested on top of a stack of papers to his left. He grinned when I came in—one of those wolfish grins with too many pearly whites that's been known to undo women of lesser mettle—and nodded toward the couch.

"That's great," he said into the phone. "I'll let her know. Yeah—thanks."

He snapped his phone shut. "How was the run?"

"Super, thanks. Very invigorating."

He eyed my knee, but wisely made no comment.

"Who was that?" I asked.

"Editor at the *Quebec Chronicle*." He looked pleased with himself. "Ask me if I found anything out."

I arched an eyebrow and waited without a word.

"Killjoy. Well, I did find something." He nodded toward the door, refocusing his attention on his computer screen. "Why don't you hit the showers, and I'll fill you in at ten. I just want to make one more call."

I started to protest, but my knee stung and my stings ached and my hair was definitely not doing what I'd intended when I set out that morning. Besides which, I might as well be trying to pry information from a Chia Pet when Diggs decided he didn't want to share.

He called after me as I was walking out. "First aid kit's still in the medicine cabinet, Flo-Jo."

I made an impolite hand gesture in his general direction and hit the showers.

Once I'd gotten the gravel out of my knee and wrestled my hair into the requisite ponytail, I returned to the office to find Diggs deep in conversation with an unnervingly tall brunette seated on the edge of his desk. A quick flash of what looked a lot like guilt crossed his face when I came in; my stomach bottomed out in that way it does when you get bad news or eat bad clams. Einstein was curled up on the couch glowering at the stranger, which made me feel only marginally better.

"Sol, this is Andie. She just took over the Lifestyle section here." He made no effort to tell Andie who I was. I took a step toward her and extended my hand.

"Erin Solomon," I said.

"Oh, I know," Andie said. She had curves that I lacked and a brighter smile and she was still sitting on Diggs' desk. I managed to suppress the urge to push her off, but just barely. "I've heard all about you, trust me." The way she said it made me think those stories hadn't been entirely flattering. "You left out how cute she is though, Diggs."

I flashed a brilliant smile. "Yeah, he always forgets that part."

She removed her shapely ass from Diggs' desk and casually brushed her hand against his shoulder, leaning in just a touch. "Well, I'll leave you to it. We still on for lunch?"

"Yeah, definitely," Diggs said. "I'll catch up with you later." He was doing his best to avoid eye contact with either one of us. Andie sashayed out the door. I fired up my laptop and settled in beside Einstein, who thumped his tail uneasily.

"She's new," Diggs said, after I'd frozen him out for a good five minutes.

"You don't say." I pulled up a page on the Gendreau murder and began reading.

"She's nice," he continued. "I think you two will hit it off."

"Super." I kept my eyes on the computer screen. "How long would you say the drive to Quebec is from here?"

"You're pissed."

Damn skippy I was pissed. I leaned into the feeling for just a second before I pulled back and got myself in hand. Diggs and I had been friends for years—I'd learned a long time ago that that was the best we could hope for. So he'd suggested a few months back that he might be interested in something more; it wasn't like he'd declared his undying love. And I was the one who took off, not him. So now... Well, now I was going to focus on work. Chase down leads. Find my father. All anything else amounted to were distractions I didn't need.

After another five seconds of silence, I almost bought it.

I met his eye. "It's fine, Diggs. I didn't call—it's not like I expected you to sit around and wait for me to come back."

"I just thought you and Juarez..."

I waved off the explanation. "Yeah, I know—I told you, no big deal. We're good. Now, what'd you find out from your contacts up north?"

He wasn't buying the act, but at least he did me the courtesy of going along with it. "I'm just waiting for a return call, then I've got a few more things to check out. Maybe we can go over everything a little later. What time's your thing with the lawyer?"

I checked my watch. "Actually, I should probably get going now." It was ten minutes 'til ten; my appointment wasn't until one. I packed up my stuff, grabbed Einstein, and took off before I had to face Amazon Andie again.

Since it was once again way too hot for any good dog to be car-bound, I left Einstein with Maya—who assured me that she and Kat would treat him like the grandson they'd never had until I returned. I left town and headed back up Route 1 into Rockport, where I swam a few laps at Walker Park and tried to clear my head. The mercury was pushing ninety that day, the park filled to the brim with trendy moms corralling trendy toddlers on the playground. I chose a picnic table as far from the action as possible, managed to tap into someone else's Wifi from one of the neighboring houses, and got my head back in the game.

At a little before one, I changed into something moderately respectable and drove the five minutes it took to get from the park to the offices of Max Richards & Sons, just over the Rockport bridge. I double checked the address I'd been given when I ended up at a huge old Victorian place badly in need of paint. Or possibly demolition. A six-foot privacy fence surrounded the perimeter. The front steps sagged, the yard was overgrown, and when I knocked it sounded like the hounds of hell were about to burst through the front door to devour me.

After some colorful language on the other side of the door, a thin, sixty-ish woman wearing a frayed housedress finally opened up. A pack of dogs ranging from ten pounds to two hundred surged toward me until the woman hissed a few more choice epithets in what sounded like French. The lot of them slunk backwards, tails low, as I crossed the threshold. The place smelled like wet dog, spoiled food, and old coffee grinds. Shredded newspapers and old books littered the entryway. Whoever this woman was, housekeeping clearly was not her forte.

"I'm sorry," I said. "I think I must have the wrong place. I'm looking for Max Richards?"

She stared at me like I'd just dropped from the sky. I persevered. "I think his office must be around here—it's a law office. Max Richards and Sons?"

The woman pointed behind her. "He's waiting for you. Down the hall and up the stairs. *Troisieme etage.* Third floor." It took me a minute to place her accent, a kind of Downeast-Meets-Cajun-N'Orleans common to the Acadian contingent in northern Maine.

One of the dogs dared to slink forward to sniff my hand. I scratched his ears and the woman smiled, revealing grey teeth and a badly receding gumline. Despite the smile, she was still staring at me like my head was on fire.

"*Il s'appelle* Midget," she said. Midget was the two-hundred pounder, a cross between a Newfie and a grizzly bear. The other dogs crept forward at my attention. "*Allez*—Go. I can only hold them so long."

I went.

Once I'd reached the top of the third flight, past peeling wallpaper and sagging steps and air so warm and so damp I felt like I was trapped at the bottom of an old gym sock, I found a long, dark hallway with a dim light burning. Classical music played behind a door to my left. I knocked, and was met with an eardrum-piercing shriek and what sounded like a bookshelf falling. Five minutes passed before a white-haired man with glasses opened the door just a crack. It was all very Dickensian.

"Erin? Come on in—nice to meet you. Mind the bird."

I ventured inside the cramped space where there was, indeed, a balding white cockatiel perched on a branch in the corner. An orange, one-eyed tomcat sat in the windowsill, tail twitching. An oscillating fan blew hot air around the room.

"You're Max Richards?"

"In the flesh," he assured me. He moved a pile of newspapers from a rickety chair with threadbare upholstering and motioned for me to sit. "Sorry for the mess. You met Bonnie?"

"Your... Uh, the woman, downstairs?"

He nodded, smiling. "She's an odd one. Nice enough, but she's not much for order. I hired a cleaning lady once—lost her, though."

Whether she'd quit or just been misplaced in the clutter was unclear. Max took a seat behind his desk, where the paperwork was piled so high I could only see the top of his glasses and his balding head.

"Hank wasn't sure you'd be by or not," he said.

"I figured I'd at least look into things. He told me to check in with you about the case files."

He hauled a box out from under his desk and nudged it toward me with his foot, then repeated the procedure with three more.

"Seriously?"

"You asked," he said. "This is everything: notes, transcripts, photos, press clippings…"

I mopped the sweat from my forehead with the back of my hand. "So you really don't think he did it?"

"Not a chance," he said without hesitation. He wasn't quite so Dickensian once I got a better look at him—or if he was, he was closer to Skimpole than Micawber. Though he was probably in his sixties, it wasn't a frail sixty and he moved with surprising agility. He wore a tweed sport coat and dress slacks, his only concession to the heat a notable lack of footwear and an unknotted plaid tie. He seemed sincere enough, but I didn't take that too seriously. He was a lawyer, after all.

"What about the confession?" I asked.

"Read the transcripts and the notes the police kept," he said. "You'll see erasure marks from the arresting officers right there—they altered the original documents. He loved Ashley. Besides which, he has no history of mental illness; it's true he was no choirboy in his youth, but there was nothing in his past to indicate something like this. There's no doubt in my mind that he didn't do it."

I opened the first box and peered inside to find three bound volumes of court testimony and a bunch of photos.

"This may take a while," I said.

"Take your time." He stood and put an expert Windsor knot in his tie without so much as a glance in the mirror. "I have meetings in Augusta this afternoon, but I'll be back when I'm through. You think you may still be here?"

"You could have meetings in Johannesburg and I'm pretty sure I'd still be here."

He chuckled. "Well, it's just the capitol for me today, so I expect we'll see each other before you go. Watch Spartacus doesn't get too close. He can be ornery."

He left before I could ask whether Spartacus was the bird or the cat. Neither of them looked that friendly. I listened to Max whistle his way down the stairwell, then once I was sure he was gone, I carried two of the boxes to a worn duvet at one side of the office and set to work.

Ashley Gendreau had just turned seventeen when she was killed, on a hot July day in a small northern town called Black Falls, population 6,093. The same Black Falls, presumably, where Hank Gendreau and my father met, according to his story. On the day she disappeared, Ashley had been in the house watching her younger sister, who was two at the time. Mrs. Gendreau—their mother—got home at four that afternoon to find Ashley's shoes by the door and her backpack still on the couch. The sister was asleep in her room.

Ashley, however, was gone. The transcripts from the original trial in 1988 were yellowed and worn inside their black binders. I paused at a section in the first trial transcripts, when Ashley's mother—Hank's ex-wife, Glenda Gendreau—had been questioned.

Q. Was your husband home when you returned that afternoon?
A. No. Nobody was there but Chloe—the baby.
Q. Did it seem strange to you that Hank was gone?
A. No. He said he was going out in the woods for a couple days. I knew he wouldn't be back. Didn't give it a second thought.
Q. Did he say what he would be doing in the woods?
A. Hank likes to go out there whenever he gets the chance, just to be with nature—sometimes he'll go out hunting, but most times he just likes to hike around.
Q. Were you aware of his drug use?
A. I knew he'd done some stuff in high school—it was the '70s. Everybody did that kind of thing.
Q. Did you know he had LSD that he intended to take that day?
A. No. I didn't think he did that stuff anymore.
Q. Prior to July 12, are you aware of the last time that your husband took LSD?
A. I'm not sure. You'd have to ask him.
Q. Can you tell the court what happened on November 2nd, 1973?

A. I don't know. That was a long time ago.
Q. I'll refresh your memory. On the evening of November 2nd, 1973, you contacted the Black Falls sheriff's department. Can you tell the court why you made that call?

What followed from there was a long, drawn-out account of a fall night in 1973 when Hank Gendreau dropped acid, had a bad trip, and wound up naked and fetal on the porch of his girlfriend's parents' house. He was twenty at the time; Ashley was three, and Ashley's mother—Glenda—was a whopping seventeen years old, still living at home with her parents while she and Hank saved to get their own place. A bad trip was hardly unheard of for college kids in those days, but Hank Gendreau wasn't a college kid, he was a deadbeat twenty-year-old who'd already knocked up a thirteen-year-old girl back when he was in high school. Not exactly the kind of guy who inspired a lot of faith in your average, God-fearing jury. When you looked at that in conjunction with the events of the day Ashley Gendreau had been killed, it established a history of drug use and what the prosecuting attorney called "deviant behavior." Hank's defense had taken a bad hit that day, and things had gone downhill from there.

The only chink in the State's case was an alternate suspect in the area at around the time of the murder, but the judge had ruled the evidence inadmissible before the jury ever heard about it. I read through appeals filed and news articles written on one Will Rainier, a convicted sex offender and one of Hank's best friends. I thought of the photo Hank had shown me: *Jeff, Will & Hank.* Though I didn't know for sure, it seemed safe to assume that the man in the photo was Will Rainier. If this Jeff kid really had been my father once upon a time, he had epically shitty taste in BFF's.

Will's alibi—a fishing trip with his father and brothers the day Ashley was killed—seemed weak to me, but apparently the judge didn't agree. Will Rainier was written off and the case moved forward without him.

I took a break about an hour in because I was about to either burst into flames or melt from the heat. The pack descended the second my feet hit the first floor, Bonnie close behind. She opened the front door and the lot of them fled for the yard.

"You look *mal,*" she said. "Come in the kitchen. I'll get you something cold."

I nodded gratefully. The kitchen was no cleaner than the rest of the house, but an ancient air conditioner roared in the window, making the temperature at least twenty degrees cooler than it had been in Max's office. Bonnie fixed me a glass of iced tea and set a plate of very stale looking Oreos in the middle of the table.

"You are investigating Hank, *non?*" she asked before I'd even had a chance to sample the iced tea.

"I'm looking into his daughter's murder, yes—Or at least that's the plan. I'm not sure what I can do, though."

"*Rien, maintenant.*"

I looked at her in surprise. My French was virtually nonexistent, but her tone came across loud and clear.

"Nothing," she said. "It is better to leave it."

She sat in a torn vinyl kitchen chair across from me and pushed the hair out of her face. Her eyes were deep-set and brown, the lashes long and dark—the kind of eyes that could make an otherwise unremarkable face stand out in a crowd. Despite a little lax hygiene now, I suspected she'd been a real beauty in her day.

"So you know Hank, then?" I asked.

"*Oui,*" she said briefly.

"What do you think of his story?"

"The day Ashley died?"

I nodded. "From what I can tell, there are quite a few people out there who think he didn't do it."

"*C'est vrai.* Red Grivois arrested him that day, but he never did believe Hank was the one."

I jotted down the name. "Hank said something about DNA evidence—do you know where that's kept at this point?"

"In Augusta—with the State. It was in a drawer here for a long time. They don't let us do that no more." She took a long, slow sip of iced tea before she spoke again. "Did Hank tell you about that day?"

I set my tea back down. Health code-wise, I figured Bonnie's kitchen was just a step above eating from a dumpster in Bangkok, so I avoided the cookies. I shook my head.

"I haven't gotten to his testimony yet," I said. "And we didn't have that much time to talk when I met with him the other day. Has he talked to you about it?"

It looked like she was about to say something important, but she changed tacks at the last second. "Your name—what is it, *s'il vous plez?*"

"Erin," I said. "Erin Solomon."

She nodded, never taking her eyes off me. "How did Hank find you?"

"I'm a reporter—he read a story I'd written, and asked me to look into this. I thought it sounded interesting. Can we get back to what you were saying a minute ago, about what Hank saw the day his daughter was killed…?"

She stood abruptly. "It was a bad day."

I'm no Sam Spade, but I'd managed to put that much together on my own. I waited for her to elaborate. She didn't. Instead, she took the still-full platter of stale cookies off the table and headed for the sink.

"How do you know Hank, exactly?" I asked.

She set the platter on the counter and started the water running in the sink. Between that and the air conditioner, it was hard to hear her when she finally spoke.

"I'm sorry," I said. "I didn't catch that."

She turned around and fixed me with that Hellraiser stare of hers again. "Don't worry about Hank. He won't hurt nobody." She stopped. Despite the fact that her eyes were drilling holes clear through me, I got the sense she wasn't seeing me at all. Then, suddenly there was a shift. She softened, and her eyes found mine. "It's G. you watch for, *oui*? Because G. will be watching for you."

A damp, icy chill climbed my spine. "Excuse me? Who's G.?"

"*Il est un diable*," she said. "The devil, *oui*? He comes out at night. *Pis* when I'm in the garden. He waits for me in my dreams. The world grows cold, and then, *voilà*. *Il est là*."

"I'm sorry—I don't think I'm following you. Who are we talking about?"

"I don't know him—I only see him. Not see him *avec mes yeux*," she laughed dryly, gesturing to her eyes. "I know he isn't there. Not truly."

Somehow, that wasn't a lot of comfort. She continued without another prompt from me.

"When he sees you, that's when he is *le diable*. Even when he doesn't want to be no more, *oui*? *Il ne peut pas arrêter*." She closed her eyes. Her voice lowered to a whisper. "When he smells blood *sous le rouge blanc et bleu—il est fait*. He is done. His eyes find yours, *pis maintenant il a besoin de vous*. You run. And don't stop."

My new psychic friend lit a cigarette with unsteady hands, took a long drag, and let it out in a slow, shaky exhale. She turned the water off in the sink.

"I should go back to work," she said.

"Just a second," I said quickly. "This man you see—this G. Can you tell me what he looks like? Is he someone you know?"

She took another pull from her cigarette. I'd quit just a couple of months ago; it was a testament to how wrapped up I was in the conversation that I didn't even notice the smell.

"I don't see him," she said. She rolled her eyes, like she knew exactly how nuts she sounded. "Not his face—*jamais. Il est un fantôme.* A ghost, *oui*? A shadow I feel sometimes. I don't know what he looks like—only what he feels. What he wants."

My fingers curled around the edge of the table in front of me. "And what does he want?"

She opened the kitchen door and started out, leaving the water in the sink and the dishes on the counter. When she turned again, there was something cold and resigned about the way she looked at me.

"*Il vous veut.* He wants you," she said. She hesitated a split second, like she was trying to decide whether or not she dared say whatever it was she'd been holding back. "For the game. He already had you one time," she said finally. "That's why he needs you again. *Il ne se reposera pas*—he won't rest after seeing you, *oui? A la pleine lune...*" She stopped, thinking about her words. "When the moon is full," she started again. "Then, the game begins. He won't stop. Not until he *est mort.*"

She walked out. The kitchen door swung shut behind her, and I was left with a knot in my stomach and the unshakeable feeling that her warning was one I should heed. Clearly she was a crackpot—she had a pack of dogs at her heels and a lawyer in her attic, all living in a filthy house about five degrees hotter than the sun. If I was looking for crazy, there was no shortage of it here. It was still hard to shake the look in her eyes, though.

I left the kitchen and headed back up to Max's office, thinking about what Bonnie had started to tell me before the whole channeling business began: something about whatever Hank had seen the day his daughter was killed. I made a mental note to reexamine the statement he'd made just after being taken into custody. And maybe figure out when the next full moon was.

Chapter Four

Ileft Max & Sons at a little after eight that night. Max never came back and Bonnie vanished with the dogs, leaving me with a notebook filled with questions and the rare opportunity to snag whatever files I wanted. Somehow, I didn't think Max would mind. Or notice, for that matter. I took a box of transcripts and some press clippings, and made sure not to let the bird or the one-eyed cat out as I left.

I was about forty-five minutes from Littlehope, where my dog and all my worldly goods—or at least my backpack and my favorite pj's—were being held hostage. I glanced at the clock, then at my phone. Tapped on the steering wheel a few times, getting progressively more irritated.

Finally, I gave up and picked up the damn phone.

"Are you coming back, or can I get rid of your bed and tell the boys at the paper we've got that scrapbooking room we've always wanted?" Diggs asked.

"I was just making sure I wouldn't be interrupting anything."

"Nope," he said breezily. "I'm running solo tonight. I've got portabella burgers for dinner and Swiss chocolate for dessert."

"You didn't invite my mother, did you?" I paused. "Or anyone else?"

"It's just you, me, and the hound tonight." He was quiet for a second. When he resumed, there was something weird in his voice—something weighted that hadn't been there before. "I found out a few things about the bodies up in Quebec you might be interested in, too."

"What?" I asked immediately.

"The usual—torture and an agonizing death, in graphic detail." He was trying to be light, but he fell considerably short on that count. "We can talk about it when you get here."

The portabella burgers weren't much of a draw, and I was rapidly reaching my limit when it came to speculation about the grisly murders of young girls. The thought of spending an evening with Diggs, Einstein, and Swiss chocolate, however, was more than enough to sway me. I told him I'd be there in an hour, put the car in gear, and headed back to Littlehope.

◊◊◊◊◊

Burgers were on the grill and Diggs had U2's The Unforgettable Fire on vinyl playing loud enough to make a lesser man's ears bleed when I arrived. My mother had dropped Einstein off earlier, sparing me the agony of trying to find common ground since Maya's revelation about the status of Kat's surgical career. My mutt thumped his tail and his ears perked up when I stepped onto the deck, but otherwise he remained focused on any table scraps that might fall his way.

Diggs wore jeans and a burgundy pullover that did ungodly things for his shoulders, his hair still wet from a recent shower. No shoes. We'd been friends long enough that it was easy to forget just how good looking he actually was—Until moments like this, when it was almost impossible to ignore.

"You mind setting the table?" he asked over his shoulder.

I cleared my throat and focused on staying focused. "Yeah, sure."

The bugs were staging a revolt, so we opted to eat inside rather than on the deck. I gathered plates and glasses and we did the polite small talk thing until dinner was ready, all the while carefully avoiding any mention of Diggs' perky new reporter at the Trib. Once the burgers were up, I grabbed a beer for myself and the requisite bottled water for Diggs, chomping at the bit to get started.

"So, what'd you find out about the case?" I asked the second he was seated.

"You're getting a little over-eager in your old age, Sol. How about a little foreplay before we dive into the heavy stuff, huh?"

"I thought this was the foreplay. Come on—I'll show you mine if you show me yours." His casual façade slipped, and I felt a sudden push of adrenaline. "You found something, didn't you?"

"I haven't eaten all day—let's have dinner first, then we can dig into it."

"Are you kidding me? Diggs—"

"Please," he said quietly. "Just have dinner with me. Then I'll tell you everything."

If it was anyone but Diggs, I would have told them to go to hell. But he didn't ask for much from me these days... The least I could do was have dinner. I took a bite of my portabella burger—which, it turned out, was a thousand times tastier than I'd ever imagined fungi could be. When that single bite didn't prompt Diggs to spill his guts, I took another.

"So, why don't you tell me what you found while you were at the lawyer's place?" he asked.

The man was impossible.

For the next half hour, I told him everything I'd learned about the Gendreau case: about the alternate suspect and the endless transcripts and Max and his balding bird and Psychic Bonnie and her pack of dogs. I left out her grim prediction about my fate, since it seemed to me we'd had enough of that sort of thing in the past few months.

Diggs switched U2 out for Dusty Springfield for dinner, her voice sad and silky and the perfect compliment to our quiet night. When we were done eating, we took the dishes into the kitchen and he washed while I dried.

"You're stalling," I finally said. He was scrubbing the last pan, and my patience had worn thin about an hour earlier.

"Maybe."

"Is it about my father?" I asked, though I already knew the answer. There was only one reason Diggs would have his knickers this twisted.

"Finish up and meet me in the living room."

His good humor had vanished about halfway through the dishes. Now, he looked conflicted and concerned and a little bit sad, and he wouldn't look me in the eye. He left me in the kitchen, where I focused on drying the last beads of water from his cast iron skillet. Whatever he knew, it wasn't good—that much was clear. The thought that the delicate cocoon I'd woven around my sanity in recent months was about to unravel was unsettling, but it still couldn't compete with the thought that Diggs might actually have a lead that could bring me closer to learning the truth about my father.

Diggs was on the couch with Einstein beside him and a manila folder in his lap when I came in. He nudged the dog to the floor and nodded to the spot Stein had grudgingly vacated.

"Have a seat."

"Are you trying to freak me out with this act, or is that just a side benefit?"

He grinned—a wide, rakish smile that never came close to touching his eyes. "Sorry. I guess I'm a little off my game tonight."

I sat down yogi-style, facing him on the couch. When I reached for the manila folder in his hands, he held it just out of my reach.

"What the hell is wrong with you?" I finally demanded. "Just give me the friggin' thing, Diggs."

"Just relax for a second. There's a preamble to this file." Arguing was pointless. I shut up and let him have the floor. "I talked to my guys in Quebec today. They told me the police up there have a suspect they're looking at."

"Who?"

"His name's Jeff Lincoln." He watched me closely when he said the name. "It turns out he's originally from Black Falls—where Ashley Gendreau was killed."

I flashed on Hank's picture again: *Jeff, Will & Hank, Summer 1968.*

"Jeff Lincoln," I said, half to myself. I had a hard time finding my voice. "Why do they suspect him of the murders? Where is he?"

"They're looking for him," Diggs said. "He's been a fugitive for almost thirty years now." He'd already figured out there was a connection between Jeff Lincoln and my father—I could see it in his eye. He handed me the file.

There were photocopied news articles and a couple of stories Diggs had printed off from online sites. I started with the top of the stack: a story from the *Bangor Daily News*, dated September 28, 1970.

```
Fifteen-year-old    Jeffrey    Lincoln   and
twelve-year-old   Erin   Rae   Lincoln   were
both reported missing after their boat was
found capsized on Eagle Lake early Saturday
morning. A search party has been organized,
and area residents are asked to lend their
assistance.
```

"Erin Rae," Diggs said when I'd finished reading. "That's your name, right?"

I nodded. My reaction was immediate, and a lot stronger than I'd expected it to be—I felt like I'd just been side swiped by a steam engine.

"This is him," I said. "He always told me I was named after his sister. This has to be my father."

"Keep reading," he said. He didn't look happy.

The next article was dated two weeks later, also from the *Bangor Daily.*

BRUTAL MURDER SHAKES COMMUNITY

The body of Erin Rae Lincoln was discovered
by workers on a logging road fifteen miles
from Eagle Lake, where the Lincolns' boat
was found abandoned earlier this month.
According to sources inside the police
department, twelve-year-old Lincoln was
tortured and strangled shortly after her
disappearance. Fifteen-year-old Jeffrey
Lincoln, who also went missing at the time,
has still not been located. Authorities
will not specify whether or not he is a
suspect in his sister's murder. A service
will be held for Miss Lincoln at the Black
Falls Baptist Church this Saturday at 1
p.m.

I closed the file and set it down between us. The remnants of my portabella burger was lodged halfway up my gullet, and my heart was pounding.

"He didn't do this," I said.

"I had the State M.E. fax me a copy of the coroner's report. You might want to take a look."

I reopened the file and leafed through until I found the report. Autopsies forty years ago weren't all that different than they are today, and the details of Erin Lincoln's death were just as disturbing now as they had been then. She'd been raped, stabbed multiple times, and finally strangled to death with a leather belt that had been identified as belonging to her brother, Jeffrey Lincoln. Post mortem, a single letter had been carved into her chest: J.

I thought of the father I'd known growing up on Payson Isle—of tending the garden with him, playing games, going to church services. The man I'd known had never even raised his voice. He loved animals, and the outdoors, and sunsets over the water. I shook my head, refusing to cave at the threat of tears. I closed the file and pushed it away again. If I looked at it one more time, there was no way I'd keep dinner down.

"He didn't do it," I said again.

"That's not all that's in there," Diggs said. I fought the urge to put my hands over my ears. "Jeff Lincoln resurfaced in 1972. He spent two weeks in a psych ward in Lansing, Michigan, before he escaped and disappeared. No one ever saw him again—he stayed under everyone's radar after that."

"So how does that have anything to do with the girls they just dug up on the border?"

He paused. The music had ended, the house now quiet and warm and cast in shadow.

"While he was in the hospital in Lansing, they got his fingerprints," he said.

I couldn't get the image of Erin Lincoln's body out of my head. "They found his prints at the grave site in Quebec," I guessed.

He nodded.

"It wasn't him," I said. "He was on the island in the '80s. He couldn't have done it." I didn't know who I was trying to convince more—Diggs or myself.

"He visited the mainland a lot though, didn't he?" Diggs pressed. "You said he had buying trips, right? He did the shopping for the church. Went to craft fairs to sell the dolls the Paysons made." He touched my arm. "As much as you might think you knew your father, maybe you didn't really know him at all. You've painted this rosy picture of who you imagined him to be, the same way you painted this rosy picture of what your childhood in that church was like. How much of that is actually based in reality, though?"

"I sure as hell knew him well enough to know he didn't do this," I said angrily. I stood and walked across the room, putting as much distance as possible between myself and the gruesome photos. "He never would have done that."

"Did he ever tell you what happened to his sister?"

I turned on him. "Why the fuck would he name me after somebody he raped and murdered?" I shouted. "The hooded man—"

Diggs was on his feet at that. He stayed where he was, but I could feel his frustration all the way across the room. "The hooded man *what*, Sol? You're really gonna stand there and tell me that the phantom you say set the Payson Church on fire did this, too? *He* killed your aunt, then twenty years later tortured and murdered another handful of girls and planted your father's fingerprints before he buried his victims so far in the middle of nowhere they'd likely never be found? If he was gonna frame your father, why would he go to that much trouble to get rid of the bodies? Think about it!"

I was thinking about it; that was the problem. I shook my head. I had an overpowering urge to hit something. "So you think Gendreau brought me in on this because he thinks my father killed his daughter? His whole point was to use me to track Dad down when no one else could?"

"I think you should ask him that."

I ran a hand through my hair and tried to get a handle on this latest information. What the hell had I expected I'd find when I finally got some insight into my father's past? That he'd had an apple-pie-and-board-games childhood with a loving family somewhere, and then on a whim just decided to change his name and hide out for the rest of his life on some island with a bunch of religious nut jobs? I'd known it had to be bad… I'd never imagined something like this, though.

I went to the window and stared out into the darkness, my reflection superimposed over a canvas of blue-black night and trees cast in shadow. Diggs came over and stood beside me.

"I assume this means you'll be headed up north next?" he asked.

"Yeah. I want to get up there as soon as I can. I won't be able to figure any of this out until I'm actually able to sit down with some of the key players to ask a few questions. And if Dad really is from up there…" My voice faded. If he was really up there, what? I'd like a reunion with the old family, if any of them are still alive? I'd like to find out every last detail of the brutal murder that took the sister I'd been named for?

I still felt sick, my arms crossed over my stomach as I tried to erase the images I'd seen in both girls' files now—Ashley Gendreau and Erin Lincoln. Unlike the victims in Canada, buried so long that most traces of the crime had been erased by time, the brutality of Ashley's attack had been captured in half a dozen different mediums. Her mother sat through the trial; went through Technicolor photos that left no doubt about the kind of hell her daughter had endured in the hours before her death.

And now it seemed my aunt had endured the same hell.

If she had, what did my father know about both girls' deaths?

Diggs leaned against me, staring out into the same black night. "I could come with you."

I leaned back for just a second before I remembered the stacked brunette now keeping his office stocked with fresh wildflowers and Post-it notes. I straightened up. Shook my head. "You don't need to do that—I've got it covered. You've got too much going on here, anyway."

He looked like he was about to argue when his phone rang. The expression on his face was all I needed to confirm that that very same stacked brunette was on the other end of the line.

"I can call her back later," he said.

"Nah, answer it," I said quickly. I grabbed Jeff Lincoln's file and the dog. "If I don't see you tomorrow, I'll catch up with you another time. Thanks for this." I nodded toward the file numbly. Diggs answered the call as I was headed down the hallway, but I made a point not to listen.

◊◊◊◊◊

Two minutes. Growing up, my mother used to say that was all the time anyone needed for even the worst emotional shit-storm before a woman with any true substance could get control and soldier on. Dad was more forgiving of emotional shit-storms—or at least I thought he was, but since I hadn't had a meaningful conversation with the man since I was nine, it was becoming a lot harder to remember his views on life.

As a general rule, I tried to avoid taking Kat's advice on anything beyond basic medical care—and even that was sketchy—but at the moment, the two-minute rule seemed like a good idea.

I gave myself a minute and forty-five seconds of tears and a borderline panic attack over Jeff and Erin Lincoln, the connection to my father, and the recognition that, whatever the truth might be, there was no way it could possibly be good. I refused to acknowledge that any of my inner turmoil might have something to do with Diggs and his new lady friend. When my time was up, I took a deep breath, set my files and my laptop on the bed, and pulled myself together. I changed into boxers and a t-shirt, washed my face, and brushed my teeth. Then, I got into bed with Einstein, opened the first file I found, and dove in

Chapter Five

Diggs was gone when I got up the next morning, though he'd left a note on the fridge instructing me to give him a call before I left town. Childishly, I did not. I packed up the Jetta with Einstein, what little gear I'd brought with me, some bottled water, and a couple of peanut butter and jelly sandwiches for the trip. I didn't bother saying goodbye to Kat or Maya on the way out of town, reasoning that I could just call them from the road or drop a line once the story was done and I was settled back in Portland. I didn't stop by the *Trib*. The sun was bright and I played Jenny Lewis too loud with Einstein hanging his head out the window all the way down 97 toward Route 1, desperate to get the hell out of Dodge.

Before I hit Route 1, however, I cleared the front gate and found a shady parking spot at the state prison. It was unexpectedly cool, so at least I had that going for me. I set Einstein up with some water and a well-worn Kong, and then I went inside to take my rage out on the man who'd introduced me to Jeff Lincoln and all his demons in the first place: Hank Gendreau.

I hadn't had the foresight to set up a meeting with Hank before I showed up, which turned out to be a problem. It took almost an hour before things got straightened out and the warden agreed to give me ten minutes. The visiting room wasn't available, so a stocky guard with a buzz cut led me to a smaller, private room where I suspected inmates usually met with lawyers. The guard remained posted at the door, though as far as I was concerned Hank Gendreau had a lot more to worry about than I did.

Hank must have known why I was there, because he didn't look nearly so happy to see me this time around as he had before. He was already seated when I got to the room, but I remained standing.

"Tell me about Jeff Lincoln," I said before he could say a word.

"Do you know where he is?" he asked immediately.

The same kind of wood-veneer table that had separated us two days before was between us now, but the civility was nowhere to be found.

"Tell me what you know about his sister first," I said. "What happened on that lake? Did you see her brother again after they disappeared?"

"I wasn't there—I don't know where he went after. I don't have a clue what happened on the lake the day they went missing."

"You must have heard something, though. Did you know her?"

"Of course I knew her," he snapped. "You grew up in a small town—you know what it's like. We all knew each other."

"I went to see your lawyer yesterday," I said, trying a different tack. "I got a chance to talk to the woman who lives there—Bonnie. Do you know her?"

"Yeah, I know her." He rolled his eyes at me. "She's my sister."

Some investigative reporter I was. That explained the way she'd been staring at me the day before, though: She must have seen the same resemblance Hank had when he'd found the picture of my father and me in the paper.

"She said you told the cops something when they first picked you up the day of your daughter's murder. That you'd seen someone else out there?"

That fear returned to his eyes for just an instant before it vanished. "Jeff," he said, after just a second's hesitation. "I saw Jeff out there."

I didn't say anything. The fear vanished from his eyes, replaced with pure bile. I sat down. Wet my lips.

"You're lying," I said. My voice was barely more than a whisper. "You would have told the police if you'd seen him that day."

"I did tell them. Red Grivois—he was the first cop on the scene. I told him. Ask him. But I was out of my mind, between the drugs and what I'd seen. Who the hell do you think's gonna believe somebody like that—covered in his daughter's blood, raving about a kid who went missing seventeen years before? I might as well have told them Bigfoot did it."

I struggled to get my voice back. "Your sister said she saw something—or that she sees someone. Does she think the killer is Jeff Lincoln, too?"

"I don't know what she thinks anymore; you can't go by her. You go by me. I was there." The harmless do-gooder I'd met before had vanished, now that we were alone. His eyes burned with grief and rage and a kind of madness that I suspected no one ever really came back from.

"What do you want from me?" I asked. "Why did you send that picture to me? What's supposed to happen next here?"

"I want you to find him," he said. "And then if I can't kill him myself, I want him to rot in here. You saw what he did to my daughter. What he did to those other girls… And God knows who else. I know he's your father, but he's not human. You must be able to see that by now."

His voice had lowered to a harsh whisper. The guard shifted behind me. I tried to move my chair back, but it was bolted to the floor.

"Go to hell," I said softly. "You're wrong. It wasn't him—you don't know what you're talking about." I made an effort to keep my voice level. "He wouldn't do this."

"I knew him," Gendreau said. "He was cold. Mean. And maybe he thought he had a right to do what he did…" I looked at him in confusion. He shook his head. "But nobody has a right to do something like that."

If the table hadn't been between us and a guard hadn't been two feet away with his hand wrapped around the Mace at his belt, I'm not sure what I would have done. I stood, my palms on the table as I leaned in. "Why the hell would anyone believe you? You said it yourself: you were out of your mind that day. You were the one they found covered in Ashley's blood. You've got everything to gain by palming all this shit off on my father."

Gendreau looked at the guard, stood, and backed up until he was pressed against the concrete wall, as far from me as possible. The hate in his eyes was unmistakable.

"Get her out of here," he said.

The guard tried to pull me away, but I wasn't finished yet.

"How does anyone know you aren't the one who killed those other girls, too? You could have killed Erin Lincoln for all I know. You got a thirteen-year-old girl pregnant, for Christ's sake. Maybe you've had a hard on for little girls for as far back as you¬—"

He lunged for me suddenly, everything about him coiled as tight as a fist. The guard got between us before Gendreau ever touched me, and pushed me roughly toward the door. An alarm went off, bouncing off the concrete walls.

"It was him," Gendreau called after me. "Your father's the monster. He did this!"

Another guard arrived and pulled me out of the room before I went in for another shot at him, my blood boiling. Once we were a few feet down the corridor, I pulled my arm out of the guard's grasp. He didn't press the issue, but he also didn't make any move to let go of his Mace.

"I'll need to report this," the guard said to me. He had dark hair and a square jaw and a pug nose that didn't fit his face. He was very unhappy with me. "I doubt you'll be allowed back in here."

"Fine by me. I don't want to come back here."

My cheeks were burning, though it was more from embarrassment than rage once I got some distance. Half a dozen burly guards had gathered at the security station when we returned. A couple of them looked at me like I was clearly Satan's spawn, while the rest just ignored me outright. My pug-nosed escort walked me back through the main entrance and all the way to the parking lot before he'd let me go.

"You'll be all right from here, Miss?" he asked.

I nodded. "I'm fine. Thank you."

He remained at the gate, watching me go. I could still hear the alarm blaring inside the building.

◊◊◊◊◊

I'd just managed to pull myself together—or as close as I was likely to come as long as people were saying my father was a crazed psychopath who butchered young girls—when I got to my car. Or rather, the spot where my car had been when I left it. In its place was a worn blue Jeep with a kayak strapped to the top. Inside, a very wet Einstein greeted me with tail wagging, his paws on the dashboard. All my stuff had mysteriously repacked itself into the back. Diggs—also wet—reclined in the front with his feet on the dash and his arms crossed over his chest, his straw hat pushed low over his eyes.

"A prison riot, Solomon? Seriously?" he casually pushed the hat back so I could see his eyes, but otherwise didn't move. "I can't leave you alone for a second."

I felt a rush of relief so sweet I almost sank to my knees. "I didn't start the damn thing," I said. "And it wasn't technically a riot. What'd you do with my car?"

"Sent it back with one of the boys from the paper. Don't worry—it's in good hands. Then Stein and I went for a swim."

"And now you're here because..."

He removed his feet from the dash and sat up. "You really thought I'd let you head sixty miles north of the Arctic Circle on your own to chase a psychotic serial killer who may or may not be your old man? Give me a little credit, Sol."

"What about the paper?"

"Eh." He waved his hand vaguely. "I took a few days off. I'm not the only one who works there—they can handle it. The only time anything worth reporting happens around here is when you're in town anyway, so I think we're safe."

"And Andie?"

The humor vanished for just an instant. His eyes drifted from mine. "We're good. She understands."

Bullshit was on the tip of my tongue, but I kept it to myself.

"Do you know where we're going?" I asked.

"Head north 'til you see the Mounties?"

Pretty much. I went around to the passenger's side, forced Einstein into the backseat, and got in. Diggs ground the Jeep into gear. I put my seatbelt on as a sudden rush of emotion—fear or grief or a residual adrenaline rush from my encounter with Gendreau—washed over me. Out of the corner of my eye, I saw Diggs glance at me.

"You okay?"

"Yeah," I said. I wet my lips. Cleared my throat.

He took a bottled water from his center console, uncapped it, and handed it to me without taking his eyes off the road. "I'm here, Sol," he said. "Whatever we find up there… We can handle it."

I wiped my eyes with the back of my hand, then took a good slug of water and focused on keeping it together before I disgraced myself entirely.

"Even if it turns out my old man was a card-carrying psycho who used to party with Charlie Manson himself?" I asked.

He smiled. "Yeah," he said. "Even then.

PART II.
BLACK FALLS

Chapter Six

We hit the requisite stops on the way through the Midcoast: coffee and scones in the vault at the Thomaston Highlands; the best ice cream in the state at Dorman's for dessert; and a quick stop at Rockland's Loyal Biscuit so Einstein could rub elbows with Chuck, sniff out the latest cats up for adoption, and pick out some choice treats for the trip. Once we were well down the road on Route 1, I got out my cell phone and dialed Max Richards' number. Max himself answered on the second ring.

"Ms. Solomon," he said smoothly. "Sorry I missed you last night. Did you find everything you needed?"

Not by a long shot, but I kept that to myself. "Actually, I was calling about your…" I wasn't sure what to call her. Housekeeper seemed wildly off the mark, but guest didn't seem right, either. "Bonnie. I need to speak with her."

There was a long pause on the other end of the line, during which the cockatiel let out a couple of ear-piercing shrieks. Between the bird and the prison alarm, it wasn't a good day for eardrums.

"She's not here, I'm afraid," he said.

"Do you know when she'll be back?"

"I don't, sorry. I woke up this morning and she was gone—took the dogs and everything. No note. Nothing. She does that sometimes… Eventually she'll be back."

"Do you have a number where I could reach her?"

He chuckled. "Bonnie isn't really the cell phone type. You might consider sending a message out to the universe… She'll find you if it's important."

I asked him a couple of questions about the Gendreau case and Ashley's death, not really paying attention to his answers. Bonnie Saucier was missing. I thought of what she'd said to me: It's G. you need to watch for. He'll be looking for you.

Who the hell was G?

◊◊◊◊◊

We traveled Route 1 up to 1A, past farm stands and pickup trucks selling fresh lobster and crab on the side of the road, past bookstores and bars and all the picture postcard scenes that continue to make Maine one of my favorite destinations. I shed my shoes and rode with my bare feet on the dash while Springsteen blared from Diggs' formidable car stereo and memories of a hundred drives much like this ran through my head. The sun was shining and the Atlantic was a pure, deep blue that we traveled alongside for as long as possible before I convinced Diggs there was no way in hell we were adding three hours to the journey so he could avoid the highway in favor of a summer jaunt along Route 1.

"You were a lot more fun when you were younger, you know," he said.

"You just think that because you were always high back then," I said. "I've never actually been that much fun."

He didn't argue with that.

I fell asleep sometime after the sixth moose crossing sign on I-95. When I woke up, it was just after two o'clock and Diggs was leaving 95 for Route 1 up in Houlton. We stopped at a scale model of Saturn so Einstein could pee, then ate a late lunch on the hood of Diggs' Jeep while summer traffic whizzed by and birds chirped and bees buzzed. Diggs got his old Gazetteer and half a dozen other faded maps from the glove compartment and hopped up beside me again.

"I didn't think they actually made those anymore," I said.

"Don't mock. These things have gotten me a lot of places over the years." He opened the Gazetteer to Maine and handed a topographic map to me. Most of Aroostook County was covered with an old coffee stain, and a deep burgundy streak obliterated much of Piscataquis.

"I'm getting you a GPS for your next birthday. What happened to this thing?"

"Roadside mishap." He looked downright nostalgic. "Have I taught you nothing, Sol? GPS is for people who don't appreciate that travel's all about the journey. Logging roads, caves, fire towers, the American dream... Try to find that with GPS."

"That's because most of those logging roads and fire towers don't exist anymore. And I'm pretty sure even Hunter S. gave up looking for the American dream a while ago."

He heaved a weary sigh. "You disappoint me. The day they invent a

GPS that can evoke the same feelings a moldering map can, I'll be first in line to get one. Now—Where the hell are we going? On a need to know basis, I feel like I should be in the loop at this point."

I pulled a wrinkled newspaper clipping from my pocket and handed it to him. He read it silently, then glanced at me.

"Where'd you get this?" he asked.

"It was in with the files I took from Max Richards' place."

"Why was Erin Lincoln's obituary with Hank Gendreau's files?"

"Good question, isn't it? I looked up the cemetery they mention in there—where she and her family are buried. I'd like to start there."

I could feel him looking at me, but I kept my gaze fixed on the coffee-stained County. Diggs slid back to the ground and held out his hand. I took it just long enough for my flip flops to hit the dirt before I pulled away.

"So, you don't mind? I don't know how much we'll actually find out there."

"I don't mind," he said. "It's a good idea—a place to start, anyway."

I doubted that, actually, but I didn't say anything. We got back in the Jeep, and neither of us spoke while we drove the rest of the way up Route 1, toward an abandoned cemetery that held a family I'd never even known I had.

◊◊◊◊◊

It turned out to be a good thing that Diggs had packed his Gazetteer, because there was no way in hell GPS ever would have found the Forest Grove Cemetery. We turned off Route 1 about ten miles south of Black Falls, onto a steep, overgrown dirt road that led up a forty-five degree incline into no man's land. It was late afternoon, the sun still high in the sky, but minimal light made it through the canopy of thick forest. After about ten minutes creeping along a barely discernible dirt road, I spotted a lopsided, rough-hewn gravestone.

"Hang on—I think that's it."

I got out and made straight for the trees while Diggs was still trying to figure out where to pull over. The grave belonged to Jason Saucier, who'd died in 1922. That stone marked the beginning of a rough path littered with Bud cans and cigarette butts. I forged ahead without waiting for Einstein or Diggs, following the path to a cluster of lichen-covered headstones scattered seemingly haphazard in an overgrown field. Wildflowers grew in knots of color. Bees buzzed. A mosquito the size of my thumb set up camp just below my left ear until I had the presence of mind to swat it.

I kept walking.

Diggs and Einstein caught up to me somewhere along the line. Sweat trickled down the back of my neck and my t-shirt clung to the small of my back. The forest got thicker, as did the mosquitoes and blackflies. The trail of beer cans and butts dried up. I could hear water rushing somewhere nearby.

"You're sure it's out here?" Diggs asked.

"It should be," I said.

When it was clear that Erin Lincoln's grave wasn't among the ones we'd found so far, I followed a path deeper into the woods. Einstein ran on ahead, while Diggs lingered behind. We'd gone about fifty yards beyond the first graveyard when the path opened up again. I came out of the woods to find myself at the edge of another overgrown field, this one on a hillside. A single crumbling headstone was planted halfway down the hill. Through a grove of spruce at the bottom, I could see and hear white water rushing past. I stopped and crouched to read the stone.

Wallace Lincoln
1925 – 1972

Jeff and Erin's father. Erin Lincoln's headstone wasn't there, but I didn't have to look far before I found it. At the bottom of the hill were two immaculate gravesites overlooking a waterfall that dropped into a clear, peaceful stretch of the Aroostook River. The cemetery plot had been mowed recently, and fresh wildflowers decorated both graves. The headstones were made of marble. Both were elegant, oversized, and undoubtedly expensive.

The stone to the left belonged to Willa Lincoln—my grandmother, or so the theory went. According to Erin Lincoln's obituary, Willa had died of pneumonia in '68. The inscription said simply, Taken too soon. The second stone belonged to Erin Rae Lincoln. Below her name, etched in an elegant script, were the words, A better world awaits.

Diggs came over and stood beside me silently.

"You okay?" he asked.

I didn't trust my voice, so I just nodded. There was no evidence of Jeff Lincoln here—no sign that anyone mourned his passing, or missed him in his absence… No sign that he'd existed at all.

"Someone's been taking care of it," I noted when I could finally speak.

Diggs pointed into the woods to our left. It took me a second before I saw what he was pointing to: a cabin, just barely visible from our vantage. A quick look around revealed a path leading straight to it.

"It doesn't seem vaguely creepy that there's a house out here in the middle of nowhere, and the only neighbors for twenty miles are…"

"Dead?" Diggs finished for me. "It's a hell of a lot more than vaguely creepy, but I don't see a lot of choices here. If you want to talk to the crypt keeper, this looks like the best bet."

I hated it when he was logical. "Right. Absolutely right."

I whistled for Einstein, who came galloping toward us a few seconds later, delirious at his newly-earned freedom after almost eight hours on the road. I started down the path to the house. When I realized I was alone, I glanced over my shoulder.

"Are you coming?"

Diggs grimaced. "I don't know how I keep ending up in situations like this with you."

"Suck it up," I said. "Do you know how long I tagged after you on your undercover stories from hell? How many creepy freaks I distracted with my feminine wiles while you got your scoops?"

That nostalgic gleam I'd been seeing so much of lately resurfaced. "Ahh… The good old days." He nodded, resolute, and hurried to catch up. "You're right. Let's do this thing."

The cabin had a garden out back and flowers out front and three goats and a lame donkey in a fenced area off to the side. Deep-throated barking came from within the second my feet touched the doorstep. Diggs put Einstein's leash back on and held him a few steps back while I knocked.

A tall, sturdy man who could have been thirty or could have been eighty answered. His eyes were dark and his beard freshly trimmed. When he saw me, he took a step back and just stared, an unmistakable simplicity in his eyes. He wore a meticulously pressed, peach-colored dress shirt beneath a pair of equally well-pressed overalls. He remained in the doorway staring at us with his mouth open before he suddenly turned his head and shouted over his shoulder.

"Sarah!"

I looked at Diggs, who just shrugged. A huge, shaggy white dog peered out at us from behind the man's left hip. Einstein whined behind me. The man shouted the same name again—twice—without ever making a move to let us in. Or shut us out, for that matter. The shaggy dog pushed past him and padded out to meet us with tail wagging. Einstein took one look at her and his dogged heart was a goner. While we waited for this mysterious Sarah to appear, the two dogs did a quick sniff test before Diggs unhooked Stein and they took off for the wild blue.

Eventually, a woman as tall and twice as broad as the man at the door appeared from the back, spitting what was either pig Latin or pissed-off French.

She stopped the second she saw me, blinked once or twice, then pulled the man away from the door and took his place, her hands on her wide hips.

"What you want here?" She had the voice of a lifetime smoker, an impressive growth of crisp black hairs sprouting from her fleshy chin, and a much thicker version of the same Acadian accent I'd heard from Bonnie.

"We were just up at the cemetery there," I said, pointing over my shoulder. "We saw the path leading here. I thought you might be able to answer some questions."

"*Non*," she said briefly. The man was standing behind her with his arms crossed over his chest, still staring at me. "We have work, *oui*? No time for tourists." She started to close the door.

I stuck my foot in the door without a moment's hesitation. "I'm here about Erin Lincoln—she was my aunt. Or she would have been, anyway. You knew her, didn't you?" I addressed the man directly. "That's why you're looking at me that way; you can see the resemblance?"

"We don't have nothing to say about it," the woman insisted.

"Jeff was *ton pere*?" the man asked. He took a step toward me.

"He didn't use the name Jeff when he had me, but I think so, yes. I came here to find out more about him. About what happened here."

"We don't know about what happened," Sarah said. "And we have work."

The man touched her shoulder and said something in rapid-fire French, his eyes on me the whole time. I didn't need to speak the language to know he was pleading my case.

"Please," I said. "I won't take that much of your time."

She looked like she'd rather have lunch with a rabid mountain lion, but she finally opened the door again and stepped aside.

We were in.

I'd been expecting slasher-movie chic when Diggs first pointed out the cabin, but what we found inside was anything but: a mud room that opened into a sunny, spacious great room with oversized windows and plants on every surface. Matted black and white photos—a few landscapes, but most of wildlife—hung on the walls. Diggs looked around in wonder.

"Did you build this?" he asked Sarah.

She pointed at the man. "My brother did everything. Furniture, art, *et la maison.*"

The man nodded, his face shining with pride. He dug his hands into his pockets. "Sarah showed me, and then I built it. We worked together."

Diggs ran his hand reverently along the pale, wooded walls. "I built a place a couple of years ago," he said. "It's good work—peaceful. A good way to get your head together. Mine didn't come out anything like this, though," he added.

I looked at him in surprise. Diggs had returned to Maine after his third marriage failed a little over three years before, resolutely sober and uncharacteristically celibate, but that was about all I knew—he'd never shared any details beyond that. Sarah softened at his words, maybe seeing a glimpse of the vulnerability I'd somehow missed up to that point.

"Luke has a gift for it," she said, nodding toward her brother. "*Pis c'est vrai*—anything you can do with your hands that gets you out of your head *c'est tres bien.*" She waved toward a handmade table with matching chairs in the kitchen. "Sit if you like. I'll put on coffee."

I glanced back out the window. Einstein and his new girl were chasing each other through a field of goldenrod. Sarah followed my gaze.

"They'll be fine, *chere*. She was raised to be *maman* to everything in these woods—she looks out for everybody. She can keep him from trouble."

Despite her reassurance, I took a seat facing the window—just in case Stein decided to make a break for it, or his woolly sweetheart decided she'd had enough.

Luke made himself some tea, moving carefully around the kitchen—like he'd broken one too many things over the years, and was afraid of repeating past mistakes. Sarah set two mugs of steaming coffee in front of us, and sat down with tea for herself.

"She was *très jolie*, you know? Pretty," she said as soon as she sat down. I looked at her in surprise. "We might as well get to it, *non?* The reason you're here."

A woman after my own heart. "What do you remember about her?" I asked.

"Oh… I remember everything," she said immediately. "She was a good girl. But very…" She paused, like she was trying to find the English for what she wanted to say. "Fiery, *non?* Always fighting for something. Helping people, all the time. It's why Luke took to her."

Luke nodded. He was sitting at the edge of his chair, which he'd pushed as close to me as possible without actually landing in my lap.

"You look like her," he said. "But not so much as I thought when Bonnie said you was coming, *oui*? You have her hair. *Et la bouche, non*?" He tapped his own lips. "But not the same smile. She smiled with all her teeth." He demonstrated. "She was sad, sometimes. *Mais tu est plus triste.*"

I looked at Diggs, whose *francais* was far superior to mine. "He says you are more sad," he said.

"Oh." The heat rose in my cheeks while I tried to think of a graceful way out of that one. "Wait—Max Richards' Bonnie? Hank Gendreau's sister? You know her?"

"*Oui*," Sarah said. "She married our brother—he *est* gone now. *Mais* we are all Sauciers."

"She told us about *la rêve*," Luke said. Whatever *la rêve* was, based on the wild look in his eye, it had freaked the hell out of him. "What she saw. She says it's *pas bien*, you coming here. Not safe."

Diggs looked at me, baffled. "What are they talking about?"

"Bonnie is *un taweille*," Sarah said. "Same as her *mémère*. She has the Sight. We learned many years ago not to ignore that."

"She said something about G," I said before Diggs could get in on the act, hoping to get us back on track. "How she saw someone named G, or being able to see... into them," I finished, feeling like an idiot.

"*Il est mal* to talk about what Bonnie sees," Sarah said, glancing at Luke. Based on the rocking and the clenched fists, he wasn't handling the conversation well. I understood how he felt.

"What about her brother, then—Jeff. Can you tell me anything about him?"

"He was *un monstre*," Luke said, his fists clenched on the table. The rocking sped up, his breathing along with it. I've been accused before of lacking empathy, but even I could tell this was a bad sign. Sarah touched her brother's hand; he stopped almost instantly.

"Jeff was one of the more popular kids in Black Falls," Sarah said. "On the basketball team, always in the paper for something. But he..." She hesitated.

I leaned back in my chair and attempted a reassuring smile. "It's all right. You can say whatever you want. I'm just after the truth."

She looked at Diggs for confirmation. He nodded.

"*D'accord*," she said. She looked me dead in the eye. "He was mean. Smart, but cold. Cruel."

I thought of my father and me in the greenhouse when I was a kid—tending the plants, wondering at every caterpillar and earthworm that crossed our path.

"Can you give us an example of what you're talking about?" Diggs asked. His eyes never left mine.

"He locked me in the cellar," Luke said immediately. His eyes clouded. "He told me nobody would come for me because I was *stupide*. *Il m'a laissé dans le noir.*"

"He left him in the dark," Diggs translated for me.

I swallowed past a knot that lodged itself halfway down my throat.

"It was just overnight," Sarah said, like that somehow made it better. "Only a few hours. But Jeff slipped and told Erin… She came back and let Luke out."

"I didn't think nobody would find me," Luke said. "I prayed on my knees and I tried to dig myself out. Bloodied my fingers. Hurt my head. Who would do something like that? I never did nothing to Jeff Lincoln."

"What happened when you got out?" Diggs asked, saving me the trouble of coming up with an apology for the demon my father had apparently been as a kid.

"His *père* was *très* important in town," Sarah said. "He owned a mill that shut down soon after Erin… " She stopped. "*Après tout.* But then, nobody did nothing because Mr. Lincoln would have their jobs. Jeff didn't get away with it at home, though."

Luke looked troubled.

"That bothers you?" Diggs asked.

"Erin told me things," Luke said softly, like he was revealing a long-kept secret.

I looked at him curiously. "What things?"

"About home. What *son père* would do to Jeff when nobody was there. I was trying to be his *amis* …"

"And that's when he locked you in the cellar?" Diggs asked.

"He was *tres fâché*. Angry. He told me to shut up. Hit me in the face." Luke looked down at his hands, twisting his callused fingers together. "He said I didn't know nothing about it because I was *stupide*. He told me I shouldn't talk about him again. *Jamais.*"

"When did all this happen?" I asked.

Sarah looked at Luke. "It was after Mrs. Lincoln died, *oui*?"

He nodded. "*Dans l'été.* In summer."

"*Oui*," she agreed. "Not long before they found Erin."

So, mere months before Jeff Lincoln dropped out of sight and his sister was found murdered, he'd been beating up mentally challenged neighbors and locking them in the cellar. I couldn't imagine any of it. The man I'd known—the one who raised me and kept me safe for the first nine years of my life—might as well have never existed.

I took out the photo I had of the two of us out on the island together and slid it across the table to her.

"Do you recognize him?" I asked. "The boy you're talking about— Could this be him?"

Sarah and Luke both leaned over the photo, looking at it closely. After a minute or two, they both eased back. The look on their faces was enough.

"He looks nicer, there," Luke said. "*Un bon père, oui?* A good father?"

"*Oui,*" I agreed softly.

"How did Jeff get along with his sister?" Diggs asked. He glanced at me to see if I was still in the game. I managed a naked smile, but nothing more.

"He never left her side," Sarah said. "They were like magnets, *non?* Opposites, but they fit. There was three, four years between them, but that didn't matter. *Il est très…*" she hesitated again, looking for the word. "Protective. Very protective"

I held on tight to that tenuous lifeline. "And no one thought it was a little weird that he would do... well, everything that was done to Erin Lincoln before she died? Given that she was the only one he ever actually seemed to like?"

"She was afraid of him," Luke said. "He didn't want her to have no other friends. *Jamais.*"

"It wasn't affection," Sarah agreed. "He owned her. She was his pet. It was okay when she was younger. By the time she died, she didn't like it no more."

"You knew her, then," I said.

Her eyes clouded. She didn't say a word.

"Sarah and Erin were *amis*. Best friends. Together always. Sarah even went dancing *avec* Jeff. It wasn't a good date, though," Luke said. "She came back crying, *pis* cried for two more days."

She took a long sip of tea and set the mug down carefully. The look in her eye was all I needed.

"How old were you?" I asked. My voice was barely above a whisper.

"Thirteen," she said. She held herself carefully upright. "He was handsome. Very charming, when he wanted to be."

She put a hand over Luke's and nodded toward the door, issuing an order in French. Luke got up without any fuss, said a quick goodbye to Diggs and me, and headed for the door. Sarah waited until he'd gone before she said anything more.

"I am sorry I can't tell you better things about your father," she said.

"He raped you," I said. I couldn't seem to get my voice back.

"It wasn't like that," she said quickly. "He didn't beat me, nothing like that. He gave me beer. Was nice to me—and careful, so there wasn't no worry about *un bébé*. But then when it was over, he wouldn't talk to me no more. He drove me home, *pis* then he stayed away from me. He tried to make Erin stop spending time with me and Luke, *mais non*. She never did listen to him."

"I'm sorry," I said. The apology hung in the air, grossly inadequate considering the damage Jeff Lincoln—my father—had inflicted on this woman more than forty years ago. I stood numbly. "We should probably go."

Diggs got up and took our dishes to the sink.

"You should talk to Red Grivois," Sarah said, just as the dogs came bursting through the door with Luke on their heels. "He was with the state police for many years. He found Erin, and investigated the case. He's been fishing, but he's back *maintenant*. I'll call and tell him to expect you."

"Wasn't he the same one who was first on scene when they found Ashley Gendreau?" I asked.

"We don't have many police up this way—every *mal* thing that happened here for many years, Red was the one had to pick up after it. It wasn't a good job."

I supposed not. Still, he was definitely high on my list of people to talk to while I was in Black Falls. While Sarah made her phone call, Luke and I occupied ourselves picking burrs out of the dogs' fur and Diggs studied the photos on the walls. When Sarah hung up, he nodded toward the prints.

"These are all Luke's?" he asked.

She nodded, her eye on her brother. "*Oui*. There are many things he can't do. Neither one of us was nothing much in school, *mais* there are things he takes to. God's way, I like to think. There is balance, always."

Except for Erin Lincoln, of course, raped and murdered at twelve years old. And Ashley Gendreau. And any of the other victims of the monster we were trying to find.

Sarah walked us to the door. We said brief goodbyes, but I was so stuck on her revelations about my father that she might as well have gone back to French. We were on our way out when Diggs stopped for one last question.

"What about Hank Gendreau? Did you know him, too?"

"*Oui.* We know his sister Bonnie, *bien sûr.* Hank was friends with Jeff, though," she said. She didn't look happy about that. "*Pis* Will Rainier. We didn't spend lots of time together."

"So what happened with his daughter… You know about that."

It's not like everything we'd been talking about had been a walk in the park, but this was the first time I saw a genuinely emotional reaction. Her eyes swam with tears. She brushed them away and nodded. "*Mais oui.* Everybody remembers here."

"Do you think it was a coincidence that Ashley died the same way Erin Lincoln died?" Diggs asked.

"*Non,*" she said shortly. "Coincidence… I don't believe in that. Hank left after Erin and Jeff went missing; we thought then he must know something. *Après* Ashley… *Non.* No coincidence," she said again.

"Do you think Hank and my father were both responsible for Erin's death, then?" I asked.

She shook her head. "*Je ne sais pas.* Everybody's thought about it, everybody still thinks about it. Nobody knows, *mais Jeff pis Hank pis Will. Mais ton père* wasn't the only *monstre* in this town. Hank was just wild—too many drugs. But Will was just *mauvais.*"

She took my hand at the door and held it tightly. "There are some things it is better not to know. This may be one, *oui?*"

I didn't say anything, not sure what kind of response was required in that situation. When she let me go, I joined Diggs on the front step. We were silent the entire trek back to the Jeep

Chapter Seven

Diggs and I rented a couple of rooms at a Budget Inn on Route 1 a few miles shy of Black Falls, stopped long enough to dump our stuff, and within twenty minutes were on the road again.

Black Falls was an old mill town built on the Aroostook River, with railroad tracks running clear through town to connect it to the rest of the country. Now, the mills and the railroad were shut down, the economy had tanked years ago, and as far as I could tell all that was left were a few potato farms and a main stretch through town with more FOR SALE OR RENT signs than actual businesses.

Red Grivois lived in a little house in the heart of town, an old pickup on cement blocks in his well-groomed front yard. When we pulled in, he sat at a pine picnic table with a half-full bottle of Black Label and a twelve pack of Bud beside him. He had thick white hair and thick white eyebrows and a red nose that suggested this wasn't the first night he'd knocked a fifth back on his own. Diggs looked at me before we got out of the Jeep.

"This should be fun," he said.

"Yup. How do you wanna play it?"

"This is your story... I'm pretty sure he'll want to talk to you a lot more than me, anyway. You've got nicer legs."

"Don't sell yourself short, Diggs," I said.

I grabbed my bag and put Einstein on his leash without waiting for a reply. Then, I strolled across the lawn and took a seat on the bench opposite Grivois without waiting for an invitation.

He looked up, grimaced at the sight of me, and looked back down at his red Solo cup of whiskey, clearly remembering another girl, another time. As superpowers went, I'd take flying or invisibility over the ability to freak out the locals just by showing my face, any day of the week.

"So, what do you want to know?" he asked. There was no trace of the

Acadian accent; I could barely detect a Maine one. He lit a Camel and pushed a warm beer toward me, which I accepted.

Diggs came over and sat down beside me. Grivois didn't offer him anything, which was just as well. Better to be left out than forced to refuse.

"You were the one who found Erin Lincoln's body," I said. I took the file from my bag and set it on the table between us.

"Well, you've got me there. Is that it?" he said.

"Not quite. I just have a few questions about that day. And about the investigation afterward."

"I'll tell you all I can," Grivois said, "but I can't make any promises. My memory isn't what it used to be."

Diggs glanced at the half-dozen empty beer cans beside him, but didn't say a word.

"How long had you been looking before you found the body?" I began.

"That's not in the file?"

"I just want it in your words, if that's okay."

He frowned. "Six days. We got a call about coyotes showing up closer to the camps than we like out at Eagle Lake, so I went to look. There was enough woods then that they usually kept to themselves; if they were coming that close to the camps, I knew there had to be a reason."

"And what did you find?"

He took the cap off the Black Label and dumped the rest of the whiskey into his cup. His frown deepened.

"You know what I found," he said quietly.

I glanced at Diggs. He shrugged, his meaning clear: This was my play.

"I understand you not wanting to think about it," I said. "But if my father did this, I'd like to know. I need to." It was a naked admission I hadn't intended to make, but it did the trick. Grivois eyed me speculatively before he nodded.

"She'd only been there a day, maybe," he said. "The coroner said she'd been alive up to then—running for maybe the full week before he caught her and killed her. Broken bones were healing; cuts had scabbed over." He stared at the table, stone faced. "She'd been raped. Strangled to the point of death, then brought back."

It was all information I'd read in the coroner's report, but it didn't make it any easier to hear.

"And what about the brother—Jeff?" I asked. "Did you find any trace of him?"

He hardened at mention of the name. When he met my gaze this time, there was a righteous fury I'd seen in cops before—the look of someone who'd seen the worst, and had no qualms about demanding justice in its purist form for the evildoers. Someone else who wanted Jeff Lincoln dead, then.

"You mean besides his belt wrapped around her throat? The same belt that was used to whip her backside 'til it was raw? Besides his initial carved in her chest? Or the fact that he disappeared the same time she went missing? Besides what we know happened later?"

"What do you mean by that?" I asked. "What happened later?"

"The nut house in Michigan," he said impatiently. "And now the bodies on the border... You need more than that?"

"But you don't have any hard proof that it was him," I said. "I mean—there's no witness who actually saw him do this. Everything else... There could be an explanation for that." I sounded like a delusional kid, intent on believing a fairy tale the rest of the world had given up on years ago.

Grivois set his cup down. He straightened in his seat, folding his hands in front of him on the table. He looked at me calmly.

"I know he was your father," he said. "But I knew Jeff Lincoln was trouble the day he set foot in this town. He was mean. Spiteful. It was his daddy's fault—we all knew that. But he was dark in a way young people shouldn't know to be dark. I wish I could tell you something else, but those are the facts. There wasn't any doubt in my mind then that Jeff Lincoln did this, and there's no doubt now."

"What about alternate suspects?" I asked stubbornly. "There must have been someone else you looked at, right? Summer in a popular spot, there has to be someone other than my father who could have done this."

Grivois looked at Diggs like he was hoping for some kind of intervention, but Diggs stayed quiet.

"What about G?" I asked suddenly, recalling Bonnie's warning to me. "Does that name mean anything to you? Or just the letter?"

He looked genuinely perplexed. Diggs spoke up. "When Bonnie said that to you, was it with a soft *jh* sound to it?"

I nodded. Based on the look on his face, I was guessing that wasn't a good thing.

"*Jhee* is French for the letter J," he explained. "It would make sense, considering the J on Erin Lincoln's chest."

I took barely a second to digest that before I moved on, refusing to be thrown. "What about Hank Gendreau? Seventeen years after Erin Lincoln is raped and murdered, his own daughter is tracked in the woods and killed in almost exactly the same way? You really think that was coincidence?"

"Some people still think Hank didn't get a fair trial in that case," he said.

"And you're one of them," I said, recalling both Hank and Bonnie's words to that effect. "What do you think happened?"

He didn't say anything for a while, staring into his whiskey. "It was too much like another girl I found—I knew who did that one. There was every reason to believe the bastard who killed Erin Lincoln killed Ashley Gendreau, too."

"Except for the fact that the bastard who *allegedly* killed Erin Lincoln had been missing for seventeen years," I said. "And Hank Gendreau was right there."

"He saw somebody in those woods that day."

"Jeff Lincoln," I said with a nod. "According to his story. You really believe that?"

The look in his eye made it clear that he did, as a matter of fact. My guess was he'd go to his grave believing it.

"This alibi Hank had for Erin Lincoln's murder; can you tell me what that was? I haven't been able to get access to those files yet."

He took another drink. "He and a couple of his buddies were up in Quebec that weekend. We double-checked at the border—he wasn't at Eagle Lake. Your father was. It's as simple as that."

I started to argue with him, but Diggs wrapped his hand around my arm and stood. "We should go," he said. "Thanks for your time."

I knew he was right. The sun was down and Givrois was obviously done talking. I got up reluctantly. "Do you mind if I contact you with anything else?"

Givrois tipped the last of his whiskey back, cracked open a beer, and looked around. I wondered if he had any family. There was no sign of someone inside the house: no curtains in the windows, no toys in the yard. Not even a dog prowling around somewhere, with the exception of my own mutt. He blinked bloodshot eyes and stared back at the table.

"Go ahead. I'm not going anywhere."

◊◊◊◊◊

It was after ten by the time we finally got to the motel for good that night. That far up north, Route 1 is a ribbon of hills and dense woods, where locals share the road with deer and moose, black bear and coyotes. The Budget Inn was on a stretch with one other hotel, but just behind both of them was a stand of trees so thick it seemed like they were just waiting to creep closer the second your back was turned—like some primeval game of red light green light. The woods were definitely winning.

Diggs bumped my shoulder when he noticed me staring at the tree line. "Relax, Sol. I won't let Sasquatch get you."

I thought of what Red Grivois had described of Erin Lincoln's final week on the planet. I shivered despite the warm night air.

"I'm not worried about Sasquatch."

Diggs walked me to my room, though the fact that he was right next door made it seem a little silly. It didn't matter, though—I was grateful for the company. I hadn't said much since our meeting with Luke and Sarah, and even less since talking to Red Grivois. Diggs tipped his head sideways and studied me while I tried to make my key card work. Half of me wanted him to just go and leave me to stew. The other half had never wanted to be alone less in my life.

The light turned green and the door buzzed. I pushed it open. Einstein just about knocked me over to get inside, while I stayed in the doorway with Diggs.

"You'll be okay?" he asked.

"I think I can handle a motel room, Diggs. Compared to the rest of the day, this should be a cake walk."

He still made no move to go. "We got some good information today."

I laughed. "Did we? I guess if what we were shooting for was confirmation that my father was a monster…"

He didn't say anything to that. A baby cried in a room down the hall. Next door, someone was watching baseball with the volume too high; the Sox were up by two.

"We should get some rest," I said. "I'm just gonna hit the showers. And I imagine Andie's waiting for an update."

He nodded guiltily. Stepped back. "Yeah, you're right. I'll see you in the morning, I guess."

"I hope so—otherwise it's gonna be a hell of a long walk back to civilization."

He turned and started to walk away. I stood there debating for a second before I went after him and grabbed his arm. It was warm and strong and when he turned to look at me, there was something dark in his eyes—like a war was waging in that pretty blond head of his. I let go, wishing I hadn't stopped him.

"What?" he asked.

"I just wanted to thank you."

"Stop doing that," he said irritably. "You don't have to thank me for this... For being here. This is what we do. If it were me, you'd be here. Why would you think it would be any different for you?"

"Well, I still appreciate it. I just don't want you to think it doesn't mean anything."

"I know that."

Then we stood there for another six or seven days, staring into each other's eyes. I raised my eyebrows. This was when being half in the bag would really come in handy.

"Should we hug it out now?" I asked.

He kicked up a little smile, blue eyes sparkling. "I'm good. You?"

"I think I'm okay."

"Okay," he said. "I'm just gonna go scrub some of this road dust off. Give a shout if you need anything, though."

I told him I would, and went inside my room alone. A few minutes later, I heard his TV come on next door. The shower followed. For a few seconds I just stood there, my hand on the wall separating us. I'd been sleeping alone a lot lately; it turned out it didn't come as easily as I would have liked. I looked at Einstein, who had already settled himself on the bed.

"I know," I said. "It's not gonna happen."

He looked fleetingly concerned, but that vanished as soon as I opened my pack and started rooting around for treats. I gave him one and found a half-melted Hershey bar for myself, and went into the bathroom to drown my sorrows in the tub.

I went through the case files while I was soaking in tepid bath water. The bathroom fan was broken—it sounded like a DC-10 was landing in the next room, which proved to be too much for Einstein to handle. Between his whining and the content I was going through, I finally gave up on the idea of a relaxing bath and got out.

I turned the TV on, forgoing the local news in favor of a Firefly marathon on Syfy. I was half-dressed and just starting to lose myself on Serenity with the rest of the crew when Einstein bolted up from a seemingly dead sleep and started barking like a banshee, all his fury directed at a picture window on the other side of the room.

The drapes were drawn and the air conditioner was going, but that didn't stop him. I glanced at my phone. A call to Diggs would be not only cowardly but also too easily misconstrued as something else; I dismissed the idea outright. Instead, I opened the drapes. The glass was thick and both windows were locked securely.

"We've talked about this before, Stein." He looked at me guiltily. "I can't bring you if you're gonna freak out over every little bump in the night."

I stared through the glass into the night outside, waiting for the face of some deranged killer to appear in front of me. The only deranged face I saw was mine, however, so I closed the curtains and silently directed my heart to get a hold of itself.

I spent the next hour trying to convince Einstein that he didn't really need to go out for the final pee of the night, but that was a wasted effort. Eventually, after Stein had been dancing at the door shooting reproachful glances my way for half an hour, I surrendered. At eleven that night, I grabbed the dog's leash, my jacket, room key, and phone, and headed for the door.

Despite whatever scary-movie vibe the night may have had, it was still undeniably gorgeous out. The moon was full, an expanse of stars and the pale blur of the Milky Way overhead. The air had that summer smell to it: pine and earth, the cool, fragrant clean of a world in bloom. It wasn't like the stories I'd been hearing all day hadn't made an impression, though—I could have been in heaven itself and I don't think I would have strayed too far from a cell tower and a helping hand. I stuck as close to the motel as possible without actually encouraging Einstein to relieve himself on someone's doorstep. Even then, most of the windows in the place were dark, and between the trees and the stars and the silence, the whole scene had a very end-of-the-world quality to it.

When Einstein started getting more insistent about heading toward the woods, I drew the line and redirected our course toward the single-lane stretch of highway running past. An eighteen wheeler sped by, kicking up dust in its wake. Across the road at another cheap hotel, a couple got out of an SUV with two bikes strapped to the back and a canoe on top. The woman hauled a car seat from the passenger's side; I heard a baby start to cry. Einstein and I kept walking.

We continued for a while—long enough for the knots in my shoulders to loosen and that tight ache in my chest to ease, anyway. I kept returning to everything I'd been hearing about my father over the past few days: the abuse and the anger, the loss and the depravity. Yet again, I tried to connect all everyone had been telling me with the man I'd known on Payson Isle.

I named you after my sister, I remembered my father saying to me once. *Because she was from heaven. She changed everything. God took her, but he gave me you.*

The day he told me that, we'd found an orphaned fawn out behind the greenhouse on the island. We'd been debating about names. We settled on Ruby for reasons I couldn't even remember anymore, and for the next month he tended to that deer like she was his own child. She lived in the boarding house with us, trailing baby deer turds in her wake until Isaac—the head of the Payson Church—had had enough and insisted she at least be relegated to the barn. When Ruby took sick that fall, Dad lived in the barn with her for a week before she finally passed one night with both my father and me by her side.

I couldn't explain the horror stories people were telling me now, but at the end of the day it didn't matter: The man I'd known may have been a bastard as a kid, but something huge had changed him by the time I came along. I'd stake my life on the fact that he'd never been a murderer, and he sure as hell hadn't grown up to be a serial killer. There had to be another explanation.

I got Stein turned around and started back toward the hotel, feeling better than I had since Diggs had given me the news about Jeff Lincoln the night before. There were no cars on the road, Route 1 stretching as far as the eye could see in the deep blue of the moonlit night. Einstein growled just as we went 'round a bend that brought the motel back in sight, his attention suddenly on the night behind us. I instinctively reached for my cell phone. Stein started back despite my clear intent on the road ahead, whining softly, his body tensed. I turned, prepared to confront a behemoth madman with red eyes and an axe.

Instead, across the road and well back from us, I spotted yellow eyes. No axe. A coyote, thin and mangy, loped into the road with its head down. It held something in its mouth—a rabbit, judging by the size. I ordered Einstein to settle his ass down; he whined one more time, then sat. The coyote got halfway across the road then paused, head up now, sniffing the wind. She must have caught our scent, because she froze. Her yellow eyes found mine. I tightened my hold on Stein's leash and held my breath.

A tenth of a second might have passed while she stayed there, trying to make her decision: go back, or continue. Then, suddenly, a truck engine roared to life. The coyote perked her ears in the direction of the noise, then quickly turned and adjusted her course—back into the woods, her body moving with that grace and assurance wild things have when left to their own devices.

The owner of the monster truck, meanwhile, revved his engine in the distance. I gave Einstein a perfunctory head pat for being more alert than I was when it came to up-close-and-personal wildlife experiences in the making, and we got back on track to the motel. We were still maybe fifty yards from the Budget Inn parking lot when what I could now see was a very jacked-up pickup, revved its engine one more time, spun its wheels in the gravel, and shot out of the lot with no headlights on.

I spent more Saturdays than I can count back in Littlehope as a teenager watching the locals do donuts on every habitable surface in their 4x4's, so I know a little about the peculiar driving habits of Men With Trucks. Rule number one? Stay the hell out of the way. I was preparing to do exactly that when the truck picked up speed and the headlights came on suddenly, blinding me. For one endless moment, I was frozen in a dream-state, watching the truck barrel toward me. The lights got brighter, the engine louder. I kept waiting for the driver to swerve.

When it dawned on me that the lunatic driver wasn't planning on changing course before he mowed me down, I finally yanked Einstein's leash and dove off the road. I took a digger in the gravel on my already-skinned knee, but managed to get both Stein and me out of the truck's path just as the horn blared. The driver jerked the wheel to the right and sped away.

Afterward, I sat on the side of the road beside Einstein for a good five minutes, trying to pry my heart out of my throat. I was just getting my knees back under me when my phone rang. My hands were shaking as I pulled it out of my pocket.

"Where the hell are you?" Diggs demanded before I had the chance to say a word.

"I had to walk Einstein."

He breathed an audible sigh of relief. Whatever de-stressing I might have managed in the past half-hour was officially undone.

"What happened?" I asked.

"Where are you right now?"

I started back toward the motel, now just a stone's throw away. "I'm outside. I'll be right in—why, where are you?"

"Just get back here. Please."

When I got back to the room, Diggs was sitting on my bed surrounded by my files.

"How'd you get in here?" I asked.

"Door was open," he said. "When I came in, that was here." He nodded toward an old Polaroid snapshot on the dresser. I took a closer look, and regretted it immediately. I pushed it away and took a step back.

"What the hell is that?"

He didn't say anything. He didn't have to. In the picture, a red-haired girl lay nude on a dirt path, her eyes wide, her mouth open in a scream frozen in time.

"That's not the only picture there," he said grimly.

I pushed the Polaroid aside with my index finger, reluctant to touch it. There was a digital shot beneath it that had obviously come from a laser printer—and a lousy one at that. It didn't make the content any less disturbing, though. In the photo, Diggs and I sat at a pine picnic table with Red Grivois. Someone had drawn a heart around my face with red marker.

I wet my lips, trying to find my voice. "The girl in the first picture—that's Erin Lincoln. And that's not a shot from the crime scene. She's still alive there."

"I know," Diggs said.

"I know everyone else is saying my father did this," I said. I kept my eyes on the ground. My stomach felt like I'd been on rough seas for days. "But they're wrong. He wouldn't do this, Diggs. I don't care what anyone else says—whatever he did or didn't do, he wouldn't hurt me."

He didn't say anything. He hadn't moved from his seat at the edge of the bed. For the first time, I noticed how pale he was. His hair was still wet, and he was wearing only boxers and a t-shirt.

"I'm okay, Diggs," I said.

He shook his head. Diggs is usually a cool customer, but the way he looked at me just then, it was like he'd been stripped bare and run through.

"I thought he got you," he said. "I heard something next door—I think he dropped something while he was here. So I came over to check... I just had this feeling. And then your door was open and I found those pictures..." He wouldn't look at me. I sat down beside him and put my hand over his.

"Hey—I'm serious. I'm right here, Diggs. Nothing happened."

He squeezed my fingers so tight the blood stopped flowing. A second passed, then another, before he took a deep breath and let it out nice and slow. He let go of my hand and shook his head again, running his fingers through his hair.

"Jesus Christ, Sol," he said. He managed a strangled laugh. "Seriously—just call me before you walk the damn dog, huh? At least until we're done with this thing."

I would have made fun of him normally, but the Polaroid on the dresser had effectively killed my rapier wit. Diggs gave me a thorough once-over for the first time since I'd come in, just noticing my torn jeans and bloody knees.

"What the hell happened to you?"

The short version of the story seemed like a good bet at the moment. "I fell."

"I'm getting you a helmet and kneepads for your next birthday," he said. "Get into something more comfortable—I'll be back in a minute."

I changed into pajama bottoms and a t-shirt while he was gone, and returned from the bathroom to find Diggs, now in jeans and a jersey, sitting on the floor with the first aid kit he'd been carrying with him for as long as I could remember. He nodded toward the edge of the bed. I sat. He knelt at my feet and used a damp washcloth to clean the gravel out of my knee for the second time in as many days. I'd had worse, but it still stung like hell. I flinched when he dabbed at it with peroxide.

"Sorry," he said.

He curled one hand around my calf, holding me in place. I felt his touch on a cellular level, stoking something I was doing my damnedest to keep un-stoked. His thumb grazed the sensitive skin behind my knee. He was close enough that I could feel his breath, the tension still obvious in his shoulders. When he was finished, he moved back to give us both some much-needed space.

"That was a pretty good tumble you took out there. What happened?" he asked.

When I didn't answer right away, he looked up. His eyes narrowed. "Sol?"

I'd promised after the last story that I wouldn't keep things from him anymore—a reasonable request given that a slew of people hadn't made it off Payson Isle alive. A more transparent research process seemed advisable. I took a long, slow breath, and scooted backward on the bed. Diggs got up and took a seat next to me.

"I think I saw the guy who broke into my room."

His Adam's apple moved when he swallowed hard, the fear I'd seen before back in his eyes.

"Say something," I said.

"What? I don't know what to say to you anymore. Or what to do. We're chasing a *serial killer*—do you get that? A lunatic who gets his rocks off torturing and killing little girls.”

“Well, see—there you go. I’m not his type. In case you haven’t noticed, I’m not a little girl anymore, Diggs.”

“Don’t,” he said shortly. I raised my eyebrows innocently, but he didn’t crack a smile. “Don’t turn this into a joke. Have you actually looked at these pictures?” He got up and took the one of Erin Lincoln off the dresser, then came over and held it in front of me. My stomach turned, but I didn’t look away.

“Trust me, I’ve seen them, Diggs,” I said.

“Then why the fuck aren’t you terrified? He was *in this room.* He tried to run you down. This woman—this Bonnie Saucier. What did she tell you?”

I pushed the picture away. “What, you suddenly believe in psychics? It’s a bunch of bullshit—you know that.”

“Sarah Saucier obviously doesn’t think so. How do you know Hank Gendreau didn’t set you up when he got in touch with you in the first place? Maybe he worked with an accomplice all those years ago, and this is… I don’t know, some grand scheme to lure you out here.”

“So this is a conspiracy? To do what, exactly? No offense, Diggs, but I think you’re overestimating my appeal here.”

He walked away and paced the room, his shoulders so tense that I figured it was only a matter of time before he burst something critical. I went to him and touched his arm, forcing him to stop and look at me.

“I feel like a goddamn broken record,” he said, his voice still tight with anger. “Do you really not see that you’re putting yourself in danger here? Or is it that you honestly don’t give a shit?”

“Of course I give a shit,” I said, my own anger on the rise. “But this is my father. Everything I thought I knew about my life got flushed down the toilet last spring, and apparently that was just the beginning. I need to know where he is. Who he was.” My voice rose. “And don’t talk to me about not giving a shit whether I live or die. Do you know how many times I scraped you off the bathroom floor of sleazy dives from Portland to LA and back? How many bar fights and eight balls and bimbos I watched you burn through before you finally pulled your head out of your ass?”

“That’s not the same thing—”

“Why not? Because you were working and this is just some personal crusade for me? Because I—”

“Because it’s you,” he said, suddenly quiet. All the fight had gone from his eyes. He looked terrified. And very, very tired. He shook his head. “I couldn’t lose you this way, Sol.” His eyes were swimming when he looked at me again. "I couldn't lose you any way, but this... I can't protect you from something like this."

"I'm not asking you to."

He took a step closer. I didn't move. "It's not like I'm some crack shot with a black belt and an arsenal in my trunk. I'm a reporter. I know shorthand and surfing and Guitar God. Other than that, I'm no help here."

I met his eye. "That's not true."

I don't know who stepped where next, but somehow a second later we were right there—not quite touching yet, but close enough that I could already feel his energy like an electrical current.

He brushed the hair back from my forehead. I closed my eyes. Fisted the front of his t-shirt in my hands, and remained there, suspended, not quite touching and not quite... Not. I could feel his heart beating; the soft warmth of his breath on my face when he leaned in and rested his forehead against mine. His hands were on my shoulders—I couldn't tell whether it was to push me away or keep me close. Neither of us moved.

"We should get some sleep," he whispered.

I nodded, our heads still touching. He palmed the back of my neck with one hand and pressed a long, lingering kiss to my forehead.

"I'm sorry I'm a pain in the ass," I said, fighting an unwelcome surge of emotion of my own.

He laughed, his lips humming against my skin. "You should be. You're gonna be the death of me, Solomon." He stepped back and combed his fingers through his hair again with a long, slow exhale. "I'm staying here tonight—No way I'm leaving you in this room alone now."

I wasn't about to argue.

Chapter Eight

At 7:02 the next morning, there was a knock on my motel room door and Einstein completely lost his shit. I groaned and burrowed deeper into the blankets. Diggs came out of the bathroom in his shorts, his hair wet and a towel draped over his naked shoulders.

"Morning, sunshine," he said.

I groaned again, louder this time. Diggs went to the door and looked through the peephole.

"Cavalry's here, Sol—come on, get up."

"Go away," I said. "And tell whoever's here to go with you." I pulled the pillow over my head. In case there's any question, I will never be mistaken for a morning person.

I heard the door open.

"You made good time," Diggs said.

"I flew into Presque Isle last night. The case was already on our radar—it wasn't hard to convince the director to send me out." A male voice. Low, a little smoky, with a barely detectable touch of Cuban flavor in there.

Crap.

I was wide awake the instant I realized who it was. I prayed for invisibility.

"Is she hiding?" he asked.

"Mornings," Diggs said. Like that explained everything. He plucked the pillow off my head. "Come on, Sol, up and at 'em. The Feds wait for no one."

I made a half-assed attempt to smooth my hair out and rub the sleep from my eyes before facing Jack Juarez, who stood at our door in a freshly pressed suit with three coffees in his hands. He didn't even try to hide his amusement.

"How did you know we were here?" I asked.

"I called him," Diggs said.

"You couldn't have given me a heads up?"

"I thought it would be more fun this way," Diggs said. He gave me a sexy little eyebrow pump. "I was right, too."

"You're such an ass."

Juarez looked around the room. Diggs was still half naked, but both hotel beds in the room had clearly been slept in. Not that I was concerned my virtue might come into question—Juarez and I had tangled enough the last time he was in town that I'd never be mistaken for a virgin in his eyes.

My favorite Fed set the coffees on the dresser. He looked tanned and surprisingly well rested considering he must have taken a red eye to make it to the ends of the earth so quickly, or so I assumed. His dark hair was a little longer than I remembered it, his body a little leaner. He looked good. I hadn't known Juarez long, but based on my experience thus far, this wasn't unusual. Juarez always looked good.

"You don't have to look so appalled," he said to me with a smile. "You're going after a serial killer, aren't you? That is kind of my area. I promise I'll let you play, too."

I thought of Diggs' words the night before; how completely haunted he'd seemed by them. *I can't protect you.*

So he'd called in someone who could. Since it didn't seem I had much choice, I surrendered and got out of bed. My pj bottoms had hitched down and my tank top had twisted sideways, giving both boys an excellent view of my unmentionables before I managed to pull myself together.

"When did he call you?" I asked.

"Yesterday afternoon," Juarez said.

I looked at Diggs in surprise, but he was suddenly very focused on his coffee. "When yesterday afternoon?"

Juarez shifted uncomfortably. Diggs set his coffee down and looked me in the eye. "While you were asleep on the drive up here. I had some time to think about it, and I decided then that our best-case scenario was still more than you and I could handle on our own." He set his jaw. "You can be pissed if you want, but I'm not sorry. Especially after last night."

"What happened last night?" Juarez asked immediately.

I suppressed a groan and excused myself to find something decent to wear—it wasn't like I needed to be there while they rolled their eyes and moaned about what a lost cause I was.

When I returned to the fold, Juarez was sitting on the bed going through my files. Diggs and Einstein were nowhere to be found.

"He took the dog for a walk," Juarez said before I could ask. "They shouldn't be gone long."

I'd put on shorts and a t-shirt. My hair was still wet, but I felt at least moderately prepared to face the world now. I sat on the bed beside him, inching closer to get a glimpse of the file he held.

"I'm assuming Diggs told you about my father's possible connection to the case?"

He nodded. "I did a little research of my own to learn more after I spoke with him. And I'm meeting with the coroner in Quebec tomorrow."

"And today?"

He got up and retrieved his briefcase, pulling out a stack of files three inches thick. He tossed them all onto the bed next to me.

"I shouldn't actually be showing you these," he said.

"So why are you?"

It took Juarez a few seconds before he had an answer for that. "Because based on what happened last night, I'd say you've struck a nerve with someone—someone who is unfortunately very much alive, and not keen on sharing his secrets. And since you're obviously not going to back down…"

"Obviously," I agreed.

He grimaced. "Obviously. So that means it's in everyone's best interest to catch this lunatic as quickly as possible. I think you could be the key to making that happen."

I picked up the files and began thumbing through. With each one, my anxiety ratcheted up a notch. I recognized a few of the names, but most I'd never heard of before.

"What are these?"

There were at least fifteen files, each with a photo clipped to the front. Every photo was of a different girl, ranging in age from sixteen to over thirty.

"Between 1981 and 1990, eight girls between the ages of seventeen and twenty-two disappeared in northern and central Maine. Five of them were found in that grave across the Canadian border."

"So who are all the others?"

He didn't answer. I looked through more carefully, studying the faces. They were all white, with fair skin and slender builds. Several were redheads, but not all. Locations centered around northern New England, primarily Maine, New Hampshire, and Vermont. I cleared my throat.

"Who are they, Jack?"

"I searched the database for a certain body type, facial features," he finally answered. "And cross referenced with geographic area and similarities to each of the disappearances: victims who disappeared from their homes without a struggle, leaving behind shoes, purses, younger siblings or children…"

"You don't actually think my father killed all these people," I said.

"At four of the sites in those files, one man's fingerprints were found."

I pushed the files away. "Jeff Lincoln," I guessed.

"Jeff Lincoln," he agreed.

"My father was living out on Payson Isle when a lot of these happened," I argued.

"There are boats to the mainland. You were with him part of that time, but not all. Right?"

I pulled one of the files out of the stack, opened it, and stared at the photo inside. Ashley Gendreau. The photo on top was her senior picture, taken in a pasture I assumed must be around here somewhere. She'd had a nice smile—the kind you'd expect to precede a great laugh. I closed the file again.

"Diggs told you what happened last night?" I asked.

"Someone broke into the room and left a photo of Erin Lincoln," he said. "Someone who's been following you and Diggs."

"My father wouldn't have done that," I said.

He didn't say anything.

"Diggs doesn't think he would have, either," I lied.

Diggs came through the door just in time to catch me in the act. "Diggs doesn't think who would have done what?"

"You don't think her father would have broken into the room?" Juarez asked curiously.

"I didn't say that."

My frustration was building fast. I turned on him while he was still unsnapping the leash from Einstein's collar. "If my father was this psychotic killer, don't you think I would have noticed? Wouldn't there have been some sign?" I asked. "And why would he leave me that picture of his sister last night?"

"To scare you off," Diggs said.

"He knows me better than that," I said. "After everything that happened out on Payson Isle, you really think he'd believe a friggin' snapshot would make me turn tail and run?"

"Look, whether it's your father or someone else is moot at the moment," Juarez interrupted. "I think the point we should be focusing on is that *someone* broke into this room last night and left a photo clearly incriminating them in not only a vicious murder forty years ago, but of stalking you now."

Diggs raised his coffee cup. "Exactly. Listen to the Fed, Sol."

I couldn't really argue either of those points, so I didn't bother trying. "Fine, whatever—there's a killer with his sights set on me. What else is new? You've already said you're not gonna try to make me go home. So, what's the next step?"

Juarez and Diggs shared a commiserating glance. "All five of the victims found on the border were from Aroostook County," Juarez said. "I've contacted the families. The plan is for me to speak with them today to see if I can get any information before meeting with the coroner in Quebec tomorrow."

"Excellent," I said. "We'll come along—I'd like a chance to talk to them myself."

His gaze flickered back toward Diggs. It was nice to know that, despite everything, the bromance was alive and well.

"I was actually thinking you two could stay around here," Juarez said, "and keep asking questions about the Erin Lincoln murder. That's the coldest of seven very cold cases at this point, but I think it could tell us a lot about the killer."

To my surprise—and Juarez's, judging by the look on his face—Diggs shook his head. "I think that's a bad idea. She should stick with you today."

Juarez frowned. "I'll be back here tonight—just don't get in any trouble."

"Have you *met* Solomon?"

I crumpled a piece of paper and threw it at Diggs. It glanced off his shoulder, doing precious little to drive my point home. "I know I'm no Bella fucking Swan, but could one of you at least pretend to want me along for the ride?"

Diggs quirked an eyebrow at Juarez. "Does that make me the vamp or the wolf?"

"I will hurt you," I said.

The humor vanished from Diggs' eyes. "I think she should go with you," he said to Juarez again. "We'll meet back here tonight, and then we'll head to Quebec together tomorrow."

"You're sure?" Juarez asked.

"Oh for crying out loud," I said. I looked at Diggs, who'd taken on the same haunted fifty-yard stare he'd had the night before. "I can stay with you," I said quietly. Juarez went to the door, giving us as much privacy as was possible in a ten-by-twenty motel room.

I sat down on the bed. Diggs came over and joined me. I heard the door open and close, and knew Juarez had left the building.

"If the guy in the truck last night really was *the* guy, he could have killed me right then..." I began.

"You need to stop acting like you're bulletproof," he interrupted before I could finish. "Or, if you're not going to stop, you at least need someone who can keep you safe. Juarez knows what he's doing—just listen to me for once in your life, and stick with him. He's a good guy."

"All right, fine. But you'll be here when we get back, right?"

"I'll be here."

He grabbed his backpack and started for the door, then stopped at the threshold. "I'll take Stein with me; we'll cruise the countryside, see what we can find out." He got quiet again. "Be careful, okay?"

I nodded. "You too."

"Yeah," he agreed. "I will. I'll see you tonight."

I sat on the edge of the bed for a minute or more after he left, staring at the door like that would somehow bring him back. And maybe even convince him to stay.

It didn't.

◊◊◊◊◊

The first stop with Juarez was to the home of Jenny Bishop—or the home of Jenny Bishop's father, anyway. Her parents had divorced not long after her disappearance in 1982. Now, her mother lived in a retirement home in Jersey, while Brian Bishop remained in the same house where his daughter had last been seen thirty years before.

Juarez and I pulled into a winding private drive in Houlton at just past eleven that morning. A whitewashed fence ran the length of the property, three chestnut horses grazing in the distance. The Bishops had done well for themselves, and apparently tragedy hadn't changed that: the front yard was landscaped within an inch of its life, the grounds mowed golf-green short.

I'd put on my Sunday best and was sweating in a very unladylike fashion, even though my Sunday best was just a skirt and blazer. Juarez was trussed and trimmed, his necktie knotted to within an inch of its life, and he'd never looked cooler. I knew it wasn't his fault he had better genes than me, but I found myself a little resentful all the same.

An old white farmhouse sat at the back of the Bishop property with an exact, scaled-down replica built closer to the drive. I paused in front of it, recalling Jenny Bishop's file: A model student, lifetime horse lover, only child. The apple of her father's eye.

Juarez looked at me. "Are you coming?" he asked.

"Yeah. I just…" I gestured toward the playhouse, then looked around at the rest of the grounds. "It seems a little…"

"Sad?" he finished for me.

"I was thinking creepy, actually—but sad works, too."

"These kinds of interviews are never easy," he said. "Are you sure you want to do this?"

"I just rode two hours listening to American Idol's Greatest Hits; I'm thinking it can't get much more painful than that."

"That was nothing," he said, surprising me. "I'm saving the good stuff for the trip back."

"I can't wait."

I wiped my damp palms on my skirt and waited for Juarez to take the lead up the walk. He was right, actually: there was something sad about this place, a kind of emptiness that went much deeper than the well-groomed façade. This was where the story led next, so I wouldn't hesitate to go in and ask Brian Bishop whatever questions needed asking. It didn't mean I had to like it, though.

Brian Bishop was thin and drawn and had a way about him that suggested he'd been an old man for a long, long time. He stood aside as we walked through the front door, then led us into a living room that had probably been the height of fashion in 1982. Based on the décor, however, it hadn't had an update since that time. It was like the whole house was holding its breath, frozen in time. Waiting for Jenny Bishop to come home.

Photographs covered the tops of two antique dressers and most available wall space. A little blonde girl with glasses was featured in most of them; her life had been well documented. Baby pictures, first steps, school photos, birthdays… A pudgy toddler grew into a lean, smiling little girl with pigtails, and eventually into a pretty, athletic teen. Photos of dance recitals and gymnastics trials followed every stage of her development, all the way through high school to the first day of college. And then, suddenly, they simply… Stopped.

There were only a few pictures on the wall taken more recently than the '80s, mostly school photos of other kids—cousins and other family members, some of whom had a vague resemblance to the daughter the Bishops lost. I got the sense that those other shots had been put up under duress. If he had his way, I had little doubt that Brian Bishop would have gotten rid of anything and everything that wasn't his daughter.

Juarez sat down at one end of an outdated floral sofa. I followed his lead and sat next to him. Brian sat in a recliner a few feet away.

"You've talked to the police," Juarez said. "About the bodies they recovered…?"

Brian nodded. He wore thick-framed glasses and pants two sizes too large, held up with black-and-white checked suspenders.

"They're sure it's her?" he asked. "I don't see how they'd know so fast, this long after… How could they know so soon?"

"They had the records you provided when Jenny first went missing," Juarez said. "They're very good at what they do—it wouldn't have taken that long. I'm very sorry, but there's no question that one of the bodies belonged to your daughter."

The old man nodded again. As much as a minute went by while we waited for him to say something. When he didn't, Juarez continued.

"I know a lot of time has passed," Juarez said, "but I was hoping you could walk me through that day one more time."

Brian took his glasses off and rubbed his eyes. "Of course," he said wearily. "Whatever you need."

"Jenny was home for the summer?" Juarez looked at the file briefly, but I could tell he didn't really need to. He may have just gotten the assignment, but it was obvious he already knew this case cold.

"Yes," Brian confirmed. "It was her first year at UMaine Machias. She'd never been away from home before; it wasn't an easy year for her."

"Did she have any problems with boyfriends, or any men she might have known on campus that she said made her uncomfortable?"

"No. Nothing like that. No confrontations, no men we'd seen lurking around, no suspicious friends." He said it like he'd been through this many, many times before.

"Did you ever spend any time in Black Falls?" I asked.

Juarez looked at me sharply.

Brian shook his head, confused. "Up at the border? No. Why? You think that's where the man who did this was from?"

"We don't know," Juarez said quickly. "It's just one of many leads we're following right now. Let's get back to that day, if it's all right."

Brian went through the entire day for us: breakfast together on the deck since it was warm out, then Jenny had planned on spending the day riding the trails with some friends. The friends got to the stable at about eleven that morning, where they found Jenny's jacket and her backpack. There'd been no sign of a struggle. Her favorite horse was already saddled and in the paddock; it looked as though she'd been riding when she was interrupted. The nearest neighbors were miles away, and no passersby reported seeing anything unusual in the area that day.

It was like she'd just dropped off the face of the earth.

"What was going on for you at the time?" Juarez asked. "Was there anyone you'd met in your business dealings who made you uneasy? Anyone who commented on your family, maybe asked about your daughter?"

He shook his head. "No. There was nothing like that. We'd just received a settlement after I filed a suit against a manufacturer in Detroit about a year before, but that was a large corporation—there was nothing personal about any of it. The only time I even had to go to court was for the settlement conference in Augusta."

"Which firm represented you?" Juarez asked.

"The same one that represents me today: Whitman, Myer & Goldman. They're out of Hartford, where I'm from originally. We dealt with a large firm out of New York."

While Juarez jotted that information down, Brian's gaze shifted to the wall of photos in his living room.

"I thought she'd come home, you know," he said to me. "You always hear people say they'd know if their child was gone; somehow, they'd know. But I never did. My wife told me years ago it was time to move on." He looked around the room helplessly. Behind his thick lenses, his eyes swam with tears. "I could never figure it out, though. How to do that."

He stood, went to one of the dressers, and picked up a photo of Jenny at four or five. She was sitting on a horse, Brian behind her in the saddle. They were both laughing.

"She was everything," he said, still looking at the picture. "Sun and moon. I didn't want anything else, once she was born. Didn't need anything else. And then once she was gone…" He looked around again, like he was searching for something he knew he'd never find again. "Then, I just wanted her back."

"I know how hard this is, but we won't take much more of your time," Juarez said. "I have a few photos I'd like you to look at. If you could just tell me if you recognize any of these men…"

Brian nodded. Juarez set a photo album on the coffee table and flipped to a page bookmarked with a yellow Post-it. Amid a half-dozen shady villains I'd never seen before was a single face I knew well: My father. I held my breath while Bishop scanned the pictures, then flipped to the next page.

He'd barely glanced at Dad's picture.

At sight of one of the men on the next page, however, Bishop went completely rigid. He looked up at Juarez, his eyes wide.

"This is Hank Gendreau," he said. "The man who killed his daughter back a few years after Jenny disappeared. Why is he here?" He choked on the words, his breath suddenly coming harder. "Are you saying... The way his daughter died. Is that what happened to Jenny?"

He'd gone deathly pale. I sat back to give him some space. Juarez set the album aside and slid to the edge of the couch, closer to Bishop. He put his hand on the man's knee.

"I'd like you to sit back and take a couple of deep breaths," he said. His voice was almost mesmerizing, it was so calm. "I know how hard this is."

"You didn't answer my question," Bishop said stubbornly, still fixated on the now-closed photo album. "Is that how she died? I remember that case—every bit of it. Jenny..."

"We don't have the coroner's findings yet," Juarez said smoothly. "There's no hard evidence that that's how she died."

It was a lie, I knew. Considering the look on Bishop's face, I couldn't imagine telling him anything else.

We didn't learn much more from Brian Bishop after that. He gave us the same details he'd given investigators thirty years ago, and didn't recognize anyone else from the album of suspects—including my father—as far as he could recall. Considering how many years had passed since that time, however, I wasn't ready to take that single win as a sign that dear old Dad was in the clear.

As we were leaving, Juarez took Bishop aside and asked if there was anyone he could call.

Bishop said no.

I thought of Red Grivois, a retired cop haunted by the broken bodies of two girls he hadn't been able to save. How many others' lives had been destroyed by whoever had killed these girls? How many more interviews would we have to do like this?

And what did my father have to do with any of it?

Juarez was quiet as we pulled out of the drive, back past the rolling hills and the chestnut horses.

"They thought it was a kidnapping at first," he said out of the blue. He stopped at the end of the drive, staring blankly at the road ahead. "That settlement Brian was talking about was huge—it was in all the papers. They waited a solid week for a ransom demand."

"So whoever this was—or is—has no interest in money," I concluded.

"That much is clear, at least," Juarez agreed. "The killer has never made any attempt to contact the families, keeps his victims' bodies well hidden after the fact, doesn't seem to feel the need to be in the public eye or involved with the investigation like so many serial killers. Dennis Rader, Javed Iqbal, Gacy… They were all bold, occasionally even flamboyant. Lived to taunt the cops and shock the public."

"So the act of killing is the reward for him," I guessed. "It's not about the publicity."

"There's something else that's been bothering me. The bodies they found buried in Canada were wrapped," he said.

I looked at him in surprise. "What do you mean?"

"In a sheet, buried with their faces covered. He tortured them when they were alive, but the way he disposed of the bodies suggests he felt some remorse. Or at least showed the victims some respect after their deaths."

I considered this. Bright sunshine had given way to dark clouds rolling in fast, the heat as oppressive as ever. I pulled my hair up off my neck and stared at the approaching storm. When I looked back at Juarez, he was watching me. I gave him an awkward smile.

"What a shitty case," I said.

He nodded. "It is."

"Is it the worst you've ever seen?"

He shook his head.

"Top five?"

He thought for a second or two before shaking his head again.

"Top ten?" I persisted.

"Top ten," he agreed.

I shook my head. "Jesus. How do you do this day after day? I mean, I'm assuming there aren't a lot of happy endings for homicide cases—the final bell's pretty much rung by the time you come in."

"It's a good ending if we can catch someone. Prevent them from killing again. It's not a happy ending… But it's a good one. Sometimes, it's the only solace you can provide a victim's family."

Something about the way he said it made me think this wasn't just idle speculation on his part; he was speaking from experience. I thought back to a rainy night in Littlehope last spring in Juarez's arms. A tan line on his ring finger. *You're married*, I'd said. *Not anymore. Not for a long time.*

"Your wife…" I began.

There was no guile in his eyes when he looked at me, no mask. "Lucia. She was killed six years ago, in Guatemala. She'd been volunteering at a school there."

"I'm sorry."

"Yes. As am I." He disappeared for a second or two, lost in his memories. Then, he met my eye and smiled. "It was a long time before I could think of anything that reminded me of her. Remember any of the reasons that I loved her."

"But you can now?"

"It seemed dishonorable not to. I couldn't protect her before she died; the least I could do was honor her memory after she was gone."

Honor. It wasn't a word people used that much anymore, but it seemed completely natural hearing it fall from Juarez's lips—a tenet he held fast to. "And you found the person who did it? The man who killed her?"

He shook his head. "Not yet. But I will."

He put the car back in gear before I could comment any further, already speculating about the woman who had first stolen Jack Juarez's heart, and the tragic end that she met. She would have been beautiful, I was sure. Someone who shared his faith, his unshakable sense of right and wrong.

After a few minutes of silence, Juarez now lost in his own thoughts, I turned the radio on. I barely winced when Clay Aiken launched into Somewhere Over the Rainbow. Hell, if I spent enough time in Juarez's dark, dark world, I suspected I might even start to see the charm in Taylor Swift.

◊◊◊◊◊

The remaining four interviews that day weren't any more helpful than the first, and they definitely weren't any more fun. After Brian Bishop's reaction, Juarez wisely took Hank Gendreau's photo out of the mix in his Big Book of Suspects. Two mothers we talked to thought they'd seen my father's face before, but they couldn't say for sure. Beyond the loss of their daughters and the fact that they lived in northern Maine, there didn't seem to be any tie between the victims' families. The Bishops were a respectable, upper middle-class family, while eighteen-year-old Grace Starke's father was cooling his heels in jail on drug charges when she was taken. Seventeen-year-old Becca Martineau was a high school soccer star active in student government; nineteen-year-old Stacy Long was a high school dropout whom everyone thought had run away until her body was discovered in that grave just north of the Maine/Canada border. One of the victims was still unknown, but Riley Thibodeau was a cheerleader from Madawaska who survived lead poisoning at eighteen only to be murdered in the woods two years later.

The only thing all the victims had in common was the fact that they were all young, pretty, active girls of a certain age. And they'd all suffered unspeakable physical pain and mental torment before they were finally killed and buried in a shallow grave deep in the woods. And, of course, the prime suspect in each of their murders just happened to be my father.

Things lightened up on the drive back to the Budget Inn, thanks in large part to Juarez, who seemed to take murder and mutilation in stride. It was a little disconcerting, actually. We stopped for dinner at a dingy roadside diner with red and white checked tablecloths and mind-blowing bacon Swiss burgers. I whipped his delectable ass at a game of pinball at the back of the diner, all the while grilling him about the case.

When we sat down for dessert, I pulled out the files again.

"We should go over what we have so far," I said.

He looked around, a spoonful of ice cream halfway to his mouth. "Here?"

"Here," I confirmed. I dug out pen and paper and started writing. "We can start with Erin and Jeff Lincoln's disappearance in 1970."

"That sounds reasonable."

I wrote down *Erin Lincoln murdered: October 1970*

"Then came Jeff Lincoln's stay in the psychiatric ward in Michigan," Juarez said.

"1972, right?" He nodded without consulting any notes. I wrote it down.

"And then he drops off the radar," I said.

"When did your father join the Payson Church?"

"1978."

"And he never said anything about where he'd been before that?"

I shook my head. He didn't say anything, eying my notes. I finally gave in and scribbled: *Adam Solomon joins Payson Church of Tomorrow: December 1978*

"And then in 1982, Jenny Bishop disappears from her house in Houlton, Maine," Juarez said.

"And five years later, Hank Gendreau finds his daughter murdered in the woods. According to Gendreau, Jeff Lincoln was there."

From there, we outlined the remaining disappearances Juarez had dug up from '81 to '90. He had specific dates for all of them, but I was lost when it came to figuring out where my father might have been for each one. The Paysons lived on an island ten miles off the Maine coast; we prayed and baked and grew tomatoes. Calendars weren't really a priority.

When I was done writing everything out, the timeline was holier than the good book itself. Juarez and Diggs were both right about one thing, though: the only consistent thread in any of it seemed to be Jeff Lincoln. He was with Erin Lincoln; Hank Gendreau claimed he'd been at the scene the day Ashley was killed; his fingerprints placed him at the body dump in Canada, and at several of the crime scenes of other victims along the way.

"Erin and Jeff went to Eagle Lake alone the weekend they disappeared?" Juarez asked out of the blue.

"That's the story."

He didn't look convinced.

"Why?" I asked. "You think someone else might have been there?"

"I know you said they were close, but it still doesn't seem like the kind of trip a fifteen-year-old boy would take his little sister on without a reason."

"That reason being?"

He shrugged. "I have no idea, really. But having been a fifteen-year-old boy myself, I can tell you that, if I had a sister, there were probably only two things that could have convinced me to take off into the woods with her."

"Unless you really are a saint, a girl has to be at least one of those things."

He nodded. "Or a party."

"Or some combination of the two?" I guessed. It was a good point—one I should have thought of before. Score one for the Fed. "Okay... So, whatever the reason was, we know at the very least that Jeff and Erin went camping that weekend. Then in 1987, Hank—" I stopped. "Do you have anything in that big thick file of yours about the cops questioning Hank after the Lincoln murder?"

The waitress approached while Juarez was leafing through the file and left us with the check. Three minutes in, he'd found what I was looking for.

"Here it is. I don't think they questioned him after the body was found—just when Jeff and Erin first went missing. Since he'd been in Quebec at the time, they never followed up."

He handed the pages to me. I scanned through until a single name stopped me dead in my tracks. Juarez had gone to powder his nose; by the time he came back, I was on my feet with my jacket in hand, ready to declare the entire case solved.

"What?" he asked cautiously.

I looked up from cruising the white pages on my iPhone. "We need to get back to Black Falls," I said.

"For?"

"Will Rainier." Juarez looked at me blankly.

"Will Rainier was Hank's alibi when Erin Lincoln went missing." He still wasn't making the connection. I reminded myself that just because I'd committed the entire case to memory didn't mean the rest of the world had. "Will Rainier was the third member of their trio in the picture Hank showed me at the prison. He also happened to be the only suspect in the Ashley Gendreau murder, besides Hank himself."

Chapter Nine

Diggs, Einstein, and the Jeep were all missing when Juarez and I got back to the motel. Juarez returned to his room pleading official FBI business—whatever that meant—and I tried to reach Diggs for an hour before he finally deigned to call back, at just past nine that night. I could hear a crowd in the background and Waylon Jennings on the jukebox. It took a couple of false starts shouting over one another before I heard a door close and things quieted on the other end of the line.

"Where the hell are you?" I asked.

"I got a lead—I'm just down the road a ways. Grab the Fed and come meet me."

I tried to tell him about the Will Rainier tie-in I'd found between the Lincoln and Gendreau murders, but there was way too much excitement on Diggs' end for me to get far. I gave up, got directions on where to meet him, and went to fetch Juarez.

The Black Falls VFW was on a dead end street in the center of town, just over the railroad tracks. There was no parking lot per se, which meant trucks and beaten-down SUVs lined both sides of the road going back a good half mile. Juarez and I parked on the next street over, in front of a trailer with freshly-mown grass and a muddy ATV in the yard. What had been an uncomfortably warm day had cooled to sweater weather, though a cluster of boys we passed on the street were still playing soccer in shorts and t-shirts. Juarez and I took a shortcut along the railroad tracks through patchy woods, and came out the other side to find a couple of teenagers locked in a steamy embrace and a few others with cigarettes and beer hanging out by a giant boulder and a few scrubby spruce trees. Apparently, this was the place to be on a Friday night in Black Falls.

The jukebox was going strong and the party was going stronger when

Juarez and I walked through the front door of the VFW. A giant American flag, a slightly smaller Acadian one, and three mounted moose heads were the first things patrons saw on their way inside. Diggs was holding court at a pool table at the center of the action, a pool cue in one hand, cigarette dangling from his lips, fedora perched far back on his head. He winked at me as I joined him at the table.

"I found the party."

Great. I eyed the nearly-empty glass at the edge of the table.

"Just Coke, Mom," he said. "I'm soaking up the local color."

"I'm happy for you. What'd you do with my dog?"

He pointed to a pretty, dark-haired girl who couldn't have been more than twenty, working behind the bar. She had a gap between her teeth, a sizable chest, and a rose tattoo that twisted around her muscular left arm. "Rosie's taking care of him."

Sure enough, when I went over and looked behind the bar, Einstein was lying comfortably at the girl's feet. He got up as soon as he saw me and ambled over to say hello, tail wagging. Rosie poured two drinks without looking at either one, her eyes on me instead.

"*Il est bon chien, oui*? Great dog."

"He is. Thanks for looking out for him."

She finished pouring the drinks, then said something in French to an older, significantly fleshier woman behind the bar. Apparently her shift was up, because she handed me a couple of beers without asking for our order, poured another Coke for Diggs, and followed me over to the pool table. She sidled up to Diggs with unmistakable interest, nodding toward the table.

"We playing?"

I looked at Juarez, who shrugged agreeably. He'd changed from his FBI gear to jeans and a fitted black tee. It fitted very well.

Diggs racked 'em up while a Nickelback triple play started on the jukebox. I checked out the bar, where an odd mix of mellowed old-timers and hard-drinking youngsters rubbed elbows over beer and French fries drowned in gravy. Luke Saucier—the resident grave keeper—was at one end of the bar, his sister nowhere in sight. He sat apart from everyone else, a beer in one hand and a bowl of pretzels in front of him. I smiled and gave a little bit of a wave in his direction when our eyes met. He waved back, then frowned and focused on his pretzels.

Once we started playing, I was relieved to find that, despite her age, Rosie wasn't the kind of girl who needed a man to guide her through every corner shot. I'm no Minnesota Fats, but I can hold my own in a pinch; she made me look like a chump, and didn't make Diggs look much better. In between, she still managed to cop a feel or flash her cleavage every time she passed Diggs.

Juarez proved surprisingly good with a pool cue in his hand. He loosened up after a couple of beers, moving with ease around the table as he chose his next shot. I hip-checked him when he rejoined me after his second successful jump shot.

"Where'd you learn to play like that? I thought you were a good Catholic boy."

He leaned in, his breath warm in my ear. "I'm not that good."

My game faltered after that.

Half an hour later, we were getting ready to wrap up our game when Juarez pulled me aside, suddenly serious.

"That man over there," he said quietly. "At the bar. Do you know him?"

I looked in the direction he'd indicated. Luke Saucier was staring at me openly now, something haunted in his gaze. "Diggs and I met him and his sister yesterday—the Sauciers," I said. "They were friends with Erin Lincoln. I think he's got some kind of autism... He's harmless."

"No." He shook his head, subtly taking my elbow to turn me a little to the left. "Not that guy. That one."

On the other side of the bar, about four seats over from Luke, was a mountain of a man with a full-on Grizzly Adams beard and small, piercing eyes. He dropped his gaze the second I looked at him.

I snagged Rosie on her next pass through after molesting Diggs. "That guy at the bar—the one who looks like he had gravel for breakfast and now he's having trouble passing the stones... With the beard?"

She followed my gaze, neither of us taking much care to be subtle. "Will?" she asked.

My heart may have stopped, for just a second there. "Will Rainier?"

"Oui. He practically lives here. You know him?"

Not yet, but I planned to. I started toward the bar, but Juarez caught me by the elbow and reeled me back in. "Where are you going?"

"You heard her: That's Will Rainier. I'm going to talk to him."

Juarez pulled me a little farther aside. "I'll talk to him tomorrow. Not here."

"Are you nuts? He's half in the bag, not expecting it, and he's in a public place. In my world, that's what we call a perfect storm. I just want to ask him a couple of questions."

Juarez shook his head. "Just trust me, all right? This isn't the way to go about it—I'll have a conversation with him, but this isn't the time."

"So you have a conversation with him some other time. I'm talking to him now."

I started toward him again. Juarez blocked my path. Over his shoulder, I could see Will Rainier watching the entire exchange. This time when he realized I was watching him, he didn't look away. His eyes had all the warmth of a rattlesnake, and none of the charm.

"Listen to me," Juarez said quietly. "Whatever we may know, I don't want to tip him off until I'm able to confirm a couple of things through my office and do a proper interview. Tomorrow. Away from here. If you want to find out what really happened to your father and his sister, you need to trust that I know what I'm doing."

I caught Diggs' eye. He was watching all of this with great interest, waiting to see what I would do next. I looked at Rainier one more time. His mouth quirked up in a faint half-smile, as though he knew exactly what was happening.

I nodded. "Yeah," I said to Juarez. "Okay, fine. I'll wait until tomorrow."

"Good. Thank you."

We got back to the game, but from that point on every time I looked up, Rainier was watching me. Juarez was clearly aware, but he seemed dead set on questioning him on his own Feeb timeline. I was a good girl, though, and minded my own business through the entire game. Sure, there may have been the occasional furtive glance, but otherwise I showed remarkable restraint. We surrendered the pool table to the natives at a little after ten and stopped to refuel. Rosie chose a booth for us at the back, in front of a wall of photos with the words *Never Forget* written in red, white, and blue above them.

Juarez slid in beside me, Diggs across from us. As the night progressed, the music had gotten louder, the patrons considerably rowdier. A knot of women in skin-tight jeans and tank tops were on the dance floor gyrating to Lynyrd Skynyrd, but Will Rainier still only had eyes for me. Luke Saucier took off at some point, and then the former sheriff, Red Grivois, showed up and took the stool beside Rainier. The two exchanged a manly nod, but otherwise I didn't see them speak to one another. Mostly, Red drank steadily with his eyes on the bar while Rainier drank steadily with his eyes on me. And still, I stayed away.

When Rosie returned from fetching refreshments for the gang, she nodded toward the wall of photos beside us.

"I thought you might be interested in this."

It took me a minute to understand what she meant. Most of the pictures were of fallen soldiers with painfully young grins and buzz cuts, dating as far back as WWI. Two of the pictures were set apart from the others, however. Below them was an inscription written in calligraphy on a faded piece of blue construction paper:

Taken by the devil
Returned to the angels
Now safe with Jesus

Erin Lincoln and Ashley Gendreau smiled back at us.

"I see what you mean about the resemblance," Rosie said to Diggs, looking from me to the photo of Erin Lincoln and back again.

"So, you know the story, too—you've heard of both girls?" I asked.

"*Oui,*" she said. "They were a little before my time, but everyone's heard their stories."

"Rosie's grandma is kind of the local historian; Rosie's following in her footsteps," Diggs explained. She downed half her beer and turned a pretty pink at Diggs' attention. "So, I was hoping maybe you could answer something for us," he continued, his focus entirely on her. "Lincoln isn't exactly a common name around here, and we didn't see anyone dating farther back than Wallace Lincoln in the graveyard out by the Sauciers' place. Do you know where he came from?"

"*Non,*" Rosie said. "There was talk—a lot of rumors over the years. But my *mémère* said Wallace Lincoln had no family when he came here. Just the wife and kids."

Another mystery. Wonderful.

"Sarah Saucier said Wallace Lincoln was a bigwig in town," I said. "Do you know what he did?"

"He bought one of the local lumber mills," she said. "Came from away, moved in, and hired half the town. Fired half the town, too. Nobody liked him too much. People here have long memories—most anyone would say the same. Everybody liked the girl, though."

Rosie gave us a little more background info from there, sprinkled in with the occasional juicy tidbit and a lot of sexy innuendo directed at Diggs. Eventually, her spiel devolved into a rant about the boys in town and how little they knew about the ways of the world. According to her, other men—

presumably scruffy tow-headed reporters of a certain age—were much more her speed.

"We should probably talk about what's happening tomorrow," Diggs interrupted, heading that particular topic off at the pass. "The big trek across the border."

"I have a meeting in Montreal at eleven a.m.," Juarez said. "There's a pilot meeting us at a private airstrip at seven-thirty."

"What about Einstein?" I asked. "Can he fly on your fancy government charter?"

Juarez didn't look over the moon about that idea.

"Rosie dog-sits," Diggs said. "Don't you, Rose? You think you could handle Einstein for a few hours?"

She nodded eagerly, but I was already hedging. "I don't know… He can be kind of high maintenance."

"What are you talking about?" Diggs asked. "I've never met a lower maintenance dog in my life. He'll be fine."

"I worked at the vet's up the road for a couple years in high school, until I realized how much more I could make working here. I can handle it."

"It would actually be better if I didn't show up in Montreal with two reporters and a dog," Juarez said. "Two reporters is hard enough to explain."

"One reporter, actually," Diggs said. I started to protest, but he held up his hand. "I've got a lead I want to check out in Quebec City. And Juarez said it himself—two reporters will be hard to get through the front door. This way, you can check out the hallowed inner sanctum at le Laboratoire, and I can do my thing without freaking my sources out by showing up with the Feebs."

"Shouldn't I be with you when you're checking out these leads, though?" I asked.

"A few of those leads have to do with my own stories, actually," he said. "Contrary to popular belief, we can't all spend every waking minute trying to track down your dad. There is one guy I'd like you to talk to, though. I was thinking maybe we could rendezvous in the city after you two finish up with the bones in Montreal. If Juarez can entertain himself for an hour or two, we can run through those interviews together."

With the logistics set for the day to come, I waited until Diggs, Juarez, and Rosie were deep in conversation before I politely excused myself to take a powder. The moment I said, it, Diggs' eyes were on me. I waited, holding my breath to see if he'd say anything. He stayed quiet, but it was clear that he knew exactly what I was up to.

In all fairness, I did actually go to the restroom. I just took a little bit of a detour on the way back. Wonder of wonders, I wound up right beside Will Rainier.

I took the stool beside him, ordered myself a fresh beer, and leaned past him to talk to Red Grivois, seated on the next stool over.

"Hey, Red," I said. "Great place you've got here."

Red looked at me like he expected me to singlehandedly infect the entire establishment with a nasty case of feminine itching.

"It's late," he said. "You should probably get on home."

"That's all right," I said. I took a slug of ice cold Molson Golden and set it down a little too hard on the bar. "I'm kind of a night owl." I looked at Rainier. "What about you... Will, isn't it? You a man of the night?"

He sipped at his own beer. His mouth twitched. This close up, I realized that I'd underestimated his size—he was monstrous. Monstrous and bearded and dark-eyed and drunk. Just the kind of man you don't want to bother when he's drinking alone on a Saturday night.

"Depends on the company," he said.

I let that slide. "I think you knew my father. Jeff Lincoln?"

He took another drink and nodded meditatively. "That I did."

"And you knew his sister—Erin Lincoln?"

Red started to get up, clearly intending to intervene. Rainier slapped his hand over the old man's arm before he could stand. He did it so quickly I barely saw him move. Red stayed where he was.

"Yeah. I knew Erin, too. What's it to you?"

"What about Ashley Gendreau?" I asked. "Did you know Ashley Gendreau?"

That sly little half-smile never left his lips. He kept looking straight ahead, sipping at his beer. "Yeah," he said. "I knew Ashley Gendreau. You plan on going through the whole phone book this way? It's a small town—not a lot of people, but I know all of 'em."

"I think it would be best if you moved along, Ms. Solomon," Red said to me.

Rainier smiled more widely. "Solomon, huh? That's nice. Got a nice ring to it. You don't have to go on my account, *Miz* Solomon. Stay right here, no skin off my balls."

Lovely.

He turned to face me. His eyes had a feverish quality common to those with a serious drug problem or some very dark demons. My guess was that Will Rainier had probably battled both in his day.

"You come on back to my place, little girl, and I'll tell you all about who I know and how I know 'em."

I heard someone clear his throat behind me. When I turned, Juarez was standing there with his arms crossed over his chest and a colossally unamused look on his face.

"We missed you over there," he said. "Why don't you come back to the table?" Technically, it was a question. He didn't make it sound like I had much choice, though.

"Why don't you leave her alone, Pablo?" Rainier said. "Girl wants to talk to me, there's not much you can do about it, is there?" He turned to Red. "When'd we start letting wetbacks in here, anyway? This still America, or did I miss a memo?"

"Erin," Juarez said quietly.

That unconcerned half-smile Rainier had been smiling before had gotten harder. I stayed where I was regardless.

"That weekend Jeff and Erin Lincoln went missing in 1970, where were you?" I asked. Juarez looked like he was about to physically eject me from the conversation. And possibly the planet.

Rainier pretended to think about it for a minute. "1970, huh? That was a long time ago, you're gonna have to refresh my memory. Which weekend was that, now?"

"They found the boat Saturday, September 27th," I said patiently.

He thought some more. "September 27... Yeah, I think old Hank Gendreau and me were up in Quebec that weekend. Had a little rite of passage that Saturday night, if you know what I mean. Pretty little thing, too." He winked at me, then licked his lips. "Come to think of it, she looked a little like you."

The words had enough meaning behind them to push me back for a second. Before I could respond, Juarez took my arm, clearly intent on getting me out of there. Rainier got off his stool with surprising speed and pushed Juarez back. He was big enough that just about anyone but Juarez would have probably hit the floor; Juarez barely budged. Red Grivois got up off his stool, as did half the bar. At our table in the back, Diggs had his hand wrapped tight around Einstein's collar to keep him from jumping into the fray.

I stayed seated for the moment, uncertain what the best move might be. Red tried to steer Rainier toward the door.

"Come on, Will. I'll give you a ride home—you can go sleep this off before things get ugly."

Rainier shook his head. "You go on. The day I let a spic and a Jew girl chase me out of my own bar's the day I retire from this whole fuckin' planet. I told you," he said to Juarez. "Back the hell off. We're having a conversation."

Juarez ignored him completely, his attention focused on me instead. Daughtry was playing in the background, but nobody was dancing anymore.

"Are you ready?" he asked.

"Yeah, fine," I agreed reluctantly. "Let's go."

I hopped down from my stool, but I'd gotten no more than a step before a big, meaty hand closed around my upper arm. Before I felt so much as a gram of pressure, Juarez whirled. He struck once with the heel of his hand, and Rainier went down like a sack of Aroostook's finest russets, blood pouring from his nose.

Rainier held one hand over his face. With the other, he started to push himself back up off the floor.

"Don't," Juarez said quietly, his eyes steady on Rainier's. Rainier thought about it for a second, then sat back down. It was a very Eastwood moment. Juarez looked at Red. "See that he gets home safe?"

Red nodded. "Will do."

Juarez started to walk away, but I didn't move until he returned and physically herded me back to the table like a willful little lamb. He didn't say a word, and he definitely didn't look happy. He wasn't the only one, though. The second we were back to the table, I pulled my arm away.

"I had it under control," I said when he sat down. Einstein greeted me with wagging tail and an anxious whimper. I crouched to reassure the dog, too pissed to even look at the Fed.

"Not for long, you wouldn't have. And I told you that I'd talk to him tomorrow," Juarez said evenly.

I looked at Diggs, who was very determinedly not looking back. "It's a room full of people. What's he gonna do, attack me here?" I demanded. "The worst that happens in that situation is that he maybe gets one pop in before somebody takes him down and he goes straight to jail for a few days. You think I can't take a punch here and there?"

Juarez just shook his head, like I was too crazy to even argue with.

"I bet you could take a punch," Rosie volunteered. Juarez might have thought my most recent stunt made me certifiable, but I'd clearly gained some street cred in the eyes of our chesty young barkeep.

"Damn straight I can. And I can throw a punch, too, so it's not like I can't defend myself in a pinch."

"She does throw a mean right hook," Diggs said. He touched his jaw. "Trust a man who's been on the receiving end before."

"Exactly," I agreed. "I can handle myself just fine."

"I'm not going to fight with you," Juarez said. "I'm in the middle of an investigation—I can't just have you interrogating my suspects. It doesn't work that way. Particularly if I believe it's putting you in danger."

"I'm in the middle of an investigation too, you know," I said. I wasn't doing the whole unflappable thing nearly as well as he was. "You act like I called you out here and now I'm working for you or something."

"I apologize if it upset you," Juarez said. "But it doesn't mean I won't do exactly the same thing again if I have to."

"It's not that big a deal," Rosie assured us both, trying to smooth things over. "Will goes off the reservation about once a month, anyway. Trust me, this isn't the first time a little blood was spilled *sous le rouge blanc et bleu.*"

Rosie continued chattering, primarily about the number of brawls the Black Falls VFW saw on your typical Saturday night. Juarez was notably quiet, and Diggs was still not-so-subtly watching me to see what I might do next. Red Grivois had taken Will home, just as Juarez had advised, but otherwise the bar showed no signs of slowing down. In all the chaos, it took a good five minutes before the comment Rosie had made finally sank in.

"The French you used a few minutes ago—*sue la rouge.* What does that mean?"

She gestured toward the American flag hanging above the front door. "*Sous le rouge blanc pis ble*u—Under the red, white, and blue... The flag over there, you know? Why?"

Suddenly, I was back in Max Richards's filthy kitchen. What had Bonnie said? When he smells blood *sous le rouge blanc pis bleu—il est fait.*

"It was just something Bonnie Saucier said to me the other day," I explained. All eyes were on me. I expected Diggs to make fun of me, but he remained quiet. "You get that she's crazy though, right?" I insisted. "I mean... I didn't really take her seriously."

Rosie didn't look convinced. "She's *un taweille.* She sees things."

"Sarah used that word the other day," Diggs said. "It's a witch?"

"*Oui.* Her *mémère*—her grandma, *oui*?—was from the tribe in Madawaska. Very powerful. She's predicted all sorts of things over the years. What did she say to you?"

I shrugged. "Forget it, it's nothing. And most of it was in French, so... Even if it was something, it was lost on me."

On the other side of the booth, our nubile friend had migrated closer to Diggs. Much closer. She wasn't actually in his lap, but I had a feeling it wouldn't take much to get her there—maybe another whiskey shooter. Or a stiff breeze. It was nearly midnight, and I was starting to feel the effects of a series of emotionally draining days and not enough sleep.

"We should probably get going," I said. "We've got an early morning tomorrow."

Rosie made a face. "Do you have to?" She tucked her hand through Diggs' arm, her big, wet brown eyes on his. "You promised me a dance."

Diggs got up eagerly, trying in vain to disentangle himself. "She's right, actually. We do have an early morning. Raincheck?"

She wasn't happy about it, but short of tying him to the booth it wasn't like she had much choice. "*D'accord.*" I noticed that she hadn't actually loosed her grip on him, though. "Maybe I could take you to see the old Lincoln place before you go. You can't leave Black Falls without seeing it, oui?"

That was all it took for me to get my second wind. Diggs had finally extricated himself and was putting on his jacket, but I held up my hand for him to wait.

"You know where the old Lincoln place is?"

"*Oui.* Everybody who grew up here does." A flash of inspiration crossed her face. "We could go now, *non*? This is the best time to see them."

"The best time to see who, exactly?" Juarez asked for me. He didn't look that sure he wanted the answer.

Rosie got serious for the first time all night. "Erin Lincoln," she said. "And her *maman.* They walk at night, in the field by their house. Out near where Mrs. Lincoln died."

Chapter Ten

"Erin Lincoln and her mother still walk the fields outside their old house," Diggs said when no one else spoke. "And you've seen them, I suppose?"

"Make fun if you want—anyone around here will tell you," Rosie said. She looked at me knowingly. "You want to see, *oui*?"

I really, really did. I looked at the guys. Diggs had been around me long enough to know what was coming next, but Juarez was still in the dark.

"Is it far from here?" I asked.

She grinned. "*Non*. Just a few miles. I'll get my coat."

"What happened to having an early morning tomorrow?" Juarez asked. He looked genuinely pained at the turn of events.

"You heard her," I said. "It won't take long. Anyway, you can go back to the motel if you want—we'll just meet up in the morning."

He looked like he was seriously considering it until Diggs gave him the eye. "Come on, Jacky Boy. They must cover this at Quantico."

"Almost none of what I learned at Quantico seems to apply when Erin's in the picture," he said. He seemed a little depressed by that fact.

We decided to take Juarez's rental, since there was more room for the five of us—Jack and Rosie in the front so she could navigate, much to Rosie's chagrin, and Diggs, Einstein, and me in the back. Einstein required a window seat, which meant Diggs and I were forced to vie for space beside him.

"You take up a lot more room than someone your size technically should," Diggs complained after I'd elbowed him in the side for the third time since we'd set out.

"I could go up front and let Rosie sit with you," I whispered. "I'm sure she'd be more than happy to cuddle up back here."

He stopped complaining after that.

What started as a lark got progressively more serious the farther we got from town, passing trailers and abandoned houses and an old, ruined mill along the way. Rosie gave us a surprisingly in-depth history of the town, but I was barely listening—too busy trying to imagine my father as a kid in this desolate little backwoods world. When I was growing up on Payson Isle, he never talked about his past. I could remember him reading to me, teaching me, praying with me (a lot)… But somehow in all that, the subject of his childhood never really came up. If it had been as bleak as I was starting to suspect, I could understand why he hadn't been eager to amble down memory lane with me.

About twenty minutes after we'd piled into the car back at the VFW, Rosie directed Juarez down a dirt drive almost completely obscured by overgrown brush.

Not far in, our headlights hit on a sprawling colonial with the windows broken out and the front portico caving in. The shutters were half off and a picket fence around the perimeter had been torn to shreds by weather and unruly teens.

Einstein and I were the first ones out after Juarez stopped the car. "It doesn't look so bad," I said, studying the place with a critical eye.

A car door shut behind me, then another. "Says the woman who spent a solid week wandering the paths of Payson Isle alone," Diggs said.

"If I didn't see any goblins there…" I began.

"Maybe you just weren't paying attention," Juarez said. He shined his flashlight across the property, landing the beam on a No Trespassing sign riddled with bullet holes. "You know, legally that sign is all that's needed to make going in there a prosecutable offense."

"Pfft," I said. "It's fine."

"Pfft?" Juarez asked. "What does that even mean?"

"Get used to it," Diggs said. "That's Solomon's number one comeback when she knows you're right but she's gonna do it anyway."

"Shouldn't we at least wait until daylight for this?" Juarez pressed.

"Our plane leaves for Quebec at dawn—we won't have time before we go. I just want to check it out. It'll be fine."

"Where have I heard those words before?" Diggs said.

"I'm with you," Rosie said. She abandoned Diggs and took my arm. "You boys can hang out back here like a couple of little girls, but we're going in. Right?"

I wasn't used to having an ally in my madness, but I wasn't about to question it. Still arm in arm, Rosie and I waded through thigh-high grass with a bravado borne of too much alcohol and not a lot of common sense. We were halfway there before I heard Diggs and Juarez start out behind us.

The front door of casa Lincoln was falling off its hinges—admittedly a little more so after I was done trying to pry it open, but I comforted myself with the knowledge that a wrecking ball would be a kindness there.

It had been a gorgeous house once upon a time, opening into a grand hall with high ceilings, a butterfly staircase, and a chandelier that I suspected would have fetched a pretty penny if it didn't appear that hooligans had spent the past thirty years swinging from it.

The entire house had been graffiti'd within an inch of its life, and the floors were littered with old beer cans and cigarette butts. Whatever ghosts may have been in residence, they apparently weren't enough to dissuade the locals looking for a den of iniquity in their own backyard. Juarez hung back with Einstein, while Diggs, Rosie, and I forged ahead to the second floor. Our flashlight beams bounced in tandem through each of the rooms, over broken glass and spent condoms and the occasional stray pair of underpants.

"Do you have any idea what you're looking for?" Diggs asked when we'd hit nearly every room on the second floor, and I still hadn't ventured farther than the threshold in a single one.

I didn't have a clue what I was looking for. It wasn't like I was expecting Erin Lincoln and my grandmother to spontaneously appear before us. I was just looking for a connection, I think… To feel as though, somehow, I belonged to this place. Or my father had, anyway.

"I don't know," I admitted to Diggs. "I just want to look around a little."

Downstairs, I heard something skitter across the floorboards. Einstein whined, but he made no move to leave us. We walked down another short corridor tagged with clever slogans from the locals, none of them all terribly original. They kept up like that all the way to the end of the hall, with one notable exception: The last door on the left was closed. There were no beer bottles or cigarette butts in front of it. No sign that someone had used the door for target practice; no food or condom wrappers. The only graffiti was three words written across the center in large letters:

HERE BE DRAGONS

I looked over my shoulder at Rosie. Her bravado was wearing thin.

"Nobody goes in there," she said. "*Jamais.* That's the rule… Do whatever you like to the rest of the place. Just don't touch that room."

I don't really believe in portents from beyond the grave or ghosts or ghouls, and the only creatures of the night I'm especially fond of can be found on primetime. But for the first nine years of my life, I was raised by a man who believed in all of them—his conviction in the afterlife and the spirits who roamed the shadow world was nothing short of fanatical. Regardless of how pragmatic Kat may have raised me to be after the fact, it was hard to simply dismiss those early years when Dad was running from every bump in the night.

Rosie took a few steps back to join Juarez and Einstein. Diggs, the perennial skeptic, took his rightful place by my side.

"There's no such thing as spooks, kids," he said calmly. He pushed at the door, but it didn't budge. He tried pulling; still nothing.

"Is it locked?" I asked.

"Must be," he said. "I don't think it's moving."

I shouldered him aside to give it a go myself. I'd barely touched the knob before it opened.

"Very funny," I said.

He frowned. I can usually tell when he's kidding, but when my flashlight beam caught him this time there was no telltale spark to his baby blues.

"I must have loosened it for you," he said.

That ghostly chill I'd been feeling ever since I'd started chasing the Gendreau/Lincoln story took up permanent residence at the base of my spine and the back of my neck as the old door creaked open. I shined the flashlight across the walls and the floorboards. Unlike the rest of the house, this room was untouched: no graffiti, no bottles, no condoms. There was no furniture. The only things that remained in the room were an old rocking horse and a baby doll that would have given me the willies on my best day.

"This must have been her room, don't you think?" I asked. I didn't go in.

Diggs passed the threshold and shined his flashlight along the walls, treading carefully to avoid rotted floorboards. He stopped at the other side of the room and focused his light on a section of the wall where the wainscoting had broken away.

"Come take a look," he said to me.

I crept across the floor, just waiting for the ground to fall away beneath my feet. When I reached Diggs, I crouched beside him. My flashlight beam joined his. There on the wall, hidden behind the wainscoting, the letter J had been carved into the wood. Beneath it, smaller but no less distinct, was the letter E. Jeff and Erin. Under the initials, someone had carved an arrow pointing all the way down to the floor.

I tried to imagine the two of them—these siblings Sarah Saucier said were too close, one light and one dark—making their mark on this home they barely knew, then covering it back up so only they would know their secret.

I knelt in the filth and checked out the floorboards directly below the arrow. What I suspected had once been the best hardwood flooring money could buy was now so rotted that it took no time at all to find the board Jeff and Erin had been pointing to. Einstein came over and tried to help, but he just ended up giving himself a sneezing fit by snuffling too much dust. He was relegated to the sidelines with Juarez and Rosie; Diggs took his place. He knelt beside me while Juarez manned the flashlight. Darkness shrouded the scene. We worked on the loose board for less than a minute before we were able to pry it up with Diggs' utility knife.

Juarez shined his light inside the compartment we'd found in the floor. There, hidden beneath more dust and dirt, was a filthy old t-shirt. I took it out gingerly, disappointed until I felt the weight of something wrapped inside.

I peeled the shirt away. Inside was an old diary, worn and faded. The inscription on the inside cover was written in a child's sloping handwriting:

The Journal of Erin Rae Lincoln
PRIVATE!!!

◊◊◊◊◊

We dropped Rosie at her grandmother's place—a double-wide trailer on a dead end street not far from the VFW—and then waited until the light came on inside before we pulled away. By the time Juarez and I got back to the motel after getting rid of Rosie and dropping Diggs at his Jeep, it was almost one a.m. Juarez had been quiet all night—or at least since my little rebellion back at the bar. He and I walked Einstein together, on the same abandoned stretch of Route 1 I'd nearly been run down on twenty-four hours before. We were almost back at the motel before I finally broke the silence.

"Are you all right?" I asked.

"Maybe I should be asking you that," he said. "It's been a long day."

That it had. "I feel like we're getting closer, though," I said. "The thing with Will Rainier is big; you might not see that yet, but you will. The fact that those three names—Jeff Lincoln, Will Rainier, Hank Gendreau—keep coming up can't be a coincidence."

"Will and Hank's names only come up in connection with Erin Lincoln and Ashley Gendreau," he pointed out. "There's nothing to indicate they had any involvement with any of the victims found in Canada."

"You've looked into it?"

He stopped walking and turned to face me, an amused glint in his eye. "I get the feeling you must not think I'm very good at this job."

"That's not true. I think you're probably very good at your job. But things get missed... I just want to make sure that doesn't happen with my father. I mean, look at Hank Gendreau."

"There's every indication that Hank Gendreau did, in fact, murder his daughter. So far I haven't seen a thing in the file to convince me otherwise."

"Have you talked to him? If you do, you might change your mind."

He shook his head. Einstein sighed beside me, no doubt wondering when—if ever—we were going to bed. I reached down and scratched behind his ears while I waited for Juarez's response. His amusement had given way to annoyance, or at least a hybrid of the two.

"You really are just..."

I quirked an eyebrow and waited for him to continue. "Just...?" I finally prompted.

He didn't answer. Instead, he pulled my jacket up around me more tightly and straightened my collar. His hands were warm. He ran his knuckles lightly against my neck and up along my jawline.

"Impossible," he said softly.

He leaned down. I met him halfway, one hand resting on his chest. A full beat, maybe more, passed before he finally made his move. Once he did, I remembered why kissing Juarez was a memorable experience. There was no epic longing with him, no torturous denial... There was just Juarez, solid and strong and more present than anyone I had ever met before. His tongue pressed past my lips and his fingers twisted in my hair as the kiss deepened. By the time we parted, my head was a little light and my nethers a little moist and, if asked, I would have been hard pressed to remember my own name, let alone the names of all the ghosts I was chasing.

It was the first time I'd kissed him since our farewell in Littlehope in the spring—regardless of what Diggs may have thought happened while we were all in Washington. I made a promise to myself not to let another three months pass before we did it again.

A few years ago, making out with a man like Juarez under a full moon in the middle of nowhere would have led one place and one place only. But I was older now. Wiser. And there was that little matter of Erin Lincoln's journal, burning a hole in the writing bag slung over my shoulder. Juarez walked Einstein and me to my room. I turned at the door.

"We really do have an early morning tomorrow," I said regretfully.

"We do," he agreed. He made no move to leave, though.

"So, we should probably just… You know. Raincheck."

He nodded again. And stayed planted firmly behind me.

I leaned up and gave him another long, lingering kiss. "So… Goodnight." I turned to unlock the door. And still, Juarez remained where he was. I turned to look at him one more time. "What are you doing?"

He looked at me like I was hopeless. Or daft. "My job," he said. "Someone broke into your room last night, leaving evidence that you're being stalked and that they have intimate knowledge of Erin Lincoln's murder—and quite possibly the deaths of at least half a dozen other girls. I can't just leave you on the doorstep when there's the possibility someone could be waiting inside to butcher you. That kind of thing tends to make a man look bad."

Right. That.

What followed was Juarez's impressive impersonation of every cop from every primetime police saga I'd ever seen, as he drew his gun (!) and checked every square inch of the motel room, from the bathroom to the closets, behind the drapes and under the bed. When he was satisfied that no one was lurking in the shadows, he kissed me again and then advised me to lock the door behind him when he left. Which I did.

Diggs had returned to his own room now that Juarez was in town, which meant I had the place to myself. I washed my face and brushed my teeth, changed into my pajamas, and then curled up in bed. Einstein waited for my perfunctory invitation before he hopped up and lay down, stretched out with his head on the pillow beside me. I pulled Erin Lincoln's ancient journal from my writing bag, dusted it off, and began with the first entry.

Christmas 1969

J. got this book for me—he says I need to write things down now, so when I'm famous people will be able to look back and see what I used to be like. He's so weird sometimes. Anyway… It was Christmas today. Daddy barely spoke, and we just sat around looking at the spot where Mama would have been, but won't ever be again. I asked J. if he believes

she's in heaven looking down on us, and he said that was stupid.
"Dead is dead." That's what he told me.

It made me cry later, but I didn't let him see—it would just make him feel bad, and if Daddy saw me crying because of something he said, it would be all over but the shouting.

I remember when we were little, how much we used to love Christmas back in Lynn. Mama made everything magic. I tried to do the same thing this year without her—decorating the house, making Christmas dinner, everything you're supposed to do to make it perfect. It didn't matter, though.

From now on, I think Christmas will be the saddest day of the year in this house.

Chapter Eleven

The next morning, my alarm went off at five a.m. I stumbled into the shower and managed to get myself dressed and walk the dog without ever actually opening my eyes, and then at five-thirty on the dot, Juarez was at my door with coffee and that just-pressed grin he wore so well.

"You ready?"

I nodded, but still had no words—they don't usually come until at least eight a.m.

The next stop was Rosie's, to drop off Einstein. It was barely six o'clock, but she looked fresh as a daisy when she answered the front door of her grandma's double wide. Oh, to be nineteen again.

Stein greeted her like an old friend, dropping into a play bow before he tried to take off for a sprint around the yard. I convinced him that as long as he was still on leash—and it was still seven a.m.—there would be no sprinting. Then, once I'd gotten him settled down, I gave Rosie his bag. At the doggy daycares Einstein frequented in Portland and Boston, this is standard procedure. Rosie just stared at it.

"What is this?"

"It's his stuff," I explained. "His treats, and his food. And his toys. He also has allergy meds, in case he starts scratching. And sometimes he gets a little lame in his hind leg, so just watch out for that when he's playing. If it gets very bad, I've got a recipe and the ingredients for a poultice."

She and Juarez were both looking at me like a crazy person. Clearly, they had no concept of the bond between a childless woman and her dog. Rosie at least had the decency to humor me, though. She took the bag and slung it over her shoulder, then took Einstein's leash from me.

"He'll be fine. We'll just hang out, maybe go for a swim."

"I'll be back by tonight," I assured her.

"Take your time," she said. "If you're not back by the time it's my shift at the bar, I'll bring him with me. *C'est bien.* You'll have Diggs with you when you come back though, *oui?*"

"Definitely," I promised. "And you have my phone number. If there are any problems, you can just call."

She nodded. I kissed Einstein's head and told him when I'd be back. Then, I manned up and left the dog.

If I'd had any idea how long it would be and how much would happen before I saw him again, no one on the planet could have pried me away.

◊◊◊◊◊

After that, Juarez pointed the car south along Route 1 and I tried to catch a little more sleep before the day got rolling. When we pulled into a tiny dirt parking lot beside a tiny dirt airstrip about an hour later, he woke me with his hand on my knee and his mouth at my ear.

"Rise and shine, princess." Princess. I opened one eye and glared at him, but he just laughed. "You really don't like mornings."

"No sane person likes mornings."

He nipped my earlobe. "I bet I could make you like them," he whispered. With the smoky accent and the deep dark eyes and the way his hand traveled up my thigh, I almost believed him. If anyone could make me embrace a new day, it would be Juarez.

If I hadn't had drool on my chin and there hadn't been a gear shift between us and a plane waiting to take us to a world-renowned morgue to talk about young women being tortured and killed, things may have gotten sexy at that point. Instead, I kissed him very briefly on the mouth and we prepared to take to the friendly skies.

A little twin engine something-or-other was waiting for us in a dome-shaped hangar in the middle of nowhere. Curly's Charters was written on a faded wooden sign just outside the building. Our pilot was a small, wiry man whose moniker was refreshingly free of irony. Besides an impressive head of dark curls, Curly was notable because he was missing two fingers on his left hand. He joked about losing them in a plane crash. Juarez didn't look like he appreciated the humor.

Once we took off, I read Erin Lincoln's journals while Juarez looked out the window beside me.

"It doesn't make you sick to read in this thing?" he asked after we'd been in the air for about half an hour.

I shook my head. "Kat says motion sickness is all about mind over matter.

She says nausea's a sure sign of someone lacking character." I hesitated. "Or someone lacking moral fortitude… I can't remember, exactly. It's one of those."

"Well, I must have no character at all then," he said. Now that he mentioned it, he did look a little green.

"You get airsick?"

"It's just the height," he explained. "And the speed. I'm not actually that fond of the motion, either. I should be used to it by now. Perhaps I should talk to your mother."

"She'd cure you in no time," I agreed. "She'll fuck you up in sixteen other ways in the process, but you probably won't get nauseas as much."

He tapped the journal in my lap. "So, have you learned anything? What did Erin Lincoln have to say about the world?"

Quite a bit, as it turned out. She was a bright kid, but none of her entries were all that revealing. She talked about what they had for dinner, what kind of grades she was getting, where she passed her afternoons. She didn't say anything about someone stalking her. Jeff was a pain in the ass who definitely pushed the limits sometimes, but so far she hadn't said anything about him being a crazed sadist in the making, just waiting to torture and murder the town's fairest daughters.

I turned the pages until I found one of the more interesting entries so far, and read aloud.

January 9, 1970

J. says this house is haunted. He says he saw Mama at the top of the stairs last night, and he sees a little girl here sometimes who looks like me. Wednesday night, he said he thought it was me when we were going downstairs to meet Creepy Will and Hank Gendreau. But the ghost girl didn't say anything to him, and then she just disappeared.

He said she was crying.

I don't mind the idea of Mama being here, as long as she's okay. It would be better if she was in heaven, I know, but maybe she just doesn't want to leave us alone with Daddy. I could understand that. The little girl makes me nervous, though.

I don't like this house.

I finished and looked at Juarez. "Creepy, right?"

"Very," he agreed. "Her brother could just be teasing her, though."

"My father believed in ghosts," I said. "I remember that about him, at least. Everything Isaac Payson talked about in church services, he bought hook, line, and sinker. Maybe it was because he thought he really did see something in that house."

Diggs would have shot that down in a second. Juarez just nodded. "Anything's possible, I suppose. What about the final entry? Don't tell me you're not the kind of woman who'll skip to the end to see how everything turns out."

"Only when it's merited."

That last entry was actually one of the first things I'd read the night before. It turned out to be disappointingly innocuous. I flipped to the entry again and read to Juarez.

September 19, 1970
Daddy went to Quebec for the weekend, leaving Jeff and me. Jeff says he does business up there, like he used to in Lynn. I told him he doesn't know that for sure. Sarah and Luke came over, and I helped them with their homework. Luke gets so frustrated. Jeff came in and made fun of him, but I told him to get lost. He started in all over again about how Luke's got a crush on me, and why did I want to spend time with those townie losers, anyway. He's one to talk, with CW and H. trailing after him all the time. Talk about townie losers. Thank Gawd Mr. E's in town a little while longer. I never would have made it through the summer without him.

"Who's Mystery?" Juarez asked.

"Mister E," I corrected him. "I don't know. I think he stayed that summer with them—Erin mentions him a few times. She never calls him anything but that, though."

"According to the Sauciers, that previous spring was when Jeff shut Luke in the basement, wasn't it? And that was when the whole incident with Sarah Saucier took place."

The 'incident.' I nodded, reluctant to talk about it. Or think about it.

"Their mom died in the winter of 1968," I said. "Erin writes in here that they moved to Black Falls in '66. Considering that and the shitty way their father treated Jeff, it's not surprising that he went off the rails. He was fighting in school. Drinking and staying out all night with Will and Hank…"

"The next logical question," Juarez said, "is whether all those incidents were really just him acting out against a home life turned upside down, or if this behavior started earlier. She doesn't mention anything about that?"

"You mean something like, *'Got an A on my math test today; Jeff skinned Mister Whiskers and left him in the neighbor's kiddie pool?'*"

He smiled. "Something like that, yes."

"Not a word. In fact, so far the only thing that sounds remotely like my father in all this is when Erin talks about how he was with animals. There are a couple of entries where she talks about him feeding the birds... And he refuses to go bear baiting with Will and Hank that summer. That doesn't sound like the kind of guy who'd get his rocks off torturing teenage girls, does it?"

Juarez considered that. "No, it doesn't. I'm not ready to make up my mind one way or the other just yet, but that's definitely a point in your father's favor."

"Well, that's something, at least. Right now, I'll take any points I can get."

We touched down in Montreal at ten-thirty, and stepped off our little twin-engine straight into a hip, bustling European furnace. The temperature had to top ninety, and the humidity was enough to make even Juarez break a sweat. According to the GPS in our little rental car, it was supposedly a straight shot to drive from the airport to *le Laboratoire de Médecine Légale*, but in reality it was a harrowing thirty-minute drive, navigating through construction and detours and an unholy mess of one-way streets. When we finally did arrive, Juarez pulled into a lot reserved for staff, and we went inside a surprisingly modern facility to find a veritable ghost town.

"They take weekends off here," Juarez said to me as I joined him on the elevator. "Unlike we Americans." He pressed the button for the basement. Once the doors were closed, he turned to face me.

"So, you're clear on the rules, right?"

"Everything's off the record," I parroted back. During the car ride over, this had been our primary topic. "No touching anything. Only speak when spoken to. Chew with my mouth closed."

"The last two are just personal preferences," he said. "The first two are critical, if you ever want to be invited back."

"I know," I agreed. "I've got it, don't worry." I moved in a little closer. Juarez was in another of his standard-issue FBI suits. Despite the heat and the lack of sleep, he still managed to wear it well. "You're cute when you're official, you know." I bumped my hip against his.

"And you're cute when you're impossible," he returned evenly. He returned the hip bump just as we reached the basement, then raised it with a light slap to my backside as he stepped out of the elevator. "Which is almost always."

I followed Juarez down a deserted, dimly lit corridor to a locked door marked *Laboratoire de Pathologie*. He was just about to hit the buzzer when a small, gray-haired woman in a lab coat appeared down the hall.

She strode the rest of the way to us and met Juarez with a hug before greeting me with a perfunctory nod.

"Dr. Sophie Laurent, this is Erin Solomon. That friend I was telling you about."

She looked me up and down with keen gray eyes, then responded in completely unintelligible French—or at least it was unintelligible to me. Apparently it wasn't to Juarez, who surprised me by laughing and then launching into a lengthy dialogue of his own, also in French. I held up my hand.

"Hey, no fair."

Juarez winked at the woman. "Sorry, Sophie. English, *oui?*"

"English it is, then," she agreed. There was only the slightest trace of an accent.

She let us into the lab, a relatively small, overly bright room that smelled like bleach and chemicals. I waited for that stench of death writers are always talking about, but none came; no doubt an advantage to working with bones versus flesh. Four steel gurneys were lined up against one wall, each holding a different set of remains. The bones were clean, the skeletons completely disassembled. Dr. Laurent turned on a series of light boxes above each table, all holding x-rays.

"Where are the other victims?" Juarez asked, indicating the four bodies present and accounted for.

"I'm having a student run some tests. I'll let you know what we find. We've identified all six girls now," Dr. Laurent said. "You have the first five files?"

Juarez nodded, pulling them from his briefcase.

"The sixth victim was a transient from Boston: Kelsey Whitehart. Based on her history, it's possible she'd been hitchhiking in Maine or New Hampshire when the killer picked her up."

"Can you run me through the details of the attacks?" Juarez asked. "You said you had some new information."

"*Oui*," she agreed. "You're free to do whatever exams and tests you want once we release the remains, of course, but these preliminary findings should give you a place to begin."

She opened her own file and began listing details that I assumed Juarez had already known, since he didn't ask her to slow down. Juarez had already made me promise I wouldn't take notes or record the session, but I was sorely tempted to renege on that promise when I realized just how much information Laurent was providing.

"All six victims stabbed multiple times; based on the bone markers we found, it appears the attacks were centered around the abdomen, upper torso, and face."

I winced. Juarez caught me and raised an eyebrow. "You okay?"

"Yeah, of course," I said quickly. "Go on."

"All six had nicks in the second, third, and fourth ribs consistent with a straight razor, which was used to carve what we believe was the letter J into each woman's chest." She paused when Juarez jotted something down, then looked at Laurent to indicate he was ready for her to continue. "There are a couple of other details I think you'll find interesting."

She went to the light boxes and pointed at two x-rays—one of a leg, one of a foot.

"You see this?" She pointed to the x-ray of the leg. "The victim, Jennifer Bishop, fractured her tibia, but there was already some mending taking place. If you look here, you'll see a metatarsal stress fracture in the left foot, suggesting that she had been running barefoot for an extended period of time before she was killed."

I thought of Brian Bishop. He was already broken, but he'd never survive if he found out this was how his daughter spent the last days of her life.

"Can you tell if there was any sexual assault?" I asked.

She shook her head. "Not this long after the fact, no. The cloth the victims were wrapped in was too degraded to learn anything, and of course there was no genetic material to test from the victims themselves."

"What about the other victims?" Juarez asked.

"Those particular details are the same for all six women: damage consistent with running for an extended period of time, no sign of rape from the admittedly limited testing we're able to do at this stage of decomposition. The differences are what I found particularly intriguing."

Juarez and I both remained silent, waiting for her to elaborate.

She walked to the table farthest from us and stopped at the remains. "This is Jennifer Bishop," she said. I thought of the girl in the photos: the pudgy four-year-old with glasses and pigtails who grew to become the lean, smiling blonde teen on horseback. Dr. Laurent went to the next table. "And this is Stacy Long." The nineteen-year-old high school dropout.

"According to the missing persons reports," Juarez said, "they disappeared in 1982, within two months of each other. Jennifer Bishop at the end of May, Rebecca toward the end of July."

"*Oui*," Laurent said. She flipped a few pages in her file and handed it to Juarez. I leaned in closer to see what she'd given him. "As I mentioned, there is no genetic material on which to do a chemical or nutritional analysis, but we can look at bone density and some other orthopedic abnormalities to find out about these young women in their early lives. Stacy Long, for example, was already showing some signs of osteoporosis consistent with poor nutrition as a child. Ms. Bishop, alternatively, had strong bones, the best dental care, and a fairly expensive procedure to mend a broken clavicle when she was between eight and ten years old."

So far, these were all things I'd known from reading the files. I kept quiet, waiting for her to get to the point. It didn't take long.

"In the last months of her life, however, it appears based on a bone density scan my assistant just completed, that Ms. Bishop suffered from severe malnutrition. She also had stress fractures in both wrists and ankles that indicate she was bound for an extended period of time."

"He kept her," I said softly.

Dr. Laurent nodded. "Very good. Yes… He kept her. I believe she was imprisoned in a small space for some time—a matter of weeks, at least, and possibly months— before the next phase of her torture began."

"Do you think he let her go when he kidnapped Stacy Long?" Juarez asked.

" 'Let go' may be a bit generous," Laurent said. "That was when the hunt began. What was of particular interest to us was the fact that there are no indications that Stacy Long suffered through the same type of imprisonment that Jennifer did."

"So, he kidnaps Jenny Bishop," I said. My voice faltered. "Makes her his prisoner for two months, and then kidnaps Stacy Long. Brings them back to the same stretch of woods and… What? Hunts them both?"

"That would be conjecture on my part," Dr. Laurent said. "But the theory is supported by the evidence we've collected thus far. The same pattern was repeated on the other four victims."

"One victim kidnapped first, held captive, then a second kidnapped. Both released and hunted together," Juarez summed up. I was starting to feel sick. I took a deep breath and backed away from the remains, working hard to keep my cool. I didn't miss the look that passed between Juarez and Laurent.

At the moment, I couldn't seem to do much about it, though.

Juarez guided me toward the door, his hand at the small of my back.

"I should probably speak with Dr. Laurent alone for a few minutes. Would you mind waiting for me outside?"

Diggs would have hidden his head in shame; I was so much better than this kind of reaction. I couldn't help it, though—my breath was coming harder and the room was getting smaller and I knew if I didn't get air soon, things would get ugly. I nodded.

"Yeah. Okay. I'll meet you out there."

Juarez may have meant for me to just wait in the hall, but I chose to believe he'd be all right if I left the whole damned building behind. The air was still stifling when I burst through the side entrance, but at least there was no chemical smell. No tiny mortician telling me in graphic detail about the horrific ways six young girls were tortured before they finally met an equally horrific end.

It was just past eleven o'clock. I paced the sidewalk until sweat dripped from my forehead and clung to the small of my back. The only solace I took from any of this was my renewed certainty about one thing:

My father could never have done this.

Juarez met me outside twenty minutes later. I'd managed to avoid a full-on anxiety attack, but just barely. We walked back to the car in relative silence. It wasn't until we were back on the road headed for lunch that he spoke.

"You're very quiet. No jokes? No theories?"

I shook my head. I hadn't even asked what else Dr. Laurent had told him after I left. I wasn't sure I wanted to know. I couldn't stop imagining Jenny Bishop—the girl who loved horses and didn't like college because it was too far from home—caged like an animal. Tortured and hunted and tortured again. And what about Stacy Long? What role had she played? Ally? Foe?

"No jokes," I said finally, when I could find my voice. "I'm just trying to imagine how anyone could do that to another human being."

Juarez nodded grimly. "Welcome to my world."

◊◊◊◊◊

After a very good lunch and a fairly dull meeting back at the *Laboratoire* with the crime scene guys who had analyzed the body dump site, we headed for Quebec City. We'd taken longer in Montreal than anticipated, which meant Diggs had already done whatever research and interviews he'd needed to do in the city by the time we got there. We met him in Quebec's Old Port at a little after five that evening, at Mistral Gagnant—a little restaurant with a distinctly Provencal flair and a menu to die for, enough off the beaten path that it took Juarez and me half an hour wandering the narrow streets before we finally found the place. Diggs was already busy writing at a corner table, a tall glass of water and a nearly-empty bowl of potato leek soup off to the side while his fingers flew over his keyboard.

Unlike me, it looked like he'd actually gotten a full night's rest. All the time he'd spent with the top down riding around the countryside these last few days meant his hair was starting to bleach out again in the sun, and his face had taken on a beach bum glow I hadn't seen in a while. I wondered what it said about me that I was only attracted to men who seemed to thrive on murder and mayhem.

He took one look at my expression as I approached the table, however, and much of the sunshine vanished from his.

"That bad, huh?" he asked when Juarez and I sat down.

I shrugged, affecting my most hardened who-gives-a-shit air. "It wasn't a picnic. I've seen worse, though."

Diggs' mouth twitched. "Oh yeah, Ace? I forgot about all those years you were embedded on Beantown's traffic beat. That's rough stuff."

I flipped him the bird, a gesture that was not entirely appreciated by our waiter or fellow patrons. We ordered and then, once the waiter was gone, Diggs moved in closer and lowered his voice—as only seems appropriate when discussing serial killers over dinner.

"Let's hear it: What's the latest?"

Juarez gave him a very abbreviated version of what we'd learned back in Montreal. Then, he looked at me.

"There was actually something else—Sophie gave me some more information after you left."

Diggs caught the look that passed between us, but made no comment.

"You couldn't have mentioned that in the six hours we've been together since then?"

Juarez looked profoundly uncomfortable. Right. He hadn't wanted to upset me. I'd become that girl in his eyes—the delicate flower men had to protect from harsh reality.

"Okay, so… Spill. What else did you find?" I asked.

He lowered his voice. "The cause of death—strangulation. For all six, the injury to the hyoid and some of the other indicators on the bones were consistent with strangulation, with the killer most likely using a thick belt or strap."

"Isn't that what we expected?" Diggs asked. "I mean… If this is, in fact, the same guy who killed Erin Lincoln and maybe even Ashley Gendreau, wouldn't the COD remain basically the same? Especially if that's the thing he gets off on the most?"

Juarez nodded. "True. What came as a surprise was the fact that the same amount of pressure wasn't exerted with every victim."

"I'm not following," I said.

"Four of the six girls were strangled with the kind of force consistent with a man between two-hundred and two-hundred-and-fifty pounds."

"And the other two?" Diggs asked.

"The hyoid bones weren't broken," Juarez said. "Less damage, indicating less pressure, because the killers were smaller."

"How much smaller?" I asked.

"Sophie believes it was probably a female—one hundred to one hundred and ten pounds."

"What about Jenny Bishop? Does Sophie know whether it was the man who killed her, or a woman?"

"It was the man—definitely. Or at least a man. Same with Stacy Long. The only two who weren't killed by him were Grace Starke and Kelsey Whitehart."

"Who were they taken with?" I asked.

Juarez checked his notes. "Grace Starke was taken three months after Becca Martineau, in '84. Kelsey Whitehart was never actually reported missing, so it's hard to pinpoint exactly when she was taken or when she died, but Riley Thibodeau went missing in '85."

"Is it possible that he took Becca Martineau and *she* killed Grace Starke three months after she'd been taken?" I asked. "And then in 1985, he presumably did the same thing with Whitehart and Thibodeau?"

"That's my theory at this point," Juarez confirmed.

"And you honestly think the guy who raped, hunted, and killed Erin Lincoln in 1970 is the same nut job who started taking girls ten years later and running them through his own private death matches somewhere deep in the woods?" Diggs asked. "How does Hank Gendreau's daughter fit into all this?"

I looked at Juarez as he weighed those questions. "Ashley Gendreau doesn't fit—at least, not in my mind. She was killed on site, no J carved into her chest, no body dump, no hunt… And it was all too rushed. Whoever he was, J. liked to take his time. More than anything else, he thrived on the fear, and the feeling of power derived from controlling every aspect of these girls' lives. Ashley Gendreau was hunted for a few hours, no more, before she was killed."

"What about Erin Lincoln?" I asked.

He hesitated. "If J. killed her as well, I believe she was his first kill. The hunt was unorganized, the method of torture and killing very… frenzied. Based on the evidence gleaned from the bodies in Quebec, we're looking for someone fully in control of his impulses. A deeply methodical, highly organized individual with a history of sexual abuse—"

"Why sexual?" Diggs asked. "So far the only evidence you've seen of rape was in Erin Lincoln's case, right? Ashley wasn't touched, and though it's hard to tell so far, there's no indication that any of these other girls were, either."

"The obsessive need for control," I answered for Juarez, glancing at him to see if I was on the right track. He nodded. "Victims of severe sexual abuse who act out later in life typically have a need to either control or be controlled. They have a hard time relating in any other context."

Diggs raised an eyebrow in question.

"That piece I wrote for the *Globe* a couple years back," I explained.

"Right." Diggs nodded, then looked from me to Juarez and back again. "So, what else are we looking for?"

Juarez looked at Diggs' laptop, now safely stowed in a bag at his feet. "You do know this is all off the record, right? You're here because Erin is here, and Erin is here because of the potential link to her father."

"And because there's no way in hell you could have convinced her not to pursue it on her own," Diggs added.

"She's sitting right here, actually," I said. "And she hates it when you talk about her like she's not in the room."

"Does that mean you do or don't understand that this is all off the record?" Juarez asked.

"Scout's honor," Diggs said, three fingers raised. I thought it best not to mention that Diggs never made it past Cub status in the Scouts, kicked out after only a week for consorting with a couple of cute Brownies in the classroom next door.

Juarez started to dig out the files in his ever-present FBI tote when his phone rang. The whole restaurant turned to shoot appalled glares at him for the very American intrusion on their Sunday. He apologized to us and the world at large, then stepped outside to take the call.

"So, what happened at the *Laboratoire*?" Diggs asked the second Juarez was out the door.

"Nothing. It was interesting." I kept my eye on Juarez in the vain hope that Diggs might let it go. Because there's a first time for everything.

"So interesting you had to walk out before the good doctor was finished?"

Based on the pacing and the furrow in his well-formed brow, both of which I could see through the wall of windows looking out on the street, Juarez wasn't happy with whomever was on the other end of the line. I turned my attention back to Diggs, who was looking right through me in that irritating way of his.

"I got a little queasy, that's all," I said. "And you don't have to tell me—I know they were just bones, so I shouldn't have been bothered. I think it was the heat."

Instead of making fun, he shrugged. "This case is insane... I'm a little queasy myself, believe it or not. It happens to the best of us, Sol."

I sincerely doubted that, but I did appreciate the gesture. "I'm over it now. No big deal."

"Sure."

He took another bite of his salad and I took another bite of mine. I could feel him watching me. Before the silence got awkward—or, worse, he did something completely insensitive like try to make me feel better, Juarez returned.

"What's going on?" Diggs and I asked at the same time.

"There's been a new development in Black Falls," Juarez said. "I'm sorry—I have to leave."

"Wait a second; what do you mean, you have to leave?" I demanded.

He sat back down. "The police will be waiting for me when I get back," he told us both. "I'll go straight to the airport from here; I have a plane waiting."

"What about me?" I asked. "What am I supposed to do in all this, exactly?"

"I'd like you and Diggs to go to Montreal," Juarez said hesitantly. "Get a hotel. Lay low, just for the night."

Clearly, he'd lost his mind. "We're not going back to Montreal; my dog is in Black Falls. Why can't we just stay with you? What the hell happened?"

"I can't say anything about it right now," he insisted. He lowered his voice. "I'll just tell you that as of this afternoon, the case is no longer cold."

"You have a new victim?" Diggs asked.

Juarez bit his lip, giving the very slightest of nods before he went all business again. "Which means I can't be seen with either of you right now."

I'm a pain in the ass, I know, but even I understood the position Juarez had put himself in by including me in the investigation up to that point.

"Are you in trouble?" I asked.

Diggs looked at me in surprise.

"What? I can be sensitive."

Diggs didn't look like he bought it. Juarez shook his head. "Nothing I can't handle."

"What happened to the whole objective of keeping Solomon with you so she'd be safe from the nut job out there?" Diggs asked. "Particularly if he's gotten a taste for killing again. And who did you say that victim was again?"

"I didn't," Juarez said flatly. "And as for keeping her safe, that's where the hotel in Montreal comes in. I'll arrange for a guard to be stationed there to be doubly sure. I don't think it should be an issue, but I don't want to take any chances."

"Why wouldn't it be an issue? Because you've already caught the guy?" I asked.

Juarez stood, hands raised. "Sorry, that's the end of that interview, or you really will get me fired." He turned his attention to Diggs. "Is this all right? I'm sorry—it's not the way we planned it, but I don't have a lot of options at this point."

"A night in Montreal living the high life sounds just fine to me," Diggs said. He looked at me, his meaning clear. "I'm not the one you have to worry about, though."

I suspected Juarez knew that quite well. He nodded toward the exit. "Can I talk to you for a minute?"

I followed him out to the sidewalk. We'd gone from the dead heat of an August morning in Montreal to the cool breeze and casual crowds of evening in Quebec City. Juarez found a secluded corner and led me that way, his hand at the small of my back.

"Can you just tell me if this means my father's cleared?" I asked.

He shook his head. "I don't know yet—I'm sorry."

"But you'd tell me if you did know, right?"

He hesitated.

"Jack, come on. You can't seriously think I'm gonna leave my dog, turn my back on a story, and go spend the night in a friggin' hotel in Montreal while you solve the case. You have to give me something here."

We were in an alley off to the side of everything, cool brick at my back. Juarez advanced on me, pressing me against the wall.

"I'm no closer to finding your father than I was when I first arrived in Black Falls," he said quietly. "And I don't believe he has anything to do with this latest victim." He pushed my hair back off my forehead, his body trapping mine, his eyes dark and unfathomable.

"But you won't tell me who that victim was," I persisted. "Will Rainier? Sarah Saucier?" I watched his face closely, but saw no sign that I was on the right track.

"Erin." There was a definite edge to his voice.

"I know. Go with Diggs."

"Please." He kissed me slowly and very, very sweetly, his hand on my cheek. His body was warm and solid against mine and I could feel my own responding despite the circumstances. After what was rapidly becoming an indecent display for passersby, he pulled back and looked at me seriously. "I'll talk to you as soon as I can. The police will meet you in Montreal, but I don't think you'll have any trouble between here and there. Just stay on main roads, no detours. Call me on my cell or at this number if you have any problems." He handed me a piece of paper with a couple of numbers written on it. "If you can't reach me, you can speak with anyone at that second number. Just tell them who you are, and give them the code beside it when they ask about your emergency."

I rolled my eyes. "Yes, Dad."

He rolled his eyes right back at me. "As soon as I can tell you something, I will. For now, just stick with Diggs. Go back to Montreal. Be safe. And when this is over…" He kissed me again.

"When this is over, what?" I asked.

"When this is over, we're taking a weekend," he said. "Somewhere nice. And quiet. No dead bodies, no long-buried secrets." He kissed me one more time, with a little more heat. "Just you and me."

"And Einstein," I added.

"Right," he agreed. He didn't look as enthusiastic about that as I would have hoped. "You, me, the dog, and a romantic weekend away."

I stood on my tiptoes and gave him one last peck on the lips. "I think that could be arranged."

Chapter Twelve

As soon as we were back in Diggs' Jeep with Juarez safely on his way, Diggs turned to me with waggling eyebrows and a devilish grin.

"So, ready to tear it up on Uncle Sam's dime in lovely Montreal this evening?"

Clearly, he'd lost his mind. "Are you kidding—what kind of reporter are you? We're going back to Black Falls."

"Oh no we're not," Diggs said immediately. "J-Fed was very clear on that one—it's Montreal or bust for you, young lady." He put the Jeep in gear and headed out.

"You heard Jack: They've already got the guy. This is overkill. I just want to get back to Black Falls, pick up Einstein, and figure out what the hell's going on."

"And we can do that," he agreed. "Tomorrow."

"Dammit, Diggs." Fury built like a storm cloud in my chest, quickly obliterating any good humor I might have had about the situation. "I'm going back to Black Falls—you can't just abscond with me and dump me in Montreal."

"It's my Jeep, I can do whatever I damn well please."

"Fine, then." I waited until he'd stopped at a streetlight and hopped out of the car. I leaned in before he took off. "I'll just rent a car. No problem. I'll see you back in Black Falls tomorrow."

I tossed my bag over my shoulder and headed off in the opposite direction. I'd already googled the nearest rental place on my phone and was working out the logistics of actually getting to it when I heard tires squeal and Diggs pulled up beside me.

"Get in the fucking car," he said. He didn't look amused.

"I'm not going to Montreal," I said again. "You do whatever you want, but unless you're planning on tying me up and gagging me, there's no way

I'm going anywhere but Black Falls tonight. Just go on without me, it's no big deal."

"No big…" He shook his head. He looked like he was about to blow a gasket. "Did you not hear what Juarez said? Have you been listening to me at all since we started on this thing?"

"I've heard both of you. And I appreciate the concern, don't get me wrong," I said evenly. "But I'm a grown woman. If I want to take chances, that's my right. It's my life, Diggs."

A horn honked behind him. Diggs glanced back over his shoulder, then at me. His hands were clenched so tight around the wheel I expected his knuckles to pop clear through the skin.

"You don't have to worry about it," I said. "I told you—I'll just rent a car."

He sped ahead a few feet, found a place to pull over, and slammed the Jeep into park. I wasn't sure about the wisdom of the whole tying-up-and-gagging comment; based on the look on his face, he was seriously considering it. I walked over to the passenger's side door, but made no move to get in.

"You don't have to get so pissed off about this," I said. I was starting to get a little pissed off myself. "I can take care of myself. I'm not some helpless little fool who needs to be protected all the time."

"Then stop acting like one!" Diggs shouted. People were staring at us. "I called Juarez the other day because I thought maybe he'd have better luck convincing you you're not invincible, but you're still picking fights with rednecks in bars and ghost hunting in the middle of the night. He's right—the only way to keep you safe is to take you out of the equation completely."

"I never asked anyone to keep me safe."

"Right, I forgot. We should just let you go get yourself killed, then."

"You should just let me do what I do, and stop freaking out about it. Now, if you don't mind, I need to call a cab so I can get a car before it's too late."

I turned my back on him and started dialing. Ten seconds later, Diggs was in front of me with his eyes blazing.

"You're driving me nuts—you know that, right?" he asked.

"I'm not all that crazy about you right now, either," I said. "What happened to the man who'd do anything to get a story? Since when do you listen to the freaking Feds when they tell you to take a hike?"

He threw his hands in the air and walked away. He was talking to himself; more people were staring. I wished he'd just go already—I was

~ 122 ~

more than happy to take off on my own. Hell, by that time I was looking forward to it. Instead, he came back around and took me by the arm.

"Get in the car."

"Excuse me?"

"If you're going to Black Falls, you're not going alone. Get in."

I looked at him suspiciously. "This isn't a trick, right? You don't have a bottle of chloroform and some shackles in that magic bag of yours?"

"Please." He was quieter now. A little desperate. Very tired. "Just get in the Jeep."

I got in the Jeep.

Just as we were heading out of Quebec City bound for Maine, I called Rosie for the third time that day to check on Einstein, and let her know we were on our way back. She told me for the third time that day that everything was fine, and we planned to rendezvous at her place as soon as Diggs and I hit town—even though that likely wouldn't be before midnight. Rosie assured me she'd still be there with bells on, just waiting for Diggs to show his pretty face.

The sun was already low on the horizon by the time we were out of Quebec City for good, and well and truly on our way back to Maine. Diggs wasn't speaking to me. I didn't blame him, necessarily, but it didn't make the trip any more pleasant. He was going through some kind of U2 retrospective phase; he'd programmed their entire playlist for the trek, from *Boy* all the way to *No Line on the Horizon*, including their live albums and a couple of bootlegs, which meant we basically had enough, music to carry us through all of New England and the better part of the eastern seaboard.

We were deep in Bono's early '80s bouffant days before Diggs finally spoke again. He nodded toward the backseat. "Grab my bag, would you? I got something for you."

"What is it?"

"Just grab it, Solomon. Jesus."

I did as I was told, hauling the backpack into the front seat with me. "What am I looking for?"

"A manila folder—it should be in the front pocket."

It wasn't in the front pocket, or the second front pocket. "What, exactly, do you need all this shit for?" I asked. I dumped the contents onto my lap. "Survival knife, tape recorder, extra tape recorder, waterproof pens, waterproof matches, waterproof camera, waterproof bandages… Was there a flood warning I missed?"

"You can never be over-prepared—especially when I'm traveling with you. Check the back pocket, then."

I did. "Eureka." I opened the folder and started thumbing through about a dozen black-and-white, very dated photos of crowds in bars. "What am I looking for?"

He leaned toward me slightly, going back and forth between watching the road and checking the folder. I would have been alarmed with anyone else, but I'd been driving with Diggs since I was fifteen. Almost eighteen years, and we had yet to crash and burn. Going through the stack again, he stopped me at the third photo.

"Take a look at that one, would you? It was for a story they were doing on underage Americans coming across the border to get wasted. You might need the magnifying glass."

Which he, of course, had. I took a good long look. It wasn't until I reached the lower left corner that I realized why the photo was significant. I looked at the date stamp at the bottom: *Sept. 26, 1970.* The day before Jeff and Erin Lincoln's boat was found on Eagle Lake.

"Where is this?" I asked.

"A bar in Quebec City," he said.

I studied the blurred faces in the photo. There was no doubt—I'd been looking at old pictures of the same two boys *ad nauseam* for the past week. Hank Gendreau and Will Rainier, this time with another boy whose face was blocked from the camera. All three had beers in their hands, Will and Hank each grinning broadly.

"So, Hank and Will's alibi holds up then," I said, making no effort to hide my disappointment. "They really were in Quebec City."

"Take a closer look," he said.

I did, while he sped along at a racer's clip and the sun set on the horizon. He had to give me another couple of clues before I finally figured out what he was talking about.

Around Hank Gendreau's waist, plain as day once I actually looked for it, was a belt. Wide and leather, with a gaudy buckle whose insignia I couldn't quite make out. I didn't need to, though; I'd seen that belt before.

It was the same one found around Erin Lincoln's neck just outside Eagle Lake two weeks later.

◊◊◊◊◊

"This blows their whole story to pieces," I said. We'd gone nearly one hundred miles over the course of an hour and a half. The tension had lightened between us since our fight, but I knew we'd hardly reached a resolution. Juarez had called twice since we left; I hadn't taken either call. In the meantime, I was still focused on Hank Gendreau and his snazzy incriminating belt.

"This is it. Hank Gendreau did it," I said. "Will Rainier must have helped. I bet they worked together all those years."

"Maybe," Diggs said. He didn't sound convinced.

"What? You don't think so?"

"All the reasons Hank's given for why we should believe he's innocent actually do make sense—why would he ask for DNA testing? Why would he consent to psych test after psych test? Why would he get in touch with you?"

Rather than biting his head off, I took a few seconds to think about his questions. "Okay… So, maybe he didn't do it. Maybe it really was Rainier."

"But then why would Hank blame your dad? Why go to all the trouble of getting you involved, unless he genuinely believed your father was to blame for killing Ashley?"

I'd been wondering the same thing, though I was loathe to admit it. Diggs turned off the highway onto Route 289. We were making good time, thanks to surprisingly light traffic for a Sunday night in August and what I suspected was Diggs' conviction that the sooner he could get us back to Black Falls, the sooner he could just wash his hands of me entirely.

We'd been neck and neck with a family in a station wagon for close to an hour, two wild-eyed boys making faces every time we got close. Other than that, it was just a black pickup that we'd been playing leap frog with for hours, the windows tinted and one headlight broken out.

The Edge was just kicking into the first strains of his solo in One Tree Hill and we were still a good two hours from Black Falls the third time Juarez called. Diggs glanced at me. "You could at least let the guy know you're okay."

I shook my head. "I will, I just want to make sure we're close enough to Black Falls that he can't have me arrested and held in some Quebec prison indefinitely. You think he knows by now that we didn't go back to Montreal?"

"Probably."

I felt a twinge of guilt when I thought of how intent Juarez had been about keeping me safe. "He'll be all right. Once we get there, I can talk to him."

"Right," he agreed. "Bat your eyelashes and tell him whatever it is he wants to hear, then turn around and do whatever you damned well please all over again. It'll be great."

"If I'd told him I wasn't going to Montreal, he would have... I don't know, handcuffed me or something. This way, he doesn't have to be culpable for whatever might happen, and I get to follow the story," I said. "Everybody wins."

"Yeah. Until you get one of us killed."

I let that one slide. "Let's just drop it, talk about something else. How's Andie these days?"

He glared at me. I smirked at him. The moon shone overhead and the world flew by as Bono sang about that age-old conundrum, living with or without. The Jeep hurtled onward.

We hit the border crossing into Maine at just past ten that night. The guards were nice enough to me, but they seemed to view Diggs as an imminent threat to national security and all we Americans hold dear. After he was frisked and searched and his backpack thoroughly ransacked, they proceeded to do the same with the Jeep. They seemed genuinely disappointed when they didn't find anything more suspicious than Diggs' survival gear and a couple of specialty teas I'd picked up for Maya in Montreal.

It was eleven by the time we were cleared and on our way, with another forty-five minutes or so before we'd get back into Black Falls. We were deep into Rattle and Hum by then, but at least the tension had dissipated.

"I can drive the rest of the way if you want," I offered. "I do have a license, you know."

Diggs shook his head. "We're almost there—I'm good. Besides, when have I ever let you drive this baby unless I was literally too incapacitated to see straight? You just lie back and rest that pretty head. You'll need your wits about you when you have to face the Fed this time."

"He'll be fine." I leaned back in the seat and yawned. "Don't forget we have to stop for Einstein before we go back to the motel."

"Got it."

I was just drifting off when Diggs swore under his breath and the Jeep shimmied on the road. I opened my eyes.

"Problem?"

"Just the idiot behind us," he said.

The family in the station wagon was long gone. I'd seen the pickup with the busted headlight waved through the border crossing well before us, but suddenly a vehicle very much like it was behind us again. He had his high beams on, riding our bumper despite the fact that there wasn't another soul on the road in any direction. A dull edge of fear cut through that bulletproof fantasy Diggs had been bitching about for so long now.

"Is that the same guy we've been traveling with since Quebec?" I asked.

Judging by the tension in Diggs' jaw, he'd noticed, too. "Call Juarez."

For once, I didn't argue. The truck behind us had eased off a little by the time Juarez picked up, but he was still traveling too close, his headlights blinding in the rearview mirror.

"Where the hell are you?" Juarez asked as soon as he picked up the phone.

"On our way back," I said. The connection between us was bad, and the truck on our ass was picking up speed again. I cut to the chase. "We're about half an hour outside Black Falls," I said. "There's a truck—"

"Solomon!" Diggs yelled. He put his arm in front of me to keep me from hitting the dash as the jackass behind us suddenly stomped on the gas. Metal hit metal with a bone-jarring crunch and we shot forward, swerving dangerously close to the curb.

"Erin? Tell me where you are." Jack's voice faded in and out, but there was no mistaking his urgency.

I looked at Diggs. "Where are we?"

"Smugglers Road," he shouted. Both hands were tight on the steering wheel. The truck had backed off again, giving us some space. Playing with us.

"Smugglers Road," I said to Juarez. I had to repeat it twice, then lost the connection before I was sure he'd heard me.

Just after the call got dropped, the pickup shot out ahead of us again. It roared past and then continued on the wrong side of the road with its red taillights blazing in the darkness until, eventually, it faded into the horizon.

"What the fuck was that?" Diggs asked. "Call Juarez again."

I checked my phone. "There's no reception out here. I'll have to wait. Where the hell is Smugglers Road?"

"It's a short cut," he said reluctantly. "Rosie told me about it yesterday; I just added it to the map then."

"How far do we have to go before we get back to civilization?"

"Just another ten miles or so and we're back on the road that'll bring us into Black Falls."

I dug the map out of the glove compartment. When the turnoff was in sight, Diggs started to slow down. He was getting ready to make the turn when I realized we were headed straight for a truck parked in the middle of the road, its headlights off. I screamed just as the truck's high beams came on and it barreled toward us, engine roaring. Diggs had no alternative but to swerve and either stop entirely or continue along Smugglers Road. I clung to the edge of my seat as he chose to swerve, narrowly missing the truck, and adjusted his course. We continued along Smugglers Road, the roar of the pickup close on our tailpipe as it followed behind.

While Diggs looked for some way to get us out of the path of the lunatic behind us, I kept checking my phone for reception. There was none.

"I think he's been waiting to make his move until we were out of cell range," Diggs said after I checked my phone for the sixth time.

"Do you know where we are?" I asked.

He shook his head grimly. "Still on that same logging road... Rosie said they used to use it to bring contraband in and out of Canada. After that main turnoff, I don't have a clue where it leads next, though."

"How far are we from the main road?" I made a concerted effort not to panic.

"About half an hour—maybe thirty miles by now."

I thought of the bodies that had been discovered; all we'd learned about how the victims had died... The hell they'd gone through beforehand. "Do you think it's J.?"

"I don't want to think about that right now. Can you check out that topo map again?"

I did, bouncing almost out of my seat when he hit a pothole the size of a moon crater. I sat back and braced myself with my feet against the dash while I lit the map with my phone. Diggs reached over and tapped my knee with one hand, then quickly returned it to the wheel.

"Feet down," he said briefly. "If we crash, you'll break your legs."

Of course.

I put my feet down, and did my best to keep myself in the seat aided only by my seatbelt and sheer willpower while I checked the map.

"What the hell am I looking for?" I asked hopelessly.

"The logging roads. They're in red on there—I turned onto Smugglers Road off the main stretch. I want to see if there's another road coming up that might bring us back to a highway."

I leaned in and focused my light on a network of thin red lines taking up the entire upper left quadrant of the state. Traveling on a rocky road at a high speed in the dark, for the record? An excellent way to test your map-reading skills.

"Shit! Solomon," Diggs warned. I looked behind us as he stepped on the gas. The truck was closing in fast.

"Can't you just pull into a side road before he knows you're doing it and trick him into passing?" I asked.

"What side road?" he asked. "Tell me where there's a side road and I'll gladly turn into it."

"Well, don't get pissed at me," I said. "I'm doing the best I can here."

"I don't think it matters, anyway," he said from between clenched teeth. "I think he knows this place backward and forward—the few side roads I have seen, he speeds up just before we hit them so there's no way I can make the turn."

"He's herding us," I said. Sure enough, another logging road sped by. The second it was behind us, our pursuer dropped back. "God knows where he's taking us." I clutched the dashboard as I looked over my shoulder again. "We have to get the upper hand here. Or at least get some semblance of control."

He nodded. "Well, I'm open to suggestions." He flexed his fingers on the wheel and glanced at me again. "I want you to get everything we'll need, okay?"

"Everything we'll need for what?"

He didn't answer me. "The first aid kit and my pack are in the back there. That map. Both our phones. Make sure we can grab them as soon as we hit. Any food you've got stowed away. My sleeping bag."

The truck sped up behind us again. I unfastened my seatbelt and angled myself into the backseat, grabbing everything he'd told me to—plus Erin Lincoln's journal and my flash drive, of course—and then Diggs warned me to get back in my seat. The truck's engine cycled a tone higher behind us. I'd just managed to get myself buckled in again when the pickup hit once more, its front end smashing against Diggs' back bumper. The Jeep swerved off course. Diggs recovered at the last minute and got us back on the road.

"You have everything?" he asked.

"I think so," I said. "First aid kit, pack, map, phones, sleeping bag. What about water?"

"Just one bottle—we're close enough to the river here, we'll just head there first and follow it back to civilization."

The truck hit again, harder this time. I flew forward, my forehead bouncing off the dash.

"Goddammit," Diggs shouted over his shoulder, followed by a long string of language more colorful than I'd heard from him in years. He took a breath, his hand on my arm. "Are you okay?"

I touched my head gingerly. "Yeah—It'll leave a mark, but I'm fine."

"Check the phone again."

I did. "No bars."

The road was getting more narrow, pocked with holes, trees encroaching on both sides. Up ahead, I could see a steep incline lit by the glare of our headlights and a full moon overhead. Diggs looked around, his fingers flexing around the steering wheel again. His shoulders were rigid.

"What are you thinking?"

"If we can get out of here now—"

Before he could finish, the truck struck again. This time after the impact, the driver didn't back off. Instead, he kept our bumpers locked and started pushing the Jeep up the hill. Diggs tried stomping on the brakes; threw the emergency brake; shifted it in reverse as gears screamed and the truck behind us just roared with that much more fury. It barely slowed down. The road leveled out at the crest of the hill, but on the left was a steep wooded ravine—I grabbed Diggs' arm when I realized what was happening.

"I know," he said. I'd never seen him look more terrified. He tried to jerk the wheel to the side, but it didn't make any difference—we were headed in one direction, and one direction only.

Just as we went over, Diggs abandoned the wheel and pushed my head down. "Just hang on," he shouted over the sound of screaming engines. I clutched the dashboard with one hand, the other holding tight to Diggs. The world spun and kept spinning, end over end, until I felt a sharp pain in my temple and darkness fell.

◊◊◊◊◊

"We've gotta go. Come on—Erin, wake up. Please."

I floated for a while, halfway between consciousness and something infinitely nicer, before Diggs' voice finally registered. Pain came next, accompanied by a wave of nausea and the even less pleasant memory of what the hell I'd gotten us into.

I was on my back outside the Jeep, beneath a star-filled sky and a canopy of forest. Bono was still singing somewhere far off. Diggs tried to pick me up, but I squeezed his arm to let him know I was awake.

"I can do it," I whispered.

I caught a glimpse of his face: blood down the side, terror in his eyes. The terror vanished the second he realized I was with him, replaced almost instantly with a determination I'd come to know well over the years.

"Come on," he said. "We have to go. Can you walk?"

I sincerely doubted it, but I made the effort anyway. My right leg folded beneath me, but no real pain came until Diggs grabbed my arm to keep me on my feet. I cried out. He let go.

"Sorry—"

My head spun, darkness closing in again. Diggs stopped long enough to face me, still holding me up with his hand under my other arm. He looked me in the eye.

"We have to do this," he said.

I nodded, though even that small movement brought back the nausea. He lifted my chin with one hand, his eyes boring into mine.

"You're okay," he said. "We're alive. I won't let him near you." I'd never seen him look so fierce. "We're getting out of this, Sol. We just have to keep moving."

If he'd expected an argument from me, he wasn't getting one. I nodded gamely. "Okay. Let's go."

He took my good hand. He had his backpack on and a bottle of water in the mesh side pocket, a map clutched in his other hand.

"You ready?"

I swallowed past all the fear and doubt, pushing it far away. There was no room for it here. "I'm ready."

III.
OVER THE RIVER,
THROUGH THE WOODS

Chapter Thirteen
Juarez

Juarez's plane touched back down in Black Falls at ten o'clock Sunday night. The landing could have been smoother, but wasn't the worst he'd ever had. He dug his nails into the arms of his seat and thought of Erin's words that morning: *Mind over matter.* It was the sort of thing someone who had never experienced aviophobia would say—to Juarez, she may just as easily have told him to will his way to time travel, or sprouting a dorsal fin. He'd been afraid to fly for as long as he could remember, all the way back to thirteen years old, when the sisters would wake him from nightmares in which airplanes crashed into a sea of fire off the Miami coast.

All of that required more of an explanation than he was prepared to give Erin that morning, however. Besides, she'd been sweet enough to be concerned, and kind enough to distract him until the plane landed. If he had to fly, that wasn't a bad way to go.

He tried Erin's cell phone when he landed, but she didn't answer. He frowned. He'd already tried her once before, with the same result. He called the hotel he'd booked for her and Diggs, and was told they hadn't checked in yet. It had been nearly four hours since he'd left the two of them at the restaurant; more than enough time for them to make the trek from Quebec City to Montreal. A pinprick of concern needled its way beneath his skin.

He made sure that his phone was on, put it in his pocket, and offered up a quick, silent prayer that for once Erin had decided to go against her nature and listen to someone else for a change. If she hadn't, and arrived in Black Falls while this latest development was still unfolding, he would simply have to deal with it. For the moment, there was very little he could do about any of it.

From the air field, Juarez drove straight to the Black Falls police station, where Sheriff Nathan Cyr was waiting for him. There were seven others in the cramped police station, most of them in civilian clothes. Juarez offered a perfunctory nod when he came through the door, then asked to speak with the sheriff alone.

"Who's at the crime scene now?" Juarez asked the moment they were shut in Cyr's office. A deer's head was mounted on the wall, along with framed photos of the sheriff's family. The sheriff himself was likely in his fifties, with dark hair and a dark moustache and a beer belly that hung over the belt of his uniform.

"I just left Teddy—my deputy—over there. He knows not to touch anything."

"There's no question it's Bonnie Saucier?"

"Not one," the sheriff confirmed. Juarez was surprised he didn't look more shaken, considering what he was dealing with. "She'd only been out there a few hours, so no problem with ID there."

"And you still believe there are other bodies buried there?"

"We're not positive, but it looks that way," Cyr said. "We're basing some of that on what Bonnie said to Red when she called this afternoon. But there are a few mounds in that area, about the right size. I figured I'd leave that to you to figure out."

"Can you take me out there?"

"Now?" Cyr hesitated. "You don't want to go out in the morning? There's not much you can tell right now. We've got a couple of guys up there to make sure no animals go for the body overnight... She'll be just as dead come morning."

Juarez didn't even dignify that with a response.

It took half an hour driving through dense woods before they reached the site. During that time, Juarez went over everything that had happened in Black Falls since he and Erin had left town that morning, point by point, starting with a phone call Red Grivois had received from Bonnie Saucier at three o'clock that afternoon.

"Did she say where she was calling from?" Juarez asked.

The sheriff shook his head. "If she did, Red didn't recall. It was late afternoon... After church is out, Red likes to tip back a few. Just to relax, you know. There were a few things he wasn't completely clear on, thanks to that."

Juarez nodded. "So, he got the call from this woman. And she said...?"

"She gave him directions to this spot. Said she'd seen blood—that it all came to her in a dream... And around here, of course, we all know about

Bonnie's dreams. Nobody really questions 'em anymore. He called me, and we went out there together."

Cyr continued talking for the remainder of the drive, but Juarez wasn't listening. He didn't like to know that much about a crime scene before he arrived, preferring to come to his own conclusions about what may or may not have transpired.

When they had driven as close as possible to the site, the sheriff parked behind another police car pulled off to the side of a narrow dirt road. The moon was full overhead, the air cool. The deputy, Teddy, was waiting in his car. He was no more than twenty-two or twenty-three, and looked terrified. The sheriff told him to go home, but Juarez stopped him.

"I'd like you to stay a little longer, if you don't mind. So I can get your impressions of what you've seen."

And find out whether or not the deputy had compromised his crime scene, of course. He left that part out.

A narrow path littered with beer cans and cigarette butts led to an overgrown field where the gravestones from an old, forgotten cemetery were scattered in a distinctly haphazard fashion. The sheriff continued on through the first field and back onto another path in the woods. Juarez could hear the river nearby. The moon was bright enough that they barely needed flashlights, though he used one regardless. When they reached the cabin where Luke and Sarah Saucier lived, Sarah was waiting on the path with a large white dog. Teddy and the sheriff forged on ahead, but Juarez stopped and stood there for a moment, listening to the scene.

He disliked having others with him in these situations—particularly those he didn't know well. It was a common requirement for him to work with local law enforcement, however, and over the years he'd become used to simply taking the time he needed. If his pace was too slow for those around him, it was rare for them to come right out and say so; and once they saw the results he typically got, they stopped complaining.

The house was well cared for, with a flourishing flower garden in front and a pen off to the side containing three goats, a donkey, and a well-made henhouse. A man, presumably Luke Saucier, sat on the front steps. He was rocking slowly, his gaze focused on the ground. According to the sheriff, the man suffered some type of mental deficit (*He's not all there, if you know what I mean*, were the sheriff's exact words). Juarez turned his attention to Sarah Saucier next.

She was a large woman, though she moved well for her size—five-foot-eight or nine and easily two hundred pounds. He guessed her to be in her mid-fifties. She bypassed both the sheriff and his deputy and went straight to Juarez.

"*Ou est Bonnie? C'est vrai—elle est morte?*"

Juarez put his hand on her shoulder, guiding her away from the sheriff and his deputy. The dog growled at him; Juarez ignored it.

"Ms. Saucier, can you tell me what happened?"

"*Oui.* I came in to cook, *pis* Tulip—*le chienne*—was barking. I called for Luke, *mon frère, mais* he is not home. Red came to the door. He said Bonnie called, *pis* could he come inside."

She was close to hyperventilating. Juarez led her to the front door, his hand at the small of her back.

"Why don't you go inside," he said quietly. "And if you would please put on some tea—you have tea?"

She nodded. "*Oui.*"

"Good. If you would put on some tea, I'll have the sheriff show me the scene. The deputy will go inside with you and your dog. I'll be in shortly to speak with you."

With Sarah Saucier, her dog, and the deputy out of the way, Juarez followed Sheriff Cyr out to a path behind the house. He tried Erin again, with no more satisfying results than he'd gotten all night. After a brief internal debate, he paused to contact the police in Quebec, leaving instructions that Erin and/or Diggs be detained and he be called immediately should they attempt to cross the border. Then, satisfied that he had done everything he could, he rejoined the sheriff.

They continued walking for as much as half a mile through dense underbrush and thick mosquitoes before the sheriff finally stopped at the edge of a small clearing. Juarez noted that the man didn't venture any farther.

"This is it," he said.

Juarez walked past him and surveyed the scene: A circular clearing ringed by evergreens, perhaps ten yards in diameter. A body encased in a white sheet lay at one edge of the clearing. When Juarez got closer, he could see that the sheet had been pulled away from the victim's face, revealing a gray-haired woman in her fifties or sixties. Juarez crouched beside the body and pushed the sheet aside, holding the edge with a glove-clad thumb and forefinger.

"Did anyone move the body?" Juarez asked the sheriff.

"No, sir," Cyr said immediately. "We don't deal with these things much, but we know protocol. We moved the sheet enough to see who it was, then called you."

"But you didn't put it back the way it was before?"

"No, but I had Teddy take pictures before I checked to see who it was. We've got 'em back at the station."

"And other than that you haven't examined the body?"

"I haven't," he confirmed. "And nobody else has—at least, not that I know of."

Juarez nodded, satisfied. It was more than he usually got. He noted bruising around the woman's neck and a bluish tint to her lips. He lowered the sheet, but stopped after only a few inches at what he found. The sheriff scratched his head and crouched beside him.

"What the heck is that?"

"Can you get photos of this?" Juarez asked. "I need to send them to someone immediately." He stared at the woman's thin chest. The letter inscribed there wasn't unexpected, but it still sent a chill through him. What *was* unexpected was the age of the injury: The J carved into Bonnie Saucier's chest had scarred over completely. She'd likely been living with the mark for decades.

Once he'd examined Bonnie Saucier's body, Juarez refocused his attention on the immediate area around him. He stood and walked three paces, stopping when his feet hit an area where the earth was piled slightly higher than anywhere else. He set an evidence marker down beside the mound. Another six paces, and he found another. Ten paces more, and there was another. By the time he had carefully walked the entire area, he'd found four such mounds.

"And Sarah Saucier says she knows nothing about these?" Juarez asked.

Sheriff Cyr hurried over to stand beside him, now at the center of the circle. "They don't usually come out this way—or at least she doesn't."

"But Luke Saucier does?"

"She claims she doesn't know," the sheriff said uncomfortably. "This land's been in the Saucier family for a lot of years... They're old timers around here—traditional. Superstitious."

It was cool here—colder than the surrounding woods, at least. The moon was low and white, the sky filled with clouds. Jack took it all in, listening for those things that might not be visible to the naked eye.

"Is there a story attached to this land?" At the look on the sheriff's face, he added quickly, "I've studied these types of things before. It's not to say we believe any of it is real, of course... Simply that legends and superstitions handed down over the years can influence behavior."

The sheriff scratched his chin. "From back at the turn of the century—around 1915, 1920, I think. About a local Indian girl who got killed out here."

"Who killed her?"

"Supposedly, Luke and Sarah's great great granddaddy," the sheriff said, warming to the subject. "He had a bit of a reputation with the girls back then. Young girls. Apparently things got out of hand with this Indian, and he wound up killing her while he was trying to… Well, you know. So, he tried to bury her out in this spot. Only she wouldn't stay buried. According to the legend, her *maman* was a witch. Old Jason Saucier'd dream of her in the night and come back to make sure she was still here, and the grave would be half dug up. So he'd bury her again. Go back to bed. Come out the next day, and there she'd be, half out of the ground all over again."

Juarez studied the area, considering it with fresh eyes within the context of the story. "How did anyone find out about what he'd done?"

"He finally admitted to it," the sheriff said. "I guess he thought he'd go crazy if he didn't. He brought his wife out here to show her what he'd done, but the body was gone. He dug up the first spot where he thought he buried her, but she wasn't there. Then he dug up the whole rest of this plot, trying to find her."

Juarez felt a familiar chill wrap itself around his shoulders. He considered the story, imagining the white man desperately searching for the ghost he would never be rid of.

"He never found her," he guessed.

"Not according to the story," Cyr confirmed. "He started the cemetery out here after that, supposedly so he'd be able to keep track of his dead from then on. He was never the same, though. His grave is up there, too." He gestured back toward the house. "Jason Saucier. He died in 1922. I don't think he made it to forty."

Another young girl raped and murdered—this one a Native American with strong ties to the spirit world.

"How did he die?" Juarez asked.

"Suicide," Cyr said. "He hung himself from a tree not far from here."

"And the girl? Any idea how she was killed?"

Cyr looked uncomfortable. His gaze drifted to Bonnie Saucier's inert form. "Strangled. That was his thing, I guess you could say. He liked to choke the girls while he was, well… In the middle of things, if you know what I mean. As far as I know that Acadian was the only one he killed, though."

Juarez walked the area once more, while the sheriff remained beside the lifeless body of Bonnie Saucier. Based on what he'd seen thus far, he would guess that there were four bodies buried here, at least—possibly more. And now he had the story of an ancestor tormented after raping and killing a local Native American girl. Plus Erin Lincoln, Ashley Gendreau, and six other girls, kidnapped, hunted, and killed in pairs by an unnamed male who may or may not have been Jeff Lincoln.

And now Bonnie Saucier. If Bonnie had been J.'s victim all those years ago, how had she survived? And why kill her now?

Juarez rejoined the sheriff. "I'll have a team out here from D.C. tomorrow—if it's all right, I'd prefer if they handled the crime scene. If you could just cordon it off, I would appreciate it. Keep predators away, and make sure no one disturbs anything."

"Fine by me," the sheriff said, clearly relieved. "I'll get Teddy and a couple of the other boys to babysit out here overnight. Then it's all yours. We should probably get back to Sarah now, don't you think? Try to figure out what's going on there?"

Juarez agreed. "Just give me a minute, if you don't mind," he said. "You can go on ahead. I'll find my way back."

Cyr didn't look very sure about that. "I can just stand by, if you want. Teddy'll be back before too long to keep the scene secure 'til we can get the crime scene boys out here. These woods can be hard to find your way out of sometimes, especially this time of night."

"I have my phone—I'll call if I have any trouble. Just a few minutes please, Sheriff." It wasn't a request. The sheriff didn't take it as such.

When he was alone, Juarez took some time to view the scene again. Bonnie would have come down the same path he and the sheriff had traveled; he didn't see any other way to get here, unless it was straight through dense forest. Or was she killed elsewhere, and brought here after the fact? Red Grivois received his phone call at three o'clock. Based on lividity, Juarez estimated that Bonnie had to have been dead at least a few hours. She planned on coming here to meet him. Said she saw blood in her dreams…

And now here she was.

She hadn't been buried, which was surprising considering the killer's usual M.O. The way she'd been wrapped in the sheet suggested, once again, that J. had some respect for the dead. From the admittedly cursory exam Juarez had done, it didn't appear she had struggled while being strangled; there were no immediately obvious bruises or lacerations like the other victims, so it didn't even appear she had been tortured beforehand. She seemed utterly at peace.

He thought of Lucia—something he did frequently at crime scenes. Lucia had not been at peace. The energy here felt much different than that Guatemalan jungle had, but it still was not a place he'd willingly stay for long. He paced the clearing again, his eyes on the ground this time, and tried to push any dark thoughts aside. The spirits were restless here; he felt them reaching up from the ground with bony fingers, heard them whispering in low voices of their sad endings. If Erin knew the tumult of his subconscious, Juarez thought ruefully, he was certain she would run for the hills.

And perhaps she should.

He stopped at the center of the circle and turned the full three hundred and sixty degrees, trying to imagine the killer. What would he be thinking? Why carve the *J.* on his victims' chests? When one marked something with one's initials, it denoted property. *This is mine—no one else's.* If it wasn't an initial, however, it could be a message to others meant to say something about the victims. But then, why not just write the word out?

No… It had to be an initial.

The clearing got very quiet suddenly, as though all the voices of the forest—in this world and beyond—had been hushed. The bony fingers of the afterlife vanished. In their place was a familiar, much more tangible force. Behind him, he heard rustling in the undergrowth.

Juarez turned, expecting to see a deer, or possibly a coyote or a fox— it was that kind of an energy. Someone accustomed to travel in darkness, skirting in the shadows. Instead of a wild thing, however, a tall, lean, bearded man peered out from the trees. Juarez stood perfectly still. The man stared at him with clear, serious eyes. Years had passed since his last photo, but Juarez recognized him regardless.

"Jeff?" he said, as quietly as if it actually had been an animal that he'd heard.

The man didn't move. He held something in his hands, out in front of his body but too shrouded in darkness for Juarez to make out.

"I'd like to talk to you about what's been going on out here all these years," Juarez said, his tone still gentling. "I don't believe you did these things; murdered these girls. Other people may, but I have a feeling they're wrong. Your daughter doesn't believe it, either. I know she'd like to see you."

Erin's father took a step forward. He looked solid and well cared for, not at all the shadow Juarez had imagined. When he emerged from the trees, Juarez could finally make out what it was that he held in his hands:

A belt.

Juarez's certainty wavered.

"Stay right there, if you would," he said. He kept his tone as conversational as possible. "If you could just drop that belt..."

The man did as directed. They were still dueling distance from one another—perhaps fifteen, twenty strides.

"Good," Juarez said. "Thank you, Jeff."

"I don't go by that anymore," the man said. His voice was quiet, almost musical in cadence. "I haven't gone by that for a very long time."

Someone was coming up the path toward them—probably the deputy coming to keep watch. Juarez resisted the urge to turn and see who it was; maybe signal them back, even.

"What would you like me to call you?" he asked, trying to cover the noise in the brush with his own voice.

The man wasn't fooled—he tilted his head slightly, listening to the approaching footsteps. Juarez could see his body tense as he weighed his options. "You can call me Adam," he said. "I need to go now. Please don't tell Erin you saw me... Not until this is over."

"Wait," Juarez said quickly. He eased his hand toward his gun. "I'd like your help. Do you know who did this?"

"I can't help you," Adam said, just as quickly. He took a step backward, edging toward the trees once more. "When I help, people die. *En masse.*" He followed Juarez's movement knowingly, nodding his head toward the gun still in its holster. "Please don't do that; if you bring me in, I'll be dead within the hour. I'll stop this myself. I should have done it years ago. You just keep my daughter safe."

Juarez drew his gun just as the deputy emerged from the path, turning to wave the officer back where he'd come from. In the same instant, his phone rang. When he turned back, Adam was gone—vanished like a ghost in the moonlit night. Juarez ignored the deputy, palming his gun in his left hand as he checked the phone with his right. The number on the display belonged to Erin. He made a snap decision and answered the phone as he was headed into the woods after Adam, his heart pounding.

"Where the hell are you?" he demanded.

All he got was static on the other end of the line. He stopped running a few feet in and swept his flashlight through the trees, searching for some indication of where Adam may have gone. There was nothing. He returned his attention to the phone call.

"Erin?" he asked again, his anxiety ratcheting higher at the lack of response. There was static on the other end of the line, punctuated by a couple of barely decipherable phrases.

"Erin? I can't hear you. Where are you?"

All he got was white noise before he heard Diggs shout something in the background. Erin screamed, and Juarez lost the signal. He called back immediately, but got a message saying the user was out of range. He'd gone cold.

"Trouble?" The deputy asked with obvious concern, when Juarez had returned to the clearing.

He took a moment to order his thoughts. "I think so," he said. He picked up the belt Adam had dropped and deposited it in an evidence bag. This was the point when he should be reporting to someone what he'd seen: Jeff Lincoln, in these very woods. Holding the belt that had killed Bonnie Saucier. It didn't really get any clearer than that.

If you bring me in, I'll be dead within the hour.

He thought of Matt Perkins, the closest thing he'd ever had to a father, dying in his arms. The church on Payson Isle. Jane Bellows. Noel Hammond. Joe and Rebecca Ashmont. And now these girls…

There seemed no end to the bodies in Jeff Lincoln/Adam Solomon's wake. "I need to get the park service and some officers out here," he said finally. "I just spotted Jeff Lincoln."

The deputy couldn't have looked more alarmed if Juarez had said he'd spotted Satan himself. "Where did he go?"

Juarez shook his head. "I don't know. That's why we need the team." He thought of Erin's voice on the phone. Adam's words: *Just keep my daughter safe.* Diggs' panicked shout echoed in his mind.

He dialed her again, but hung up in frustration when he got the same message saying she was out of range. When he called Diggs, he got the same result.

"Agent?" the deputy prompted.

Juarez hung up his phone and focused on the deputy. Every cell in his body was screaming to get out of there; go find Erin. He ordered himself to stay calm. Do his job. "I don't think he's coming back here," he said. "But I don't want you alone out here, all right? Two guards on duty at all times throughout the night."

"You think we're in danger?"

Juarez shook his head as he headed back up the path toward the house, Erin's desperate cry still ringing in his ears.

"I wish I knew."

Chapter Fourteen

For two hours, Diggs and I ran north through thick brush and brambles. There were no trails but the ones we forged, no light but the moon overhead, no sounds but the wild ones that hadn't been part of my world since I was a kid: bats and deer and frogs whose low warbling voices sounded creepily human in the stillness. Diggs wouldn't let me stop, even to tend the gash in his leg, still oozing blood. I held my arm as close to my body as possible, trying not to jar it—something that's technically impossible when you're running for your life in the dark woods, incidentally.

We stopped when he tripped on a root and lay gasping on the forest floor. I knelt beside him.

"I think this is the part where I tell you to go on without me," he said. "Save yourself." We'd been moving too fast for me to get a good look at the cut in his temple. Now that I had, my stomach turned. I shook my head.

"We're not there yet," I said. "I'll let you know. We need to find a place to stop, though."

"I know," he agreed. He held up his hand to let me know he needed a second. He crawled away a few feet. I closed my eyes while he puked in the bushes, then stood and limped back to me. I handed him the water. He took a single gulp before he handed it back.

"You can have more," I said.

"Not 'til we get to the river."

Based on sound alone, it couldn't be far—somewhere to our right I heard rushing water. "How far behind us do you think he is?"

Diggs shrugged. He was leaning against a birch tree, his head resting against the trunk. I didn't like the way his eyes looked: glassy, the pupils too large. I touched his forehead.

"You think you can make it a little longer?"

"I should be asking you that," he said, nodding toward my mangled wrist. "What about your hand?"

"It's fine," I lied.

"It's broken."

I glanced at it, bent at a weird angle and already about twice its normal size. So much for the stiff upper lip. "Well... Yeah, I think so. But other than that, it's fine."

He shook his head. "Sure. Other than that." He took a SAM splint—a roll of soft aluminum I'd seen my mother use innumerable times when she was doctoring the locals of Littlehope—from his bag, then started to shape the splint.

"A T-curve would probably be better out here," I said.

He glared at me. I shut up.

He silently unrolled the aluminum, folded it over itself, strengthened it with a series of strategically placed curves, and then molded it to his own wrist. Then, he gently eased my wrist into the finished split and secured it with a waterproof wrap. Even with that small amount of movement, the pain rocked me to the bone. The world swam. Diggs held my other hand, searching my face.

"You still with me?"

I pushed past the pain and nodded, resolute. "I'm okay. We need to get moving again."

"Just tell me if it gets too bad, or you don't think you can keep going."

I didn't know what he planned to do if that happened, but I assured him I would. Behind us, a branch snapped.

We ran.

◊◊◊◊◊

Half an hour later, we found the river. The water was ice cold and running fast, the rocks slick under our feet. I wanted to stop to check Diggs out, but he insisted we keep moving. We waded in the shallows because it was easier to avoid leaving a trail behind us for J. to follow, but that meant we were more exposed than we would have been traveling in the woods, and progress was slower because now we were battling injuries, fatigue, and the current. Diggs walked behind me the whole way—picking me up when I stumbled, pushing me onward when I slowed. We didn't talk. Diggs had his compass and seemed to have a destination—something I was admittedly lacking. I let him lead for a change, and kept my mouth shut.

I don't know how long we'd been moving when we reached a section of the river where the water moved slower and the moonlight shone pure white on the surface. However long it had been, we'd heard no sign of someone behind us—no snapping branches, no rustling through the brush... Nothing. Diggs and I had both slowed, and two or three times when I looked over my shoulder, it seemed he was having trouble keeping up. I stopped beside a fallen tree where the water was shallow and we were more concealed than we had been.

"I want to take a look at your head," I said to Diggs when he caught up. "Have a seat."

"We don't have time."

"If you drop dead from blood loss or shock, I'm thinking that'll slow me down a lot more. Just sit."

He sat. I searched through his industrial first aid kit until I found a cloth and soaked it with river water, then gently cleaned away the blood on his forehead.

"It's not as bad as I thought," I told him, relieved to find only a shallow cut across his left temple. "Head wounds always bleed a lot... This isn't deep, though. Might not even leave a scar."

"Well, I dodged a bullet there," he said. "Chase me, torture me, kill me, but God forbid anybody scars this face."

I wet his hair with the cloth, then smoothed it back. He closed his eyes. "That feels good."

"I do what I can." And not much more, I thought silently.

The moonlight turned everything a deep, deep blue, the water black at our feet. I put some gauze over the cut on his head and then turned my attention to his leg.

"We shouldn't waste time on that right now," he said. "It's not bad. We need to keep moving."

"Humor me."

He didn't put up any more of a fight, but sat there silently while I checked him over. He was right, though: the gash was deep, but not nearly as bad as it could have been. I cleaned it as well and as fast as I could, then wrapped it with gauze and a bandage. He helped me up when I was through, and I sat down beside him on the fallen tree.

"I haven't heard any sign of anyone behind us, have you?" I asked.

Diggs shook his head. "Not for a while, no."

"Maybe we lost him."

He looked around. The forest was thick on all sides; I hadn't seen a trace of civilization since we went off the road. Wherever we were, J. had done

one hell of a job making sure we wouldn't be found.

"I don't think so," he said. "We need to keep moving."

"Keep moving where, though? If on the off chance Juarez actually did understand what I told him—"

Before I could continue, there was a splash just up the river from us—a lot louder than what you'd hear from some old fish belly slapping the water's surface. Then another. A flash of panic touched Diggs' face. He held his finger to his lips, and I nodded. In an instant, my heart was racing again, my pulse pounding in my ears. He pushed me down behind the felled tree, then crouched beside me. There was another splash—this one close enough that I could see the stone when it hit the water.

Someone began to whistle, low and tuneless. I clutched Diggs' arm, peering into the moonlit night in search of whoever was out there. The whistling stopped as suddenly as it had begun. The splashing ceased. And then, I heard it: a click, followed by the smooth slide of metal on metal. Diggs grabbed my bad arm and pulled me into the woods before I knew what was happening. We were already on the run, crashing through the underbrush so fast that I knew nothing beyond the tangled ground beneath my feet and the trees and brush that clawed at me on the way through, when we heard the shot behind us. It was loud enough to shake the ground; loud enough to make the world go silent for long seconds afterward, before the next shot cracked the world wide open once more.

"That's your warning," a man's voice shouted after us. I didn't recognize it. "That's all you get. You won't hear me coming again."

We kept running.

Chapter Fifteen
Juarez

It was one of the more idiotic moments of his professional career, this naïve leap of faith Juarez had made with Erin. He stood in front of a wall map of the Allagash Wilderness beside the sheriff and his deputy and half a dozen others who'd been called out for two searches now: one for Adam Solomon, and one for his daughter. It was almost three a.m. For the past three hours, he had been silently chastising himself for how poorly he'd handled Erin from the start. He should have had a police escort take her straight to Montreal. Or just kept her with him.

Go back to Montreal. Wait for my call.

Right.

The problem, as he saw it, was that he didn't have any idea how else to deal with her. He should have listened to Diggs: A stern warning was hardly enough for a woman like her. He'd be lucky if titanium handcuffs and a horse tranquilizer would be adequate. He should have known something wasn't right when she'd gone along with his instructions so readily.

He'd received a call from border patrol shortly after the one from Erin, informing him that Erin Solomon and Daniel Diggins had already passed through the Fort Kent crossing, twenty minutes before his instructions had been received. Their documents had been in order and there had been nothing suspicious about either them or their vehicle, so they were allowed through without incident. That had been at ten-thirty.

"Considering the information we got from border patrol and the fact that Erin called me approximately thirty minutes after that, we can assume she would have been somewhere in this area when I spoke with her," Juarez said. He circled a reasonably small area around the main highways and two of the more significant logging roads, then looked at the sheriff again. "And still no luck finding their vehicle?"

Cyr shook his head. "I've got some wardens out looking now. They'll call if they spot it, but so far nobody's seen anything on the main roads your friend should have been traveling."

"What about the cell phone?" the deputy asked. "You can't track that?"

"Not without cell towers to triangulate the signal," Juarez said.

"Most folks just use satellite phones out that way," Cyr told him. "Cell towers are few and far between, even on the main stretch there. If it turns out she was on one of those side roads…"

Juarez nodded. He didn't need the man to finish that particular thought. "And we have people checking the highway and the logging roads, just in case they ended up out that way for some reason?"

"We do. But you say you want to start checking the woods anyway?" Cyr asked. " 'Cause I've gotta tell you, trying to find people out there is worse than looking for a needle in a hay field. Especially when you don't have any real idea where they might be. She's only been gone what two, three hours?"

"I heard her voice," Juarez insisted. "Something was wrong. If there wasn't, she would have called back by now. You must have protocol for handling this kind of thing. If we were to do a grid search, how would that be organized?"

The sheriff looked at his deputy, the two of them silently calculating. "That whole section out there is pretty wild," he said. "There are a few hunting camps, but other than that we're talking dense woods, rough terrain, and a lot of wildlife. We can get a chopper to do a fly by once it's daylight, but in forest that thick it doesn't do a whole lot of good."

Juarez rubbed his eyes with the heels of his hands and considered his options. Erin and Diggs were out there somewhere—he knew that much at least. As was the killer. And whoever that killer was, his intent was clear. Juarez looked at the map again.

"I want you to start with helicopters at dawn, doing a fly-by of the area. Then I want men on the ground in the areas least likely to see tourist traffic this time of year—he'll keep them as far from people as possible. Wherever the woods are thickest or the terrain least hospitable, I want people searching."

"We don't have much of a budget for that—" the sheriff began. He stopped at the look on Juarez's face.

"This is a Federal investigation," Juarez said. "We'll figure it out. We've got a serial killer out there somewhere; this is our best shot at catching him."

Cyr nodded. "I'll call in the park service, let them know. Overtime?"

"Whatever you need," Juarez assured him. "I'll talk to the director and get the funds approved. In the meantime, you start getting people out there. We've wasted enough time as it is."

Cyr and his deputy went to make the necessary calls. Juarez sat down at the edge of the desk, staring at the map. Will Rainier still hadn't been brought in. Juarez couldn't stop thinking about Quebec. What the hell had happened? He could believe Erin may have resisted, but Diggs had seemed clear on the importance of keeping her away. What the hell had he been thinking?

Even as the thought crossed his mind, Juarez realized how unfair it was: He hadn't known Erin that long, and already he had given in to her demands more than once. She was infuriating. Childish. Stubborn in a way he hadn't seen in a woman since… Well, since his wife.

He closed his eyes. Rubbed his throbbing temples with his thumbs, all the while trying to think this through.

Where the hell were they?

Red Grivois arrived at the station at three-thirty. Juarez had only met him in passing on Saturday night, more concerned with getting Erin out of Rainier's way than meeting the locals. He looked oddly revitalized, considering it was deep in the night and he'd just discovered the body of an old friend and the potential of several more in the past twelve hours.

"Will's gone," Red said the moment he got through the door.

"What do you mean, Will's gone?" the sheriff asked. "Where'd he go?"

"Hell if I know," Red said. He sat behind one of the desks, put his feet up, and took a beer from his jacket pocket. "I dropped him there Saturday night, he said he was gonna sleep it off. He's not there now, though. I checked the place. His truck's gone."

"Is there somewhere else he might be? A girlfriend's? A bar?" Juarez asked.

"Bars are closed. And Will's not much for dating—he's kind of the solitary type," Red told him.

Juarez thought of the oversized, sloping man he'd seen Saturday night. He couldn't imagine anyone voluntarily going out with a man like that, but he'd been surprised more than once by the monsters women dated.

"He could have gone fishing," the sheriff suggested to Juarez. "Maybe took off after you decked him Saturday night, nursing his pride."

"That's what I'm thinking," Red agreed. "His guns are gone. A couple of his bear traps are missing, too. He always takes to the woods when he's pissed about something."

The hairs on the back of Juarez's neck stood on end. "Where would he go?"

"He's not the one you're looking for," Red said immediately. "I checked him out years ago. Will Rainier didn't kill those girls."

Juarez thought of the look in the man's eye when Erin was speaking with him at the bar: the cruelty of his gaze; how intimately he took her in, as though he were imagining scenarios that made Juarez's skin crawl just to think about.

"Where would he go?" he repeated.

The sheriff went to the map, ignoring the anger on Red's face. "Most likely over here," he said. "He likes to hunt over by the Waterway, here," he said, pointing to a stretch of river approximately fifty miles south of them. "He's been getting ready for bear season—getting the bait out there in a few spots he thinks nobody knows about. If he's in the woods anywhere, that's where he'll be."

Juarez put on his jacket. "Put out a BOLO for his truck," he instructed the sheriff. "Do you have dogs who can search the area?"

The sheriff looked at Red. "You know if Jamie's around?"

"She's back on the island," Red said. "I can give her a call, get her up here fast enough."

"She has dogs?" Juarez asked.

"The best dogs in the country, according to just about every law enforcement agency out there," the sheriff confirmed. "If that's the route you want to take, Jamie's the one to call."

He hesitated for only a moment, thinking once more of the look on Will Rainier's face when Erin confronted him.

"Call her," he said. "I need to make a couple of phone calls. When the dogs are here and you have a search party organized, I'll join you."

He looked at the clock on the wall, silently calculating. If this was J. — the man who thrived on hunting young girls for days on end so many years ago—then chances were good that his methods may have evolved, but the essence of the crime would remain the same. Age would likely have slowed him down, but now he would have the benefit of experience on his side. With Diggs and Erin together, he would have two victims, but it wouldn't be under the controlled circumstances he usually enjoyed… And Diggs was hardly his preferred prey.

Which meant J. would kill Diggs first, Juarez reasoned. Get rid of him entirely. He would keep Erin, taking her God only knew where, and seek another victim to join her later. For now, though, J. would have no interest in a man as a pawn in his game. Juarez imagined Erin out there: Possibly injured; certainly terrified. She and Diggs running for their lives in the depths of the wilderness, with no idea who was chasing them or what he had in store.

"We need to hurry," he said, addressing everyone in the room. "They won't last long out there."

Chapter Sixteen

I don't know how long we ran. I don't know how far. I don't even know where we went. All I know is that we ran. It was dark. There was no path. At some point Diggs convinced me to circle back and we were at the river again, where we silently slogged through fast-moving water up to our knees, and sometimes deeper. Eventually, the world lightened as the sun started to rise. I was numb. Shivering. We were both stumbling by the time Diggs finally stopped and nodded toward the trees.

"According to the map, there should be some caves close by." He checked his compass and looked off into the distance. All I saw was darkness and an endless expanse of trees, but I was hoping he had more vision than that. "We can't stop before we get there," he said regretfully. "If we do…"

I knew exactly what would happen if we stopped. "I know. Don't worry about it—I'm fine. Let's just go. I'm okay as long as you are."

We didn't talk much after that, too busy trying to forge our way through a wilderness that seemed intent on remaining unforged. We reached the cave just as the sun was coming up, casting the world around us in pale gold.

"You don't think it would be better to stay by the river?" I whispered. The entrance to the cave was hidden beneath an overhang of not-terribly-solid-looking boulders, and it didn't look like what I'd always known caves to be: dark and dank, sure, but still reasonably maneuverable when push came to shove.

The gaping fissure Diggs brought us to didn't look remotely maneuverable in the best of circumstances.

"That's what he'll expect us to do," Diggs said. "We've got enough water to get us through a day in here, and it'll give us some time to regroup and get a few hours' rest."

"What if he knows about it?"

"There's a long network of tunnels in here; not many people have been through the whole thing." He tapped the map clutched in his left hand. "Let's see your GPS get us through here."

He pulled himself up the rock and into the tunnel. I watched as he was gradually swallowed by the earth, inch by inch.

I followed.

Once we got through the opening, I was surprised to find myself in what did look like a real, honest-to-god cave: a low, smooth ceiling and a wet floor, the sunlight just barely making it through the narrow entrance.

"It'll be tight in places," Diggs said over his shoulder.

"I know. I'll be okay."

"Your arm…" he began.

"I'm all right, Diggs. I can handle it."

Within a few steps, we were plunged into a deeper kind of darkness than any I'd ever experienced before—an absence of light so profound that it felt like a physical presence. Diggs shined his flashlight along low walls and a low ceiling, stalactites hanging down far enough to brain us if we weren't careful. I crept behind him until he found the first fissure.

"You're sure that's the way?" I asked as he approached the crevice.

"No," he said. "But the map is pretty clear." He pulled a coil of rope from his pack and tied a length around his waist, then repeated the process with me.

"So we don't get separated," he explained. "We won't have far to go, but I don't want to take any chances."

"Agreed."

"If you can keep your bad arm still, and just use the other hand and push off with your feet, that'll make it easier."

"I know." He didn't look convinced. "I can do this, Diggs. I'll be fine."

The first leg of the journey was so narrow I had to push my pack ahead of me through fissures and winding crevices, pressed so tight against the rock that I could taste the damp limestone. I held my hand close to my body as much as possible, trying to avoid using it whenever I could. Because I was horizontal a lot of the time, crawling through the earth on my belly like some subterranean soldier, most of my weight rested on my broken wrist. A couple of times, the pain got bad enough that I had to stop and pull myself together, sure I was about to either pass out or lose my lunch. I didn't say a word, though; we were there because of me—I wasn't blind to that fact. As far as I was concerned, Diggs had every right to try and get as far from me as possible, and never look back.

I had no right to complain about anything.

We continued on for maybe twenty minutes. Maybe two hours. Time had become a useless construct—all that existed was darkness and pain and the knowledge of the monster on our heels. Diggs' presence up ahead was detectable only through the occasional whisper back to me, accompanied by a tug on the rope. Otherwise, it felt like the entire world had vanished without a trace.

With the notable lack of sights and sounds, everything filtered down to my remaining senses: the feel of my body pressed to the cool rock; the smell and the taste of damp earth and crumbling limestone. At a particularly tight pass, Diggs whispered back to me.

"Hang on. I don't know if I can get through here." His voice was tight, something that sounded a lot like panic just under the surface. I forced myself to take as deep a breath as possible.

"Do you want me to go back?" I asked.

He didn't say anything for a few seconds. His breathing was labored. Now that I wasn't moving, just lying still and belly-down between a rock and a hard place, I could hear movement in the tunnel behind us—a slither and drag that made my heart speed up and my stomach bottom out. I wet my parched lips and closed my eyes. The sound wasn't heavy enough to be a person. A snake, then? Spiders? What the hell else gravitated to a netherworld like this?

"How are you doing?" I asked. I fought to keep my voice steady.

"I think I can make it. Just a second."

I heard the shimmy and shudder of his body against the rock and then, finally, a tug on the rope at my waist.

"I'm through," he said. There was no missing the relief in his voice. "It's not much farther now. That should have been the tightest pass for now."

For now.

I pulled myself forward with one arm and pushed with the toes of my sneakers hooked into every hold I could find, my mind still on the body slithering behind me. I kept moving.

Diggs was right: It wasn't that much farther before I heard him whisper "Thank Christ," and then call back to me. "We're here, Sol. Just a few more feet."

He was waiting for me at the mouth of the crevice, his hair and clothes caked with dirt. I took the hand he offered and half-stepped, half-tumbled from the crevice into a larger cavern just barely illuminated by the pale beam of his flashlight.

I sat on the hard ground and closed my eyes, able to take my first real breath since we'd started inside the cave. Diggs sank down beside me.

"You okay?"

I leaned against him and nodded. I'd never wanted sleep so badly in my life. That would have to wait, though.

"How's your leg?" I asked.

He just grunted.

I took the first aid kit from his bag and eyed the bandage around his thigh, now stiff with dirt and blood.

"I need to wash that out again," I said. "And get a clean dressing on it."

He didn't even open his eyes. "Try not to use much—I don't have a lifetime supply in there. Otherwise, have at it. Just let me know if you're gonna need to amputate."

I pushed the leg of his shorts up as far as it would go, and gently unwound the bandage. When I'd finished washing and re-dressing the gash—not quite so deep as I'd thought, but already showing signs of infection—I patted his knee.

"Looks like you'll be able to keep it. At least for now."

"Thanks." He opened his eyes. They were a startling blue in the darkness. "Your turn next, right?"

"I'm okay," I said.

"If it's all the same to you, I'd like to take a look anyway."

We swapped places, and I sat in the darkness while he checked my fingers to make sure blood was still circulating. Even that small amount of jostling turned my stomach inside out.

"There's a lot of swelling," he said. "How are you feeling otherwise? Chills, nausea… Think you might pass out?"

"We were in a car crash a few hours ago, and there's a psychotic killer on our heels. You're telling me you don't feel a little off?"

"I'm just worried about—"

"Shock," I finished for him. "I know. I'm fine."

He got out a Power Bar that we shared, and three ibuprofen for me. We washed everything down with lukewarm water.

"Is there anything you don't have in that kit of yours?" I asked.

"When your ten-year-old brother dies in your arms because you don't have a clue what to do to save him, you tend to start over-thinking the old emergency kit."

"I guess you would," I said quietly. "I'm sorry. I didn't even think about that."

He shrugged. "Don't worry about it. It is what it is."

We were both quiet for a few seconds, locked in our separate—no doubt equally dark—thoughts.

"I'm sorry about this, too," I said, finally. "About putting you in this position." It wasn't the kind of admission that came easy to me—I felt inexcusably bitter for having to say the words at all. Whatever I'd hoped to do differently growing up, whoever I'd hoped to become, hardly mattered now; I was officially my mother's daughter. I couldn't even say 'I'm sorry' without getting pissed off at the universe for putting me in that position. Diggs didn't say anything for a long, long time. Decades passed. Mountains crumbled. Finally, he cleared his throat.

"I can't pretend it's no big deal this time," he said quietly. He ran a hand through his hair. His eyes were shadowed in the scant light of the flashlight between us. "You push and you push and it's like you don't care about anyone—"

"I do, though." I interrupted him, swallowing past the boulder lodged in my throat. "I care about you. I've always cared about you. I just didn't think—"

"And that's the crux of it, isn't it?" he asked. His voice was strained, like it was an effort to keep from screaming bloody murder. Not that I could blame him. "You don't think. You never think. Your mother almost dies trying to protect you from some secret monster who's apparently had your number since birth, and you don't even think to call her afterward. Don't imagine that things may have changed for her. We go to Washington and you wander around hand-in-hand with another man for three days, and you don't think at that point I might decide I missed my shot. You leave town without a word. Don't call. Don't visit. And you don't think I might move on? And then this…" He stood and walked away.

I sat there in the failing light, cold and alone. "Where are you going?" I asked.

"I'm getting the sleeping bag," he said. The anger was gone from his voice, but there was a coolness in its place that felt a thousand times worse. He brought the sleeping bag back over and unrolled it beside me. "You should get some sleep. I'll wake you in a couple of hours."

"I should take the first shift," I said. "You can sleep."

"You're hurt worse," he said briefly. "You need it more. Besides, I need a little time to think."

I caught the fabric of his shorts in my hand and held on tight. I couldn't think of anything to say. All at once, I thought of the first time we'd ever met, in Bennett's Lobster Shanty one Friday night more than fifteen years before. I was just a teenager at the time—awkward, lonely. Lost. Hanging out at the bar waiting for my mother to decide who she was taking home for the night. And then, suddenly, there was Diggs: Twenty-three years old, cigarette dangling from his lips, beer in hand. Cocky. Sophisticated. But beyond that, what resonated for me then—and what resonated for me still—was that he'd been just as lost, just as lonely, as I was.

He crouched to disentangle my hand from his shorts and set it back in my lap.

"Get some rest," he said. All the warmth, every ounce of connection I'd once felt between us, was gone. I nodded blindly.

"Wake me in an hour," I said. "I'll take over then."

He didn't answer.

Chapter Seventeen
Juarez

A woman answered when Juarez called the *Downeast Daily Tribune* at eight o'clock the next morning. She sounded young, but competent—though not professional enough to be a secretary. Another reporter was Juarez's guess. Just who he felt like talking to.

"My name is Jack Juarez. I'm a Special Agent with the FBI—"

"Juarez?" the woman asked. "Hang on just a second, I'll send it right over."

He paused, wondering if he'd missed something. When Erin and Diggs were back where they belonged, a good night's sleep was definitely in order.

"I'm sorry—you know who I am?"

"Diggs said you might be calling," she explained. "If you have an e-mail address, I'll send it now."

"Can you tell me when you spoke with him last?"

She didn't answer for a few seconds. When she did, a faint touch of concern bled through her cool professionalism. "What happened? Is he all right?"

Juarez hesitated. "He just hasn't checked in for a couple of hours. We think they probably got lost," he lied. "Did he contact you last night?"

"Yesterday afternoon. He was at the *Quebec Chronicle*... He e-mailed me something; told me to send it to you if you called. You're sure he's all right?"

"We don't know for certain," he admitted. "But if it is something more than them just getting off track, time is critical. This attachment that he sent—can you forward that to me?"

"Of course," she answered immediately. He gave her his e-mail address and waited while she typed out a message. "I'll get it right to you. Is there anything else I can do? Where are you?"

"Northern Maine," he answered vaguely, already checking his e-mail. Within a minute, he had the photograph Diggs had scanned and sent to the newspaper. It was a faded black-and-white picture of a bar, packed full. Two teenage boys had been circled in red. Juarez checked the date, recognizing them immediately. Another circle in yellow was drawn around Hank Gendreau's midsection. It was encircling a belt that looked very much like the one used to strangle Erin Lincoln.

By nine o'clock, the Black Falls police station was packed tight with state and local police officers, park service employees, volunteer searchers, and four search and rescue dogs tended by a slender young blonde woman the sheriff introduced as Jamie Flint, as well as a teenage boy and a trio of overly pierced, tattooed women Juarez suspected were ex-cons. Juarez stood with Sheriff Cyr at the head of the small room, surrounded by wood paneling and half a dozen maps.

"We have two priorities right now," Juarez told the group. "The first is to find Will Rainier." He tacked a photo of Rainier on the bulletin board, with a photo of the man's black pickup truck beside it. "The second is to find Erin Solomon and Daniel Diggins." He added photos of each of them to the board. "They were last seen at the border station in Fort Kent at ten-thirty last night. It's been confirmed that Will Rainier also crossed at that station, at ten-forty-five. He was driving this pickup truck.

"Erin and Diggs—Daniel, sorry," he corrected himself, "were traveling in a blue 1996 Jeep Wrangler. We believe at this point that that vehicle may be off the road, though so far we've received no accident reports in the areas we're searching, and no one has spotted it if it went off the road. They would have been traveling toward Black Falls on a road with spotty or nonexistent cell service."

"Most of the woods out there have spotty or nonexistent cell service," the blonde woman said. She had a southern accent Juarez hadn't expected, and she was tall and angular—striking, actually, with clear blue eyes and a ballerina's build. Her nose was pierced, her hair pulled up in a dancer's bun. Despite the activity in the room, all four of her dogs were lying down, seemingly unconcerned. "And the woods out that way are thick enough on some of those logging roads that you wouldn't even see a vehicle if it'd gone into the trees."

"Which is why I think it's important we do more than fly-bys trying to find them," Juarez said.

"As long as we have the rough area down like you say," the woman said,

"I'll take the guys out there and we'll get started. I'm more concerned about Rainier, though."

Cyr spoke up. "We'll be careful, James," he said to her. "You don't need to worry about that."

She leveled him with an icy stare. "The hell I don't—I've been getting that party line too long now. I'm assuming he's armed, yeah?"

Juarez nodded.

"Yeah," she said with a frown. "Exactly. So if we're out there looking for him, I want some fire power on my side. And I'd encourage anybody who runs across him to shoot first and ask questions later. Especially now."

"Let's just hold on with that, all right?" Juarez interrupted. "Nobody's shooting anyone—especially not when Diggs and Erin may be in the immediate vicinity and there's a forest full of search-and-rescue wandering around. Let's put the emphasis on the 'rescue' in that phrase, please."

She looked at him like he was a complete idiot, but she didn't argue.

"I have a press conference here at ten o'clock," Juarez continued. "At this point, I don't want any of this information going out to the public. I'll release Rainier's photo with instructions to contact the authorities if he's spotted. News of Bonnie Saucier's death has already been leaked, but I don't want anyone breathing a word about anything else that was discovered there. That means no one should be discussing any theories you might have about what happened or didn't happen or what else may be linked to this case. If you need to speculate, I'd appreciate it if you kept those speculations to yourself. Do not discuss this case with anyone."

Two more officers entered at the back of the room and looked meaningfully at Juarez. He nodded to them, then returned his attention to the rest of the group.

"Everyone should have my cell number. Please don't hesitate to contact me if you have any questions or any thoughts that might prove helpful in the search. I'll join you out there myself as soon as possible."

He dismissed the group and watched as they filed out, talking quietly amongst themselves. The dog woman waited until everyone was gone, then approached. Her dogs—a bloodhound, two German shepherds, and what looked like a pit bull mix of some kind—all remained where they were.

"You know about Rainier?" she asked Juarez as soon as they were alone.

"Know what about Rainier?" The dogs were watching him with unnerving attention.

"Know he's a psychopath," she said. "Ask any woman around here—they'll tell you. I've been saying it for years now. It's nice somebody's finally listening."

"I'd prefer it if people go out there without the idea that they're on a kill-or-be-killed manhunt, though," Juarez said. He thought of Erin again, flashing once more on the way Rainier had looked at her the other night at the bar. He let his curiosity get the better of him for a moment. "What do you know about Rainier?"

"He raped one of my girls," she said promptly. "One of the women who works with me. We were up here looking for some kids, and she ended up on his property. Killed one of my best dogs, too."

Juarez tightened his hands around the folder he held, struggling to keep his face impassive. "Why isn't he in jail?"

"The girl was scared," Jamie said briefly. "And I could never prove what he did to my dog. But trust me... You don't want your girlfriend out there alone with this guy."

Juarez started to deny the charge. At the look in her eyes, he shut his mouth. Instead, he gave her a few parting instructions that he suspected she would ignore, then watched as she whistled for the dogs and all four sprang to life. As she was leaving, the cops who had signaled Juarez during the meeting reappeared. This time, they flanked a prisoner in a blue jumpsuit and shackles. He shied away from the dogs as they passed.

"You're Hank Gendreau?" Juarez asked.

Hank nodded. He looked tired and confused, and more than slightly anxious at the marked disruptions to his routine at the state prison. Juarez nodded to the sheriff's office, now empty. The guards led Hank through the door. Juarez followed behind. Once they were inside, he nodded to Hank's wrists.

"You can remove the handcuffs," he said. One of the officers started to protest. Juarez looked at him evenly. "I'll take responsibility if anything happens. Uncuff him, please. Then you can leave us."

The moment they were alone, Juarez pushed the photograph Diggs had found across the desk toward him.

"Do you recognize that?" he asked.

Gendreau looked puzzled for a moment before a flicker of panic crossed his face. He did his best to get the reaction under control, but failed. A bad liar, then.

"That's me and Will Rainier when we were kids. What about it?"

"Look at the date on there," Juarez instructed.

He did, then looked away for another moment before he recovered.

"September twenty-seventh. So what?"

"That's the weekend Jeff and Erin Lincoln disappeared," Juarez said.

"I was in Quebec that weekend." Hank shrugged. "That's been my story all along—how's this picture supposed to be a bad thing for me?"

"It's not so much the when or the where," Juarez said casually. "As it is what you're wearing. That belt…?"

It was over from there. Hank blanched and stuttered and started a few stories before Juarez cut him off at the pass.

"You killed Erin Lincoln," he said calmly. "You raped and murdered a twelve-year-old girl, and then seventeen years later you tortured and strangled your own daughter." He made no attempt to keep the revulsion from his voice. "And along the way, you and Will Rainier killed how many others?"

Hank shook his head frantically. "No! It wasn't me—I'm telling you, I didn't have a thing to do with any of it. I didn't kill any of those girls."

"You were there when Erin Lincoln died," Juarez continued, undeterred by the man's denial. He stood, planting his hands on the table, and leaned in until he was just inches from Hank's face. "You tortured her for a week, you raped her, you strangled her nearly to death, and then you let her go so you could do it all over again—"

"No!" Hank shouted. He slammed his fist on the desk. "No, goddammit, I'm telling you. We didn't kill her."

"But you were there that weekend," Juarez said. "How did that belt wind up around her neck? The same belt you were wearing the day her boat was found capsized in the middle of Eagle Lake?"

"I want my lawyer," Hank said suddenly. His face had gone from terrified to that impenetrable mask Juarez had seen in countless interrogations before. "I want to talk to Max. I'm telling you, I didn't kill Erin Lincoln."

"Look, I can bring your lawyer into this. Which means word will probably get out back at the prison that we're looking at you for the deaths of a bunch of other girls besides your own daughter. If that's the way you want it, that's fine with me. I've read your file—I know how hard you've worked to convince the other inmates there that you're innocent… How many do you think will believe you when they find out you're connected with the murders of these other girls? Once they get the details of all that was done to this twelve-year-old child?"

"You can't do that."

Juarez didn't blink. "Watch me." He straightened and retrieved his cell phone. He was just walking toward the door when Hank stopped him.

"Wait!"

Juarez turned calmly. The man looked terrified. His eyes shone with tears Juarez was certain would fall before he was through.

"What happened that weekend?"

"It wasn't me," Hank repeated. "I didn't do any of it."

Juarez sat down at the table again. He leaned back, calmer now. "So who did?"

Hank hesitated. All Juarez had to do was look toward the door this time before the man folded. "It was Will," he said brokenly. "It was this stupid thing we did... I didn't kill her. I didn't kill any of them. Will did Erin, but it was all Jeff's idea. That was where it all started. Jeff Lincoln started everything."

Chapter Eighteen

I woke in the cave an indeterminate amount of time later to pain—the kind that digs in deep and holds on so tight it feels like your whole body's being rung out. I reached for my phone and turned it on long enough to get my bearings. Light filtered in through an entrance above us that I hadn't noticed before, so at least I could see something of what was going on around me. According to the iPhone gods, it was ten o'clock in the morning. Diggs was sitting on the ground with his back against the cave wall, his eyes closed. It was warmer than it had been, but it was still damp and dark and dank. Still a cave, in other words.

"You okay?" Diggs asked.

Our fight came back immediately: everything he'd said. Everything I'd said. All I'd done to get us here.

"Yeah," I said. "I'm good. Why don't you get some sleep? I'm up."

"You haven't been out that long. I can stay up a little longer."

"I'm all right. I won't be able to get back to sleep anyway. You go ahead."

He came over and waited while I extricated myself from the sleeping bag. I put too much pressure on my broken wrist and had to stop for a second, waiting it out while the world dipped and spun. I felt Diggs' hand at the small of my back.

"Sol?"

I got up. Backed away a little. "I'm fine—I just need to be a little more careful. What about you?"

"I'm good. Or as good as can be expected given the circumstances."

I gave a stilted laugh that sounded even more stilted in our subterranean prison. When I stopped, the whole world went silent. Diggs stood a foot away from me, but it was like the Berlin Wall had been resurrected between us.

"Well… I'll just go over there," I said. "Let me know if you need anything."

"Sure thing."

I walked past him, thinking of his words this morning: *You don't think.* And look where it had gotten us.

I sat down on the cool ground, trying not to see any of the unknown creepy crawlies I was bound to find if I looked too hard. Diggs cleared his throat.

"Hey, Sol?"

I looked up. "Yeah?"

There was a long pause. I saw him shake his head. "Nothing, forget it. Just wake me if you get tired."

"I will."

I sat there in the semi-darkness and watched him toss and turn until eventually his breathing evened out.

While Diggs slept the sleep of the damned, I dug out Erin Lincoln's journal and sat in the miniscule shaft of light funneling in from outside. I opened to the entry I'd left off at, and happily retreated to the past.

January 20, 1970

Me and Bonnie and Sarah had a sleepover last night at Sarah's house. I didn't want to go—I don't like to leave J. and Daddy alone together after last time, but J. said he'd spend the night at Hank's. Sarah's mother (Maman) had so much food I thought I'd split, and then Luke came in and drew a picture of me while we were sitting there. He says I'm an angel. I told him angels can't spit halfway across the room or land a free throw better than any boy in town.

Hank and J. and Creepy Will tried to sneak in the window but Sarah screamed and got her Maman. She came running in and told the boys to get the HELL out of there or they'd be sorry. Then she made Luke go to bed, too.

Bonnie says she can see the future, because her mémère could. She's an Indian, and a witch. She says she can see everything that ever happened when me and J. were in Lynn. She says Daddy is a bad man.

I told J. what she said, but he said not to get too worried. He says you don't have to be a fortune teller to know Daddy's no good.

February 3, 1970

I haven't written in a while because J. got sick again. I've been taking care of him. He's been coughing and had a fever and he's got the

*same white patches all up and down his throat as he did last time. I
finally convinced him to go to the doctor on his own, because Daddy won't
ever take him. All I'd need to do is sneeze and Daddy would move heaven
and earth to get me to the finest doctor in New England. J. could be dying
and Daddy would just let him go, same as he did with Mama.*

*He has strep throat, and the doctor said maybe he should get his
tonsils removed since this is the third time this year.*

*If he'd stop kissing so many gross townie girls, I bet he wouldn't get
it at all.*

Most of the entries continued along those lines, giving me some insight
into my father's life as a child, but providing very few clues as to what had
happened to him and his sister that fateful weekend in September of 1970.
Until I found this entry, that is:

May 19, 1970

*Jeff's mad at me because I won't call him J. anymore. I never would
have started in the first place if I'd known what it was all about. Sarah
told me. We were at her house while her Maman was cooking, and Bonnie
and Luke and Sarah took me out to the back of their property—way out
in the woods. I told them I didn't like it out there, and Bonnie says it's
because the woods there are filled with ghosts.*

*Sarah told me that her great great grandpa (or something) was
buried there. She said he'd been très mauvais (very bad), and he killed a
girl our age. His name was Jason Saucier, and him and these two other
boys had a club where they had S_ _ with every girl they could, and
whoever did it the most got a hundred dollars.*

Then she told me Jeff has the same kind of club.

*She said he did it to her, and he and Hank and Creepy Will were
all in the club. That's why Jeff wants to be called J. now—because of Jason
Saucier. I called Sarah a damn liar, and I ran all the way home, even
though I was supposed to spend the night. Not that it matters. Nobody
knows if I'm here or gone, anyway.*

*I told Jeff what I found out—what Sarah told me. I wanted him
to tell me she was lying, that he'd never do that stuff, but he didn't say
anything like that. Instead, he said why pretend he's something he's not?
It's better to just be honest. And besides, everybody's gonna think he's bad
anyway because of Daddy... 'The sins of the father,' he said to me. He said
he's been paying for what Daddy did his whole life, and now he might as*

well have some fun with it.

He said he never hurts those girls, but Luke said Sarah cried after. I told him if that happened to me, I would cry.

He said nothing like that will ever happen to me, because he'll keep me safe. No matter what, he said he'll keep me safe. I told him to go to hell. How many of those girls have brothers who promised them the very same thing?

That's why I told him I won't call him J. anymore. I don't care if I never lay eyes on him again.

I closed the journal and set it down. There it was, in black and white: the key to this whole thing, I was sure. If he hadn't killed Erin—and I was still ninety-nine percent sure that was the case—then it had to have been Will or Hank. And all of it was tied to this sadistic fucking sex club my father had started as a teenager. I thought of the way Will had looked at me at the bar the other night, and what he'd said: *Had a little rite of passage that Saturday night. Come to think of it, she looked a little like you.* Had Erin Lincoln been his 'rite of passage'?

If Hank was in jail, then Will Rainier seemed like the most obvious lunatic out there stalking Diggs and me now.

Except…

I thought of the hooded man from Payson Isle—the one Kat and Diggs both kept telling me to forget. The deaths on Payson Isle and the murders of all these girls over the years couldn't be coincidence; I already knew he had *something* to do with my father's past. Was this it? Diggs had dismissed the idea that the hooded man was trying to frame my father as absurd from the start, but I wasn't so sure about that. What if that man, that mysterious specter who'd been haunting my dreams since I was a kid, was actually the one who had been kidnapping and killing teenage girls for the past forty years? If my father had known about it, that would be motive enough for the hooded man to burn down the Payson Church in a bid to maintain my father's silence, wouldn't it?

But how did my father's fingerprints end up at the crime scenes of so many of those murders over the years?

I lay my head back against the cool, damp cave wall and closed my eyes. On Payson Isle, my dad used to tuck me in every night. Some of my earliest memories were of being curled up in his arms while he read to me; walking along wooded paths, my hand in his; him singing silly nonsense songs when I was hurt or sad. I'd never felt so safe, so protected, as I had in those early years with him watching over me.

Whether he had committed the murders or not almost didn't matter; he'd done enough without that. He'd been the one to get his sister killed. The revelations last spring had been hard enough, learning that my father had sent me away when I was nine years old, relegating me to the mainland and a mother who'd never wanted me in the first place. I'd been able to rationalize that, convinced he'd done it for my own good. This, though… He really had been a monster. Hell, maybe he was a monster still.

Diggs stirred on the other side of the cave, mumbling something in his sleep. I thought of what he'd said to me: *You don't think… It's like you don't care.*

He was right. I didn't think. I didn't care. For most of my life, I'd been chasing a ghost—a man who didn't even exist. A fictional character my father played for the first nine years of my life, but in his off hours who the hell knew what he was doing. Who he really was. Had whatever he'd done as a kid paved the way for what came after? The fire on Payson Isle; the cloaked man who chased me in my dreams; the deaths out on the island last spring. My mother's attack. What if he really was at the root of all of it?

I was pulled from my thoughts when Diggs sat bolt upright in the sleeping bag. "Sol?" he called, looking around. In the dim light of the cave, I could just make out the look on his face. Sheer terror, his eyes wide.

"I'm here," I said.

Relief washed over his face. He ran a hand through what was rapidly becoming a rat's nest of greasy curls.

I went to him, but I couldn't figure out how to bridge the gap between standing there and actually *being* there—especially not after everything that had happened. So I just stood there.

"I'm right here," I said again. "Are you okay?"

"Yeah," he said. "It was just… I was in the woods. I couldn't find you."

"Oh." I started to tell him it was all right, it had just been a dream, but then I realized that the reality was probably worse than any dream his subconscious could come up with. At least if it was a nightmare, he could wake up. "Well… I'm here."

"Right," Diggs said. He still looked a little bleary. "I see that."

He sat and I stood, that chasm still between us.

"You could go back to sleep," I finally said. "You weren't out that long."

"I'm set," he said. "We should probably get a move on anyway."

He started to get up with some difficulty. I resisted the urge to offer any help, knowing he wanted nothing to do with me, and instead shoved my good hand in my pocket while the other just hung there, useless. When he was up, he started to go for his pack at the same time I went to roll the sleeping bag back up, thus managing to block his progress completely. We did an awkward little dance to try and get out of each other's way.

"Sorry," I said.

"It's okay. I'll go this way."

We ducked around each other and worked in silence. I'd just packed the sleeping bag and Erin Lincoln's journal when he returned to my side. He put half a Power Bar in my hand without a word.

"I'm all right. You eat it," I said.

"I've got my half. If we're both getting out of this, we need to keep up our strength." No arguments, in other words.

I ate it without further comment, though I will say now that surviving exclusively on Power Bars and warm water isn't something I would recommend. My stomach was grinding, and there were other issues I'd eventually have to address… I was just hoping we'd be able to leave the confines of the cave before I did.

It wasn't quite noon; we'd been out here more than twelve hours. Juarez had to be looking for us by now. At least I hoped he was. Even if he'd decided I wasn't worth the effort after this latest stunt, I was reasonably sure he wouldn't just let Diggs die.

I finished my half of the Power Bar and put the wrapper in my bag. Diggs handed me some more warm water to wash it down. I reached for it, but somehow in the process ended up knocking it over rather than grabbing hold of it. Before I could fumble the damn thing upright again, half the contents had spilled.

"Shit! I'm sorry." I put the cap back on the half-empty bottle and patted ineptly at the wet cave floor.

"Relax—It's okay," he said.

"No, it's not."

He actually laughed, pulling me up before I went completely apoplectic. "I'm thinking a little water won't do this place a lot of harm."

"But I shouldn't be wasting our supplies," I insisted. "Like I haven't caused enough problems, now I'm just dumping your water out willy nilly."

"We're fifty yards from a fast-flowing river, Solomon. I've got plenty more iodine tabs; we're not gonna die of thirst out here. I can think of about a dozen *other* ways we might die… But we'll be well hydrated when we go."

I didn't crack a smile. "It was still stupid, though. I'm sorry."

"Stop apologizing," he said. A trace of irritation crept back into his voice. "I don't want to spend the last days of my life listening to you say you're sorry."

That was all it took to push me over the edge. I looked him in the eye. A tear or two escaped and spilled down my cheeks. I could barely breathe. "But I am sorry," I managed in a choked whisper. Another tear fell.

Diggs brushed it away with his thumb. "I know you are," he said softly. He pulled me into his arms.

"It's all right if you want to go," I said. I pulled back so I could look at him, trying to get hold of myself again. Unsuccessfully, I might add. "I wouldn't blame you if you just took off—honestly. You really should save yourself. I could even create a diversion and you could run. I'd understand."

His mouth twitched, a hint of amusement touching his eyes. Which was annoying, considering the fact that I was completely serious. "What kind of diversion did you have in mind?"

"I don't know," I admitted. "I thought about a fire, but then I'd end up burning down the whole friggin' forest. Like my karma isn't bad enough with a sociopathic father intent on deflowering tweens in the backwoods of Maine, then I'd be responsible for the fiery deaths of millions of woodland creatures."

"It could take a while to hit nirvana with that kind of cred," Diggs agreed.

He was kidding, but I chose to ignore that. "He doesn't want you," I said. "He's only after me. I could distract him. You could run."

"Run where, exactly?"

"I don't know—go find help. I could keep him busy."

"Yeah, I imagine rape and torture would probably keep his attention diverted," he said, his eyes suddenly hard again. "Jesus, Solomon. I'm not leaving you. It's not going to happen, so just forget it. If you die out here, I'm dying with you."

"You don't have to—"

"I know I don't have to," he interrupted. "I didn't have to come with you in the first place; I didn't have to leave the safety of my desk in Littlehope. I didn't have to agree to that bogus interview you concocted when you were fifteen just so I'd let you come hang out at the Trib. But I did, and as far as I can tell I'm gonna keep agreeing to shit I probably shouldn't where you're concerned." He studied me intently. "And you'll keep doing the same for me. Because that's what we do."

I lay my head against his chest. He stroked my hair while I listened to his heartbeat. "So, if you're not leaving me here to die, do you have another plan?" I murmured into his chest. "Because I'm thinking we're gonna need one."

I felt his lips brush the top of my head. "As a matter of fact, I do."

Diggs wanted us to leave the safety of the caves and head for a fire tower about twenty miles northeast of us. I wanted to stick to the caves, with the assumption that if we continued within the network of tunnels, eventually we would find some adventure-seeking spelunkers who could help us get to safety.

"He won't let us get that far," Diggs said. His tone changed when he said it, took on an edge we'd managed to avoid for the past hour. The words made something sink like a stone in my gut.

"What do you mean, 'let us'?"

"I mean 'let us,'" he said. "He's holding all the cards here. I think he knows every move we're gonna make before we make it... He might even know where we are right now."

"And he's just out there... What? Following us? Watching us right now?"

"Possibly. Yeah."

The thought chilled me to the bone: the idea that he—whoever he was—was just waiting, biding his time until he decided it was time to make the sky fall. And once he did, there wasn't a damn thing we could do about it.

"How do we level the playing field?" I asked. "He knows these woods; we don't. He has weapons; we don't. He has access to food and water and shelter, presumably."

"It's not exactly sporting," Diggs agreed. He looked around our homey little hovel. "I think the best thing we can do at this point is figure out an easy way out of here and get moving again. I'm gonna go on ahead and check out the tunnels, just to see where we come out. You mind waiting here for a few minutes?"

I minded very much, as a matter of fact. "I thought you said we should stick together."

"I won't be gone long. But there's a limit to how much of this tunneling you'll be able to do with that wrist. If I go ahead, I can figure out the most efficient way for us to get out of here."

"What about the opening up top there? Why don't we just go out that way?"

"I checked it out while you were asleep," he said, shaking his head. "It's too high up—there's no way to reach it. Just trust me, okay? I'll be gone twenty minutes. If you hear anyone coming, just follow me inside. You'll have hold of the rope; we won't get separated."

I'd never felt so clingy in my life. "Twenty minutes?" I asked.

"At most. I'll be back before you know it."

Famous last words.

I watched Diggs disappear into the tunnels a minute later, while I held tight to the other end of his rope like it was my only lifeline. Which it very well may have been. We'd been trying to conserve the power on our phones so that if we ever did come within range of a cell tower again we might be able to make a call, but now I kept mine on and watched the minutes tick by the entire time that Diggs was gone. It was five thirty-two in the evening when Diggs left. There were some kind of cave dwellers—crickets or frogs or something—that had been cheeping incessantly since we got there. Their chatter got louder while Diggs was gone, until it felt like that was the only sound on the planet. Occasionally, I'd tug on the rope just to make sure someone was on the other end; within a second or two, Diggs would return the tug, but the interim until that happened lasted years.

The fourth time I tugged the rope, at five forty-seven, there was no answering tug. A minute passed. Then two.

"Diggs?" I called into the tunnel softly.

No response. I tugged the rope again.

Another thirty seconds passed. The cave dwellers had fallen silent.

And then, deep in the network of tunnels, I heard the shuffle and shimmy of someone moving. I wet my lips, trying to slow my heart. Somewhere so far off it sounded more like imagination than reality, a song bubbled up from the rock. I strained to hear, my ear pressed to the cave wall. My hands were sweating, goose bumps up and down my arms. When I realized what I was hearing, fear moved like an electric shock through my system:

That same low, tuneless whistle we'd heard back at the river.

"Diggs?" I whispered again. I tugged hard enough on the rope that I figured there was no way in hell he couldn't feel it. The whistling got louder, but the main tunnel Diggs had gone into branched off in three different directions. I couldn't tell which tunnel the whistling was coming from.

I knew what Diggs' answer to the dilemma would be: Run. Save yourself. My feet remained rooted to the spot.

I was just getting ready to go in after him when I felt a hard tug on the other end of the rope. Seconds later, Diggs appeared a few yards into the tunnel, moving fast on his belly. "Get our stuff," he whispered frantically. "Then run."

I grabbed his pack and mine, and stuffed the flashlight into my belt. We had three choices of escape in our dismal little cavern: the entrance at the top of the cave that Diggs had already said was too high up, the network of tunnels Diggs was just emerging from—where J. was apparently gaining on him fast—or an almost impossibly narrow fissure in the opposite cave wall.

Diggs made it the final few feet through the tunnel and dove out, pushing me toward the entrance in the cave ceiling he'd told me not half an hour ago was too high for us. I stopped moving with Diggs' hand at my back and J.'s tuneless whistle ringing in my ears. Diggs almost ran me over. I pointed toward the narrow fissure I'd been hoping to avoid.

"What about that?" I asked. "We could try that way."

"If we can get up there, then we're out," he whispered. "Then if we can block up that entrance, we'll get some time on him." Before I could argue, he pushed me toward his intended escape route again. The opening was maybe ten or fifteen feet up, and I could hear J. getting closer. "Put the pack on," Diggs ordered. "I'm gonna give you a boost up."

"What about you?"

"Throw me the rope when you're up there. I'll climb." I started to argue, but he cut me off. "Just do it, dammit. I don't think he knows where we are yet, but it won't take him long."

He knelt and I clambered up his back and stood on top of his shoulders. He stood, steadying me with his hands on my calves while I tried to figure out the best way to maneuver.

"What are you doing?" he asked.

"Hang on, I'm looking for a way up."

I searched for a hold at the opening, but only succeeded in sending a cascade of stones down on both of us.

The whistling got louder suddenly, like J. had just gotten past one more barrier between us.

"Erin," Diggs whispered frantically.

"I know," I said. I tried to get hold again, but between the crumbling rock and the fact that I could only hang on with one hand, I was getting nowhere. "It's the splint. I can't maneuver with it." I tried one more time, then shook my head. "Fuck it." I ripped the splint off and tossed it up through the opening, ignoring the searing pain in my wrist as I finally caught a solid hold and pulled myself up and through.

Once I'd birthed myself through the opening, I turned around and tossed one end of the rope back to Diggs, then began searching for something to attach my end to. I'd emerged at the top of a bare rock wall, surrounded by little but other rocks, smaller pebbles, and some scrubby brush. There were no trees to speak of. I couldn't find anything that seemed strong enough to hold a grown man's weight.

"Erin?" Diggs called. There was no missing the panic in his voice.

"Just a second, I'm almost there."

"I don't know if I have a second." He didn't sound good. "If I tell you to run, I want you to do it, all right?"

"Forget it," I said. "I'm not running anywhere without you." My hands were shaking. I expected my heart to fly right out of my chest at any minute, but I finally found a rock that was narrow enough to tie the rope around, but solid enough that it wouldn't dislodge when Diggs started climbing. I peered through the entrance.

"It's solid," I said. "Come on."

He tugged on the rope, just in case. Miraculously, it held.

He heaved himself up.

Somewhere in the cavern below, I heard a single refrain of something familiar: The Battle Hymn of the Republic. Then, it stopped. Diggs was only a foot from me now. I could see his face—the fear in his eyes, the determined set of his jaw. And then, suddenly, just when I was sure he would make it, someone jerked the rope. When the whistling started this time, it was directly below us. I couldn't see past Diggs to figure out who was down there, or what the hell he was doing.

"You have to go, Solomon," Diggs ground out. He wasn't climbing anymore. It took me a minute to realize why:

He couldn't.

"I'm not leaving without you." I lay on my stomach and peered down at him; reached down and grabbed his hand. "You're almost there."

Diggs clung to the rope, his eyes as cold and as hard as blue steel, while J. tried to pull him down. Diggs kicked out and I heard the sound of his foot connecting with something—a body, presumably. He scrambled up the rest of the way, his head just clearing the opening.

I grabbed hold of his arm to try and help pull him through. His shoulders and chest were clear when I heard the sickeningly wet sound of a knife slicing through flesh. Diggs screamed. I reached for him as he fell, my hand touching his on the way down, but the contact was fleeting. He was in my grasp... And then he was gone.

When I peered down inside the cave, Diggs was lying on the ground, gasping for breath. Standing above him, his eyes fixed on mine, was Will Rainier.

Chapter Nineteen
Juarez

After his conversation with Hank Gendreau, Juarez held a press conference in front of the Black Falls police station. Word hadn't spread that far yet about Bonnie Saucier or the other bodies that had been found. He knew from experience that it wouldn't take long before crews were arriving from far and wide, however, all of them intent on getting the latest scoop on a case sure to make national headlines. After the press conference came status updates, none of which showed any promise, and then a call from Dr. Sophie Laurent—who had been called in to consult on the case, and who'd been at the Saucier grave site since 6:30 that morning. Now, it was eleven o'clock. The heat was rising, the woods behind Luke and Sarah Saucier's home was crawling with crime scene techs and police and investigators, and Juarez could think of little beyond the fact that Erin had been missing for a full twelve hours now. He returned to the relative coolness of the barren police station and took Sophie's call.

"It seems we're spending a great deal of time together, Agent Juarez," she said. "We've found four females, approximately eighteen to twenty-four years of age," she began. "Three were killed within the past two to three years; one was more recent."

"How recent?" Juarez asked.

"Within three to four months. All have the same mark I found on the victims in Quebec: the J. carved into the chest."

"Sexual assault?"

"I'll need to conduct more tests for that. I've seen no evidence of it yet, however—no seminal fluid or spermicide present on any of the remaining clothing, at any rate. We haven't done a thorough examination of the bodies, of course, and it's difficult to determine something like that with any certainty this long after the fact."

"And no idea who the victims were?"

"Two look as though they may be indigents—possibly from Mexico or Central America. Definitely third world."

"The farms up here hire migrant workers, don't they? Is it possible these girls came from that type of situation?"

"That's what I was thinking," she agreed. "It's too early for positive IDs on the others yet, of course, but we have a couple of leads."

It would take a more detailed examination before anyone would know the finer points of the victims' final days: whether they had been imprisoned, the presence of any genetic material the killer may have left behind, the physical state of the victims when they were killed. Like Bonnie Saucier, strangulation was the probable cause of death. Juarez gave Sophie the go-ahead to prepare the bodies for transport, but he'd already been given instructions to have all remains shipped to D.C. No one argued that detail with him. From everything he'd seen thus far, the authorities in Maine couldn't get rid of this case fast enough.

When Juarez emerged from the sheriff's office, an attractive dark-haired woman was waiting for him in the lobby. Though he had only seen her once before, in less than ideal circumstances, he still placed her immediately.

"Dr. Everett," he said, extending his hand to Erin's mother as he strode forward. "Thank you for coming."

"What do you know so far?" she demanded, ignoring his proffered hand. "Where are your people looking?"

"Why don't you sit," he suggested. "Can I get you something?"

"I'm not here for the hospitality," she said wearily. "I've been driving since five o'clock this morning… I just want to know what the hell's happening. What's the last thing you heard from my daughter?"

He gave her the details of the search, providing cursory details of Will Rainier and the current theory about where he might be now. Juarez poured a cup of coffee for Kat and then one for himself, and sat on the edge of an unoccupied desk. Kat sat in a nearby office chair, holding the coffee mug with both hands. She was small like Erin—perhaps two or three inches taller with a few more curves, but hardly the larger-than-life monster Erin portrayed.

"You're Erin's G-man, aren't you?" she asked. "Juarez?"

He raised his eyebrows in surprise. She dismissed him with a wave of her hand. "She never said anything to me—we don't discuss those things. But Maya told me. They talk."

She sat with her back rigid, her green eyes—eyes Erin had inherited from her—taking in everything.

"I wanted to talk to you about your ex-husband," he said. She didn't look at him. Said nothing. He continued. "Erin said you told her you didn't know what happened to his sister. That you didn't know he and Hank Gendreau grew up together. That's true?"

"I never said I didn't know about his sister. She never asked me. And as for his link with Hank... I don't see how that's pertinent now."

"I'm just trying to get any information I can that might help us find Erin. It's hard to tell sometimes what's pertinent and what's not. You knew about Adam's sister, then?"

"I know too much to keep track of anymore," she said vaguely. "It's hard to remember which secrets I can tell and which ones need to stay buried..."

He ignored that, irritated at her unwillingness to cooperate when Erin's life hung in the balance.

"Did you know Adam is in the area again?" he asked. She tried very hard not to react, but he saw the barely perceptible tensing of her shoulder, a telltale spasm in her jaw. "I believe whoever killed Erin Lincoln is now after your daughter... Hank says it was either Will Rainier or your ex-husband. I don't believe it's your ex doing this."

"Where did you see him last?"

"No one's spotted him since he left the bar Saturday night—"

"Not Rainier," she interrupted. "Adam. You said you saw him?"

Juarez hesitated. "Yes... He was at the crime scene where Bonnie Saucier's body was found. Why?"

"No reason. I was just curious." She looked around the room restlessly. "What else do you need from me? I'm assuming you called me here for a reason."

With the exception of a couple of volunteers manning the phones, the little police station was empty. Juarez stood and went to the map, taking a moment to control his temper. He thought of Erin, suddenly—those vulnerable moments when he felt like he was actually connecting with something beyond that hard, flippant shell. With a mother like Kat Everett, it was no wonder she had difficulty showing her softer side.

"I called you because I wanted to know if Adam ever told you what happened the weekend he went to Eagle Lake. The night that Will Rainier and Hank Gendreau stormed their campsite in the middle of the night and Will raped his sister," he said. Anger burned in the words.

She turned on him, surveying him coolly—as though she viewed his emotional response as some kind of weakness. "He didn't want Erin to know about that," she said. "I honored his wishes. What good would it have done?"

"Did he tell you who killed his sister?" Juarez asked.

"Gendreau didn't tell you?" she asked. She was watching him closely, something wary in her eyes.

"He said he didn't know," Juarez said. He thought of Hank's tears when he'd told the story. *We got to the campsite late that night. Jeff and Bonnie were there, passed out in the other tent. Will and I went in to wake up Erin... It was just supposed to be part of the game, you know? That's what we did—Jeff was the one who came up with the whole thing, for Christ's sake. He was already doing my sister; what right did he have to tell us Erin was off limits?*

"Jeff—or Adam, whatever you want to call him—woke up when Erin started screaming. According to Hank, he went crazy and went after them both. Hank thought he was going to kill them. Jeff and Will started fighting; Hank took off."

She turned her back on him halfway through the story and went to the map. No reaction. Not a word.

"Do *you* think Will Rainier killed her?" he asked her.

"That's not really for me to say, is it?" She remained focused on the map, touching the colored pins with a shaking hand. It took a moment before he realized there was a physiological reason for the tremor beyond just anxiety. "Do you think he did it?"

"Maybe," he said honestly. "But I think if he did, there was someone else pulling the strings." She turned and met his eye, waiting for him to continue. "I don't think Will Rainier would have the patience, the intelligence, or even the attention span to come up with the elaborate games J. —our serial killer—has been playing for the past forty years. Will is a sexual sadist who likes little girls. Most of the victims we've found recently haven't even shown obvious signs of sexual assault."

"But you don't think Adam did it, either?"

"From a purely logistical standpoint, it doesn't seem that plausible," he said. "He would have been gone for long periods of time while he was keeping and hunting these girls in the '80s, while he was living out on Payson Isle with your daughter. Even if he was just checking up on them every day or so, it would have required much more than the occasional shopping trip to the mainland."

She looked relieved, though she tried to hide it. "Well... There you go, then. I guess it must have been someone else."

"In Erin Lincoln's journal, she mentions someone named Mister E. Do you know who that might be?"

For the first time, he saw a flash of genuine emotion: Fear. Terror, as a matter of fact. She recovered quickly, but there was no mistaking it. She shook her head and turned back to the map.

"Can't say that I do," he said. "Is that the only way she refers to him? Never by any other name?"

"I don't know. Your daughter hadn't finished reading it when I left her and Diggs in Quebec. She didn't say anything about it, though."

"It was probably just one of those silly codes kids have sometimes."

He was debating throttling her when the door opened behind him. A moment later a furry white thing came barreling toward them, headed straight for Erin's mother. Rosie, the young bartender they'd met at the bar Saturday night, followed close behind.

"I'm so sorry," the girl apologized, clearly mortified at the dog's behavior. Kat paid no attention, already on her knees to greet Einstein. "I heard what happened," Rosie continued. "I knew something must have happened when Erin and Diggs didn't show up to get him last night. I kept him as long as I could, but I've got classes this afternoon..."

"I'll look after him," Kat said immediately. "You don't need to worry about it."

"Oh—uh, I don't know. Erin seems pretty attached..."

"It's all right," Juarez reassured the girl. "This is Erin's mother; she'll take good care of him until Erin's back."

Rosie breathed a sigh of relief. "*D'accord. Bien.* It wouldn't be a problem, except for those damn classes."

Kat still ignored them both. Einstein wagged his tail ecstatically, lapping her face. She got off the floor with some difficulty and took the dog's bag from Rosie without a word. "I'll just take him for a walk, then," she said.

Juarez hurried after her. He stopped her with a hand on her shoulder just outside the door. "Hang on—I still have questions."

"Which I'll answer shortly," she said. She glared at the hand still touching her. He removed it before she removed it for him. "I just want to stretch my legs. I'm not under arrest, am I? I'm assuming I'm not a suspect in all this..."

"I just thought you might be anxious to do whatever you could to ensure Erin was returned safely. I mean... You do want her returned safely, don't you?"

Anger flashed in her eyes. "Don't make assumptions about what I do and don't want for my daughter. You don't know the first thing about me. Now,

I'll be back in a moment. Don't you have work you need to do somewhere around here?"

She stalked out without waiting for an answer. Juarez wasn't at all surprised when she headed straight for a silver Prius in the parking lot out front, put the dog inside, and drove away.

Erin and all of her hang-ups were making more sense by the second.

Rosie was still in the station when he returned, studying the maps on the wood paneled walls intently. Juarez grabbed his jacket with the intention of going after Kat for a few follow-up questions.

"I can walk you out," he said to the girl. "Wouldn't want you to miss your classes."

She made no move to leave. "So, it's true, then?" she asked. "Bonnie Saucier is dead? And still no sign of Erin or Diggs?"

He stopped, a wave of fatigue washing over him. It had been too long since he'd eaten, and far longer since he'd slept last. Lucia's sweet voice whispered in his head. *How do you expect to save the world if you can't even save yourself?*

He turned and faced the girl. "It's true," he confirmed.

"And there were other bodies, *oui*?"

"I can't really discuss that…"

"Ah," she said. She nodded understandingly. "*Pas de problème.* You think Will did it, though?"

"We don't know anything yet. We're investigating every possible lead."

"But he's one of the leads you're investigating, *non*?"

"What's this about, Rose?" he asked wearily. "Is there something I can answer for you?"

She hesitated. Her fingernails were painted bright fuchsia; she gnawed on her thumbnail and stared back at the map for another minute or more before she finally spoke.

"When I was *une petite fille, ma mère* dated Will Rainier one summer, *d'accord*?"

Suddenly Juarez was all ears. "Okay," he said cautiously.

"She broke up with him and went away at the end of the summer, *parce que* she found him… With me, you know? I moved in with my *mémère* after that."

He thought of Jamie Flint's story, about the woman who worked for her. The dog Rainier had killed. How much damage had this man done over the years? And why the hell hadn't anyone stopped him? "I'm sorry," he said sincerely. "I didn't know…"

She waved him off. "*Non, c'est bien.* I screamed like a banshee. Just about bit his pecker off, too. He probably would've killed me if my *mémère* didn't tell him she'd finish the job if he ever came near me again. He stayed away after that, *oui.*"

Juarez squelched a smile. "Well… Good for you. And that's good information about Will—"

"That's not why I'm telling you." She shook her head rapidly. "One night we were at his house, and I was sleeping on his couch—he didn't have a spare bedroom or nothing. Sometimes I'd sleep in his bed with *ma mère* when he was out wandering in the woods with Sheriff Grivois. They was always out there together, drinking and shooting and drinking some more… But that night he was home, so I was on the couch and this friend came to visit. My *maman* didn't like him—she wouldn't come out, and she told me one time that Will might be bad but he wasn't so bad as his friend."

"What friend, Rose? Did you get a name?"

"Maman called him Mister E—that's what he called himself, *pis* maman said he was *un idiot* for doing it. But that's what she always called him, 'Mister E.' And this one night he came over late, so I heard them…"

Juarez thought immediately of the journal entry Erin had read to him. The mysterious Mister E.

"Did you hear any of their conversation?" he prompted. "Do you know what the E stood for?"

"They were fighting… I know that. The man told Will he was a *mal* partner, never helping. I couldn't understand everything they said—it didn't make no sense, and Will was getting angry so I was trying to hide. But he said he didn't want to do it no more… If the man wanted anybody else, he had to find them himself."

"Find them for what?" he asked. His fatigue vanished.

She bit her lip. He was reminded how young she was. "That's what I didn't understand," she said. "He said they were for the test, *oui*? Or the experiment… He said Bonnie—she was the only one who passed the test. Bonnie and Will. Mais he wanted more like them. Hank and Jeff failed. Everybody else failed."

Juarez perched on the edge of the desk and looked intently at the girl. "I'd like you to think about that night, Rose. Did he ever say the man's name? Or maybe your mom mentioned something? Can you remember anything at all about him?"

She thought carefully for a couple of minutes, her forehead furrowed in concentration. Suddenly, her face lit up. "Eliot," she said. "I remember because I just watched E.T., *oui*? And I remember thinking of that… I forgot, 'til now."

Mr. E. Juarez thought of the journal entry Erin had read him… Something about a Mr. E spending the summer with Jeff Lincoln.

It couldn't really be a coincidence, could it?

He thanked Rosie and assured her that he'd contact her when he knew anything about Erin or Diggs. He ushered her out, and was on the phone the instant he was alone. Mr. Eliot… He just needed to figure out who that was. Once he did, maybe this whole mystery would unravel. And then, God willing, he'd be able to get Erin home again.

Chapter Twenty

I stayed at the cavern entrance peering down, lying on my stomach with my heart in my throat, for what felt like a lifetime. Waiting for Diggs to move. Speak. Something. Rainier smiled up at me.

"You can run if you want, but we're not done with you yet. And the more you run, the more he suffers. Trust me on that one."

"Just go, dammit," Diggs said when he could finally speak again. He sat up. His left leg was bleeding badly. He waited until he had my eye before he spoke again. "You come down here and we both die, right? What good does that do anyone? Run."

I couldn't get my breath. Couldn't find my voice. I shook my head. "I'm not leaving you."

"Yeah, you are," Diggs said evenly. I expected him to be angry—to rant and rail and lecture while Rainier beat him to death. Instead, he looked at me with a kind smile, his eyes wet. "You know what you need to do. Go on, Sol."

"If it was me, you wouldn't leave," I said, my voice barely above a whisper.

"This is sweet," Rainier said. He hauled Diggs up by the back of his t-shirt, a knife pressed to his throat. "But we're done here—you've got a choice, little sister. Get down here, or start running."

Diggs never took his eyes from mine. "Please, Solomon." His voice didn't waver. "Go."

I stood.

Rainier smiled at me, waiting for me to decide. He pressed the knife into Diggs' throat, his eyes alight with a frenzied kind of madness. I could barely see through my tears.

"What'll it be?" Rainier asked. He twisted the knife, pressing it deeper. Diggs didn't even flinch, his eyes still on mine.

"You can do this," he said.
I turned away.
And ran.

◊◊◊◊◊

I stumbled down over limestone and shale, slipping more than once in a cascade of loose rock. The sun was high overhead, the air thick. If I'd known where to go to run for help, I might have done that—might have actually left Diggs alone to fend for himself, with the vague hope that I could find someone to save our asses. But as far as I knew, we were on our own; I'd seen no sign that the cavalry was on the horizon. Lacking that, I tried to come up with a plan to save our asses myself.

Once I'd descended from the rocky outer face of the network of caverns, I crept along the treeline, searching for another entrance into the cave. Half an hour passed while I stumbled along in a panic, trying to find a way back in, all the while imagining what Rainier was doing with Diggs by now… Wondering whether he'd even be alive when I returned. When I finally found another way in, I set everything but my survival knife down outside and prepared to go in. I tried to still my shaking hands; quiet my pounding heart. I was already on my way in when I heard voices. It took me a second to reassure myself that they weren't in my head. I pressed my back against the rocks and listened. When I turned, I caught sight of Diggs limping along the treeline not twenty yards from me, Rainier close behind.

I grabbed my stuff and crouched behind a boulder.

Diggs and Rainier continued past, apparently oblivious to my presence just above them. Diggs was using a tree branch as a crutch. Rainier held a rifle at his back. They passed so close that I could see the sweat traveling in beaded rivers down Diggs' face. When Rainier went by, I held my breath, watching the sloping way that he walked, the power in his shoulders, the confidence in the way he held the gun. I clutched the survival knife more tightly and closed my eyes. The sound of my beating heart was deafening. I felt sure Rainier would hear it—would sense the blood rushing through my veins.

If I made a move, I realized, I would have to be absolutely certain of what I was doing. Rainier wouldn't go down without a fight—and as long as he held that gun, I knew he would take one or both of us with him before that fight was done. They kept walking; I didn't stop them. As they disappeared back into the woods, I heard Diggs' voice reciting half-forgotten lyrics in a soft, easy tenor:

She's got fuck me eyes and a fuck you smile
My red haired, silver tongued, steel toed wild child

I stifled a laugh, my eyes filling with more useless tears. Like that, I was nineteen again, wrapped in a bed sheet in a too-warm Bridgeport apartment, while Diggs strummed his guitar and made up country songs just to make me smile. I remembered the feel of his body against mine for the very first time; the way he'd tasted that night, of cigarettes and Jameson's whiskey. The way he'd moved. The way he'd known me. *This would be a good night to live in*, he'd said later, his arms around me. *No morning after. No 'What happens next?' Let's just stay here.*

"Stop," Rainier said, before Diggs got any farther into the song.

"Just thought a little mood music was in order," Diggs said.

"It's not. I need to hear. Keep moving—and keep your mouth shut."

Diggs moved on, Rainier behind. I waited until they were far enough ahead before I followed their path into the woods.

◊◊◊◊◊

I followed Diggs and Rainier for an hour before Diggs began to drag. Rainier pushed him on, but it was clear he was fading fast.

"Keep moving," Rainier growled when Diggs slowed to catch his breath.

"I'd be faster if you hadn't knifed me," Diggs said. His speech was slurred. "It slows a man down."

"I barely touched you," Rainier said. "Rule number one: Don't hurt the subjects before the experiment begins. Gotta be healthy enough to run, but hurt enough to fight."

"What's rule number two?" Diggs asked.

"None of your fucking business. Move." Rainier pushed him in the back, hard enough that Diggs fell. He righted himself with a herculean effort, and forged on.

By hour two, I was covered with bites, sunburned, and parched. My head was pounding from the sun and lack of food or water, my body moving on muscle memory alone. We reached the river at three o'clock. Rainier tied Diggs' wrists and ankles, ordered him to stay put, and disappeared back into the woods.

I waited until I was sure he was gone before I crept forward. Diggs was sitting against a fallen tree, his head back and his eyes closed. His body was caked with mud and blood, bites and scrapes. Either he or Rainier had done a surprisingly good job of dressing the knife wound on his calf, but now the bandage was filthy. The gash in his thigh had been neglected—it was an angry red beneath the grime, swollen and festering.

"I thought I told you to go," he said, eyes still closed.

"And I told you I wouldn't. How'd you know it was me?"

"Because I know you. And you're not as sneaky as you think." He opened his eyes. They were glassy and distant, the pupils dilated. It took a minute before he actually focused on me.

I started carving at the ropes around his wrists with my knife.

"We can't just run away from this, Sol," he whispered. "You can't just untie me, and we'll skip off into the sunset. We either stop him, or he keeps coming at us."

I continued struggling with the ropes—not an easy task with one hand. "I know that. But I have your knife. And if we can get his gun..."

"Then what? We just blow him away?"

"Then we make him tell us how to get out of here," I said, shaking my head. "Nobody's blowing anyone away."

"Right," Diggs said dryly. "Because that would be wrong."

"No. Because we're not killers—that's his thing, not ours."

I thought of this game Rainier had been playing all these years—this bizarre, deadly match he'd set up between young girls from vastly different worlds. It must have taken planning; patience. Intelligence. As far as I could tell so far, Rainier might be as mean as a snake, but he wasn't much brighter than one.

"Where do you think he's taking you?" I asked.

He shook his head. Before he could answer, I heard Rainier coming up the path again. I severed the ropes at Diggs' wrists at the last minute, then put the knife in his hand before I sprinted for the trees. He looked after me wildly, but there was no time for him to argue. When I looked back, just a few yards away but safely hidden in the trees, Rainier was looking directly my way, his gaze clear and cold.

"You talking to someone?" he asked Diggs.

"Just myself. I got lonely."

Rainier eyed him doubtfully, then looked back toward the spot where I was hiding. "Too bad your girlfriend turned tail," he said. "Bitches. They'd just as soon stab you as give you the time of day."

"They can be moody," Diggs agreed dryly. "You're taking it pretty well—

Erin ditching us, I mean. I thought she was the whole point of all this."

"She's not," Rainier said. "But she's not done yet, anyway. She won't get far. We're just getting started."

Diggs was still seated with his back against the tree with his hands behind him, the knife clasped there. Rainier prodded him with his rifle. "Get up."

"I can't," he said. "Not until you untie my ankles."

I held my breath, watching to see if Rainier would actually fall for it. He leaned forward, the gun loose at his side. I could see how tense Diggs was. I crept forward. A horsefly followed me, lighting on my neck. I ignored it. All Diggs needed to do was make Rainier drop the gun, and I could race in and grab it. We were just one well-placed knife slash away, and the balance of power would shift. The horsefly dug in and started to feed just below my ear; I didn't flinch.

Rainier set the gun down and knelt on one knee, slowly working on the knots at Diggs' ankles. Diggs eased his hands out from behind his back. The steel of the knife blade shone in the sun. I held my breath, waiting for Rainier to notice.

He didn't.

I crawled another foot.

Rainier bowed his head, focused entirely on untying Diggs' ropes. Diggs waited until I was just a foot or so from the gun, barely concealed by the brush around us, before he raised the knife.

He brought it down in a single, swift arc—that missed its target completely. Rainier never even looked up before he snapped one hand out and knocked the knife away. Then, in a lightning-quick move I never would have dreamed possible for a man that big, he was up and after me. I almost reached the trees before he grabbed me by the hair and pulled me back into him. Diggs tried to get to the gun in time, but with his ankles still tied there was no way.

Rainier smiled, pulling me closer.

"I wondered when you'd come back to me," he said softly, his mouth at my ear. He twisted my hair painfully and nipped my earlobe. "Now comes the fun part. Pick up the knife."

I shook my head, my eyes on Diggs. Rainier jabbed the gun into my back. "It wasn't a request. Pick it up."

I picked it up.

"Get on your knees."

I stayed where I was, clutching the knife. Diggs untied the ropes around his ankles while Rainier was focused on me, though it was clear he didn't give a rat's ass whether Rainier found him out or not.

"Leave her alone." He stood on shaky feet and limped to my side.

Rainier watched the whole thing play out with his rifle still in hand, a faint smile hiding behind his Grizzly Adams beard.

"Oh… This really is gonna be fun."

He took the knife from me, then bound Diggs' and my hands. When he was doing mine, he twisted my broken wrist until I bit through my lip to keep from crying out. Diggs remained silent, ashen and shaking beside me. Rainier marched us deeper into the woods.

.

Chapter Twenty-One
Juarez

The afternoon brought no news about Diggs or Erin. Erin's mother refused to answer his calls, and between the heat and a forest fire in the area, the search party had stalled out just beyond the perimeter Juarez had established earlier in the day. He called his assistant in D.C. at three o'clock in the hope that she might have something more promising to tell him.

"Did you find them?" Mandy asked the moment she realized it was him. She was sixty-two, but remarkably adept at all the technology that stymied Juarez.

"Not yet. What do you have for me? Any background on the Lincolns?"

"You won't like it."

"Then you should probably just tell me."

"Surly today, aren't we? I looked for Wallace and Willa Lincoln in Lynn, Mass, as you suggested, but I found no record. So, I did a search for those names in every other Lynn in the country: Lynn, Georgia; Lynn, Colorado; Lynn, Texas—"

"I get the picture. What did you find?"

"Zilch," she said without hesitation. It was one thing he normally liked about her: Mandy didn't sugarcoat anything. He wasn't as happy about it today, of course. "At least, not under those names."

"Did you find something under any other names?"

"I started thinking about the fact that Erin's dad told her she was named after his sister—right? If you're going to name someone after someone, you'll do the actual name, not the name they took later on. I mean, if I changed my name to Matilda Mae now, I hope someone would have the good sense to name their child Amanda Paulette if they were going to pay homage. You see what I mean? So, even if these Lincolns changed their names at some point along the lines, I thought, 'I bet they kept their first names, thinking no one would tie them together if they moved.' "

Juarez rubbed his temples. "Mandy…"

"I know, I know… The point. Keep your britches on, stud. The point is: A Wallace and Willa Monroe lived in Lynn, Indiana, up until 1965. They'd moved there from Chicago. Sweet old Wally was up on prostitution and racketeering charges, but he managed to finagle himself out of that by agreeing to testify against some very nasty folks in Chi-Town. At the last minute, Wally flaked on the whole arrangement, and his whole family went missing."

"When they moved to northern Maine."

"That's my guess," she agreed.

"So… What about this Mr. E? Anything at all about any Eliot?"

"So far, no luck. If he was in a mob family, who knows what his real name might have been. Or whether he was from Chicago or Lynn. Or somewhere else, for that matter."

"You'll keep looking?"

"I'll keep looking. How you holding up?"

"I'll be better when we find her," he said.

"I know you will. Just keep the faith—and don't forget to eat. And sleep. Where'll I be if you up and drop dead in the boonies somewhere?"

He smiled. "As long as you were still there, they wouldn't even notice I was gone. I'll talk to you soon."

"Yes, you will."

After she'd hung up, Juarez considered the information she had provided. Wallace Lincoln had been a mobster… Not only that, but he'd been a mobster on the run from both the mob and the government. It was no wonder young Jeff had some issues growing up.

Juarez left the police station and headed for the Sauciers' at shortly after four that afternoon, after attending to paperwork and reporters' inquiries and the dozens of other administrative details that drove him up the wall when he was dealing with a case of this magnitude. All he really wanted was to get back in the field, where he might actually make a difference in getting Diggs and Erin home again.

When he arrived at the Sauciers', Sarah was working in her garden. She wore overalls and a sleeveless t-shirt, her fleshy arms surprisingly muscular considering her size. Juarez took off his suit jacket and tie, rolled up his sleeves, and joined her in the soil.

"Your brother isn't out here helping with this?" he asked.

She looked up in surprise at his appearance, wiping the sweat from her brow with the back of her arm. "Non," she said. "All the police scared him. Pis Bonnie... He works inside on mal days like this."

"I can understand him being upset," Juarez said. "You must not be crazy about having people tearing up your property, either." He knelt and pulled a couple of carrots from the ground, adding them to a canvas bag already overflowing with fresh vegetables.

"You shouldn't be out here," she said disapprovingly. "Your suit..."

He shrugged. "That's what dry cleaners are for. It's nice to be outside. Feel the soil under my hands."

"You garden at home?"

"Not now—I live in the city. When I was a teenager, we had fruit trees." He thought of Sister Mary Louise, watching him with her sharp eyes under the brutal Miami summer sun while he helped pick bananas and mango, grapefruit and oranges. He didn't mention Lucia's garden in Santa Rosa; kissing her after a day's work, when she smelled of strawberries and sunlight.

"Where was this?" she asked.

"Miami. The sisters at the place where I grew up loved having fresh fruit. They had no problem putting me to work."

"Ah," she said. "*C'est bien.* It's good putting boys to work. Less trouble, *non?*"

He couldn't argue with that. A giant, long-haired gray cat strolled into the garden and made for Juarez directly, rubbing against him with a low, rumbling purr. He held up his hand and she butted her head against it, tail twitching.

"Miranda," Sarah said to the cat. "*Va-t'en.*"

"It's all right," Juarez said. "Don't tell anyone, but I'm more of a cat person anyway... Let her stay." He resumed working in the soil while Miranda wove around him.

"When you were growing up," he asked after they'd worked in silence for a short time, "did Bonnie ever talk to you about being at Eagle Lake the weekend Jeff and Erin went missing?"

She didn't answer.

"Sarah?" he pressed.

She looked at him unhappily, her lips in a tight line. "Her and Jeff— they were together sometimes, *oui*? He didn't usually date just one girl, *mais* he liked Bonnie. All the boys liked her. *Elle est très jolie.*"

"Did you know a Mr. E—or an Eliot, maybe—who spent time with them, too? Or maybe hear them talking about someone with that name?"

To his surprise, she nodded readily. *"Bien sûr.* He came to stay that summer. *Avec Jeff pis Erin."*

"So you knew him?"

"Oui."

"Do you know where he is now? Or have any idea what he did after they disappeared in 1970?"

She shook her head. *"Non,"* she said. "He wasn't here long. Everybody liked him, though. He never did nothing *mal* the way they did. He was *très intelligent.* Very quick."

So, nothing since 1970 according to Sarah. Except that if Rosie really had heard this Eliot at Will Rainier's when she was a child, that couldn't have been longer ago than the late '90s. Juarez excused himself and left Sarah and Miranda to finish in their garden. He jogged along the by-now well-traveled path to the crime scene, his head clearing with the movement.

Sophie Laurent, the medical examiner, was just finishing up when Juarez arrived. The entire clearing had been taped off. Stakes and string cordoned off the sites where each of the bodies had been buried. Bonnie Saucier and all four of the other bodies had already been excavated and were now in transit. A small team from CSU was all that remained now, painstakingly covering every inch of the area to ensure no evidence had been missed.

Sophie finished discussing something with the crime scene techs and greeted him with a pleased smile.

"I was just getting ready to call you. We have some interesting developments I wanted to speak with you about." He waited while she leafed through her paperwork.

"First," she began. "Bonnie Saucier… Something seemed a bit off with her COD, so I had someone double check something for me." She consulted one of the reports again. "She died of asphyxiation, as I suspected when first examining her. The distribution of weight and the pattern left by the belt were inconsistent with strangulation, however."

"So how did she die?"

"Suicide would be my guess," she said promptly. "Off the record until a thorough examination can verify that, of course. Hanging."

"And someone moved the body here," Juarez said. He thought of Red Grivois' story about the phone call he'd received at three o'clock the previous afternoon. "Can you tell when that was done?"

"Oui. Time of death would have been between noon and four p.m. yesterday, based on liver temp and lividity."

"You can't pinpoint any closer?"

"Not until further tests can be done."

"That's all right, I understand," he assured her. "That's a good start." He made a mental note to speak with Red Grivois again about that phone call. "Was there anything else?"

"I spoke with the technicians about that belt you wanted analyzed for fingerprints." Juarez was still stuck on the revelation about Bonnie's suicide, but nodded absently for her to continue.

"Ms. Saucier's fingerprints were on the belt, of course, so no surprise there. But Jeff Lincoln's prints were not. There were fingerprints from an unidentified male who was not in the system, but there was no trace of Lincoln's."

"That's impossible," Juarez said. "I saw him holding it. He dropped it right in front of me; there was no time for him to wipe his prints, and he wasn't wearing gloves. You're positive about that?"

"I knew you'd ask, so I had them run it through twice. There's no question."

His head was awhirl with questions. Everyone to that point had agreed that Adam Solomon and Jeff Lincoln were the same person; that the teenager in Black Falls was the same man in the photos on Payson Isle years later. He excused himself, already dialing Mandy as he walked back up the path toward his car. It felt as though a huge piece of the puzzle was about to drop into place.

"I need a photo of Jeff Lincoln," he told her. "One taken directly from the Lansing asylum where he was held in '72. The place where we first got prints on him."

"That won't be easy," she said immediately. "This is an awful lot of years later… I doubt they even have anything like that."

"You said I should keep the faith. Right now, it's all wrapped up in you," he said.

He could practically hear her roll her eyes. "That's low, Jack. But I'll see what I can do."

He hung up and stood there for a moment, his body humming. The assumption up to that point had been that the Jeff Lincoln who went missing from Eagle Lake in 1970 was the same Jeff Lincoln who resurfaced in Lansing in 1972, was fingerprinted, and then escaped two weeks later. But what if that had merely been someone posing as Jeff? Someone who knew the scant details necessary to steal someone's identity in the '70s. If the mysterious Mr. E was a friend of Jeff's at the time, he would know the time and place of Jeff's birth, and would likely have access to his social security number, as well.

He could have killed Erin Lincoln, then left her brother reeling and in shock in the woods… Juarez had no idea where the fifteen-year-old might have gone from there, but it made sense that he might simply disappear rather than going home to tell his abusive father what had happened. He became someone else… And Jeff Lincoln was reborn a monster.

Chapter Twenty-Two

I don't know how long we'd been going before Rainier slowed. Diggs and I had been silent through most of the trek, my body sapped of strength, running far too long with no food or water or sleep. It turns out it's basically impossible to maintain any kind of good humor during a death march.

We were back at the side of yet another mountain in the middle of yet another wooded glade when Rainier ordered us to stop.

"It's about fucking time," he said with a sigh. "We're here."

I looked around. All I saw were more deep woods; more horseflies; more mosquitoes and sunlight and blackflies and pain. I wondered if he was going to kill us there... If he'd rape me first, while Diggs watched. I tried to imagine my life back in the real world: shopping Trader Joe's; walking Einstein around Portland's Back Bay. I closed my eyes.

I really missed my dog.

Instead of raping me or torturing us both or even just killing us and getting it over with, Rainier pushed us toward a tangle of brambles and brush on the mountainside. We were less than two feet away before I realized he wasn't trying to force us into the side of the mountain.

Or he was... Just not in the way I'd expected.

Concealed behind the brush, painted to blend perfectly with the landscape, was a door.

Rainier brushed past us both and unlocked it with a rusted skeleton key. He stepped aside and motioned us through, then followed behind. The door echoed when it closed behind us. He snapped on the lights.

I blinked twice, taking in our new surroundings. Carved into the side of the mountain, deep in the woods and completely concealed from the rest of the world, was a simple, tastefully furnished subterranean prison.

"Welcome to the Sanctuary," Rainier said. He pushed us farther inside. "You can check out... But you'll never leave."

◊◊◊◊◊

The neatly decorated foyer was only a way station for Diggs and me before Rainier pushed us through the dimly lit living area, to a barred door with another reinforced steel one behind it. He opened both doors with his magic skeleton key, and turned on more lights inside. I could hear a generator humming somewhere inside the mountain.

"You stay here tonight," Rainier said. "I'll come for you at five o'clock tomorrow morning. Be ready. Rules are on the dresser."

He untied both of us, left the room, and closed and locked both doors behind us.

When he was gone, Diggs went straight to the dresser, while I took in our surroundings. The floor was poured concrete, with a couple of sedate throw rugs. The walls were carved into the mountain wall itself. There was a kitchenette with a stocked refrigerator, small stove, microwave, and a cabinet with a few dishes; a double bed with a down comforter and a dresser; a bathroom with a working toilet and a double shower. The medicine cabinet was stocked with first aid supplies. The apartment was notably lacking computer, telephone, or TV.

"So, we're basically being held captive in the Bat Cave," I said to Diggs. "Is that what you're getting from all this?"

"Basically," he agreed. "Listen to this." He took a placard from the dresser and sat down on the bed: " 'Welcome to the Sanctuary. During your stay, you can be assured of the following: All food is safe; All clothing, first aid supplies, and food are available for the taking; You are under neither auditory nor visual surveillance; You will not be disturbed until your prearranged wake-up call; Subjects are allowed one night in Sanctuary with a partner; After said shared night, the victor in subsequent matches will periodically be allotted additional time in Sanctuary; Suicide is discouraged, but not prohibited. Best of luck. – J.' "

I scratched my head. "What the hell is going on?"

"I don't have a clue. But would you look at this place?"

"Martha Stewart meets Soldier of Fortune. Pretty sweet." I tried to ignore the bubble of hysteria welling in my chest. "What are we supposed to do now?"

He lay back and closed his eyes. "I don't have a clue. Sleep comes to mind, though… And food. And a shower. In that order."

"You're going to sleep now? Aren't you freaked out?"

"Mm hmm," he said. "But I'm also exhausted. And so are you."

I sat there another minute or so before I knew I'd come unglued if I didn't do something. Anything. I went in the bathroom and checked the shower. The dual showerheads shuddered and sputtered, but eventually came to life with surprisingly good water pressure. I raided the medicine cabinet, pulling out bandages and ointments and everything else I could imagine us possibly needing. When I returned to the bedroom, Diggs was already asleep. I pulled the blanket around him, but I resisted the urge to lie down myself. According to the clock on the dresser, it was already after five p.m. We had less than twelve hours to figure out some kind of plan… I couldn't afford to sleep that time away.

I started by searching the place for hidden cameras or wires or any other sign that Will Rainier and whoever else was in on this was listening. I found nothing, but that didn't mean I believed for a second we were really on our own for the night. I went to the refrigerator next and surveyed the contents: bottled water, bread, eggs, cheese, bacon. Juice. Oranges. There was peanut butter and Shredded Wheat and a few canned goods in the cupboard. On the inside of the refrigerator was a note that read: *For those who have not eaten in excess of 24 hours, moderation is critical. May have difficulty digesting 'heavy' meals. – J.*

I took out the bread and cheese and sniffed them both. They smelled fine… Of course, unless they were well past the Best If Used By date or someone had laced them with almond-scented cyanide, I didn't really have a clue what the hell I should be smelling for. I made a sandwich, grabbed a bottled water and some aspirin, and sat on the floor in the far corner of our cell, my eye on the door.

I ate slowly, in case it started to feel like my intestines were filled with razor blades or the room started looking like a Degas painting. Neither of those things happened.

Diggs was snoring by the time I finished eating. I started the shower, took care of business, and then stripped out of my filthy clothes—with the exception of bra and underpants, so I wouldn't be completely vulnerable if Rainier decided now was a good time to go Psycho on me. I opened the bathroom door and kept the shower curtain partially open so I could keep an eye on Diggs… I didn't want to get out and find him murdered in bed while I'd been in the bathroom sucking up all the hot water.

The shower was one of those natural-type deals they have on HGTV a lot, with a drain in the floor and two square showerheads overhead meant to mimic rainfall. I stood beneath the spray and considered our situation. As far as I could tell so far, there wasn't a chance in hell of escape; that's one of the drawbacks of being imprisoned inside a mountain. I thought of Erin Lincoln's journal; the J carved in her chest when she died; all the other girls who'd been imprisoned and hunted... Dr. Laurent had said those girls had been bound, starved, and confined to a small area. Was that what Diggs and I had to look forward to, once these 'matches' referred to in the rules began?

I thought of Rainier again. From what I'd seen, he didn't have the intelligence, patience, or vision for this kind of lunacy. He couldn't be the one behind it all. But if it wasn't him, I honestly didn't have a clue who it was. I closed my eyes and leaned against the rock wall, letting the water wash over me. The pain in my wrist had migrated up my arm and down to my fingers... I couldn't tell where the hurt ended anymore. Quebec City seemed light years away now. I winced at the memory of that fateful fucking decision that brought Diggs and me here instead of some little motel in Montreal. If we survived this, Juarez would probably never speak to me again. I imagined him out there somewhere, trying to find us. Tracking down leads. Beating in doors. Had he learned something we hadn't?

I drifted, standing there as exhaustion moved through me. When I opened my eyes, Diggs stood at the bathroom door, watching me. He didn't look away when our eyes met. When I made no move to cover myself, he stepped into the room.

"I don't know how much hot water there is," I said. I took a breath. Thought of the rules: No surveillance. And Rainier's words: *I'll come for you... Be ready.* How did you get ready for something like this? Diggs was still watching me. His eyes were dark, filled with a kind of hunger I'd almost forgotten he possessed. "There's room for you, if you want." I couldn't look at him when I said it.

He nodded silently. I watched him strip to his boxers, taking in the battle scars—both old and new. He had a scar over his heart that he'd always refused to tell me about—a burn about the size of a silver dollar; a razor-thin scar along his jawline from a night in Tijuana that I'd missed; a cigarette burn on the inside of his right elbow from a night that summer in Bridgeport that I only wished I'd missed. Celtic tattoos on both arms. He stepped into the shower without touching me and raised his face to the spray. Between the two of us, the concrete shower floor was filthy as all the blood and the mud and the... Whatever the hell else we'd carried in with us, magically washed away. When Diggs finally made contact, it was to nudge my shoulder so that I'd turn away from him.

He took shampoo from a shower caddy in the corner and wordlessly poured some into his hand, then gently tipped my head back.

"You got burned today," he said. I looked from my vantage; Diggs upside down. Inside out. His finger skimmed my forehead.

"Yeah... I didn't have the kit with me to put any sunblock on. It's not so bad, though—we were in the woods most of the time. More bites than burns."

He put the shampoo in my hair and massaged it in until my knees had gone soft. "Close your eyes," he instructed. I did, and kept them that way while he rinsed the soap out. He turned me around. We faced off once more.

"What do you think happens tomorrow?" I asked.

He shook his head. "Nothing good."

"That was my thought."

I watched the water run down his chest, drip off his shoulders. He's bigger than most people think when they first meet him, in the office with his concert tees and jeans and vintage hats; there's a physical power there that people just don't suspect. He'd gotten a little soft in recent months, though—his arms not quite so big as I remembered them, his stomach a little soft. I thought of Andie, back in Littlehope waiting for him to come home. I stepped away.

Before I got very far, his hand skimmed my side; he pulled me back to him. His eyes were still on mine. I could tell that the same old battle was waging again: should I stay or should I go now...

I steadied myself with my good hand at his side and raised myself up on my toes, our bodies pressed close. I could feel him against me now, hard where I was soft, warm and solid. We remained that way for a few seconds, the water washing over both of us, our gazes locked. When he finally lowered his mouth to mine, all the air left the room.

The last time we'd kissed had been in his kitchen last spring. That night, I could feel him fighting it, never really giving in. That night, it had been over before it began.

This time, he didn't try to fight. One kiss and my blood caught fire. He tugged at my bottom lip with his teeth and I opened to him, his tongue pressing past my lips. His hand spanned the small of my back, pulling me closer until there was nothing left between us. I moved against him. Twisted my fingers in his hair. He pushed me back against the wall, and I remembered what it had always been like between us, that loss of reason when he wrapped his body around mine and his mouth found all the right spots and nothing mattered but touch and taste, sky blue eyes and the way my name sounded on his lips.

Eventually, however, reality set in.

"I think we're out of hot water," I said from between chattering teeth. We'd both miraculously managed to keep our underpants on, but my bra had washed away in the storm. Diggs was shivering too, his lips blue.

"I think you're right." He kissed me again. "We should probably…" He nodded toward the other room.

"Probably," I agreed. I didn't move. He kissed the tip of my nose, his hands moving over my body in an almost absent-minded way, like he didn't even know he was doing it. "Did you want me to carry you? Because I got shanked earlier… I'm not in the best shape of my life here."

"I think I'm okay."

He stepped out first. While he didn't say it was because he wasn't sure what might happen when we got out, I knew that's what I'd been thinking. Nothing hideous was waiting for us, though: no Will Rainier wielding a ten-inch blade, no mutant honeybees. Diggs toweled himself off quickly, but he took more care drying me—starting with my feet and working his way up, never quite meeting my eye. We'd both gotten quiet again.

There were thin cotton pajamas in the dresser that were just our sizes. We put them on without speaking. Diggs re-splinted my wrist; I washed out the gashes in his legs, noting that they both looked better after the shower. And still, we didn't talk. We held hands a lot, but we didn't kiss again. At just past ten o'clock, we turned off the lights and got into bed. Diggs curled his body around mine, holding me close.

"Sleep, Solomon," he whispered in my ear.

I could feel myself drifting, even though I didn't want to. I held onto the arm wrapped around my middle. "Don't let go tonight, okay?" I whispered back. "Not until you have to."

"I won't," he agreed. He tightened his arms around me. "I'll never let go, Sol."

Chapter Twenty-Three
Juarez

Juarez was headed back to the station after his conversation with Dr. Laurent when he passed Erin's mother on the highway, headed in the opposite direction. He turned around when she was well down the road, keeping two or three cars behind as he followed her south on Route 1. He wasn't that surprised when she turned onto the dirt road leading to the Sauciers.

Instead of parking behind the last crime scene van still on site and walking in from there, however, she drove past. Juarez knew the road dead ended before long, so he parked and got out. He changed into sneakers, then loped after her in his shirt sleeves and dirty slacks, wondering all the while how he'd ended up here: in an ill-fitting suit, doing paperwork and appeasing bureaucrats rather than trying to find the woman he may or may not be dating, who—he was fairly certain—was actually in love with another man.

Within minutes, Kat stopped her car, leashed Einstein, and set out on a trail Juarez suspected few even knew about. He stayed far back. He already knew where she was going, or at least who she was going to; he just didn't want to spook her before she got there.

During one of their late-night phone calls over the past few months, Erin told him once about a fight she'd had with her mother as a teenager: *She cracked the phone on my forehead. Left me concussed and took off with some sailor for three days… It wasn't a big deal, really. Mothers and daughters, right?*

He didn't know about that. Having no memory of his own parents, he supposed he could have lived through the very same kind of scenario himself as a child. Somehow, he didn't think that was true, though… He wouldn't have been quite so horrified if that had been standard protocol in his own life, would he?

He tried to imagine the woman he was following now flying into that kind of a rage. She walked with a pronounced limp over the uneven terrain, clinging tightly to Einstein's leash. The dog slowed frequently to look up at her, never going too far ahead. Kat made her careful way down the riverbank, until she reached a spot where she was almost completely hidden from view. Juarez crept forward, hiding low in the underbrush.

He didn't have to wait long.

Within five minutes, he saw a rustling in the trees to Kat's right. Einstein whined unhappily, pacing on his leash. Juarez sank down lower. Adam Solomon emerged from the trees.

Einstein barked twice, but Kat silenced him quickly. Juarez watched with great interest as Erin's parents squared off by the river. He had to strain to hear them over the water.

"Do you know where she is?" Kat demanded immediately. There was something different about the way she held herself here—a vulnerability he hadn't seen before. Adam shook his head.

"I've been looking. They're on the run somewhere... I don't know whether he's gotten to them yet."

"You need to do more than just look," she hissed. "More than just wander around in the woods, waiting for him to do this all over again. You know Rainier is out there, too?"

He shook his head, but he didn't speak. Kat went to him. She touched his face, guiding his gaze to hers in a gesture so intimate that Juarez almost felt he should turn away.

"Your sister wasn't your fault, Adam. Everything that came after... You couldn't have changed it. But this..." Her voice failed her. Adam took her hand, and Kat slid easily into his arms; more easily than Juarez would have imagined for a woman as prickly as her. Adam held her tightly.

They spoke too quietly to be heard for several seconds. Then, Kat pulled away. She looked at him seriously.

"You have to call them. Or I will. They've protected him all this time, but this... You can worry about the greater good, what the repercussions will be if they decide to teach you a lesson again. That's your prerogative. My silence is on one condition and one condition only—it always has been: Keep Erin safe. I don't care whether this was their fault or not; they have the power to stop it."

"Katie—" Adam began.

She shook her head. "No," she said fiercely. "I'm telling you: either they stop this, or I'll talk. I'll tell the world—I don't care how much power they have. Who they hurt. You call and tell them that. If Erin doesn't make it out of this because their bastard son has gone off the rails again…"

Adam nodded quickly, squeezing her hands in his own. "Okay," he agreed. "I'll call. I'll tell them." He pulled her back into his arms. Juarez actually did turn away when they embraced this time, his eyes on the ground when Adam kissed her. She was crying when they parted.

"You have to go," she said softly. "It's not safe. Call them, though. Tell them what I said—our agreement was always my silence for Erin's safety. That still stands."

Adam brushed a tear from her cheek and kissed her one more time. "Take care, Katie," he said. "I'll write again soon."

Juarez palmed his Glock. If he was going to make a move, he needed to do it now. He stood, but remained concealed in the brush. The wind shifted; Einstein whined. The dog gazed into the woods, directly at Juarez. Kat pushed Adam's chest gently.

"Go," she urged. "Before someone catches you."

He started to walk away. Juarez pointed the Glock and stepped out of the trees. "I need you to stop for me, Adam."

Adam did as he said, hands raised as he came to a halt. He glanced back toward the trees. Kat stepped in front of him. "Keep going," she told him. She looked at Juarez. "He won't stop you, will you, Jack?"

"I need to talk to you," Juarez said. "I know you're not the same person who's been posing as Jeff Lincoln all these years, killing those girls. The fingerprints in the databank don't belong to you; they belong to him. I can help you prove that."

"That doesn't matter," Adam said. "Forget it… Whether I'm guilty or innocent has never been the issue. All that matters is getting Erin back safely."

"But I can't do that if I can't unravel these final pieces," Juarez insisted. "The boy who stayed with you that summer: Eliot. Do you know where he is now? What happened to him after Eagle Lake?"

"I don't know," Adam said. He was lying—and not well. "He could be anywhere."

Einstein growled at Juarez, his eyes fixed on the gun in the agent's hand. Juarez didn't care for the way the dog was staring. While his attention was momentarily diverted from Adam, Kat crouched and touched the leash clip on Einstein's collar. The dog continued to growl.

"I don't think he likes you pointing that thing," Kat said. "There's no telling what he might do if he got loose somehow. Dogs are funny that way.

Who knows what might set them off."

Adam was easing back into the trees. Juarez kept his gun up despite the fact that the dog was looking at him like a steak after a seven-day fast.

"Keep him back," he said to Kat.

"What are you gonna do? Shoot Erin's dog?" She looked at Adam again, more confident now. "Go on. I've got this. You know he didn't do anything, anyway," she insisted to Juarez. "If you really thought bringing him in would do anything but hurt things, you would have been out here hunting for him yourself all this time."

She took a step toward Juarez, Einstein by her side. The fur along the dog's spine stood on end. "Seriously, Jack," she said reasonably. "You've got enough going against you, trying to make any progress at all when Diggs is still in the picture. But I promise: you shoot Erin's dog, and you're as good as dead."

Adam was already nearly out of sight. Juarez side-stepped Kat and the dog and started after him. Kat unclipped Einstein's leash. The moment he was free, he took off after Juarez. He tackled the agent, knocking him to the ground. Adam disappeared. Kat walked over casually and stood over Juarez while Erin's dog slobbered all over him.

He was beginning to rethink having anything to do with Erin Solomon at all.

Juarez took Kat back to the police station, following in his own car behind her Prius. She purposely drove fifteen miles under the speed limit the entire way, occasionally slamming on the brakes for no apparent reason. When they reached the station, she bypassed an almost completely empty parking lot to take the space reserved for the sheriff.

It was six-thirty on Monday evening when they walked into the station. It was virtually empty. Juarez had already seen news vans invading Black Falls, but thankfully they seemed otherwise occupied at the moment. He made himself yet another cup of bad coffee, offering one to Kat at the same time. He held the door for her and Einstein—who seemed to hold no grudge after their encounter in the woods—and followed her into the sheriff's empty office.

Kat walked around to the sheriff's desk and took his chair immediately, setting her coffee very deliberately on a stack of his papers. 'Maddening' came to mind.

"So, what can I help you with now, Agent Juarez?" she asked.

"I'd like to know what you and your ex-husband were discussing out at the river."

"Ah. That's a tough one… The problem there is that I just don't remember," she said, her eyes wide. "If you remember, I had a brain injury last spring. My memory's just gone to shit since then. Is there anything else I can do for you?"

"You told him to call someone," he persisted. "To take care of things— to protect Erin. Who was he calling?"

"And I say again: 'I don't remember.' Now really, Agent Juarez, I'm tired. I'm going to take the dog and go lie down at the hotel. And as for you… Wouldn't it be better if you were out there actually, oh I don't know, *looking for my daughter*? Instead of trying to stop me from doing the only things that will ultimately bring her home again?" She stood. "Thanks for the coffee, though."

She walked out.

Juarez didn't even try to stop her.

◊◊◊◊◊

Sheriff Cyr called when Juarez was back at the hotel, changing out of his by-now essentially ruined work clothes. His news, at least, was welcome. Sort of.

Diggs' Jeep had been found.

Juarez arrived at the site at eight o'clock that night. The Jeep was in a ravine off a dirt logging road. Someone had camouflaged it with branches and brush. It was upside down. There was blood on the dashboard. Blood on the steering wheel. The windshield was cracked. There was no sign of Diggs or Erin.

After Juarez had spoken with the sheriff and gone to take a look at the surrounding area himself, Jamie Flint met him on the path with her dogs. Her face and clothes were filthy, several angry-looking welts rising on her face and arms.

"Damned horseflies," she said when she caught him looking. "It's been a long day out here."

"And no progress?" he asked.

"We just found a couple of backpacks about ten minutes ago—one inside one of the caves, a smaller one outside."

He felt a surge of hope. "So you must be close."

She frowned. He'd seen that look on people's faces before—the day they found Lucia. Pity. "The dogs ran up and down that area, but there was no sign of them. We tracked them to the river… My guess is they traveled that way."

"So it would be harder to follow them," he said.

"That's my guess, yes." She hesitated. "I've gotta retire the dogs for the night, but we'll be back at first light tomorrow."

Her four dogs were just as dirty as she was. They lay down on the ground panting quietly while she and Juarez talked. One of them—the one who looked like a pit bull—sat close to him, resting his big block head on Juarez's shoe. They were hauling the Jeep out of the ravine now; it was totaled. He zeroed in on the windshield and saw more blood there—on the driver's side. Probably Diggs, while Erin hit the dashboard. And now God only knew where she might be.

He thought suddenly of Lucia… Lucia with the dark hair and the olive skin, with that smile that melted everything. Broken and bloody on the side of an unknown road in a country he hadn't even wanted her to visit.

"Agent Juarez?" Jamie said.

He realized she'd been trying to get his attention. He shook his head, trying to clear it of memories that he was convinced would never fade.

"I just asked if there's anything else we can do? Me and my crew were gonna grab some grub in town. You could join us if you'd like."

"I thought I'd just stay here. Maybe follow—"

She touched his arm. When she looked at him, her blue eyes burned with an intensity he found difficult to look away from. "You should get away from it for a couple of hours, okay?" she said quietly. "Trust me on that. We'll find them come morning. When's the last time you ate?"

He had to think before he could answer. "I had a sandwich at lunch, I think."

The teenage boy Juarez had noticed earlier came over and said something to the dogs—a single word Juarez couldn't make out. All four got up.

"Bear, why don't you get these guys settled in," Jamie said to the boy. "Ride back in with Cheryl. I'll catch a ride with Agent Juarez."

He didn't bother to argue. It seemed all he did these days was lose arguments with willful women.

Chapter Twenty-Four

An alarm went off at four-thirty the next morning, but Diggs and I had already been up for an hour, trying to prepare for whatever we were in for in the coming day. We'd raided the fridge and re-checked injuries and changed into the clothes provided: river pants for both of us, new boots, lots of layers. Neither of us had our backpacks anymore, which meant whatever we took with us had to either fit in our pockets or be strapped to strategically selected body parts some way or other.

We were both sitting on the bed when the alarm went off, going over our plans for getting through this whole nightmare. As soon as the bell sounded, my insides tightened into a sailor's knot—the kind nearly impossible to untie without expert assistance. Diggs' hands fisted around our down-filled comforter. The full night's sleep had done us both good, as had the food, but now all I could think about was being forced back into the forest. Rainier had gone easy on me yesterday, but I couldn't imagine that trend would last long.

"The goal should be to get as far as we can as fast as we can," Diggs said. We'd already talked about this exhaustively, but I nodded all the same. "Even if we get separated. Head to the river, and just keep moving. We can't help each other without reinforcements."

That was the part of the plan that bothered me—leaving Diggs. In theory, it sounded perfectly logical: Separately, we stood a better chance of at least one of us going in the right direction and finding someone out there who could help us. In practice, however, that meant striking out on my own, without a clue of how Diggs was faring; whether he'd even made it out alive. I thought of the bodies found in Canada, and everything those girls had been through. Diggs and I had both been putting on a brave face through most of the night, but that was faltering now that our final hour together was speeding past.

We'd made a half-assed plan to take Rainier on when he came for us that morning, but I think we both knew that would fail. Diggs held my hand, staring at it while he ran his index finger over my knuckles and veins, the lines on my palm. I kept thinking that we should say something important: tell each other everything we hadn't said. I couldn't figure out how to do that, though—where to begin, even. I stayed quiet.

When we heard someone unlocking the door, Diggs pulled me back into his arms. He kissed me and I kissed him back, fast and hard and silent. We separated before the door opened, and then stood holding hands when Rainier came in.

He wore camouflage. Lots and lots of camouflage—from the top of his billed hat to his camo combat boots, with a camouflage survival knife strapped to his camouflaged leg. He was freshly shaved and showered and bright-eyed. Clearly a man who loved his job.

"You," he said, looking straight at me. "Come with me. You stay," he ordered Diggs.

To my surprise, Diggs' hand tightened around mine. I thought we'd reconciled ourselves to this eventuality, but apparently he hadn't quite come to terms. "If you take her, you take me, too."

Rainier smiled, that sadistic light in his eyes burning a shade brighter. "I think you might be wrong on that one."

He took a single step inside and grabbed me by my broken wrist. I yelped as he yanked me toward him. I kicked him in the shin with all the strength and pure pissed-off fury I could muster. Meanwhile, Diggs got down low and drove into Rainier with the kind of power that had earned him a reputation as one of the best defensive tackles in the state way back when. Unfortunately, Rainier never let go of me while he was being tackled. When he went down, he brought me with him—wrenching my hand so hard I nearly passed out.

He got up before Diggs could do anymore damage, but he kept me on my knees with my wrist twisted. He looked at Diggs with a surprising lack of anger.

"Get back inside," he said. My stomach rolled. Diggs' eyes were wild, his hands clenched, his breath coming hard.

"Go," I said, fighting to stay strong. No tears. I waited until he'd look me in the eye, then nodded. "I'll be okay."

Diggs took a step back into our room; Rainier shut and locked both doors. He pulled me to my feet, his hand still locked around my wrist.

"It's just you and me now, Red," he said. "We're gonna have a little fun."

Rainier took me straight through the main apartment to the front door. He smiled at me when his hand touched the doorknob—the rattlesnake smile that made everything in me that might have warmed overnight run cold again.

"Ready?" he asked. "Rules change outside these walls. Just so you know."

"Maybe we should just stay here, then," I said. "I mean... It looks nice here for you, too. You could take it easy. Raping and pillaging has to take it out of a man after a while."

He licked his lips. "Yeah. Rules change outside these walls."

He opened the door and shoved me outside, then closed and locked it behind us.

It was a cool morning, the sun already lightening the horizon. We walked for maybe a mile, my blistered feet already sore, when he stopped at an olive green truck parked under the trees. He came around to the passenger side. Before I even knew what was happening, he was holding me still with one arm around my middle while he dropped a dark pillowcase over my head. The second the lights went out, I couldn't breathe. I fought until Rainier wrapped his arms around me, squeezing me so hard I thought he'd break something.

"Knock it off," he growled in my ear. His hands ran over my body possessively. In the darkness, it felt like he was everywhere. I kicked out again, but only hit air. While I fought, Rainier tied my hands in front of me. He shoved me into the truck cab, hitting my head so hard on the way in that I saw stars. Then, he buckled my seatbelt—death by exposure or shock, blood loss or strangulation was fine, but apparently vehicular manslaughter was not on J.'s agenda. Good to know.

It was impossible to tell how long we drove. I heard water nearby, but otherwise the only sound was the roar of the truck engine. The air was warm and fetid inside my hood, the smell of gasoline from the truck overwhelming in the close space. When I was sure I'd be sick, I reminded myself of that conversation with Juarez: *Mind over matter.*

I thought of Kat. Did she know anything about what was happening? Did she even care? If J. really was the hooded man from the island, why in hell had she been protecting him?

How much of this insanity were my parents a part of?

I took a breath and closed my eyes, trying to find some way to calm myself. To get clear. All the thoughts that had been swirling got more swirly for a split second before I imagined myself swimming past them. Diving down to a quieter place. I wet my lips. Found my voice.

"So, now that we're here…" I began. Trapped in the hood as I was, my voice sounded like it was underwater. Like I was locked inside my own head. Rainier laughed.

"Now that we're here what?" he prompted. He hadn't told me to shut up, though, so I counted that on the plus side.

"I wondered if you could answer some questions for me."

Another laugh. Because nothing says comedy like a woman with her head in a pillowcase. "Go ahead," he said. "Got nothing better to do. J. said you'd try this."

"This J. —So, that's not you?"

"Nope."

"Is J. my father?"

"Your father's a pantywaist, not fit to shine our shoes. Sure as hell not fit to set foot near the Sanctuary. He never had what it took for this. He thought he did; thought his fuckin' game with the little girls of Black Falls made him tough."

I slumped back in my seat as relief washed over me. J. wasn't him. Never had been.

"So, if my father isn't J., what happened on Eagle Lake?" I asked.

We traveled a long way before he answered, bouncing over potholes, traveling occasionally off-road, fording more than one stream. I fought a growing sense of hopelessness. No one would find us out here. I thought of Diggs: the way his body fit with mine, the way he knew me. I couldn't imagine us ever finding each other out here. What would they do to him, once they'd dumped me in the middle of nowhere?

Rainier didn't answer my question until he'd stopped the truck, slamming on the brakes so abruptly that I would have hit the windshield if I hadn't been buckled in.

"That night," Rainier said, "Your old man got what was coming to him. And J. was born."

He would say no more on the subject.

Instead, he got out of the truck. I was left alone for a couple of minutes before he returned and opened my door. He unbuckled my seatbelt, pressing his body unnecessarily close to mine as he did so, then pulled me outside. When he pulled my hood off, I stood there for a second blinking in the sunlight, gulping in fresh air. We were still in the woods… It could have been an entirely new spot, or Diggs and I could have traveled through this place sixteen times in the past two days.

Rainier pulled me to him by the front of my shirt. His eyes had that crazy shine I was rapidly getting used to; rapidly coming to dread.

"Here we are," he said.

"Yeah," I said. I turned my head away, leaning my body as far from him as possible. "And where is that again, exactly?"

He snaked his arms around me, pressing his body to mine while his lips fell to my neck. I closed my eyes against a surge of panic that dwarfed anything I'd felt up to that point. I was alone now. Whatever he wanted to do, I had absolutely no say. No power.

"What are you doing?" I ground out. He bit into my neck, hard enough to make me yelp in pain. I brought my knee up and got him in the groin before he could block me.

He stepped away from me—but only far enough to allow space to backhand me. The world spun. My head exploded in bright white pain. I fell backward, then scrambled up before he could pin me to the forest floor. When I could see again, he was smiling at me.

"That was just a taste," he said. He took the survival knife from the sheath at his leg, pulled me close again, and held the blade to my face. He stroked my skin, laying open a thin stinging line on my right cheek.

"Now," he breathed in my ear. "You run. And every time I catch you, I get a little more. That's the game."

He pushed me hard enough that I fell again, but I was on my feet an instant later. I ran away from the truck and up to higher ground, stumbling along the way. I didn't know where the hell I was or where the hell I was going.

I just ran.

Chapter Twenty-Five
Juarez

After a fitful night's sleep, in which Juarez chased Erin and Lucia through deep woods and city streets and a jungle without end, he woke by four a.m. and was at the police station by four-fifteen. Jamie and her dogs and the odd crew she ran with were already back out searching. Juarez tended to paperwork and checked through files and then arranged to meet with Hank Gendreau one more time before the man was returned to the Warren prison.

Mandy wasn't in yet at the D.C. office. As of last night, there still hadn't been any progress getting a photo of Jeff Lincoln from the Lansing asylum. Juarez had been trying to get in touch with Red Grivois to re-interview him about finding Bonnie and whatever it was she'd said about her dream, but so far no one had been able to locate the former sheriff.

At six a.m., just before the guards led Gendreau into Sheriff Cyr's office, Juarez got an e-mail from D.C. He opened the attachment and sat there for a long moment, studying the face that stared back at him: a gangly teenage boy with lank hair and glasses stared straight into the camera. His thin lips were quirked up in a cold smile. Juarez had never seen him before. One thing he knew with certainty, however: this sure as hell was not the real Jeff Lincoln.

A guard knocked on his door, now standing ajar. Juarez waved him in. Gendreau was behind him. He didn't look good, his eyes shadowed and rimmed with red.

Juarez got him a cup of coffee and told the guard to wait for them outside.

"I'm sorry about your sister," he began. "I know this isn't an easy time to be doing this."

"It doesn't matter," Gendreau said. "I've lost my whole family to this, one way or another. I'll do whatever you need to track down Jeff Lincoln and make him pay. Whatever it takes."

Juarez nodded understandingly. He picked up a copy of his photo of Jeff Lincoln and slid it toward Gendreau.

"Can you tell me who that is, Hank?" he asked.

Gendreau barely had to glimpse at the photo. "Yeah, of course. That's Eliot—a friend of Jeff's. He stayed with them that last summer."

Juarez made a concerted effort not to show his excitement. "Eliot what?" he pressed. "Do you have a full name for him?"

He had to think about it for a minute. "I don't think so, no. We always called him Eliot. Or Mr. E… Why?"

"And when was the last time you saw Eliot?"

"He was with us that last night in Quebec—we all went out drinking together."

"Did he come with you that night?"

Gendreau shook his head. "He wouldn't. Said it wasn't his scene; he'd catch a ride back with Red."

Juarez did a double take. "Red Grivois?"

"That's right," Gendreau said. He hesitated. "I don't want to get him in trouble now… He was always good to us. Used to buy us beer sometimes. Take us across the border with him. He always said if we were gonna party anyway, he wanted to make sure we were doing it right."

Grivois was the last one to see Bonnie alive. The one who found the body. He was the one who'd found Erin Lincoln, as well. The first one on the scene when Ashley Gendreau was murdered. He was friends with Will Rainier. Juarez thought of Rosie's words that afternoon: *When he was out wandering in the woods with Sheriff Grivois… drinking and shooting and drinking some more…*

"Did Red know Bonnie?" Juarez asked, forcing himself to finish the interview.

"Of course," Gendreau said. "Everybody knew Bonnie. My sister was the prettiest girl in the County back then. Red wasn't much older than us, you know? Early twenties—not sheriff yet, just a deputy. He liked her, I think."

Juarez stood abruptly and went to his briefcase, hauling out most of the files inside. Then he opened the office door and called for the guard. "You can take him back to his cell. I won't need him again."

Gendreau stood without any prompt from the guards. "My case… Ashley dying. Do you think whoever did all these other girls is the same one who killed Ashley?"

Normally, Juarez tried not to answer that kind of question directly—there were too many repercussions if it turned out he was wrong. This time, however, he didn't hesitate.

"I do. And I'll do everything in my power to convince the judge of that."

"I know that everything that happened with Erin Lincoln... What Will did—I can't ever make up for that. I'll never forget it. Never be able to change what we did to that girl. But if there's some way I can get out of prison now... Maybe make things up to my other kids, try to rebuild things with them. That's all I can ask for right now."

Juarez shook the man's hand. He was reminded of all the bad decisions the universe seemed to just let slide by... Until that one fateful miscalculation that invariably turned the world on its head. He thought of the four boys: Jeff, Hank, Will, and Eliot. Teenage boys who got caught up in a game more serious than they ever could have imagined, when Jeff Lincoln first came up with the idea to ply thirteen-year-old girls with beer and sweet nothings. And two of those boys took the game a step further.

"Thank you for meeting with me," Juarez said. "I hope you get that second chance."

After he was gone, Juarez spread the files out on his desk, looking at each and every victim for the link he was sure he would find. Within minutes, he had his answer.

Jenny Bishop's father had filed a lawsuit, with a hearing held in Augusta. Juarez put a call in to the FBI to have Mandy check to find out whether or not Red Grivois had a court appearance scheduled for that day. Grace Starke's father was in jail on drug charges; over the years, he'd had extensive involvement with the police. It took some time to figure out the link with Becca Martineau, but Juarez eventually found it: a trip to Augusta for the kids in student government, to meet with a group of lawyers and police officers from around the state. Red Grivois had been among those police officers. Stacy Long had been a high school dropout who'd had several brushes with the law, including a trial for aggravated assault against an abusive boyfriend.

And then there was Red Grivois himself, who'd spent a significant portion of his time in court or seminars or out on the streets, getting to know these kids. What if the mysterious Eliot wasn't the key at all... What if Red had been the one to engineer this plot all along?

Beneath his welling excitement over the thought that he may have actually cracked this case and was that much closer to finding Erin, rage settled like a growth in his chest. If Red truly was the one behind this diabolical forty-year trail of death and destruction, Juarez vowed that the man would pay.

Chapter Twenty-Six

I went straight to the river as soon as I was able, just like Diggs and I had talked about. From there, I focused on putting distance between Rainier and me. I was blistered and burned and battered from the day before, but having the ability to move freely now—after a full night's sleep and a couple of balanced meals—felt good. Or as good as running for one's life while a psychopathic rapist is hot on your trail could feel, anyway.

I thought of what I would do if I got out of this. I just had to try to find help, somewhere out here. *Try not,* I heard Diggs whisper in my ear. *Do or do not. There is no try.* I stopped myself from laughing out loud. Best to avoid outright hysteria for as long as possible. Instead, I focused on vengeance. The story at hand. Except I knew almost nothing about the story at hand. I went back to the vengeance part of the equation.

When I got out of this, I would get strong. Work out. Move more. Learn to fight... I would never be a victim again, helpless while a madman like Rainier ran his hands over me, waiting for me to break. Part Jedi, part vampire slayer.

Fueled by that thought, I kept moving. The things that I did know about the story were heartening, at least: My father wasn't the monster. J. was the monster. J. was behind the deaths of all those girls; the one who watched and took notes and treated them like lab rats while they fought for their lives. And lost.

I wouldn't lose, though.

I put on more sunscreen. Drank more water. I used a bandana I'd taken from the Sanctuary to keep my scalp from burning. It wasn't as hot as it had been, but the bugs were still thick. The air smelled clean and clear, and the sunlight felt good on my shoulders for a change, instead of debilitating. I tried to keep my wrist up and immobilized, in a sling I'd fashioned from an extra t-shirt I'd snagged from the Sanctuary. A turtle lounged on a rock in the center of the riverbed. Trout were plentiful. It was a fisherman's paradise; it couldn't possibly be completely deserted this time of year. Somewhere, there had to be a group of rogue sportsmen just dying to save a half-dead damsel from a couple of madmen.

I traveled a good part of the way in water to my knees, just because the cool on my feet and legs felt good. I stopped once to swim, and ate half the sandwich I'd brought with me by the river while three white-tail deer drank not ten feet from me. Within a couple of minutes I was restless. I set out again.

I thought of Juarez. He had to be out here somewhere by now. He'd know what was happening. People would be looking for us—Diggs and I weren't like the other victims, who'd simply vanished without a trace.

If Juarez didn't come for us, though, I would find a way to get to him. Find a way to get us out of here.

The sun was high overhead and I was lost in thought and a bizarre kind of delirium-induced zen when I heard something in the trees above. My heart took a flying leap. I sought cover in the underbrush, burrowing into a cluster of ferns and brush. I scanned the skies for some kind of genetically mutated flying machine about to devour me. When you've been held captive inside a madman's sanctuary carved inside a mountain, anything seems plausible.

I didn't see anything, though. I stayed on my belly on the ground for a few minutes, the smell of earth and greenery strong in my nose. Watching. Waiting. Rainier's words crept through my head again: *Every time I catch you, I get a little more. That's the game.*

I couldn't give him that chance.

A light breeze rustled through the canopy of greenery above. I scanned the area one more time, but there was still nothing. I got up, my eyes on the horizon.

"Psst. Solomon."

When my heart leapt this time, it was for entirely different reasons.

I peered through the trees until I spotted him: Diggs, sitting in the crotch of an old oak. He slid from his perch, stumbling when he hit the ground. My enthusiasm faded when I saw his face.

His left eye was swollen shut and his lip was bleeding. A trail of crusted blood ran from his very swollen nose.

"It looks worse than it is," he said. He limped toward me.

We met on the rocks of a riverbed so pristine it seemed man had never set foot there. Three hawks circled overhead. Diggs pulled me into his arms and held on so tight I couldn't get a breath, then inhaled sharply when I returned the embrace.

"Careful," he said. "I think my… Everything, is broken."

"What happened?"

"Rainier happened." He held me an arm's length away, studying me closely. "What about you? Are you okay? He told me…"

He stopped, his eyes tormented in a way I'd never seen before. I knew instantly exactly what Rainier had told him.

"I'm okay," I said. "He lied—whatever he said, he was lying to you. It's all part of the mind fuck. What did you do?"

"I went a little nuts," he admitted. He wouldn't look at me. "They've been jamming all this shit in our heads from the start: that picture of Erin Lincoln; you in the crosshairs. The bodies that were found. They're using all of it to get to us—figuring out which buttons to press. Apparently, they found mine."

Words failed me—a rare occurrence. "We should probably keep going," I said, in lieu of anything remotely adequate considering what he'd been through. What he'd done. "Do you think you can?"

"No problem," he said breezily. "I could do this for weeks. Or, you know… At least an hour." We parted. I watched as he struck on ahead. I thought of that night in the Black Falls motel when we were just starting out on this nightmare, when I'd gone after him for an inadequate thank you that he'd dismissed with a wave of his hand. A furrowed brow. *This is what we do.*

I went after him and touched his arm. He turned.

Before he could say a word, I stood on my toes and kissed him as gently as I could—infusing it with all the words I could never say, all the history we shared. "Thank you," I whispered.

He held me there, forehead to forehead. "I won't lose you," he said. "No matter what I have to do… If you go, I go. That's the deal."

I kissed him again, fast this time. That strength I'd been feeling since morning took root again. "Neither of us is going anywhere. Unless it's home."

At around noon, we stopped to eat what little food we had left. It was still mercifully cool out, and now overcast—which meant welcome relief from the sun. There was even enough of a breeze to keep the bugs away. We sat on a couple of boulders with our bare feet soaking in the river.

"We could get some fish, maybe," I said. "If nobody finds us by tonight—just build a fire and cook something up."

"I don't eat fish. And how are you catching them, exactly?"

"I don't think the vegetarians of the world would throw you out of their club if you ate one trout. Especially not given the circumstances. And I'd catch it with my hands. They do it in movies all the time—how hard can it be?"

"If we make out again, maybe the Capitol will send us some tofu," he said.

I laughed. "Maybe." Things got quiet again. "How are you feeling?"

"Fine. Really good." His left eye had turned a deep purple.

"Maybe you'll get another night in the Sanctuary," I suggested. "If we can't get out of here… You need to put something on those cuts."

"I don't think I'm getting another night in Sanctuary." I looked at him. His head was bowed, his eyes fixed on the water as he soaked his hands in the water.

For the first time, I focused on the damage there: swollen knuckles, bloodied cuts. *I went a little nuts.*

"What did you do to Rainier, exactly?" I asked.

"Not enough." He shrugged wearily. "I couldn't help it—not after what he said he'd done. I would have killed him if I could."

The admission didn't come easily for him. We finished the rest of our food in silence.

We kept on. Half a dozen times, we were sure we heard someone behind us or ahead, off to the side or up in the trees. Every time, we ran—always aware that if it really was Rainier or J., there was nothing we could do to stop them from doing whatever the hell they wanted to us. That sense of power I'd felt earlier drained away. We'd stopped talking and slowed down considerably when I first heard whistling again through the trees: The Battle Hymn of the Republic again, just one verse. Over and over again. Closer and closer. We ran.

No matter how far we went this time, no matter how fast, we couldn't outrun it. Eventually, after I'd been running so long that my lungs were ready to burst and my legs felt like so much dry tinder, ready to split if I took another step, I felt someone grab the back of my shirt. I screamed. Diggs pulled me back, a hand clamped over my mouth.

"It's me," he whispered in my ear. "Ssh—Listen."

I stopped running, and listened.

Beneath the thundering of my own heart, I heard birds and the rustling of wind through the trees, water rushing and frogs talking.

But no Battle Hymn.

We both stood there for a few seconds, gasping for breath. Adrenaline crashed through my veins; I felt like I'd been mainlining it for days now. I closed my eyes.

"I think we must have been near some campers," Diggs said. "He was doing what he did on the road that night—herding us as far from them as possible, so we wouldn't get help."

I couldn't speak. Rage and grief and exhaustion and terror vied for the top spot on my emotional Richter scale.

In that moment, I wanted them to die.

Rainier and J.—both of them, for what they'd done to me. What they'd done to Diggs, and the long list of victims who came before us. I wanted them to die, and I didn't care whether it was me who put them down or someone else. I just wanted them gone. Diggs squeezed my shoulder, eying me with concern. We didn't speak as we slowly made our way back to the river, and what I saw as our only hope of salvation.

We'd been there maybe two minutes before I knew Rainier was there.

There was a moment—a split second, barely detectable to the human mind—when the air changed around us. When everything hung suspended at the end of a pinpoint, ready to tip one way or the other. We would live, or we would die.

Diggs must have felt it too, because his head came up at the same time mine did. There was no time to run. After the race we'd just finished, I doubt either of us would have gotten very far, anyway. I'd just gotten my shoes off to soak my feet, now bleeding and raw, when we heard movement to our left. I scrambled for my shoes, but Diggs grabbed me and pushed me toward the forest without them.

"Just run!"

Rainier went straight past Diggs and lunged for me instead. He caught me by the ankle and I fell face first into the river, catching myself on my hands. My head went under. Then, I felt a huge, meaty hand in my hair, pushing me down farther. I fought to get free, swallowing half the river while my lungs screamed for air. Just when I was sure I'd pass out, Rainier yanked me up. Diggs went for him, but before he got close Rainier brandished a knife.

"Back up, you fucker," he hissed at Diggs. For the first time, I saw his face: His nose was broken. A lot. Both eyes were bruised and swollen, and it looked like he was missing his front teeth. If Diggs looked like he'd gone three rounds with a champ, Rainier looked like he'd gone ten. He jabbed the knife into my side, holding me still with an iron grip on my hair. Diggs stopped moving, his hands up.

"Okay, take it easy," he said quietly.

"You take it easy." He had a lisp thanks to the teeth Diggs had knocked out. If he hadn't been jabbing my kidneys with a ten-inch blade, it might have been a little funny. I saw no humor in it at that moment, however. "Who do you think is gonna pay for that stunt you pulled back at the truck?" He pressed the blade in harder, slicing my skin. I tried to get away, but he jerked my head back.

"Come on," he said to both of us, though his mouth was at my ear. "It usually takes a while before subjects get to this stage. You're special, though. J. wants to meet you."

Chapter Twenty-Seven
Juarez

Juarez met Jamie in the woods at eight o'clock that morning. Red Grivois was still missing; he hadn't been seen or heard from since Juarez had questioned him last. Police were searching his house in Black Falls, and Juarez had an entire team going through his background with a fine-tooth comb, in the hope that they might find some record of real estate holdings in the area. There was a cabin somewhere near Eagle Lake, but so far no one seemed to know where that cabin was.

When he arrived on the scene, Jamie handed him an orange vest and a bottle of water.

"Did you get some rest?" she asked.

He nodded absently.

She smiled. "Yeah, I thought not. We missed you at dinner last night—you should've come out." He didn't respond, already scanning the horizon. "All right," she said. "Let's get on with it. You ready to go find your girl?"

"More than ready," he said.

They worked with two dogs this time, the pit bull and one of the German shepherds. The other dogs were with the boy and two of the heavily tattooed, pierced women on Jamie's team. Jamie walked alongside Juarez, keeping up a steady pace, her head up and her attention focused on the dogs and the forest around them. He got the sense that she missed very little.

"So, you figured out who the bad guy is in all this?" she asked.

"I hope so." It was cooler than it had been since they'd arrived in Black Falls. That was good; Erin didn't like the heat. She called Juarez a desert flower.

She'd been missing nearly thirty-six hours now.

It had been a very long thirty-six hours.

"You really think it's Red Grivois?" Jamie asked, to his great surprise. He looked at her. "I've lived out here a good part of my life—know all the cops, retired and otherwise. They tend to talk."

"They shouldn't have said anything about that."

"Relax," she said. "It was just Nate—the sheriff, talking things through. No one else was around."

They walked on in silence for a bit longer.

"So," he finally said, when he could refrain no longer. "Do you think it could have been Red Grivois?"

"Not a chance in hell," she said without hesitation. Juarez's heart sank. She squeezed his shoulder. "Sorry—you asked. But I can't tell you how many searches I've been on with Red over the years; he feels for these girls. Bleeds for them. It's just about killed him. There's no way he's part of it. And all these years, he's tried his damnedest to turn Will into something other than the sadistic creep he is. He'll be ruined, once he hears it was Rainier behind this whole thing."

Juarez didn't know what to say. Maybe she was wrong. Maybe they would find Red Grivois and the whole thing would fall into place… Erin would be waiting for him, safe and sound.

Maybe.

Jamie tried to pull him into conversation a few times after that, but gave up eventually. They traveled over rough terrain for hours in relative silence, stopping frequently to rest the dogs. The movement felt good—Juarez never felt like he was honestly accomplishing something when he was behind a desk. But when he was out covering ground, his muscles aching, his mind occupied, then he could believe he was really doing everything in his power to bring Erin home.

During a water break around hour five, Jamie looked him up and down with clear approval. "You're holding up pretty well for a suit."

"I'm not really a suit," he said.

"Yeah, I kind of got that." When he looked up, she was watching him. He was struck again by just how attractive she was—even with the pierced nose and the tattoo. She was younger than she acted, Juarez suspected. Mid to late twenties, but no more. He thought she and the boy, Bear, must be siblings. "So," she said. "Tell me about Erin."

He was thrown. "What do you mean? You have the description, don't you?"

"Yeah. I have the description, Jack." She rolled her eyes. "I mean: Tell me about her. Why are you out here, turning yourself inside out? I like knowing about the people we find."

It was surprisingly difficult to articulate why he was out here; what it was about Erin that kept drawing him back in.

"She's funny," he said. They struck back out along the pre-established search route. The dogs—Phantom was the shepherd, Casper the pit bull—hadn't picked up a scent in some time. They kept moving regardless.

Jamie looked at him sideways. "She's funny. That's why you're out here… Because she's funny? I've seen pictures of this girl—offhand, I'd say you're probably in it for more than just a good belly laugh."

"She is very pretty," he agreed. He thought about their first—really, only—night together, back in Littlehope in the spring. And even that had been cut tragically short. "The truth is, I don't know her that well," he finally admitted. "We spent some time together last spring. Talked on the phone sporadically since then. E-mailed occasionally."

"They must've been some e-mails."

Before he could respond to that, a call came in on the satellite phone. Juarez stood off to the side of the search party, the oversized SAT phone in hand. The D.C. office had found a charge on Red Grivois' credit card statement, for a monthly delivery of specialty coffee traced to a general store in Eagle Lake.

Jamie looked at him.

"Go," she said. "I could be wrong. Or if he's not behind it, maybe you'll find something you didn't know before."

Juarez ran five miles back to his car, his heart pounding. He followed Route 11 into the tiny town of Eagle Lake, pulling into a small grocery store forty-five minutes after he'd gotten the call.

The only one working at the store was a pudgy teenage boy with bad acne. The moment Juarez mentioned the coffee delivery, however, the boy nodded knowingly.

"Yeah—Sure. Every other Tuesday Red comes in and picks up that coffee. Like clockwork, all year long. This is the wrong Tuesday, but he'll be back in again next week."

Juarez showed the boy a picture of Red. He nodded. "Yeah, that's right. That's him."

"Did you ever see him in here with anyone else? A woman, maybe? Or another man?"

The boy shook his head without hesitation. "A woman? *Jamais*. He comes in with Will sometimes, though. They wipe out our booze, then head for the lake."

"Where on the lake?"

The clerk shook his head regretfully. "We don't have any address—I just always figured it was one of those cabins, you know? Will hauls a boat with him sometimes."

"Do you have any idea of the vicinity? Or know someone who might have seen him coming or going?"

"No. Sorry... I never noticed." He hesitated at the disappointment on Juarez's face. "I could call my mom—she works here more than I do. She keeps tabs on everyone."

"Please," Juarez agreed.

A moment later, the boy was on the phone with his mother. He put his hand over the receiver to address Juarez.

"She wants to know, do you have a badge you can show me?"

Juarez got out his badge and showed the boy without argument. He was sure he'd climb out of his skin if someone didn't come up with something soon. Another moment or two, and the boy hung up.

"She says Red lives on Big Bear—the mountain. She's seen him driving out there sometimes. She doesn't know where, but she said it's on the north side. That's where she's seen him."

Juarez thanked the boy and returned to his car, where he called Jamie first thing. Within minutes, the entire search party had relocated to the north side of Big Bear Mountain. Juarez just hoped they weren't on the wrong track.

Juarez rejoined the search party at six o'clock that night. The dogs caught a scent not long after Jamie gave them a shirt taken from Red Grivois' home in Black Falls, and took off running. Juarez hung back, thinking of Jamie's words: *Not a chance in hell.* The truth was, he didn't have a good feeling about this either. He watched Jamie and the boy following the dogs, admiring the way they interacted; the effortless communication that flowed between human and canine. He thought of Einstein and Erin and shook his head. Women and their dogs.

Juarez stepped up his pace when the dogs got more frenzied and a cabin came into view. A red SUV was parked out front. He signaled everyone back, then pressed his finger to his lips. Without a word, Jamie got Bear and all four dogs back into the woods, out of sight. Sheriff Cyr and his deputy and three wardens from the park service flanked Juarez as he crept toward the sagging front steps. They creaked loudly under his weight. He searched the clearing, gun up, before he turned his attention to the front door.

"Red Grivois?" he shouted through the door. "This is Agent Juarez, with the FBI. Open up."

There was no answer.

He motioned for two officers to go around the back to make sure no one was escaping that way. Then, he tried the doorknob.

It turned easily.

He pushed the door open, gun up, heart pounding.

His pulse took a nosedive when he took in the scene they'd come upon:

The former sheriff lay on a ratty pullout sofa, eyes closed, a bottle of whiskey spilled beside him. His mouth was open. The cabin was cluttered, but clean. No sign of Erin or Diggs or any bizarre torture devices on the wall. Just a pair of snowshoes, a mounted rabbit with deer antlers on its head, and Red Grivois.

Snoring loudly, and very drunk.

Chapter Twenty-Eight

Once he'd gotten Diggs and me under control again, Rainier re-tied our wrists. If I ever got out of this, I was thinking bondage had officially lost its appeal. He put a pillowcase over my head, but he didn't use one for Diggs—presumably because wherever we were going, it didn't matter whether he saw the path we took or not. He wouldn't be leaving.

No one spoke. It was cold out now—not just cool, but cold enough that a jacket and a good wood fire wouldn't be a bad idea. Rainier kept one hand on me at all times. He'd traded in his knife for a gun that he dug into the small of my back through the whole journey. Sometime along that way, my fear had given way to anger; I'd gone from sick and hurt and tired and terrified to sick, hurt, and just plain pissed off. If they were going to kill us, I just wished someone would get on with it already.

When we reached our destination, wherever the hell that was, Rainier grabbed my bound hands and pulled me to a stop. The wrist I'd broken the day before had been jerked and snapped and pushed and pulled too many times now: when I'd caught myself as I had fallen into the river earlier, I felt the bone shift under my skin. Since then, I'd lost feeling in my fingers… If I didn't already, it was only a matter of time before I had permanent nerve damage.

I couldn't smell anything but my own warm, sour breath inside the hood. Couldn't see, obviously. There had been no temperature change, so I knew we were still outside. That was really all I knew, though. Rainier pushed me to my knees. Rage like I'd never felt before welled in my chest, with nowhere to go but in. I willed myself to keep quiet. Diggs shouted something that I couldn't make out, either because the hood kept things too muffled or simply because he'd run out of words.

We both had.

Rainier looped something over my head—I felt it brush my forehead, and then my nose and chin before it settled around my throat. Diggs screamed at them again. He sounded farther away now. Somewhere in the distance, I heard whistling.

The Battle Hymn of the Republic.

I thought of the night and that first day we'd been in the woods running: the whistling we'd heard periodically behind us. That song, in the walls of the cave while Diggs and I were trying to get out. And again today, all afternoon long. I started to shake.

Rainier tightened the belt around my neck.

The whistling got louder. And louder. Eventually, it was just a few feet from me.

Rainier pulled the hood off my head.

It was dark outside, but not so dark I couldn't see. The moon was still full. The stars still shone overhead. We were in a perfectly circular clearing, surrounded by thick woods. Diggs sat across from me, maybe ten yards away. He was close enough for me to see the hate and the terror in his eyes; far enough away that we couldn't touch. His hands were tied behind him, around the base of a pole about five feet high.

Rainier cinched the belt tighter, until it bit into my neck. The whistling stopped. A man stepped in front of me, close enough that I had to crane my neck to see who it was.

J.

Chapter Twenty-Nine
Juarez

Red Grivois had no idea what anyone was talking about when Juarez questioned him about Will Rainier. He was too drunk to answer much of anything, and Juarez wasn't interested in wasting more time when he realized they'd been pursuing the wrong man for the past six hours. He stood outside the cabin for a few minutes, taking stock. Trying to get his bearings. Jamie came over and leaned against the cabin next to him.

"Are you all right?" she asked.

He leaned his head back against the cabin, staring at the night sky. His eyes burned with fatigue. His body ached. "I'm not great," he said.

She laughed. "Well, that's the first honest thing you've said to me since we met. Where are we now? It's late, but Bear's been resting our second team for a while now. I can bring them out, retire Casper and Phantom for the night."

"I don't know where we are."

"You must have some leads though, right?" she insisted. "Don't get frustrated... Just think." She said it like it should be the easiest thing in the world.

Juarez nodded. He forced his mind back into gear. There was a quiet place in there, where answers just came... He'd been there many times before. A place where he could simply run through things without the fear of what would happen if he was wrong; if he didn't get there in time. Lucia's face flashed through his mind again, but for once he pushed her away.

Not now.

It all came back to Mister E. Every lead they had, everything they'd found, came back to him. The picture he had of Eliot from the Lansing asylum didn't come up in any facial recognition systems, and no one he had spoken with in Black Falls had seen the boy since he'd summered there with

Jeff Lincoln in 1970.

Bonnie Saucier had known J. She had known Mister E. She dated Jeff Lincoln—the real one. And she was dead now… What had Rosie said? Bonnie and Will had passed the test. They were the only ones. Will was missing. But maybe if Juarez could find the connection with Bonnie…

They were close enough to Eagle Lake, and therefore civilization, that Juarez's cell phone worked again—as long as he wandered around the area chasing bars as he talked. He called the Black Falls police station.

"I need to speak with Hank Gendreau," he said.

Gendreau was in transit. It took half an hour before anyone was able to track down the officers transporting him and get the prisoner on the phone. By that time, Juarez had driven back into town, where the reception was better. Jamie was resting her dogs. The other searchers had gathered in the parking lot of the now-closed general store, looking weary and discouraged. Juarez sat on the tailgate of one of the warden's pickup trucks, finally connected with Gendreau again.

"Did Bonnie ever talk to you about the night on Eagle Lake when Will attacked Erin Lincoln?"

"No," Hank said after a moment. "She was different after that night, though. Dropped out of school and moved to Portland not long after. She took some classes. Then she met up with Max."

"Max Richards?" Juarez asked.

"Right," Hank confirmed. "He was finishing up law school, doing a few other things on the side—he worked in a lab for a while, that kind of thing. He's richer than God, so he always paid Bonnie to help him out with whatever crazy project he had going."

Juarez's pulse kicked up a notch. "And when was this?"

"Late '70s, maybe. She got married to Luke and Sarah's brother in '79, so she stopped working for Max for a while then."

Juarez checked his notes. "And her husband died?"

"Ran off," Gendreau said. "It was a big surprise, too; we all thought he was crazy about her. She wasn't the same after that. She just hid out. Worked for Max—by then he had his own firm. He has a place up north, so Bonnie went up there whenever she could. But she was never the same, really. Then when Ashley died…" He trailed off.

Juarez barely noticed, suddenly revived. "Do you know where Max Richards is from?" he asked.

"Midwest somewhere, I think. He doesn't really talk about himself much."

"And he's been your lawyer from the start... Ever since Ashley was killed?"

"It didn't make sense to go with anybody else," Gendreau said. "Bonnie knew him, so he gave us a good deal. I couldn't have afforded half the appeals and motions he's done if it was anybody else."

Juarez got off the phone with Gendreau and called D.C. He interrupted a date Mandy was trying to have with a man twenty years her junior; someone he knew she'd been flirting with for months.

"I'll make it up to you," he promised.

"You haven't made up for the last six times you said that. What is it?"

"I need you to look into someone named Max Richards, and I need you to do it quickly. Lightning speed. He's a lawyer who practices in midcoast Maine."

Half an hour later, Mandy called from her D.C. apartment.

"He's an interesting one, this guy," she began.

"What did you find?"

"As far as I can tell, he doesn't actually practice much law. It looks like Hank Gendreau's his only client, and most of the time he's just going back and forth to Augusta filing motions or sitting in on panels or meeting with civic groups up there."

Suspect, but hardly incriminating in and of itself.

"What about fingerprints?" Juarez asked. "Aren't lawyers supposed to be fingerprinted?"

"That they are," she agreed. "Somehow, though, he's managed to get around that. I haven't been able to find any fingerprints on file for him, and almost no information about him. The guy's a ghost, Jack."

"Does it say where he's from?"

"According to what few records he does have on file, he's originally from NYC. I think that's bogus, though. I started looking in Lynn again, using the name you suggested: Max Richard Eliot. Still nothing. But I started looking at area hospital records for births around that time... That's when I hit paydirt."

It was ten o'clock at night, and he was still in the parking lot of Eagle Lake Grocery. The rest of the search party huddled in their cars, trying to get a few minutes' rest while they waited for Jack's instructions.

Juarez rubbed his head. "Mandy..."

"I know," she said. "I'm sending a picture of Max Richards to you now. I found a Max Richard Eliot Billings, born September 10, 1954. Your guy legally dropped Eliot Billings from his name in 1975, and changed to Max Richards."

Juarez took out the photo of Jeff Lincoln from the Lansing asylum, comparing it with the one of Max Richards that Mandy sent through his phone. He could understand how Gendreau and others in the town might not have recognized Max Richards as their mysterious Eliot, just ten years later. As a teenager, Max Eliot had been a small, wiry, bookish-looking boy with glasses and bad acne. Somewhere along the lines, that had changed—he had clearly gone to great lengths to tone his body, clean up his complexion, and possibly even surgically alter his appearance. All to ensure that people's perceptions of Max Richards was of a harmless, slightly eccentric and not terribly competent attorney. Meanwhile, he could live off his family's money and use his position as a lawyer to find his next victims.

They'd found Mr. E.

Now, they just needed to find Erin and Diggs.

Chapter Thirty

"I feel like we've come full circle tonight," Max Richards said to me. He clasped his hands behind his back. Instead of the suit I'd seen him in back in Rockport, tonight he wore khakis and a button-up shirt beneath a lightweight jacket. I'd been expecting a flowing robe or some kind of demonic mask... Instead, the lawyer nobody saw stood above me, gazing down with a beatific grin.

The robe and mask would have been less unnerving.

"You have questions, I expect?" Max asked.

I had a thousand of them, as a matter of fact. Instead of asking them, I kept my eyes straight ahead and my mouth clamped shut. Max chuckled.

"She is a stubborn one, eh Will? It all started when I met your father, you know..."

I lasted half a second before curiosity got the better of me. Story of my life. "Where was that?"

"Lynn," he answered promptly. "Our fathers were in business together, you could say. And then his family moved away... I had a falling out with my parents that spring, so I came up to Maine to stay with my old friend. I met Will here..." Will grunted behind me. My body was shaking from the effort of keeping still, still kneeling with Rainier's belt looped around my neck.

"Dear old J. was up to his old shenanigans with the girls of Black Falls," Max continued. "He was a real lady killer, that boy." He winked at me. "From there, it was just that cosmic perfect storm... I'd been dreaming of something like this—"

"Something like what, exactly?" Diggs asked.

Max turned so he could include him in the conversation. He waved his hand around the circle. "This, Mr. Diggins. My own anthropological Petri dish. One of the most fascinating aspects for me has been discovering the point at which empathy is cast aside in favor of self-preservation. How much it takes to drive people to kill. For Bonnie? It was a combination of things: post-hypnotic suggestion, for one. And surprisingly enough, she responded more when her animals were in danger than when she faced physical pain herself. Or when other people did, for that matter. It was fascinating, watching the way this experiment changed her over the years: from a beautiful, gregarious, bright young thing, to the eccentric shut-in you met in Rockport.

"For Will, on the other hand, it's been a series of rewards over the years… And the simple pleasure of the act itself," Max continued. "Some of our subjects have been stronger than others, of course. And you two…" He looked from Diggs to me and back again. "I wonder how much it would take—how many hours, how many days, at Will's mercy, before you agree you'll do anything for freedom."

"Anything meaning what?" I asked. "You want us to kill each other? That's your objective?" I looked past him to Diggs. "What would it take for you to put me in the ground about now, Diggsy?"

He laughed. It sounded strained and borderline hysterical, but it was still a laugh. "After this week? Not much. Maybe another night in that swank Sanctuary, and I'm there."

I looked at Max. He wasn't amused.

"And I'm on pretty much the same page here, so there you have it," I said. "Get this fucking belt off my neck, and I'll put a cap in his ass now."

Anger flashed in Max's eyes. He waved his hand toward Rainier, a kind of 'Have at it' gesture that effectively drained any *laissez faire* I'd been feeling to that point. Rainier knelt behind me, his body pressed to mine, while he cinched the belt still tighter, his mouth at my ear. The air left my lungs and the world around me blurred. Diggs shouted. Everything but Rainier's breathing in my ear, the cruel words he whispered, fell away. The world was underwater, and I was floating above it.

"That's enough," I heard Max say. Rainier loosened the belt. I gasped for air.

"There are a number of ways we've pushed our subjects to kill," Max continued. I could barely hear him above the rushing in my ears and my own hacking cough. He paused until I'd finished. "Occasionally, it's simple empathy. My subjects see how much these friends they've come to love are suffering… And they intervene."

He waved his hand again. Rainier tightened the belt around my neck. Diggs turned his head away. He was straining at the ropes, but I knew he wouldn't get free. No one would come. It felt like my lungs would explode, the belt cinching tighter around my neck, Rainier's warm breath in my ear. Spots floated in front of my eyes, getting brighter with each passing second.

And then, the angel of death appeared.

He didn't wear the cloak I remembered him in on the island at ten years old. Now, he wore jeans and a windbreaker; he might have just come from walking the dog or picking up groceries. He had a receding hairline and a thin, sharp nose, and he carried a gun. While Max and Rainier were so focused on my torture, he walked right up to them. My body screamed for air. The hooded man raised his gun. He aimed it at Rainier first, still standing right behind me. Instead of the deafening gunshot I expected, there was a muffled *snick* before the belt loosened. Rainier let go of the belt and fell backward.

Max screamed, his face red with rage. The man pointed the gun at the center of his forehead.

"You've become a liability, Max. We warned you about this when you left the fold…" He had a surprisingly gentile voice.

"My family—" Max argued.

"Your family has had enough," the hooded man said. Another muffled shot sounded in the night. Max just stood there for a second as though suspended, a hole in the center of his forehead, before he fell to his knees. He pitched forward.

The hooded man knelt beside me and untied my hands. He pulled the leather belt from around my neck, and helped me stand.

"Who are you?" I asked.

"Are you all right?"

I nodded, mute.

"Good."

Then, he walked very deliberately across the clearing toward Diggs. His gun was up again. He stopped and looked around at the bodies bleeding into the forest floor around us, then fixed his gaze on me.

"You know what I'm capable of?" he asked me.

I thought of the fire in the church; the bodies on the island last spring. My father's disappearance. Jane Bellows' murder.

"I do," I said quietly.

"Good." He released the safety on his gun and pressed the barrel into Diggs' temple, his eyes never leaving mine.

"Stop looking. If you don't, I will come back. And I will kill him. You understand?"

I nodded rapidly.

"That's good. I won't tell you again."

He removed the backpack he'd been carrying, put the safety on his gun, and backed away.

"There's water in there, and a compass. There's a search party looking for you due east of here."

"Okay," I said. I could hardly hear my voice over the thundering of my own heart.

As he was walking away, the man turned back and looked at me. He smiled. "It's always nice seeing you again, Ms. Solomon. I hope for your sake that we won't meet again for some time, though."

He holstered his gun and disappeared into the woods.

Chapter Thirty-One
Juarez

"She's unexpected," Juarez came up with finally, while he and Jamie were out searching late that night. Mandy had found an address on Three Brook Mountain where Max Richards had chartered a seaplane two years before. And now... Here they were. Searching another stretch of deserted woods in the hope that they might find something besides deer and bear and rogue vacationers.

Jamie glanced at him in surprise.

"You asked what I like about Erin," he explained. He'd been struggling with the question all night; it was a relief to finally find an answer that felt true. "Why I'm out here. Turning myself inside out."

"Unexpected?" she asked. "Explain, please."

He shrugged. An owl swooped down farther along the path. Neither of the dogs seemed concerned. "Unexpected. The things she says; the things she does. Tough one minute, crying over sick puppies the next." It wasn't coming out right, but he got the sense that Jamie understood, regardless. He continued. "Last month I had the flu. She called my assistant to find out my favorite place to eat. For three days, she had them deliver dinners, and paid extra so they'd include cold medicine and jelly beans. She has a good laugh. Is a terrible driver. And I'm ninety-nine percent certain she'd let me drown if she had to choose between me and her dog."

Jamie laughed. "And that's a good thing?"

"It shows loyalty. I like that."

"All right," she said. She'd been dragging for the past half hour— Suddenly, she seemed revitalized. "Well, now I approve. Let's find this girl, huh?"

It was midnight when Casper caught the scent and sounded off. The searchers were cold and the dogs were tired and Juarez knew that everyone should have been retired for the night hours ago. But Jamie had said they could keep on... *Just a little longer,* she'd told him. The dog's excitement this time around sent a jolt of adrenaline through his system.

When both Casper and Phantom picked up the scent, neither of them slowing down, Juarez felt a familiar comingling of anticipation and dread take root.

"Erin!" he shouted. He hurried on ahead, shining his light into the darkness. Jamie was just a step or two behind him, cautioning him to go slowly.

He paid no attention.

"Erin! Are you out here?"

He thought he heard something, but there was too much noise to tell for sure. Jamie halted the dogs. Everyone listened.

Diggs was the one who answered, his voice so faint it was hard to hear through the trees. "We're here. We need a paramedic."

The dogs led Juarez and Jamie straight to them from there, through a short stretch of woods where Diggs was sitting vigil beside Erin, who lay motionless on the ground. Her eyes were closed. Juarez's heart sank. He forced himself forward.

"She's still alive," Diggs said. He shook his head, fighting tears. "She passed out about twenty minutes ago—dehydration, maybe. Or shock. I tried to carry her..."

Jamie came over and tried to lead Diggs away, but he wouldn't leave Erin's side until the paramedics came. When they arrived and started attending to her, Erin came to with a start, fighting the moment she was conscious. Her face was a mass of cuts and bruises, her right wrist misshapen and dangerously swollen. Juarez knelt beside her.

"It's okay," he said quietly. She was shaking. "We've got you. You're all right."

She tried to get up, but the paramedics managed to convince her to stay where she was. She held tightly to Juarez's hand, her eyes wide with shock. He waited for tears.

There were none.

"I'm glad you came," she whispered to him.

He kissed the top of her head, holding her as close as he dared. Even then, it felt like she was very far away.

Chapter Thirty-Two

When I woke up, it was to white walls and white ceiling and a lovely floaty feeling I wasn't anxious to leave. The second I moved, my mother appeared. My lovely floaty feeling faded.

"You're awake," she said.

I tried to nod, but my neurons weren't firing in quite the right direction. I tried speaking instead. "Where's Diggs?" I croaked.

She gave me a look I couldn't read. I started to panic, until I realized it wasn't an *Oh God how do I tell her her best friend is dead* look so much as a *Not this again* one.

"He's in the next room—he's fine. Heavily concussed and badly dehydrated, on antibiotics for all those war wounds he got out in the field. He'll be all right." She nodded to my wrist, now in a cast. "They had to do surgery; you've got some pins in there now. You'll need at least two more before it's one hundred percent again. If it ever is."

I blinked at the ceiling. "Okay," I said.

"Is there anything I can get for you?" she asked. "Maya's on her way."

"My dog. I really miss my dog."

She actually laughed. When I looked at her, she was crying. Katherine Everett, with actual tears in her eyes. Or the morphine was working overtime. "He's been staying with me. He'll be glad to get back to you, though—I don't give him all that fruity deluxe food you do."

"It's not fruity," I said. "It's raw." I closed my eyes. Before I could drift away again, she took my hand. She squeezed it—the good one, thankfully—until I looked at her again.

"I want you to listen carefully to me," she said. "Because we won't go over this again." Her eyes were shining with a feverish intensity. "Your father died out in the woods, that day when his sister was murdered. He never got over it. After that, he did everything in his power to turn his life around...

But he never forgot that, and he made some bad decisions because of it. Got involved with the wrong people."

I thought of the man in the woods—the angel of death, his gun pointed at Diggs' temple. I didn't say anything.

"Those people are powerful, and they're deadly. If you keep looking…"

"Why did they save me this time, then?" I asked. "If they're so intent on keeping me from finding out the truth—"

"Because your father and I can turn their worlds upside down."

"Jack told me about Dad's family's tie to the mob—I know all about it now."

She looked downright disdainful. "You think this is about mobsters? These people make the mob look like a bunch of choirboys in bad suits. This isn't about them."

"But you can't tell me what it is about," I said.

"No. I can't. Your father has seen what happens when they're threatened… And I've seen it through him. As long as you stay alive, I won't tell their secrets. Not to you, not to anyone. But they only have so much patience."

"I know that," I said. My voice didn't sound like my own. "I'm done."

She couldn't have been more surprised if I'd just announced I was ditching all my worldly goods and moving to Mars.

"I'm serious," I said. "You're right—I saw what they can do. What they will do. I'm done. I'm going back to your place, and I'll write up this story and sell it to the highest bidder… Leaving out anything remotely connected to whoever the fuck this is. But that's it. I'm done. It's over."

She still didn't look convinced, but she nodded. "All right. That's good."

I studied her. The morphine was making me sentimental. "You were worried about me, huh?"

"I was annoyed by you," she corrected me. "As I usually am. Why can't you knit? Or take up some kind of light recreational drug, like the rest of the world does when they're bored."

I closed my eyes, smiling. "No. You were worried." My voice faded. I felt her kiss my forehead the way Mrs. Brady always used to when she was tucking in her brood. Morphine really was lovely.

◊◊◊◊◊

The morphine had worn off and life was considerably less lovely by the next night, when I still hadn't seen Einstein or Diggs, and nurses were coming around every half-hour to stick something in me or take something out. Juarez peered in behind a bouquet of roses. He looked a little nervous—probably because he'd already been subject to a tantrum from me earlier that day about being forced to wear paper pajamas with no backs to them.

"Up for a visitor?" he asked.

I nodded. "Please."

He set the flowers on the table and dropped a pair of my favorite pj's in my lap. "Those are for you."

"Flowers *and* pj's? You're officially my favorite person on the planet right now."

"If I'd known that was all it took, I would have sent them months ago."

He sat down. Since the rescue, in between the morphine and the bouts of unconsciousness, there'd been a tense uncertainty between us… Probably because I'd gone against his direct order to stay in Montreal for the night, thereby nearly getting myself killed. I suspected an equally large part of that was the fact that I'd been running in the woods for two days with a man Juarez had been insisting for some time now, was in love with me.

I tried to sit up. Juarez made a move to help me, but I stopped him with a glare. "So… What's the what, please? Who killed whom? And how did Max Richards fit into all of it? And why was everyone convinced my father was the bad guy?"

"Max was a friend of your father's from his hometown."

"In Lynn," I interrupted. "I got that part."

"Max got thrown out of Lynn after he set the mayor's cat on fire." I winced. "Exactly," Juarez agreed. "He came to Maine to stay with your father."

"Who was having his own little rebellion by sleeping with everything with a pulse from here to the Mason Dixon line," I added.

"Do you really need me for this?"

I closed my mouth and gave him my most winning smile. "I'll be good. Please continue."

He got serious after that. "Will Rainier took a different approach to your father's challenge than Jeff had originally intended. And when your father told him that he was absolutely, positively prohibited from touching his sister, he and Hank engineered the plot to take what Will had decided was rightfully his. Regardless of what Erin had to say about it."

I pushed away the thought of that night and everything Erin Lincoln must have gone through. It took some time before I could find my voice. Juarez took my hand.

"You want me to go on?"

I nodded. "Yeah. Please," I said quietly.

He frowned, but he did as I asked. "Max must have followed them down to Eagle Lake that night when he heard about their plan. Hank ran, but he managed to keep Bonnie and Will with him.

"We found the place where he'd been keeping all these girls over the past thirty years—his sanctuary, you said he called it? There were two separate quarters in there: a cozy little apartment with those rules you told me about. Then, on the other side, a much darker room. Cages and chains. Video equipment. He kept exhaustive notes of his 'research.'" He used air quotes on that last word, then fell silent.

"What about the other room?" I asked.

He shook his head, not sure what I was asking.

"Video equipment... Surveillance," I said. "Was there any footage of that room?"

"We didn't find anything. That's where you said you and Diggs were kept..."

I thought of Diggs' arms around me. *I'll never let go.* The look in his eye when Rainier took me away. The angel of death, his gun pressed to Diggs' temple.

I nodded. "Yeah," I said. I couldn't look at him, though. "That's where we were kept." He brushed the hair from my forehead. I changed the subject. "What about Max's records? What did you find there?"

"Everything," he said briefly. "He kept notes from the beginning, dating all the way back to that first night with Will and Bonnie and Erin Lincoln: who killed whom, how it was done. With one exception, Max never actually killed anyone. He just pulled the strings, convincing everyone else to do it for him."

"Who was the exception?" I asked.

"Mark Saucier." I looked at him blankly. "Bonnie's husband. When they got married, Bonnie stopped working for Max. Stopped doing all his dirty deeds. Apparently, Max didn't take very kindly to that. He goes into great detail about Mark's final days."

He'd gotten quiet again.

"You still say this only makes your top ten worst cases?" I asked.

"Definitely top five now."

Someone else would have stopped then. Let it drop for a while; we'd been tortured enough, hadn't we? All of us. Stopping didn't seem to be in my DNA, though.

"So, why the J. on their chests? It doesn't make sense to me, all those deaths somehow being used against my father?"

"I'm still not completely clear on that," Juarez admitted. "We know Max took Jeff Lincoln's identity when he was admitted to that psychiatric unit in Michigan, with the intention of blaming Lincoln if any fingerprints or DNA were left behind."

"But that makes no sense," I insisted. "If they actually caught my father after any of it, all they'd need to do was check his fingerprints and they'd see it clearly wasn't him."

"It was just part of the mind game," Juarez said. "A way of continually reminding Adam that he was in some way responsible for these girls' deaths. That he would always be part of it."

"What about Ashley Gendreau?" I persisted. My chest was tightening in a not-terribly-healthy way. I ignored it. "Why did Hank think he saw my father there?"

Juarez shook his head. "I'm not sure about that one—there's no mention in Max's notes of Adam being there. The whole thing was Max's idea, though: he had Bonnie give Hank the acid that day, then planned on framing him with the express purpose of representing him... Getting close enough to pull the strings on a whole new level. Will was hunting her that day, but Bonnie killed her, apparently. Max considered it a triumph: the first time she'd responded to a human being suffering."

"A mercy killing," I said. I closed my eyes.

He stroked my forehead with his thumb, his hand resting in my hair. He kissed my cheek. "You should sleep, Erin."

"I know. I will. Just... Why did Bonnie kill herself? If she was part of it all that time, what was the trigger?"

"Based on his notes, I think Bonnie blocked out a lot of what she did... You mentioned she had dreams where she saw this J., right? I think she may have done a lot of this in a sort of hypnotic state. But she started to remember..."

I opened my eyes again. Sat up. That tightness in my chest wasn't easing any. "Because I came to see her," I said. "I triggered her memories of Erin Lincoln?"

He looked at me intently. "This wasn't your fault, Erin. None of this was your fault."

I knew he was waiting for me to break; he'd been waiting for it since they found me. Waiting for me to burst into tears so he'd have some idea how to fix things. Hold me close, let me cry it out of my system.

"I know that," I said. My eyes had never been drier.

"Whoever killed Max and Rainier…" he began.

"I don't know who it was," I lied. "It doesn't matter anyway, does it? They're dead. Whoever killed them is long gone, and—let's face it—he did the world a favor, anyway."

"So it wasn't your father, then?"

I looked at him. "No, it wasn't my father. Why would you think that? My father's long gone. On the run, who knows where."

He didn't say anything to that. It looked like he wanted to, though.

"Jack—"

Before I could pursue the subject, there was a knock on the door. A pretty blonde woman walked in with a duffle bag over one shoulder, leading a giant white pit bull. Juarez got up with unmistakable relief, greeting the woman with a smile. And a hug.

Huh.

"Erin, this is Jamie Flint. She was the one who headed up the team looking for you that night."

"Just the dogs," she corrected him. "I just head up the dogs. I'm useless with people. Am I interrupting…?"

"No," Juarez said quickly. "Come in. I was just telling Erin how things were going. What we'd found."

Jamie looked at me. She wrinkled her nose. "Well, then I'm glad I came. Nobody needs to hear all that shit after what you've already been through. I brought Casper here by to meet you—I heard you like dogs."

Casper trotted my way. I sat up and greeted her happily, roughing her ears while her thin tail whipped hither and yon.

"She's a rescue dog? As in sniff-and-rescue?" She put her front paws up on the bed and licked my face, her whole body wriggling now. "I didn't know bullies were made for that kind of work."

"Depends on the bully," Jamie said. "All my dogs are rescues—I travel around, looking for the right ones to work with. Shelters call when they have somebody they think fits the bill. I met Casper; she just seemed to have the nose for it. And she definitely has the spirit."

I nodded. Something in me that hadn't been right for days gradually slid back into place. While I was bonding with the dog, Jamie produced one very grimy backpack and a writing bag from her duffle.

"I also wanted to give you this," she said. "We found them in the search. A lot of the stuff in there has had it, but there was an old journal that I thought you'd probably want back."

I kept my attention focused on the dog, thinking again of Erin Lincoln.

It took a minute before I trusted my voice. "Thank you," I said.

Jamie took her dog and left shortly thereafter. I closed my eyes, exhausted all over again. Juarez leaned in and kissed my cheek. "Why don't you get some sleep? I'm just going over to talk to Diggs for a few minutes." He hesitated. "Have you seen him yet?"

I kept my eyes closed. Shook my head. For the first time since I'd been rescued, I felt tears well somewhere down deep. I stuffed them back down.

"I'll visit soon," I said.

"Whenever you're ready," Juarez said. "I'm sure he's anxious to talk to you."

◊◊◊◊◊

I finally worked up the nerve to see Diggs that night. The hospital was quiet. I wore my favorite pajamas, but decided against bringing his backpack to him. Not yet. My stomach was tight, and the feeling of being exposed after I'd been safely shut in my hospital room for two days was unnervingly visceral.

Andie was just leaving Diggs' hospital room when I was rounding the corner: Andie of the bodacious curves, her pretty brunette head in the clouds. I waited until she'd gone before I went to his room and knocked on the door. He told me to come in.

I did.

He was all bruises and cuts and bandages. I was too, I knew, but I didn't have to look at me. I fought the urge to turn away. He smiled at me when I came in—a real, full Diggs smile, despite all the war wounds. He propped himself up more easily than I would have expected.

"Hey. I wondered when I'd see you again."

"I was just giving it some time… In case you wanted to kill me, you know. Figured I'd let that fester a little."

"Let it go, Sol. We're alive. We bested a crazed serial killer and his minions." He looked at me. "Or *someone* bested them, anyway. Your hooded knight to the rescue, huh?"

"I don't think he qualifies as a knight."

"No," he said seriously. "No, I guess he doesn't." I sat on the edge of the bed. Diggs took my hand. "How are you? Kat filled me in on the wrist, but… Other things. The death and mayhem. Torture and crazed mind games…"

"I think that takes a little longer," I agreed. I pictured the gun pressed to his temple. Thought of his body against mine. Sleeping beside him. Running for our lives, my hand in his.

"I thought we should talk about you and me, too," he said. He couldn't look at me when he said it, focused instead on our intertwined fingers. "About everything that happened… And what happens now."

"You almost died," I said. My voice was rough, but I managed to keep it under control.

He looked up, surprised. "So did you."

"I know. But with you…" My voice faded. There were people out there watching me. Watching Kat, watching my father. Now watching Diggs. I couldn't keep my parents safe, but the least I could do was make sure I never put Diggs in that kind of danger again. I wet my lips, and tried to find that molten core within that would keep me strong. I looked him in the eye. Stood.

"I think maybe we should get some distance," I said. "Just for a while… Everything we went through out there was too intense to just skate through, you know? You should go back to Littlehope. Go back to the paper, and Andie. Get back to your real life."

He tipped his head to the right, taking me in. Seeing through me the way he always had. "I'm okay, Sol. You don't need to protect me from anything. Anyone. I don't care what your phantom said when he had that gun pointed at my head… I can take care of myself."

I shook my head. Kept my eyes focused on his. And lied through my teeth. "That's not what this is," I said. "I just… I don't think it would work—You and me. There's too much history. Maybe it's better if we just don't see each other for a while."

"That's what you want?" he asked.

I nodded, never looking away. My heart ached in a way I'd never even known it could—like some vital piece was being torn away. "Yeah," I said. "I think that's what's best right now."

"Okay," he said. He still had my hand. He squeezed it, his gaze finally leaving mine. "You know if you need anything, you can come to me," he said. "Anytime. Whatever it is."

"I know." I thought of his voice in my ear that night: *I'll never let go, Sol.* I backed away from him. "It's the same for you, you know. If you need anything at all…"

"I know."

I turned my back on him. By the time I got to the door, I couldn't see through my tears. I didn't turn around when he called after me.

"I'll see you around, Sol."

I nodded blindly, but I couldn't answer. I slid out the door and closed it behind me. I managed to get down the too-bright hallway to my too-white room and climb back into my too-small hospital bed. Then, I curled up with my face buried in the pillow, and quietly fell to pieces.

Epilogue

A strong, lean forearm tightened against my jugular. I fought the familiar panic I'd been feeling like a shadow these past few months. I rode through the fear. A hand clasped my arm, holding me still. I willed myself to quiet. Steeled my body, forcing myself to a kind of fluid ease that didn't come naturally. I put my hand on my assailant's arm. Backed up, shifting my center of gravity while I used my shoulder and my momentum to flip him to the ground.

I followed him down an instant later, straddling his very toned stomach. Juarez grinned up at me.

"And that's how it's done. Very nice." He started to get up. I tightened my knees at his sides.

"Hang on, now. I'm not finished with you yet."

"Oh no?"

He rolled us both. The balance of power shifted. Einstein whimpered from the corner, where his doggy day bed was safely out of the way of the equipment I'd set up in my mother's basement. There was a heavy bag and a speed bag, an elliptical, a set of free weights, and a bar for pull ups I still hadn't quite mastered. I really liked watching Juarez do them, though. There was a Gazelle-type-thingy I'd nearly killed myself on twice now, but otherwise I was doing surprisingly well at this new, empowered leaf I'd turned.

Except that I couldn't sleep without the lights on, of course. And I wouldn't have full strength in my right hand without at least one more surgery, and would likely always feel some pain. Except Juarez had installed a deluxe security system in the house and I'd gotten a little OCD about making sure it was armed at all times. Except I hadn't spoken to Diggs in six months, and couldn't stop dreaming of him.

Otherwise, I was fine.

Juarez was watching me in that way everyone who knew about the 'incident' in the northern Maine woods watched me now: waiting to see if I was really all right. He leaned down and kissed me, then rolled us so I was on top again.

"You're getting good at this," he said.

"Because I'm part Jedi, part vampire slayer."

"Right," he agreed. "Because of that."

I kissed him again, harder this time. Einstein got up and trotted over, giving a couple of sloppy laps to Juarez's cheek.

"He only does that with you, you know. It's because you don't like dogs," I said. "He can sense it."

"I never said I don't like dogs."

"You said you like cats better. That's worse than not liking dogs."

Jack leaned up and kissed me again. I signaled for Einstein to take a hike, my body warming when I felt Juarez's begin to respond beneath me.

"You want to take this upstairs?" he whispered in my ear.

I pressed my hips against his. "Do I ever say no to that?"

I got up, then gave him a hand getting off the mat.

"We should eat something at some point this weekend," he said. "I'll raid the fridge, see what I can cook up."

We walked toward the basement stairs. Einstein scooted out in front, no doubt grateful to leave the dungeon. He wasn't a huge fan of the whole sparring thing. My cell phone rang just as Juarez hit the first step. I checked the number.

"I'm just going to take this. I'll be right up."

I didn't recognize the number, but the exchange was from Littlehope. I waited until Juarez had closed the door before I answered, my heart suddenly running off-rhythm entirely.

"Solomon," I answered.

There was a pause on the line.

"Hello?"

Whoever was there cleared her throat. "Hi. Yeah… It's Andie Reynolds—I was dating Diggs for a while. In Littlehope. I work at the paper."

"Yeah, of course," I said quickly. "What is it? Is he all right?"

"That's why I'm calling, actually," she said. "I don't know. He quit the paper about a month ago—did he tell you?"

I shook my head. "No… He didn't mention it." Because we didn't speak anymore. I left that part out. "You said you were dating for a while… you're not together anymore?"

"No. And I went by his place today to pick up some of my stuff, but he's not there. I still have a key, though, so I figured I'd just go in and get what I needed."

"And…?"

"Well, he's been gone for a while—Which I knew. He went surfing somewhere… But I checked his voicemail, because I still get some messages there sometimes."

Sure she did. Juarez poked his head back down. "Everything all right?"

"Yeah," I said. "I'll be right up." I waited until he was gone before I continued probing. "What did you find?"

"A friend of his is missing—Down in Kentucky. I didn't even know he spent any time in Kentucky. But this friend…"

"Who?" I asked immediately.

"Wyatt Durham," she said. "You know him?"

I hadn't heard the name in years. "Yeah," I said. "He used to be in a band with Diggs back when they were in college. Was it Mae who called?"

Andie sighed. "See… I knew you'd know. It was. She said she was hoping she could talk to Diggs; she thinks Wyatt's in trouble. Something about a cross… I don't know. But as far as I can tell, Diggs isn't checking his messages anymore. I thought maybe you could find him. Let him know. This woman seemed to think it was important."

Wyatt and Mae were the only happily married couple I'd ever met; he wasn't the kind of man who just up and disappeared. Not like Diggs, I thought silently.

"Erin?" Andie prompted.

"Yeah," I said. "I'll see what I can do."

I hung up the phone. Juarez appeared at the top of the stairs.

"You're officially out of food. I was thinking maybe we could go out for dinner," he said. "Maybe catch a movie in town."

I didn't say anything. He met me halfway down the stairs, studying me intently.

"No movie?" he asked.

I shook my head. "Probably not."

Coming in 2013:

SOUTHERN CROSS
Book Three in the Erin Solomon Series

Read on for an excerpt!

PROLOGUE

M̲ae was fit to be tied when Wyatt got the call—quarter past ten on a Saturday night, the first time the boys were out of the house in God knew how long, and the caller ID read Jenny Landry. Jenny Landry, whose goat's nut sac was gangrenous without a doubt and needed him out there five minutes past yesterday. Well, shoot.

"Who do they think they are, anyway?" Mae demanded, while he put on his monkey suit and his boots. "Who do they think *you* are?"

She followed him to the front door.

"They think I'm the country vet, Mae," he told her.

He sighed when she stood up on her toes and kissed him. Her face was still flushed and her lips swollen from all they'd been up to before Jenny Landry got hold of him. Mae was a good looking woman any day of the week, but with her hair down and her fire up, there wasn't anything prettier on God's green earth.

"I don't know how long I'll be—don't wait up."

She rolled her eyes. "The boys aren't back 'til tomorrow morning—I'm waiting. Put the poor thing down and get on home."

It was another hot night—not that there was any other kind in Kentucky these days. Wyatt wasn't a small man, six-foot-two in his socks, with a sturdy build that was perfect for breeding season and wrestling breach calves into the world. His big, meaty hands weren't the best for your more delicate surgeries, but he'd practiced long enough now that he could handle just about anything that came his way.

He climbed into his pickup, turned on the air conditioning, turned up the radio when Taylor Swift came on, and sang right along while he drove through the night. If Diggs and the boys saw him now, belting out sugar-coated lyrics along with a pop-country princess just this side of eighteen, he'd never hear the end of it. The band in New York and those rowdy college girls who'd just lapped up his clear, easy tenor had never seemed farther away.

He turned the radio up just a hair, and kept on singing.

Jenny Landry wasn't from around here—her boyfriend, Roger, was. Roger moved out to California after high school, started some business or other, and as far as Wyatt could tell, he'd plucked Jenny straight out of a hippie commune in San Francisco and brought her here. Backwoods Kentucky didn't suit her, and she knew it—Roger knew it too, Wyatt suspected, but they did their best to keep up appearances.

Except on nights like this. Wyatt pulled into the driveway, grabbed his bag, and stepped into the hot, dark night. Jenny was waiting for him, standing in the glow of the front porch light. She looked pale and tired, and by the look of her she'd spent the better part of the night in tears. He grimaced.

"Our boy's not doing too well?"

She shook her head. She was skinny—city skinny, with that lean, hungry look that'd always made Wyatt uneasy around the women he met back in New York. Her arms were crossed over her chest. She chewed on her upper lip for a minute before she said anything.

"Roger's inside—he said we could handle it."

Horse's ass. Wyatt nodded. "I expect he's right about that. Come on, let's have a look."

The patient was a year-old Alpine buck named Oliver, who should've been wethered about nine months ago, instead of just last week. Wyatt had known at the time that the poor bastard was too old to be banded—the goat's sac was the size of a softball, it'd take weeks before the banding took and the balls dropped off. But Roger insisted that he'd talked to one of his hippie dippie friends in San Francisco, and they said banding was the least traumatic way to go (*horse puckey*, Wyatt thought). So, he kept his mouth shut, gave the tetanus shot, got the band on there nice and tight…

The smell as soon as he hit the barn, though, was enough to tell him that something had gone wrong. He winced, taking a second to adjust to the stench. One look at the goat once the lights were on was all he needed to know Mae had been right: There was nothing he could do but end the animal's suffering as quick as he could.

The poor old boy was too far gone to struggle much—Wyatt got him around the neck and leaned into him, sinking the syringe in before the goat came to his senses. His body got heavy fast, the front legs buckled, and he went down with his tongue lolling. Jenny had gone into another stall with half-a-dozen little Alpines that couldn't have been more than two weeks' old. He could hear her crying softly.

He situated the goat respectfully in the hay, taking the time to check the scrotum to see what had gone wrong. At the sight, he clenched his jaw, scratched his neck. Tried to keep his temper.

"You mind if I go have a word with Roger?" he asked. He didn't wait for an answer, already headed for the barn door.

"He's working," Jenny said. "Can you talk to him tomorrow?"

He shook his head. "I'd rather talk to him now, if it's all the same to you. Did he try to take the band off early?"

She hesitated. Swallowed hard, looking guilty. "It looked like he was in pain—Roger thought it wasn't working, so he figured he'd just take it off."

"But the goat wouldn't let him," Wyatt guessed.

She shook her head. A white kid, a little smaller than the others, tried to jump into her arms. She pushed him down gently, thinking on her answer.

"Ollie bit him—he got angry and gave up. I tried to do it myself, but I wasn't strong enough." A long pause, the only sound in the barn the hungry suckling and occasional bleating of the babies. "Is that why it got infected?"

Wyatt scratched his head and did his damnedest not to roll his eyes or, worse, go over and throttle the woman.

"I'm just gonna have a word with Roger about it, all right? You take care of your kids, they look like they could use the attention."

He left the cool, bright barn behind, thinking of Mae waiting up for him. He could just say to hell with it, call Roger tomorrow and give him what-for then. Just shifting the band that little bit had restored enough blood flow to make the whole scrotum necrotic; Wyatt was tempted to give the idiot a taste of just how painful that must have been.

The porch light was out now, no moon and precious few stars in the cloudy sky. A thunderstorm about now would be just what the doctor ordered, but it didn't feel like one would be coming for another few hours. For now, it was just dark. Heavy and thick, crickets and cicadas screeching up a storm. He debated: Slug it out with Roger, or go home and make love to his wife.

He was halfway back to Roger's house, still thinking he was a damned fool for pursuing the whole thing instead of just going home, when he heard a car drive up behind him. He turned, caught in the glare of the headlights, and squinted to try and see who it was. The best he could make out was an SUV—a Blazer, by the look of it. He was so focused on the vehicle headed toward him that he didn't notice the noise behind until it was almost on him: a crunch of gravel underfoot; the sound of someone moving fast. Just as it registered that he wasn't alone, Wyatt felt a sharp jab dig into his neck.

He whirled, ready to fight, but there was no one there. The world slowed, dipped. He dropped to his knees. Tried to steady himself with a hand on the ground, and came up with pebbles in his palm.

Someone whispered to him. They sounded like they were underwater. Or he was. He tried to stand back up, but failed.

"Repent," the voice whispered. He blinked twice, wondering if he'd heard right.

He knelt there in the driveway on his hands and knees, his head bowed while he tried to get his bearings. Get his legs back under him. The Blazer came closer, the brights damned near blinding him.

"Who's there?" he shouted, sounding hoarse and not at all like Wyatt Durham, DVM.

The Blazer stopped moving. The driver's side door opened, then closed. Someone stepped out and walked toward him. Wyatt swayed, still on all fours. The voice whispered to him again.

"Repent," it said, lower this time.

He closed his eyes, his body getting heavier. His elbows buckled. A hand came at him from behind, pushing him gently to the ground, tender as Mae on those sweet nights when they lay together. It was all familiar— near forgotten but still there, somewhere at the back of his mind, from days gone by and a life best left behind.

Repent.

He closed his eyes, and lay still.

Chapter One
Diggs

The sun was setting over the waves of Tamarindo when I learned of Wyatt Durham's death. The air had cooled and the water had calmed and a bonfire was already blazing on the beach. I smelled like liniment and beer, and it had been too long since I'd had a good night's sleep. I limped across the sand to join the half-dozen other surfers in my party, my aching back a reminder that wipeouts weren't so easy to shake off now that forty was in the rearview mirror.

Daisy was flirting with a water rat twenty years my junior named Jason, and she wasn't being all that subtle about it. Daisy was tall and dark and tasted like good whiskey going down, with just as many regrets in the morning. She was seated on a rock leaning in to Jason, her head tilted to the side. Smiling. Jason was a couple of inches shorter than me, maybe a few IQ points lower on the scale, but he had no gray at his temples, a lot fewer creaks in his joints, and not half the demons I carry with me. The whole thing wasn't that surprising: two weeks ago, I was the one Daisy was flirting with across the fire while some other poor bastard got his ego handed to him on a paper plate. Fair was fair.

I went over and sat down. Daisy leaned back like she hadn't just propositioned another guy while I was ten feet away, and Jason jumped up like they'd already started something.

"Relax," I said. "I was just grabbing a Coke." I nodded for Jason to sit back down.

I pulled a soda from the cooler. If I said anything, there'd be a confrontation. Daisy would get pissed, say I didn't own her, and that would be the end of it. If I *didn't* say anything, on the other hand, and just played it cool for the night, I'd likely still get at least one more pretty fair roll in the hay before we parted ways. I chose the lounger on the sand instead of a piece of driftwood or a stray boulder like the whippersnappers I was traveling with were sitting on, and leaned back. Let her come to me.

Sure enough, not two minutes had passed before Daisy joined me. She ran her hand up and down my calf until my blood started to flow in other directions entirley and I'd forgotten all about my aching back and my bruised ego.

And my cell phone rang.

I didn't look at the caller ID, and made no move to answer. Daisy frowned. "Why don't you ever pick up? What if somebody needs you?"

An image of Solomon flashed through my head for some reason— Erin Solomon, of the piercing green eyes and the fiery locks and the most godawful fucking temperament on the planet. But as far as I knew, Solomon was shacked up in Maine with God's gift to the FBI, and I was… Here. I shook my head.

"Don't worry, kitten. Nobody needs me."

A slow smile touched her lips. "I need you," she whispered, low and sweet. Her hand was traveling farther up my thigh by the second.

Things were just getting good when my cell rang again.

Daisy raised an eyebrow at me. I leaned in and kissed her just as the call went to voicemail, then managed to turn the damned thing off with my other hand skirting its way to Daisy's shapely backside. Multi-tasking is a gift of mine.

I stopped kissing her, however, when I felt something solid glance off the back of my skull. I whirled. Daisy skittered backward like a long-legged, doe-eyed crab. The rest of the circle looked up with the casual disinterest of the perpetually stoned as Erin Solomon herself stalked across the sand toward me, her sandals in one hand, a backpack slung over her shoulder. She was flushed and overdressed and there was murderous intent in her eyes.

Despite everything, I don't know that I'd ever been happier to see anyone in my life.

Looking for more from Erin Solomon?
Visit http://erinsolomon.com
For short stories, trivia, and more, and sign up
for the quarterly e-magazine,
The Trib!

ABOUT THE AUTHOR

Jen Blood was born and raised in midcoast Maine. She is a freelance writer and editor with writing credits in Down East, The Bark, PIF, and a number of newspapers, websites, and periodicals around the country. She holds an MFA in Creative Writing/Popular Fiction from the University of Southern Maine, does seminars and one-on-one tutorials on writing, editing, and social media for authors, and in her free time hangs with her intrepid hounds on the Maine coast.